Seeking Justice

This book is dedicated to my son for his wisdom, my mom for her courage, my family for their love and my supporters for their encouragement. Thanks be to God.

Seeking Justice

Jordan Douglas

Library of Congress Control Number:		2015902539
ISBN:	Hardcover	978-1-5035-4466-6
	Softcover	978-1-5035-4473-4
	eBook	978-1-5035-4472-7

Print information available on the last page.

Rev. date: 02/26/2015

To order additional copies of this book, contact:
Xlibris
1-888-795-4274
www.Xlibris.com
Orders@Xlibris.com
706495

I am redeemed!

Behind the Bar

August 23 amended, amended counterclaim:

On August 23, 20xx my son and I attended court at 10:00am. We sat while the normal quick signatures were being offered by Lawyers. As one lawyer spoke before Judge Silly, he had the wrong section to the rules indicated in his application so the Judge was looking for the proper section, when Mr. Vain stood up and informed Judge Silly the section from Mr. Vain's open Rules of Court. Judge Silly announced to the court room that "Mr. Vain gets the gold star". It was my turn and Mr. Vain made his speech and then I informed Judge Silly how I was never in possession of this envelope, but he did not seem concerned that envelopes are being left in mailboxes with a Court appearance date enclosed in them.

I still don't know how an affidavit of service would be filed without it being registered or a process server having it recorded with proper identification, but then again everything to do with this case and the other seems to not go by any rules, laws or a book. I informed Judge Silly that I have an Order to Compel undertakings from 20xx and I still to date have not received any of those undertakings, but the Judge still blow it off even though Mr. Vain's client is in contempt of court which can land your Ass in jail for 2 years. I informed that there has been no correspondence for over 4 years and that there is a Statute of Limitation to this civil matter. He swayed his body back and forth as to say to me "so what". Finally, I informed Judge Silly that according to their Amended, Amended Counterclaim it is typed as being 8 pre signed cheques totalling $4x,000.00 yet Sally Liar's sworn affidavit encloses 9 cheques that Jason Jack was the only one who had signing authority of and full disclosure to, and that the total was $4x,000.00.

Judge Silly shrugged his shoulders, as to say to me "so what" and again I just would like someone to take some small sense of pride in their work and get one of these numbers correct. So I piped up and said to the Judge in a serious tone, "well I just wish someone would get the numbers correct, so we don't have to have an amended, amended, amended counterclaim. What a waste of tax payer's money. The judge did not seem to mind Mr. Vain's application and actually award him it, even though there are outstanding undertakings and I have an order to compel, and that this matter goes beyond the statute of limitations, but then again Mr. Vain did receive the gold star and if that doesn't tell you that there is a bias in our system, I am not sure what would.

August 24, 20xx I picked up my mom and my son, myself headed to the courthouse again. I had my briefcase with all my folders and after yesterdays gong show I had no idea what to expect. The doors opened shortly before 9:00am so the three of use sat in the courtroom. There was a sentencing matter before mine, but the prosecutor said the lawyer and client were not there and that they were coming from Fort Mac town, so they allowed my matter to go first. The prosecutor, Leah Back was in attendance, the Detective Away was there and a Lawyer from Simon's office, but no Simon. The judge asked me to move into the Defendants box, which I did.

Judge Main expressed his concern with the letter and the allegations of its contents. The representative from Simon's office told the Judge that Simon had some medical issues and was in the hospital, which you would think they would have conveyed to me. Judge Main asked me to attend on September 7, which I agreed too. At no time did he ask me if I was the writer of the letter. Proceedings were adjourned.

I met with the representative from Reck's office and she told me that I had better look for new legal counsel as Simon would be withdrawing from my matter. Nice how this was not mentioned before the Judge and that Simon would be contacting me shortly, but he was sick, yet she told the Judge that Simon had had medical issues and was in the hospital so which was it. I told her that I have been asking and requesting a log of my account as my family would like to see where their money want and she told me that Criminal law firms do not have to keep a log of time billed.

After getting home I called a friend and told him what had happened. He was at a loss for words and was as frustrated with the system as anyone who knows the story is. My friend told me that he would not be purchasing the new business as his lawyer had found the company had filed for Bankruptcy and did not disclose this to him. So much crap and when you attempt to clean it up you just get shafted.

I called Wayne and told him what had happened on August 23 and August 24. He could not believe that they could get an Amended Amended Counterclaim with not complying with the Order to Compel, in 20xx. I am guessing if it were me who did not comply, I am sure that things would not have played out the same. Why do we have Laws and protocol when it only applies to certain elite groups? I told Wayne what went down during proceedings today, August 24, and how Judge Main did not ask me if I was the writer and how Reck's representative told me that I had better find new legal counsel as Simon would be withdrawing from the file. Wayne was shocked that 60 seconds after being in front of the Judge she told me this. Why did she not say anything to Judge Main moments before? I told Wayne that Detective Away was at court today and he found that weird and said that Detectives don't come to court unless they are witnesses and that was not normal. We had a nice conversation and I feel blessed to have a small group of true friends. I also told Wayne about how Criminal Law firms do not have to keep a log of their billing hours according to the representative from Reck's office. Wayne was in shock that she admitted this to me, but still in shock of how she told me that Reck was going to fire me as a client. None of this crap is sitting well; hence this is why I want you the reader to know what is happening in this story.

September 7, 20xx- Mr. Reck removes himself from the file. Today I had to appear again in court for the criminal matter to deal with the fact the once the judge read the letter, my so called lawyer headed for the hills. He of course was not there again but had a representative from his firm made the motion to have Mr. Reck removed from my file. Nice considering now the judge Silly informed me that I would have to find counsel for my next appearance which was in three weeks for my sentencing. This was a complete shock as I had no idea that this was the date and now I have no money and no representation. I was going to jail for something I did not do and in a real bind. God is seeing all of this and I pray he is doing something huge.

I was sick and broken to think that this lawyer could do this and nothing. His reputation to be a good lawyer is that he really messes up people's lives. Good people and he is nowhere to be found. I left court, which my son was there with me for, and still not sure why a judge can still oversee all these matters and not be a conflict of interest, especially when this judge is favoring the crooks. I am crushed by our system, but not giving up. I have faith that something will be blessed and I will tell my story.

My son is really holding his head up high and trying to be strong for me. He is still young and to be subjected to such evil is not fair. God is the justice we need. I began searching for a lawyer to represent me for my sentencing hearing, but I first made an appointment with legal aid to see if I could get some help financially from them. You see the big crooks suck you financially and then the lawyers are so unreliable and easily bought off. There is no justice in our justice system and I have faith that one day the truth will come out. God is my justice. I was blessed with getting an appointment to meet with the legal aid panel and plea my case. It timed out perfectly and I was so fortunate to get in soon as I had very little time. I had to get my son settled, my house packed up and not much time to do it all in. I had to put aside my fears and focus on being productive. I had no time to think of myself or have any pity on my matter, I would do what I could and leave and trust in god. My son would reside with my mom and I am so thankful for her to take him in. My cat would also be subject to being uprooted. I sure hope this company and the people to fabricate all the materials are happy with themselves, as one day it will all come back to them. The truth will come out, it always does.

I presented my case to the board of legal aid representatives on September 19th, which consisted of lawyers and other professional representatives. I began with the civil case and then the criminal case and the costs and the stalling I have had to endure trying to seek justice in this very unjust system. The panel were shocked and angered by my treatment and without hesitation agreed that I would be blessed with receiving legal aids assistance. I have had to speak and tell my story so many times that I am still baffled by the reaction I received and the out pour of compassion to seek justice. After I returned home I received a message from the Legal aid department confirming I was approved as a client and I could not seek out my representation. I began making calls and was blessed with getting a meeting with a law firm to discuss taking me on as a client. The long and short of it I retained a fabulous lawyer who wanted to fight this entire case, but Mr. Reck had sailed me down the river too far and it would be very difficult to do anything now. I could appeal any decision the judge made in my sentencing but I would have to be sentenced. He seemed like the lawyer who would actually fight for a client and not be bought out. He should have the reputation Mr. Reck had unfairly.

September 21, 20xx my new counsel requested my file from Mr. Reck's office. This should have been given to me the day he stepped off my file and returned to me immediately, but now he was playing games with my new counsel and another delay tactic was being played. He would not give my new counsel anytime to properly prepare for my sentencing hearing. My new counsel asked that my sentencing date for September 28 be set over until October as he was not getting any cooperation from previous counsel and had not received my file. The crown agreed and I was told that I did not have to appear for court on September 28th and that after my new counsel would be in touch with me. He seemed to have it under control. My mom, my son and I headed to our cabin to check to make sure it was still standing that day. the three of us had a wonderful time laughing, and being together even though the day was still very emotional not knowing what was happening at court.

We headed to a local town to get some ice cream. I pulled out my cell phone and had three calls from my counsel telling me to call him now. The place where we were at was about an hour out of the city. I spoke to my counsel and he told me I had to get to court now or the judge would put out a warrant for my arrest. Shocked to know that now the prosecution wanted me in court and had pulled a fast one on my new counsel, we rushed back to town to make it in time. My gas light went on and we got lost and ever obstacle that could be placed in our way was being placed in an attempt to make us not arrive. I was not dressed or prepared for court, I had no idea what would happen and if this would be the day I was sentenced. I was not a flight risk or did I ever miss any dates. My poor family were so stressed out. My mom's health has already been taxed by this unjust process and I know my son is putting on a brave face at my expense, but this is just becoming too much for a level headed person to endure. I called my counsel and told him we were almost there and thankfully he was able to have the time moved so I would not get a failure to appear and a warrant. The judge already knew me as he was the one who had received the letter and he knew something was not right.

Once I arrived at court, Don my counsel told me he was not sure if I would be sentenced today, but prepared me in advance. God why is this happening? I had no time to say good bye to my family, this is so unfair. Once court commenced the justice had me move into the defendant box and my counsel began to tell the justice that he was told I was not required today and therefore that is why I was not there.

The prosecution never explained that this was her approval and then painted it as if she thought I was fleeing. Gosh, this woman really has blindsided by her authority. I had no conditions upon me for the entire time I was suffering in the criminal gong show courts and now she thinks I am flight risk. If I did this crime and sold my assets I would have over a million dollars and that would be when someone would flee. I did not have their crooked money and had been bled out by lawyers to keep my head above the waters or blood pool they call a system. The justice was able to see that I was not going anywhere and from my past ongoing commitment to this case I would not go anywhere, so he set the sentencing date for October 19 and that would be the day I would find out my fate.

I met with Don briefly afterwards and he told me I would get jail time so to get ready and to have a legal power of attorney document drawn up to have my son be my representative and therefore he could deal with matters outside when I was way.

Not too many lawyers really know the inside of the system and this will only be to my advantage to have been on both sides. The emotions are indescribable and beyond words. I was not so much scared for me but for my son. I was blessed to have him in the best hands, but this was not right on so many levels. I would spend the next few weeks just with my son and being with him. We would service this and we will be vindicated over this situation. Justice will prevail and God is my vindicator.

October 18, 20xx- there is nothing like getting serviced the day before I am facing jail time to have all my so called assets turned over to the crooks. I was not going to appear but Wayne told me to appear. I am so done with the lawyers, police and judges. So the crooks get a judgement of $7xx, xxx.xx, when they claim it was $6xx, xxx.xx taken.

Nice to see this judge is also putting over time on the civil matter and again was the same one who has signed off on all the restraint orders, and other matters dealing with this file. No arms length at all in our system. I let Don know that they had a judgement and sent him a copy of it. The day before I am going to jail and I have to spend my time in court for the civil crap. What does not kill you makes you stronger? That is the saying, but all I can think is only the crook get stronger as they are the ones with all the money to keep them strong. I wish the governing body that is to audit our taxes would get in and do their job and once and for all audit this massive tax evader.

My mom brought over dinner for my son and me. We had put all our small quantity of personal belongings into storage and I had made sure my son was settled at my mom's house in the meantime trying to deal emotionally and physically with mine and his world falling apart. I wonder how the individuals who did this would handle this if the roles were reversed. I would not do this to my worst enemy and yet they are just so evil and have no back bone to stand up and not do what is so wrong to keep their jobs. Guess what if this can happen to me, well it can happen to you. We had a long day tomorrow so we had some family time and called it a night.

On October 18, 20xx my now favorite Christian singer, Chris Tomlin wrote a song that would be my sign from God and when I was researching this artists I came across the story behind this song that I want to share with you now. This is off the internet and is Tomlin's story.

This is a special song, and comes from a real place. It comes from a true place and a place a lot of people come from. The song speaks an honesty that people relate to. It started with Ed Cash, and anyone who knows my music knows that Ed has been part of my songs for over a decade. He's a huge part of what I've done, and how my music sounds. We've been writing songs together for a while. We co-wrote this song together and I had this thought that I hadn't written with Ed recently and I wanted to get together with him. I had this urging and nudging to meet up with Ed. It turns out that it was the Holy Spirit nudging me.

I was visiting Nashville, and sent Ed a message that I wanted to meet up. Ed responded that in the middle of the night he had this special song he was working on and thought of me. God put us together and I couldn't get there fast enough. Ed told me his wife wakes him up in the middle of the night struggling with anxiety and fear and attacks when she's wrestling in the night and can't sleep. Those thoughts and fears come in the night and grip her. She asked him to pray for her, and not long after that he started writing this song as praise to God during the night.

There's something powerful about praying to God and praising Him during the night. When things are coming against you, prayer is the answer. Ed said he didn't even know where the words came from, but he started praying the lyrics to the song: "*I know who goes before me / I know who stands behind / The God of angel armies / is always on my side / The One who reigns forever / He is a Friend of mine.*" He played me that chorus, and I knew this song was exactly what I wanted to sing.

Did you base the song on any Bible verses?

2 Kings 6:15-18: And when the servant of the man of God arose early and went out, there was an army, surrounding the city with horses and chariots. And his servant said to him, "Alas, my master! What shall we do?" So he answered, "Do not fear, for those who are with us are more than those who are with them." And Elisha prayed, and said, "Lord, I pray, open his eyes that he may see." Then the Lord opened the eyes of the young man, and he saw. And behold, the mountain was full of horses and chariots of fire all around Elisha. So when the Syrians came down to him, Elisha prayed to the Lord, and said, "Strike this people, I pray, with blindness." And He struck them with blindness according to the word of Elisha.

How can listeners apply that message in their walks as Christians when they listen to the song?

This message is exactly what the Church needs. Our story is not a story of fear; it is a story of faith. Everywhere you turn it is fear. Fear of the economy collapsing. Fear involving relationships. Fear of cancer and sickness. Fear of divorce. Fear, anxiety and depression holds us back like we are in chains. It seems like more and more that the world is getting crazier. Fear affects old and young people.

Fear is no respecter of age, socio-economic status, or anything. It is a condition of the heart. I just think it is good to have this Truth in our hearts. Whom shall I fear? In the midst of crisis or anything that comes against, it is powerful to know who stands behind and goes before us. The God of Angel Armies is always by our side.

The Scripture really came to life for me after we wrote the song. I may have read that Bible passage from 2nd Kings before, but my eyes weren't really open to the story. When Elisha is told about the army camped outside the city, and sees the fear in his servant's eyes, he tells him, "Do not fear, for those who are with us are more than those who are with them." Then he prays for the Lord to open the eyes of his servant. Then he saw the angel armies all around their enemies.

That just really struck me. For me, for the Church, we need to be praying that same prayer for God to open our eyes. Most of the time our eyes are focused on what's in front of us. If we could see the spiritual realm, our enemy wouldn't cause us fear. Those who are with us are far more than those who are against us.

"Whom Shall I Fear (God of Angel Armies)" is chock full of the Truth that as Christians, we need to have full reliance on God to deal with the struggles of life. The song perfectly expresses that dependence: "I'm holding on to Your promises, You are faithful...I know Who goes before me, I know Who stands behind, The God of Angel armies, is always on my side, The One Who reigns forever, He is a friend of mine." All of these lyrics point to the wonders of our God combined with sweeping melodies and infectious choruses that will be replayed in your mind over and over again. You can experience the majestic nature of God in the music of Chris Tomlin. This song brilliantly sets the tone for this exceptional worship album, sure to be one of the best of the year. I am very moved by this song. I find myself raising my hands in worship and then I'm compelled to reach out horizontally to help show others the love of Jesus.

Remember that if God is for us, who can be against us? We raise our hands to celebrate and in surrender. We can lift up our hands in confidence to God and know that His mercy is unfailing. His love is never-ending. He is our refuge and our strength. God's ultimate will is not to bring affliction upon people, but to restore us so that we may experience His unfailing love.

I love the singing this song back to Jesus and telling Him plainly that I need no other than Him. What a great testimony and way to start off a new year. Make a commitment to know Jesus. My new year's resolution is to live out the faith decree of this song, «The One who reigns forever / He is a Friend of mine / The God of angel armies / Is always by my side.» Happy New Year!

Once I read this and the date I knew it was significant to my story. God was with me and he did go before me. I had nothing to fear and this song would come into play so many times during my journey. At significant times this song would play to reassure me that I was with God and he was not going to leave me. My faith was sealed, and my fate was with God.

October 19, 20xx

I did not sleep very well last night knowing that today I would most likely not return home. I had said my goodbyes to my friends and had done all the crying I could do and now as I sat outside having a cigarette I reflected on how I did the best I could to defend this matter and to have justice served, but now I would leave it in God's hands as he is much more capable of dealing with this matter.

My mom, son and I headed to the court house for 9:00am. We all were not in the mood for eating and our stomachs were in knots in anticipation of what was to come. The court house was still locked so we huddled by the door to keep warm. The three of us met Don in the cafeteria area as per our arrangement before going to the court room. I gave him the copy of the judgement to have and to give to the judge. Hopefully, he would see that they had taken everything from me and to leave me with my freedom. I had done some research on where I maybe going so that my son and my mom would know where to visit me at.

The crook and his assistant were in attendance for the sentencing. The prosecutor was not happy with some of the character reference letters I had submitted. A few of my friends had worked for the crook and were very much aware of the goings on at this company and wrote it in their letters of support for me. Well, the prosecution was not impressed with this and wanted to have these support letters removed from the judge's hands. It would be nice to have the judge see that not only was I speaking this truth, but others were also. I was asked by the judge to go and sit in the box while my counsel fought for my freedom and the prosecution argued that their position. After both sides presented their arguments, the justice asked me if I had anything to say. It was almost lunch time and I was drained. I asked the judge to think of my family and my son in sentencing. I had done my best to fight these charges, but had nothing left. I prayed he would see me and what is case was. The judge adjourned for lunch and I was taken into custody.

I was lead out of the court room and placed in a cell behind the doors of the courtroom. This is where individuals wait for their appearances. I was asked to remove items from my body such as my hair clip. I had no jewellery, no purse, and no phone as I had left all this with my family before moving to the defendant box. The courthouse guards cuffed me and padded me down. I was then put in an elevator that was more like a cage, where the guard traveled on one side and me on the other and we moved to the downstairs level. I was led down a hallway and told to put my coat on the floor and then put in a holding cell. There were four or five cells and they only had people in one so I was up into one by myself. It was very bright in it. There was a steal bench and a toilet with a small sink attached to it. Everything was exposed and no privacy. I sat down on the bench and took a deep breath. The guard offered me a bag lunch which had a couple of sandwiches, oranges, and a juice box.

It was terrible, but I was hungry and did not know what was to come. I took apart the sandwich with the mystery meat and eat the bread. The juice was quenching and now I had to wait. If you wanted to use the bathroom you did in front of the guards, either male or female. The ones on were men. No dignity left. I was done.

It was 2:00pm and I was brought up to hear what the judge had concluded. The prosecution wanted ten years and my counsel two years. I was told that it would be better to go federal as the institution was better and a lot nicer then the provincial. Provincial is two years less a day and you serve 2/3 of the sentence and federal is two years over a day and you serve 1/3 of the sentence. The judge then entered into his decision. He began with addressing both the lawyers' arguments and then asked me to stand as he read his decision. Because I had to plead guilty he could not go too lightly on my sentencing as this would set precedence for future sentencing. He was very reluctant to give me a harsh sentence and sympathized with my circumstance. I was given 3 ½ years for a crime that did not exist and that I did not do. The information that was sent to the courts along with the disc were sealed and put into the case file. Maybe one day someone will open this file and see all the wrongs that occurred. The judge knew I was not guilty and he made sure his words were put on the record as the sentence was based on precedence and not on the actual formality of the trial that never existed.

My son and mom sat in the gallery and were my rocks. I was able to give them both a hug and kiss before being lead back to the holding cell. The sheriff on staff told me that it was not permitted for me to give my family a hug. The prisoner is not allowed to touch their family before being taken into custody. I thanked the sheriff for the privilege to say good bye. My family were so strong and brave as they would leave the court house and not know what was going to take place next. My legal counsel comforted them and reassured them that I would be in touch with them soon. My legal counsel was not entirely sure of the process as most lawyers really don't know what takes place unless they have been subjected to the entire process.

Back into the holding cell and then back down to the court house jail. I waited and waited for the next move and I knew that God was with me and his angels were around me. I was called out of my cell and shackled with a line up of men being taken to another section to be processed and searched. I was the last one in the line up with three other men and me, the only women. The shackles cut into my ankles as I walked down a corridor and into a tunnel. The men in front of me were questioning me being there and how there was no way I was a criminal. They told me the system screwed me and I did not belong there.

It was very interesting how the prisoners could see I did not belong there. I was scanned and my picture was taken and then put into a very small holding cell which was occupied by at least fifteen other mates. It was so small that some mates had to stand or sit on the floor. We were sardines. I had missed dinner. so I was blessed with another bagged lunch. Mystery meat bagged lunch. The ladies moved over so I could sit down on the small wooden bench. The lady I sat beside was very nice and friendly. The lady beside her was crying. I held onto my coat and lunch bag and sat there while everyone in the cell asked me what the hell I was doing there.

I told my story and these mates became outraged at my story. The lady who was crying stopped as she hear me tell my truth and a peace came over her as she knew I was there for a crime I did not commit and how humble I was. I offered out my lunch bag to the mates in the cell and they told me to keep the drink to keep my energy up. As the minutes ticked by the mates and me each told their stories. There were four of us who really bonded and moved from this small holding cell to a bit bigger one. The guards separated our cell when it was becoming too full of laughter.

God gave me the strength to make these other mates laugh. A sense of peace and calm came over me and I no longer was afraid. We laughed and laughed and the guards got mad and separated out pod. I was placed in a new, bigger pod with my three friends. It was really late and we still had not been processed to be moved to the remand center. They had put in our pod some mates coming down off drugs and others detoxing from alcohol. One lady had to use the washroom, but no guards would open the door so she urinated in a cup she found on the floor. It was inhuman the treatment. As the pod filled up, the cup of urine spilled. The guards on staff were very upset and started screaming at the mate. She screamed back and told them she had to otherwise she would pee her pants. Gosh, are these guards really that stupid not to let some use the washroom?

One by one we were processed and moved to the remand. I had to still be processed and given jail clothing. Once I was taken into a small room and striped and searched and then given some jail attire. My street clothes were bagged and ready for transport to my final destination and I am now in the system.

I was the last of the four of us to be moved. The guards called me out of the holding cell and shuffled me up to the women's floor. There are two sides one for low risk offenders and one for high risk offenders. I was put in the low risk offenders. There was a clear bubble in the middle were the guards conjugated and the supplies were passed out. The cells were lined up on the far wall facing the outside of the jail. There was a common area in the middle with picnic benches and three phones in corner. Me and another mate that was just brought up were put into a cell. There was a bunk, a small dresser and a toilet/ sink. The cell already had one person in it, so the gal I was put in with had to get a mattress from another area and used it on the floor. I got to know the lady I was put in the cell with and she told me to take the top bunk. The one gal was coming down from drugs and the other gal was coming down from alcohol and I was coming down from nothing.

We got a blanket and a sheet and a pillow and were told to get to sleep. I had no idea where the ladies I met in the holding cells ended up, but the morning would show me. The cells locked with a big bang. If you had to use the toilet you did it in the cell with your mates. I put my head down and said a prayer and tried to get some sleep.

The next morning the door banged again and it unlocked. The other two mates has been in before so they knew the system and they were very kind to keep watch over me and show me what to do and where to go. Breakfast was only served at a certain hour, you could shower in a common area, you could get new underwear and bras in the mornings but you had to wait in line to receive them, lunch was on a schedule and so was dinner. The common area was accessed if you were not in you cell. I went out into the common area with my mates and found the girls from the holding cell. Thank goodness they were alright. It was a certain kind of sisterhood. I never felt afraid or worried for my safety. God has his army of angles with me. One evening we were able to attend a bible study. Only a certain number could attend so I had the other three mates and I go. It was lovely. We each received a chocolate bar and a bible. I gave my chocolate bar to my cell mates to share and I read my favorite passages in my bible to keep me company.

That night my mate's boyfriend set off fireworks outside. So the three of us stood at our very small window in the jail cell and enjoyed the sight. The next morning there was a message to her written in chalk. I was told that is how the outside communicates with some mates. There were phones that we could use once we were allowed to leave our cells. I called my son and mom to let them know I was okay and not to worry. I was not sure when they would be moving me but once I found out I would call them. You did not have to pay for calls, but the line ups could be long to get to use one and you certainly did not want to appear to be selfish or weak while in here. I would discuss business and then reassure them both it would all be okay. They were more afraid of me and my safety. I appreciate their love and concern so much. I worried about how they were holding up and encouraged them to stay strong.

That night we were allowed to walk the yard, so I dragged out my three amigos and we put on these big coats were escorted out into the yard. The yard was cement walls with a mess cover over the roof on the top of the holding jail, but at least it was fresh air. During my time at remand I bonded with some really wonderful women who had struggles in life, but were not bad people. I was able to make some of them laugh and give hope to others. I was being carried by God and under his angel's protection, which made me more inspired to do His works. I witnesses a lot of other women lose control and so frustrated with where, they were that it would scare someone who witnessed this in public, but our system needs more compassion and less judgment. I was learning this in my journey God had placed me on. Not once did he leave me or forsake me or my family and I am so grateful for that.

It was Sunday and the next morning the girls would be sent off to the Provincial jail to serve out their sentence or to wait until they were sentenced, but the holding jail was full and we needed to get moved. I, however, would go to the Federal jail and that taxi would come for me also on Monday but it was a special taxi that did not make this stop as frequently so I would not be given a time until they knew. As my other mates all lined up, I asked one mate to take special care of our one mate as she was fragile and would need some protection. The girls agreed to keep in touch after and we exchanged numbers and with tears and hugs said our goodbyes. Even though we had only been together for a few days when you are serving time you get to know people as that is all you have is time. These mates were kind mothers hurting and they should not be where they were at.

I sat down on the bench as the jail was almost all cleared out and it was quiet. The guard informed me I would be leaving soon also, so I called my family to let them know I was being moved and I would call them as soon as I could, but I had no information on how the next jail works. I asked them to take care of each other and told them how much I loved them both. I reassured them I was fine and not to worry. One day my story would be told and then for someone who knows nothing about the system could at least have a small glimpse into what a person deals with.

I had to get back into my court clothes for my transport. I was shackled only at my wrist this time. The guards led me down to the garage where a Sheriffs van was waiting for me. They opened up one door and I stepped in to a steel metal bench which faced sideways. Like a cage. The ride to the jail was where I met Apple, she was already in the van when they pulled up for me but I could not see her very well with the partition between us. The ride was very bumpy as we sat on a metal bench. The guards had to stop at Tim Horton's on their way to drop us off. I knew the speed bumps were big but they seemed extra big in this van. And they seemed to hit every pot hole on the road. I was the only one being transported to the federal jail that day along with Apple who came from another jail. She had the pleasure of being on this ride for over two hours already.

We arrived at the Federal institution but unfortunately we could not see much from the van. Once we arrived the guards opened up the back and Apple and I got out. I was finally able to see the lady I had been chatting with in person. We were taken into the very institutional building to be processed. We were striped searched and given sweats to wear along with a winter jacket and shoes. Our clothing we came into wearing would be returned to us once it had been logged onto our cellefex. This is a list of each inmate's belongings. Apple and I then received our pictures for our identification cards. I asked the guard if we could smile in them and she said yes, but never had anyone smile before. Apple liked this idea so she smiled in her picture also. I was not going to let this system or these crooks take anymore away from me and I was going to be the light in the darkness, as God would intend me to be. I was his servant and doing is worked in here now.

We would be granted a phone card and all the other amenities in due time, but for now we were processed and pictured and then both given two huge bags of stuff and told to follow the guards. They took us out into a beautiful court yard that had snow on it. There were houses inside the institution. It reminded me of something off Desperate House wife's and actually very nice for what a jail is. As we walked you could see faces in the houses peering out the windows watching us. Apple and I were both lead to the house furthest from the main house, or the institution headquarters. We walked in the front door and were told this would be our house for our stay. I was taken upstairs to my room and Apple was shown her room on the main floor.

Alone in my room, I sat on my bed still thinking this was so unbelievable. One of the mates came by my room and told me there was food downstairs for me if I wanted. Apple and I ate some food that seemed to taste so amazing. I was hungry, very hungry and I needed a shower something terrible. I apologized for my smell and I would take a shower very soon. I finished eating, washed my dishes and cleaned my room. I disinfected the room and began to open up the two bags of items. There was bedding so I made my bed, there was toiletries so I took a shower and got cleaned up, there were pajamas so I got into them and then I put away what I could but the clothing did not fit me so I will have to wait until they put together a smaller care package to get more clothing, but at least I had some. I met the mates and we watched some TV together. The mates walked Apple and I over the process in the house and the house rules and then told us about the institution and those rules. As night fell you could see more women moving in the yard and walking and talking and doing what a normal community would do. That was what this was, a community of convicts.

My room faced the court yard so I was able to see the action occurring in the yard. God blessed me with the most amazing sunrises. The other side of the house looked onto the road and businesses. It was a constant reminder of society outside. Across the field you could actually look onto the crooks company and see their back door. God put me in this place for a reason, not sure for what but I could keep an eye on that crooked company which was interesting. "God take care of my family, I pray."

October 22, 20xx

Dear family,

I am writing you as I have to get my access code set up and I need to do some things. I will call you as soon as my telephone access code is set up but I only have 15 minutes and a lot to get said.

A) First visitor forms and application:

Make copies of this form. Go to Wal-Mart and have the photo person at the front take the pictures so you can get them right away.

Fill out the form and sent it in ASAP, the process can take some time so the sooner you get this in the sooner we can see each other face to face.

B) Son can you come to the jail and deposit $200.00 into my canteen. This is my bank account for the jail. Just give my name and make the deposit. This should last me a while.

C) 30 days to get my care pack together: I have enclosed a list of items I am permitted to have while I am here. This is a onetime package that to be sent in. I will write out a list also.

Tomorrow I will find out about classes, courses, work and things to keep me busy and productive and self improving while I am here. I miss you guys terribly, but will remain strong for you. Please write and send pictures as nothing else will be accepted in the mail. No gifts are allowed. Son I will hopefully meet my parole officer in her tomorrow and I will let you know what she says.

I will get this letter off to you first thing tomorrow morning. The movement here is only at certain times, even though we are in a house you can only move out of it a certain times. I love and miss you both. We will survive this journey.

Visits can take a bit to get set up so until then I will be you number one pen pal and you will have to write to me. Let everyone know they can certainly write me also.

So what have you two been up too? How did the cable set up go? How is your health holding out mom? Son how are you doing, getting settled into your new 'man cave' at grandmas? How is the cat doing?

Once I have my access phone card set up we can chat every night before bed and more. It could take a bit to get things up to speed, but I will get it all organized. My new house is very nice. The housemates are very nice. There is myself, and a gal I met on the ride from the Remand Centre her name is Apple. There are a total of six women in this house, but it can hold as many as ten. It has a dorm like set up. We each have our own rooms, which contain a single bed, a comfy chair, a night stand, a table, a desk, a wardrobe closet, and a mirror. I have a window facing the courtyard. I am on the upstairs and Apple is on the main floor. There is a huge kitchen and a living room and even a bbq outside.

Tomorrow Apple and I will be getting more information and clothing. There was only one clothing pack so I will get mine tomorrow, plus the size was way too big for me and worked for Apple so that is okay.

After I get more the lay of the land here, I will ask for a family visit and maybe you could come and spend a night or two here. They do have a private family house for these visits that can range between 24 to 72 hours. We can chat later about that.

I miss you guys terrible and will remain strong for you. Please write and send pictures no other gifts will be accepted. The mail is all searched and read by the guards before we are allowed to see it. That is the same with all outgoing mail. The letters are left unsealed so the guards can read it and then they seal them.

I am meeting with my parole officer tomorrow so I will let you know what she says. I will get this letter off to you. I have to wait until movement is called so I can leave the house. Movement is on the hour and you have ten minutes to get out of the house or you have to wait until the next movement and are only until a certain hour each day. You have a chance can you please see if you can get the pen pack together, as it takes up to three months before I will receive it. All items are logged and labeled. I receive a cellefex of what is mine and if other items are in my room I can get into trouble. I am not sure why the mates would not follow the rules, but I am sure going too. Also, note that the color red is not allowed in here as this is a gang color, so no red items please. I will send you a list of items we are allowed to have in our pen pack. Since I will be here for different seasons please keep this in mind in packing.

For federal mates, you serve 1/3 of your time and for provincial mates you serve 2/3 of your time. A federal mate is a sentence two years plus a day and provincial is anything under two years. The federal jail is like a college/ university layout. You have your own rooms, TVs and space. There is one bathroom on each floor for that floor to share. In the provincial setting I was told it is like remand, whereby you are bunked with a mate and you have restricted movement. I would image it is more like the movies portray a jail to be like. You will get to see what it is like when you come to visit. You can drive by and see where I am. We are blessed to be so close. I could not even imagine living away from you guys and more distances then we are. I guess this journey is all tailored and God is keeping us close and because he knows I was not meant to be here, making sure we are blessed.

I love you both and miss you.

October 23, 20xx

I remembered a couple of things today to tell you so I will get that dealt with first. I can't have the mp3 player so could you pick up a cheap walkman and headset. Please pack a roll of stamps and I will get them as I need them. Things will be so much better once visits start so I can see you guys, but not talking to you is really painful. I will stay strong until I can talk to you and then see you. Going from seeing you every day to no contact is just heart breaking. I can't even imagine what you are going thru. My heartaches at going one more day without seeing or talking to you. I don't know if I am more upset at the system for putting me here or myself for not being stronger in fighting the system. This is completely unjust for our justice system.

How are you three doing? I am excited to talk to you and find out how you are doing and what's happening. My son can you call Don and find out what he suggests we do. If he things we should appeal or not. Gosh we should have purchase a lotto ticket as the max is 50 million dollars. God only knows we should have luck somewhere. How is grandma's health? How is she doing under all this stress? I pray you are keeping each other strong.

I start a job tomorrow working in a graphic design and sewing shops. One of my mates works there and now and another does also but she is off due to an arm/ shoulder injury. I have requested to speak to the teacher here to get some information on either the second year post secondary courses or my legal assistant program. I met with my parole officer today. Her name is Bally Weed I also met with my secondary worker here name is Seah Sutter and my primary is Bob Burger. I have not officially met him but from what the mates describe him as a very tall man. I am pretty sure I know who he is. You can pass these names onto Don.

The guards seem very nice and like I said yesterday the house mates are nice also. The house is what I would expect a dorm house to be like. One person cooks and someone else cleans up, which is fine. I am so used to having just me and my son that it is louder then what I am used too. Once I get my schooling lined up, I will spend more time in the library or putting my earplugs in.

I wonder how different this place is compared to the provincial prison. One of my new friends at the remand hopefully is adapting well to her change of environment. When the three of them left yesterday she was so sad. Charity has a five month old baby boy and was caught drinking a non alcoholic beer. Her court date is tomorrow so hopefully she will get a fine or house arrest and be returned back to her baby.

Deanna was caught on her second DUI and sentenced to four months plus two years suspense licence. She is the gal who reminds me of a girl I worked with at the crooks office. She is a fifty year old, pipe fitter and a really nice person.

Kathy had a son. He is fifteen and has the same first name as you. She has two girls from her second marriage and he husband had her arrested. He had put a restraining order on her for a scratch he received and she had to leave the house. She was not to contact him, whom she did via text message to discuss the children and he took the texts to the police. She was arrested and her court date is in November. She was so upset, so I hope my words of encouragement will keep her strong. I asked them to all look out for one another. Kathy then received a serving of separation papers just to add salt to this open cut. Gosh she soon to be ex-husband is sure a wonderful character.

One night I thought that one of the other women was going take out Kathy at the remand. There were a couple of heated moments. I saw one girl coming down off heroin, another coming of meth and another coming down from a long alcoholic binge. I can't wait to tell you the stories about from the moment I walked out of the court room saying goodbye to you until we meet here. If I don't get visits soon and phone calls sooner, I will just write to you. Save these letters so that when I get out we can read them again and see how much we have gone thru and where we are then.

I must say the food at the house is much better than the remand. At the remand they fed you a lot of bread. My lunch at the jail was a mystery meat sandwich times two, and two oranges. After justice Main handed down my sentence I was taken and given another bag lunch for dinner as I had missed the dinner menu because they take forever to process you. Well I guess you are not going anywhere anyways. I had the juice box and gave the gals in the holding cell my dinner bag. There was about twelve of us in the size room of a bathroom. This is where I met my new found friends and most of the girls who would be on the same ward as me.

Breakfast was scrambled eggs, potatoes, cereal, bread and supper was turkey, gravy, mashed potatoes, apple sauce, and more bread. There is a peanut butter and jam sandwich at bed time and with some of the meals. One time we had perogies and sausage and more bread. One meal we received and apple. Having fruit was so amazing. Jail is not a place to diet, well at least not a remand. They serve a lot of carbohydrates and starches to keep you tired. The house at the federal institution had a huge basket of apples and oranges. At the house the head mate makes the grocery list and you can put on it items you want to make a meal with. All the girls are motivated to get fit so that's great. Hopefully I might inspire them to join me at the gym once I get my runners and work out gear.

Well I want to get this letter in the mail tonight. As soon as I get my 15 minute call, I will call you. I hope it will be soon. Actually I will call when you are both there so either early morning or afternoon, but I will take whenever to hear your voices. Bally said that if I had not received the call by Thursday she would look into it and get me one as soon as possible. Gosh it will be almost a week until we can speak. Not good especially if an appeal needs to be filed.

I wish I knew how things were going on your end and I feel so helpless that I can't help you out. Remember the contact number is on the cell phone so call any of them and they will help you out. I miss you both. Stay strong and take care of one another and the cat. Did a lady call from the remand center? Her name was Kim Addison. I spoke to her before I moved over to the institution. You are in my thoughts and my prayers. I love you both.

October 24, 20xx

How are you today? How is your day today? I was hoping to be able to call you tonight but unfortunately they still have not processed my 15 minute phone call and a card so I could call collect was not available but I was told that tomorrow it would all be set up. Nice of the guard to let me know so I was not waiting for something that was not going to happen tonight.

I miss you so much, but I am trying to fill my days with productive activities. Apple, my house mate and I started our jobs today. We get paid $5.80 per day. The grocery store seems like a gold mine. Apple has sewing on the big machines experience so she works in the back part of the shop and I work in the graphics and filling orders for the correctional officers. We start at 8:00am and get lunch from 11:00-1:00pm and then work until 4:00pm. This is also when the counts are conducted. One of my other housemates has a pulled shoulder so she cooked dinner along with another housemate, who also works at the graphic place. My new bosses seem really nice. Jackie lent me some chapstick to use while I was at work, as my lips are so chapped with the house being so hot and now turning cold outside. I have a mailbox, but still no key. So any mail I can't get but still send you letters and know that they will all be read prior to me receiving them.

Did you get a hold of Don? I told my parole officer that I need my 15 minute call to find out if Don would be appealing my sentence, and would be in contact with me Thursday to make sure I have it or a conference call.

The nurse here gave me a needle when I first arrived for hepatises and she called me back to check on the results so she gave me some Vaseline which is such a relief for my lips. She is really nice. Actually, most of the guards I have interacted with are very nice, but I am a bit frustrated with the lack of organization. That's our government for you.

Apple has two girls who are with her mom so she is experiencing some of the feelings that I am, but I imagine not many parents have the kind of relationship that you and I do son, or mom.

You know I have to mention that at my job there is a zero tolerance for swearing so I really like that. Some of the other inmates have such filthy mouths it really is not nice to listen to swearing all day long. Mind you when I was working for the crook his mouth was always swearing so maybe it bothers me because it reminds me of the man. A man who should be behind the bars and not me.

December 15 is the Christmas party for families in here. It starts at 1:00-8:30pm and I would love for you both to attend. We can share a meal together and visit. After work Apple and I had supper, showered and headed over to the library. I picked up four new books to read. I plan on reading myself silly until I get into some programming here, courses at the post secondary level or a TV. The TV in the common area is controlled by Apple and myself as we are the new mates and everyone else has one in their rooms. I think that is nice of the house to implement that rule.

When you first arrive at jail you get $10.00 put into your canteen and once you receive money or earn money you pay the jail back. This money can be uses to purchase stamps, food, personal items, hygiene items and other items. You can also order from Sears or London drugs to have items bought for you and brought in. So I may have you filmy canteen/ bank account with more money and purchase a TV, alarm clock instead of you running around trying to find one that meets their code. Also, like I said before everything takes so long to get logged that this might be a better way to go. The London drugs orders come once a month, but we can discuss and see how you are making out. I don't want to stress you out more then you need to be. Once I get the card tomorrow I will call you collect, which is as weird as I am making a local call and instead of transferring money to my phone card every month. The way things run around here I would hate to not be able to talk to you because of one of the administrative errors. And after all, we are just criminals so who really cares.

My son I am looking forward to showing you and introducing you to my house mates. There is a very nice, young girl who is across the hall from me who is very sweet. So my house mate Mea is the house mom. She orders the food and her room is next door to mine. Susan and Mea are good friends and they both work in Corcan the graphics and sewing department. Max is Columbian and she actually has work release where she goes to the dump and sorts garbage. Max is one who speaks her mind and has helped me out in putting in requests for programs that will help me and look good on my file and just good to have in general. These courses will also look good on my resume when I leave this place such as construction courses, and first aid. May is the sweet on I told you about. She is off to play volleyball in the gym. She is going to school during the day and so does Max. They are getting their high school education while they are in here. Apple is a single mom with the two girls. There is four of use upstairs and two downstairs and my house is right behind the rose colored house. I am not sure if I told you this already.

At certain times of the day you have to stand for count and the guards come in and do a count. So you have to be in your room and standing at your doors. Other times of the day they guards will do a walk thru of the house. Every two hours they patrol the house. From 12:00am to 6:00am when we are asleep the guard will shine a flashlight into our rooms and make sure we are still alive. The doors lock from the inside. The first eighty dollars in your account here is set aside in case you die in here and the government uses that money for your body bag. There is a long window that is covered with fabric on the outside so when the CSC come in, that is the guard, they move the fabric and can see inside our rooms. You are too have your room doors locked at all times, which I do unless I am in my room awake, as there are serious offenders in other houses and they could come into ours at anytime. I am not too worried about my mates killing me, but the house is not locked so just to be safe.

Our house is the least restrictive so we have I think more privileges, but after all this is jail so to me we all share the same rules. Our house still h as movement the same times as the other house. Movement is where you can go from your house to the main building. I'll explain more when I see you.

Just jot down some notes to discuss with you so I don't forget anything as you won't get this letter until after our first call. I take great relief knowing you two are taking care of one another and being strong. I am so looking forward to our first meeting. After your clearance is completed we can set up visits. The visitation days are Monday, Tuesday, Wednesday, Friday 5-9pm, Saturday has three slots 9-11pm, 1-3:45pm, and 5-9pm and Sunday is 1-3:45pn and 5-9pm. I will provide you with the number to call to set up the visits.

Sorry if I am rambling on but the writing helps me stay connected and until we can talk even if you get this letter afterwards at least I can tell you what I am up too. So please tell others to write it is so nice to have outside contact if I can't see others. Well I better get this off to you. Stay strong and help one another out. I love you both xo........ forever.

October 25, 20xx

It was so amazing speaking to you both today. I am so grateful that even if I am in her that you have each other. Thank you my son for being my point man and the one who can help grandma out while I am away. And mom thanks you for your support and taking care of my number one possession, my son.

How is the cat doing? She would love it here; there are four huge rabbits in the court yard. I mean two times the size of the ones we have at home if not bigger. We had just finished dinner and Mea got homemade pizza crusts out and we each garnished our own. Today was quite a ride. I went to work this morning but before that I handed in my request form to see the doctor as I was a bit stuffed up and my throat was sore. If it takes weeks to get into the system I thought I had better request a visit to the doctors before I get too ill. I also dropped off a request form for my parole officer to set up a call as I need to talk to you about don. Then apple and I need to have our hand scanned so we could go to canteen, but the system was done and we had to come back later. So then we went to work for 8:00am. My parole officer, sorry I ran into her in the hallway on my way to work and I told her I put in a request for to speak to her. She told me I needed to talk to my primary worker, but I think Bob is off until Saturday, but when we spoke she told me to check in with her on Thursday if I had not received my call. I just look at it that I was very blessed that the other officers not only got my call but that it was over 15 minutes. Something is looking over me.

I was only at work for an hour when my parole officer came to my work and told me she had set up a call for 2:30pm. I knew where the office was but you are not allowed to knock, and I knew where the conference would be so I was excited for 2:30pm for our first call.

I had been paged to the health care unit. So my thought was the doctor wanted to see me. Great, he could check to make sure my throat was not serious. Then Apple gets called also. So we had Candice, our other boss call for a pat down. We could go to the doctors, but we had to have the pat down first and they took a while. After being cleared we headed over to the health clinic. The doctor came but it was not for my throat, she started asking me about my medical history. I told her that I was interested in having my throat checked.

Anyways, a long story short, she was there to make sure I had a clean bill of health so that if God forbid I get anything it was in here and not something I had already. We had a good laugh and she was a kind spirit who reminds me of Doctor Ruth. She looks at us as people and not criminals. Her name is Veronica. I have to write a request in one week to get my results. She asked me a list of questions about my medical history, drug history, my tattoos, which I have none, my piercings which are only in my ears and then she asked me to role play with her. She said what would my reaction be if the results of my blood work came back HIV positive, well of course I gave her the face of pure shock and told her role playing that a few curse words would come out of my mouth and then I would ask the tests to be done again. She asked me if I would be depressed or suicidal. I told her no way, I have a lot to live for my fabulous son, my wonderful mom and this is not going to define me. She loved my positive attitude and I loved the fact that we could both get a laugh in today.

I headed back to work after she took my blood, urine and she did check my throat. Unfortunately they don't give out antibiotics but that is fine as it is just the beginning of the seasonal cold and I will get rest and eat oranges and gargle with salt water.

Back at work, nothing was happening. It was lunch time and Apple was still at the health clinic, so I made her lunch as we had to go back to work at 12:45pm to get our hands scanned to go get canteen. The jail had given us the $10.00 and we both had a list of items to purchase. Apple came and ate but was called again to the health clinic. So I did laundry as you only get three t shirts, three sweaters, three sweat pants, a pair of pajamas, a housecoat, four underwear, four socks, two sport bras, and plastic flip flops.

Upon your arrival you get a hygiene kit with deodorant, tooth paste, tooth brush, a comb, shampoo/crème rinse, soap, and four towels, and four face clothes. At the remand centre there was no deodorant and the toothbrush the Brussels would get stuck in your teeth. There was a no name tooth paste and a comb. The shampoo was dish detergent and it dries out your hair.

The bedding is two pillows, two blankets, and a comforter, a top sheet and a bottom sheet. At the remand you had a sheet and a blanket but no pillow, well at least I did not, and neither did the other two girls who shared the cell. The remand cell was small and with the three girls the room was warm with body heat. The more people in a cell the more time you get accounted towards you time served. So because there were three of us the time served would be more for those waiting to be sentenced. Plus the window was very small so not much heat was lost at the remand. Some of the remand women would comment on how cold they were, so again I was grateful to be warm. The weather was bitter cold outside and that only made this time more gloomy.

Okay back to my day, after we were able to move back to work we, Apple and I stopped to see the hand scanner was working but it was still not. I got called again back to health care, so off I went and I ran into a gal who put out call thru today. She also told me last night that she would get my call set up today, so I told her that my parole officer had a 2:30pm call set up but I was still interested in getting the collect calling card. She told me she would look into that. At the health care clinic the nurse, a male nurse, looked at my throat again and told me that he could not give me anything. I told him I had it checked out earlier this morning and he my story. He is really cute so I did not mind telling the story to him.

As I headed back to work, our employer had us listening to spiels on HIV and different sexually transmitted diseases, so I listened to this speech. Some of the girls were not happy that they could get a disease from the needles they use back and forth. I am fortunate again as I work in the graphics and not the sewing. Apple and I go out hands scanned finally and after our other boss told us not to come back to work as I had my call at 2:30pm and by the time I go to work and a pat down was called and they came it would be past my call time and I did not want to miss the call. Those two ladies at work are sure understanding. Even today, the boss Jackie who lent me the lip balm, when she came in she offered it again for me to use, which was so sweet. I was blessed to have the Vaseline also. The thought was so kind. So we scanned our hands and go our federal number, we were able to get our canteen. I purchased some stamps, envelopes, peppermint tea, and Chap Stick. Some mates purchase candy, chips ect but I was only getting what I needed. Apple purchased tweezers s I will see if she will let me borrow them until next week in exchange for some tea. If not that's okay, I will get tweezers next week anyway.

While at canteen, Apple and I were called to the program trailer. We met with the lady regarding our programs we have to take while in here. It's kind of backwards as the primary worker meets with you, assesses you and the parole officer determines what you need to do before being released back into society, but that plan can take months and so I want to do as much as possible now. I want to be pro-active in my rehabilitation here. I am still waiting for the teacher so I can get some post secondary information. Most of the inmates have not completed grade 12 educations. I would like to get my next diploma so I took out a criminology book to read this weekend. I am determined to make every moment count in here.

After my session with programs I made my request for the phone call with you. I have no idea what happened to my parole officer as I was outside her office at 2:30pm waiting and nothing and even after that I was filling out the request to call you and she was busing talking to someone else.

The male nurse, John told me that Bob was a great primary worker so again I felt blessed. Finally my call was put in and I will catch you up to speed until we can talk again and see each other. I am sure my son will fill you in on everything. This event has really had to make us stronger together and test our fears, and challenge our limitations, but at the end of it all we will be more blessed, more grateful and more united the ever before.

I will call you as soon as I get the collect call card. After I hung up with you my son I took four deep breaths and the thanked the wonderful guard so much and she told me she would calmed down tonight if she can get the card for me so I will wait. If just wanted them to know how they made my day.

I headed back to the house so happy. We had pizza for dinner, I folded my laundry and Apple came back to the house. She has still not been able to get a hold of her girls and her family so I am giving her as much positive support, because I know that is what I would need if I were here. She seems fine, but I will keep giving her positive confirmations.

We got another new mate. Her name was Sally. She is from another large town nearby. She has no kids and has been here before. Apple has not been here before but has spent time in rehabs and another local jail. The other ladies have been here before except for me and I am not sure about May. One thing is for certain I will not be coming back. If I have to quit every job from now until I am retired due to a boss who is a drunk and a crook, I will be doing that. I am not going to get involve in corruption than that is what I will do. But I will speak the truth and continue to expose the corruption in this country.

Well I have just had my shower and put on my pjs. I started this book last night called "A stolen life" by Jaycee Dugard. It is a true story about an eleven year old girl who was kidnapped. I also good out a few more books to dive into and surround myself with good books.

I love you both and miss you terribly. You are in my thoughts, my prayers and always in my heart.

October 26, 20xx

How are you today? How are things going? Today was an okay day. I am sure hoping that they call me up to get my calling card, but I still plan on writing to you also. Plus, this can be the start of my new book.

Today marked one week. We headed off to work this morning, which was okay. I got to learn how to use the embroidering machine that was neat and did some free hand drawings on the computer which was interesting. After lunch I met with the Chaplin here. His name is "Whitey". He has services at different times and a full on Sundays at 4:30pm, which I plan on attending. I asked Apple if she would like to go but she has a lot of mixed feelings about religion, so I told her that she should check it out and who knows it may give her some change to start on a new path and if she doesn't get anything out of it well at least she went. Better to have checked it out than to pass up something that could be wonderful and help us while we are here.

There was sure a lot of cursing at work today. Just because we are in jail does not mean the ladies have to talk so nasty. When we were hired on Wednesday the bosses said there was a zero tolerance but today the "f" bomb was running wild. Tonight I am going to bed early I am almost over my cold and during the week the guards came into the house war so quietly to shine a flash light at you to make you move to ensure you were still alive. This is done every couple of hours so you don't' get a good night's sleep which is not healthy or wise.

At 10:00pm we have to stand at our doors so you have to be awake for that. I guess the weekends are more laid back as there is no work at the graphics place so you can sleep in for a bit. I finished my first book which was good and moving onto my second. Apple said it was really funny but I think I may be enjoying this person more in person.

I am hoping to meet my primary worker this weekend. I have put in a request for you to come to the jail and spend either 24 or 72 hours here. My parole officer got my request but I have to wait for one month and then re-apply as they have to do your clearances first. How would you like to come here for an overnight visit? There is a house we can reserve and have some quiet time together. When you come for a visit we meet in an area with a number of chairs and tables, not very private, but I will be so grateful to see you whatever the area. It was also great because Bally could witness that I was really attending work and I got a chance to tell her that I did get my call and that everything worked out great. The lady at the visiting centre is Elise who blessed us.

Weather is starting to turn into a sleep season. One thing I miss is quiet. Living with seven people in this house is anything but quiet. No one can have their TVs a t a normal volume or speak in a normal pitch, everyone shouts. And with six others there is always someone talking. You know me I am more of a quiet person.

I received my mail last night when Apple and I will walk up so she could make her 15 minute call, which she finally got thru to her girls and family. Thank you so much for coming and making a deposit into my canteen account. Please add it to the amount I owe you. I placed an order to London Drugs to order and alarm clock, and am/fm walkman and a 15" TV so you can cross those items off your list. Elise could not tell me if you were successful in getting the visitor form printed off but she explained to me that the mail can be a slow depending on when I get it in the mailbox and because they have to search everything coming in and leaving it can take a while. So hopefully you will get my daily letters and you can keep each other informed.

Back to what I wanted to tell you about my mail. I also received a note on my request to speak to the teacher about my post secondary courses, when apparently they don't usually get many mates that have their grade 12 education. Most if not all expect me don't have their grade 12 and those individuals get educated but she told me to talk to the occupational therapist and social worker to get courses via correspondence. If I can't get my classes here I will request the books and challenge the exams. Either way I is not leaving or wasting them her not being self-productive.

Can you send my manuscript of my first book to publishers? I am getting this story published one way or another.

I hate not knowing how you are doing or what you are doing so I am excited to receive your letters so get those pens moving. Jail is a place where you sharpen your pens and write, hence my daily letters. Did you hear back from Don? If not please call him again, there is a short window of time to appeal and every day counts. Also, ask how can they have a judgement and restitution? If they have a judgment then they can take the house now but have to pay the $40,000.00. With restitution that does not take place until the sentence time has lapsed and we can rent out the house. Gosh, I can't wait to tell you everything I have experienced on this crazy journey. From what it was like to be shackled and handcuffed to the lady freaking out in the holding cell, to the jail guards, to the remand, to the food, to the correctional center, to the housemates.

My son after things are settled I want you to apply for the welding or whatever post secondary education you want or if you want to work full time. I just want you to keep busy because when I get out I want to spend time being as close as we were before I came here.

Mom I want you to keep your health in check. If the doctor is not cutting it, you need to find one that is and will diagnose you properly. I need you to be in good health for when I come home. We will have a lot of living to get done.

In my brief case there is a folder outlining codes of conduct lawyers must follow. With me being her and the taxation appointment in

January, I will prepare everything I can and I have asked Wayne to help and attend with you. Have you managed to get a hold of him?

I am so looking forward to next Thursday when I can go to canteen and purchase a razor. Gosh the simple things in life are really appreciated in jail. Canteen is only Thursdays, so if you miss it too bad. Every second Thursday we get $4.00 from the government to purchase hygiene items. Did you know it costs taxpayers $140k for a federal inmate and $100k for a provincial inmate each year to house and that is now, I am sure it increases yearly. So thanks taxpayers. I am also looking forward to seeing you and having a good laugh. I have not had one since I left the remand. I know that those gals will take care of each other. I have told Apple that we should keep in contact once we are out and if she needs to call for support that I would be there for her. Apple comes from a long line of drunks and alcoholism runs in her family. I think that I could help her keep focus seeing as we are both single moms and keep her focused on her kids.

I am looking forward to getting my plan and meeting my primary. One guard I met yesterday from another jail said as we both sat on a bench that I was way to smiley being here and she could not wait to see me in a couple of months. I told her this place does not define me or my happiness. Now that I think about it I will probably be happier as I will have had many letters, telephone conversations, visits and even closer to my release date, so I will be even happier in two months.

As you two know so very well, that life has not handed me an unchallenging path, but I surely have had huge rewards at the end and I know the same will come from this journey. So we must stay strong and healthy so we will be able to enjoy the successes to come.

In our letters we can write our peaks and valley. My peak is writing to you, and maybe getting my calling card. My valley is my co-worker was being a bit of a bossy pants, but I just focused on the ability to listen to good music at work and shrugged off the rest, so it turned in to a peak.

Well I should sign off and ask my roommates for some more paper to write to you tomorrow. I borrowed Apples tweezers and paid her in tea. These gals here have been here for a while so my tea means nothing, but at least I can offer something

All my love to you both.

October 27, 20xx

Hope you are both in good spirits. I was just writing my letter to the Institution of Chartered Accountants and I was thinking that I should include the letter I sent to the judge as it explains a lot of the craziness. I should also send it to the Law Society and raise a complaint against Mr. Reck. So that being said can you please print off three copies of the judge's letter. The file is located on the desktop under judge. Just so I don't forget as I would normally just do it, but now I have to make sure I write everything down so I don't forget to tell you. Thank you so much.

Mom you can call the tax department and ask to speak to Martha's supervisor to get some contact information ask this new person why the file still has not been investigated and it was reported in August 20xx. Also, get that persons mailing address and send them a copy of the letter sent to the judge.

Sorry if this letter seems choppy, but I have enclosed two other letters. Can you please type them up and send them to Wayne for his review. Once he has replied please make the changes and make an appointment or bring them at your next visit and I will sign them.

When I went to the main house, this is the main building you see from the front of the road, I ran into my primary worker who told me he had been trying all day to get a hold of you so to confirm the phone number so I could get my calling card to you collect, but you must have been out so he told me he would try again at 4:00pm and continue all day tomorrow to get a hold of you.

My primary and I sat down for a few moments and chatted and I gave him a brief outline of my case and my goals while I was here, which included getting my post secondary education. Bob said his first priority was to get a hold of you and to get you cleared for visits. I am hoping you have filled out the forms and returned them back to the jail. Like I said before you will have to write to inform me on what is happening because it may take some time before we can talk and meet, plus it's nice to receive mail from the outside world.

I feel very out of place here. As nice as my mates are I enjoy the quiet, spiritual time and they are very loud. For example in the common area downstairs the TV will be on as high as it can go and someone else will be in the kitchen with the radio as loud as it can go. You can't even hear yourself think. My mates upstairs leave their TVs on, blaring and they are downstairs. I guess they are not thinking of others or mindful of what they are doing, but that will certainly not be acceptable once I get my course materials. I will bring it to their attention or I will purchase ear plugs.

I am also slow to process on things as all but me have been in the system before. So it is easier as most if not all of their information is there and as for me I am new to the process and the federal criminal system.

Just like I am probably the only one here pursuing a post secondary education, as everyone else in the my house either has not completed grade 12 or needs to upgrade and I am not the oldest one here. Kind of feel like a fish out of water, but that is because I don't belong here. I will make the best out of this situation and every time I get feeling a bit sad I will tell myself I have to be strong and that I am gathering information.

Tomorrow I will meet with Bob and attend church service at 4:30pm. I guess it must be that I truly came from the other side of the tracks, because being taught respect for other, kindness, and consideration and not loud or foul mouthed and I am certainly not willing to become like that, but maybe my manners will wear off on the others.

What have you been up too? Keeping busy and dealing with stuff most likely. I feel like this is a one sided conversation as I have not received any correspondence from you, but I imagine you are swamped getting settled. I will continue to tell you what is going on in here.

The address for the Law society is on the website just go to the filing a complaint link. And the institution for chartered accountants will be in the emails and on their website also. I tried to file the ICAA before the court but they said I had to send it with contact information, but the mailing address will be there.

Inside we get the movie channel so I am going to watch a movie with the mates. My mailbox number is #29 interesting as that is my birth date. I am starting to babble so I am going to end this letter and sign off until tomorrow. One week down and a couple more to go, we will survive this and be stronger and rewarded for having to have gone through this. Be strong and we will talk very soon and see each other sooner.

Good night my family. I love you and miss you. I will get this letter off to you so maybe by early next week you will have it.

October 28, 20xx

Hope all is well. I have been waiting to get my phone card and today I finally received it but the card does not work. It is extremely frustrating. I hope they can get this fixed tonight so I can call you and find out what is going on and how you are doing. This is easier for the people who are already in the system then it is for the newbie's.

As I wait for them to fix the card problem, I thought I would write you and tell you about my day and so on. After meeting with Bob yesterday, I woke up early hoping to get word that he had gotten a hold of you and approved the phone numbers. At 2:15pm, Bob gave me the approved phone number sheet but I had to wait to get the card accessed and that took forever. When I finally got the card one of my mated had been on the phone for two and half hours chatting to different people so I had to wait for her. Mea had to call her some so she told me to go ahead of her, but the card would not work so I had to wait until 6:00pm to go the main house to have them get it fixed, but visiting hour was on so the guard told me she would call me in 20 minutes, which seemed like three hours. Time has gone so slowly here but that is because I want to talk to you and see you so badly. Thank goodness for the writing it has helped me journal and communicate.

I picked up another book to read. A John Grisham and I really enjoy his style of writing. This book is called the "Innocent man" and is based on a true story.

My son can you Google search for me section 312 of the criminal code, I looked up this section and could you print it out and send it to me here along with the law of conspiracy.

Thank the good lord we got to talk tonight. Mom sorry for being short tonight. My shortness was not directed at you and I am sorry. I so appreciate all that you have done and continue to do. I certainly don't want to stress you out and have your health affected, so I promise our chats will be much better. I knew this is new to you as it is to my son and me, so the best thing to do is now we can chat more and soon see each other in person is if I ask for something to be done, I will put it in writing. I guess it is just that I have been so used to doing things myself and that I have to let you guys deal with this crap and this is not fair nor should you have too. Mom it is my frustration and not you and I am sorry. At least we got to talk and things will only get better.

If you want you can pack the cat or at least tell her if she doesn't behave she will be shipped off to see me. One of the houses they call the 'lifers' house has a cat and one of the ladies here brings her dog. Today he was dress in a prison outfit which was so cute.

Max lent me some magazines after I got off the phone with you. I am looking forward to our visit not only to give you a hug and kiss, but so you can see the environment. For your information I received a care pack which contains a small combed, deodorant, shampoo and cream rinse, toothbrush, and toothpaste, laundry detergent, tampons, and pads, and a brush. The brush makes my hair stand up with the static and it being so dry here. Once a month you are called to get refills on these items, which will help out in not having to spend my canteen money on these hygiene products.

I was going to attend church tonight, but was waiting for the phone card and more importantly to chat with you, so maybe next week I will attend as this may help. Sometimes being in the house too long can make a person a bit down. Even tonight when I was running back and forth to get the card activated just leaving the house and seeing other mates was good.

Hey how did we do on the lotto? I guess by you not mentioning our million dollars winning that must be a negative on the winnings. Well we mare much richer in other areas, like our love for each other.

When you come for your visit I will show you the canteen list. These are items we can purchase on the Thursday. Each house is called up in order and you go to the shop and place you order. This Thursday I will purchase a razor for $0.85, tweezers for $1.80, cherry halls for $1.05, q-tips for $2.35, zest for $1.00, some ibuprofen for $2.50, envelopes for $0.25, and stamps for $0.70 each and a couple of writing pads of paper for $1.65. I will only purchase what is necessary. Oh yes and some dental picks for $2.65. I sure do miss dental flaws.

We all pitched in and cleaned the house. I vacuumed and washed the upstairs floors. I am usually up early in the morning so I wash the dishes which I don't mind. There is a large window so I can look outside and see the people in their vehicles driving up and down the road. The other mates are good cooks and bakers so I have to do some walking or I will be huge by the time I am out.

My son are you still working? Thank you for being my rock. I was waiting to get my phone card and am w the list of movies they play here and one of our favorites is on the list. Fever pitch was on the list but I would only want to watch it with you guys, s ii will wait and when I get out we will watch it okay.

Miss you both, love you more than anything, and I am so grateful we talked tonight and I will call again tomorrow at lunch and again at 8:00pm

Peak was getting my phone card and actually talking to you. My valley was waiting on the card to be activates.

October 29, 20xx

It was wonderful talking to you both at lunch time today. Hearing your voices does not substitute from actually seeing you or being with you but baby steps and everyday is on day closer to being with you.

After I had my appointment with the doctor here I had to do some testing to make sure I was not crazy and to see what other programming would be required. At the doctors she gave me a hepatitis shot for A & B and explained the side effects which could be flu like symptoms and I was fine until about 4:30pm and I had to lay down and had every intention of going to the gym but was not feeling very well. I had some tea and did a few minutes on the gym machine in the house. Tomorrow I will try and go to the gym. Not sure if it was the shot or the lack of sleep. My mates upstairs get ups at 6:00am with the TV blaring. Either I have extra sensitive hearing or others have a lack of hearing, but everything has to be so loud. Good news is that the mate who works at 6:00am says it is too hot upstairs and wants to move downstairs so that might be a blessing. I will purchase some earplugs on Thursday canteen day. The doctor thinks I am funny and have a good attitude, which you have to in order to survive this journey. She makes me laugh and is just a bundle of energy.

I completed some of my testing today after my doctor's appointment. You just to answer some questions on the computer. I asked the two ladies if the write these test and they said no and asked me why. I told them the questions were depressing. One of the ladies said they probably would not be hired for her position if she took the test. Funny how they want us to answer them, yet they would not pass them or they would be assessed negatively. I view this as a set up for failure. Great system we have going down on the inside.

This afternoon I had to meet with two other ladies regarding my intake process and they gave me a bunch of paper work to fill out and answer more questions. For example, one title is work experience and a bunch of questions. Education and a bunch of questions so I will answer them and return it so they can make the appropriate assessment.

One lady was shock when she asked me if I was feeling remorse for my crime, and I told her no because I did not commit the crime. I informed her on why I pled guilty and she said she had heard many cases but nothing like mine. I told them about my booked and she said she was very interested in reading it. I asked them for a business card and then she said in all of her twenty four years of doing this job I was the first person to ask for a business card. I was shocked at this also as it just seemed natural especially when you are meeting new individuals all the time here. Keeps names and faces together.

Work was good. I learned to do engraving on tags and filled orders. My co-worker as not there today or for the rest of the week which is nice that I have to fly on my own. Tomorrow I have to see a lady about programming. These are courses that they think I should take; at least I think that is what it is for. I guess I will find out tomorrow.

The house is quiet right now. Max is at work, Mea is in pain from her sore shoulder, Susan is not feeling very well so she is sleeping, May is having a visit at the main house, Apple is doing something quiet in her room, and sally is watching TV. Sally has been here before. Like I said I am the only one with no record, and has not been here before as I have never been in trouble with the law as this is not my character as you know.

Well I am going to call you and we can chat. I love you both so much and please pass on a hi to the neighbours. Let people know I am fine and staying strong. I imagine they are also stressed over this turn of events.

October 30, 20xx

Good morning, hope you are both having a great day. I am hoping we will be able to have a visit soon as I am missing you. My son I wanted to know if you would be going to the Halloween party this weekend. I am not sure if I mentioned in my other letter this but I will mention it again, I just have so much to say, but did you not find it interesting that the letter and CD that was returned to Mr. Reck was included in the court records. I thought that these items were returned to Reck and in his possession yet the judge filed and sealed this as evidence. Reck had said he had it in his possession on august 24, 20xx.

Anyways, how are you doing? I hope you write to me also, but just know I am thinking of you and will write to you guys so you can know what is happening on the inside.

Today, I was a work in the morning and id did some embroidering. We chatted at lunch which was my peak of my day. In the afternoon, Apple and I had to attend a sexually transmitted disease information session. Wow there is a lot of really scary diseases out there. Thank goodness I have a clean bill of health and will be limiting my exposure and risk especially being in here. Apple gets a kick out of me. She has been to these sessions before so she has knowledge of what goes on.

I however have no interest in girl condoms or sharing anything with anyone especially in here. I am sure once I get a TV I will be more room bound, but for now I will read, write and workout. I have been doing some exercises in my room. I scheduled a treadmill for tonight but forgot we could not have movement until 7:00pm so my 6:00pm time did not work our very well. I'll try again tomorrow. I had a program scheduled but this sexual disease session out ranked my program so I now have that tomorrow.

My son can you get the following peoples contact information for me so I can write to them. All the information is in my phone book. I will also need this for the future. I am sure of it.

One of the girls in the house has Bob as her secondary worker and as you know he is my primary worker. Well, her primary who happens to be my secondary has gone on holidays for six weeks so now Sally is being pushy about seeing Bob and dealing with her stuff and how she needs to talk to them to get phone numbers on her card ect. I suggested she should call and find out if there is someone who is dealing with her primary workers work load as that would be very unfair to Bob, plus if he is my primary I should have first dibs on him handing my case. She took a real attitude and told me that she did not care and that she would be getting her stuff dealt with. Okay, I am not sure why people have to be so pushy, rude and inconsiderate. I put a request in to speak to Bob as we could go over the next step and because I have no idea what or who I should believe. I would rather sit down sometime this week, just so he and I can stay on the same path and headed towards the same goals.

I picked up this new book at the library; I will not be enjoying reading tonight as someone is slamming doors downstairs. These women do not know how to act. I walked over to the main house and put in a request to have Wayne number added to my phone card. I felt a really good energy outside, so if I can't book a treadmill tomorrow, I may just walk the circle and clear my thoughts. So looking forward to seeing you and working out again together and grandma you can come too.

Well I am going to sign off as I am about to call you and I don't want to miss my time again as these girls keep taking my time even when I booked it on the time schedule list. Deep breathing is essential in here. Soon we will have our visits and able to see each other in person.

October 31, 20xx

Happy Halloween! You will have to tell me all about the little monsters that came tonight. Next year hopefully we will be handling out candy together. Let's make it a date.

How was your afternoon? Mine went fast. After we spoke this morning I went to work for a while and then had to do a test to determine what programming I would be required to take, again. I am a minimum mate, so I am only required to complete one program which is mandatory for everyone anyways.

My son can you add the vital statistics to the list to get my sin number. I am not sure why I can't just give the number, but they require the actual card. I pull the University course booklet from my second year of courses, but I am not sure if this university offers correspondence courses in here.

In another University course booklet the registration number is as follows and the courses I would like to take are the ones we discussed on the phone. Can you see if this University will offer the correspondence courses in here?

Tonight was a really good night. We had a great supper, Sally cooked chicken, pasta, and vegetables. We received a treat bag for the house from the jail which consisted of cans of pop, some chocolate, candy, chips, fizzy pops and more. We headed over to the gym for some treats and pop. There was a costume contest which was really good. The pregnant nun won. Kind of funny, I thought the hippy should have won as she was all decked out and even had a joint. There was an eating contest where you could not use your hands, a musical chair game and a spin of a minute to win it. It was very entertaining to say the least. When we got back to the house, I called you which are my highlight of all my days.

The girls were getting these scary pictures to put in one of the mates room. She is scared of scary movies and since she would not be home until after we had all gone to bed, they wanted to scare her. Mea has a picture of Chucky in her window door. After I got off the phone with you Mea was showing me what it looked like. I told her that will look really freaky especially when the guards come in and shine their flashlights on it.

Apple won the contest for guessing the correct number of movies she won a loot bag of goodies which was awesome for her. She loves scary movies.

It timed out great because Apple had the post secondary catalogue I needed to look at so I was able to view it tonight. Apple can't attend post secondary yet but I was thankful she had it. Perfect timing. Well I want to get this letter off to you. I love you both and still missing you each moment. I long for the days we will be together.

November 1, 20xx

Day 14 already, October is done and gone and we are into November. Time is going fast, not fast enough until I am with you again, but just think soon we should be getting visits in person. That means a huge hug and kiss.

Happy days today I am going to purchase a razor, tweezers and ear plugs. No more jungle legs, unibrown and a good night's sleep. Mind you last night was a good night sleep, but after half a month of crazy sleep I am over due for one solid night sleep and by the sounds of it none of us are getting good night sleeps. Mom is going to the bathroom every couple of hours, my son is dealing with the daycare kid lets and me and the roommates and two hour flashlight checks. So just please of mind knowing we are all sleeping deprived. Have to wait until next time for the earplugs.

Thanks so much for all your hard work getting the house taken care of, making phone calls, covering my financial obligations, getting my pen pack together and all that you two have been doing for me. It means the world to know you two have my best interest at heart. I love you both and I am so grateful for everything.

On my way to work this morning, I popped my letter in the mail to you and ran into Bob. He asked me if I had received my phone card and that we would sit down in the next couple of days. I asked him also to sit down just so he could know what was going on and to check in the told me he would check on the visitation approval so that should be in the works and next on the important list of to do's. Just as he was leaving, my parole officer greeted me with a good morning and that was wonderful to see her also. What a great start to the day. We had canteen so at lunch I fixed my unibrow and now have two eyebrows.

I loved chatting with you at lunch, and as always my highlight of my day. I made a grill cheese sandwich for lunch and for Apple and Sally. It is a very fitting for a snowy day. For dinner Susan is making beef barley soup, which sounds very yummy and healthy.

I was called to A & D (arrivals and departures as I call it) to pick up my clothes that I came in wearing. So I now have my runners for the gym and I am very excited they sent my shoe laces in. At the remand you have to remove your shoe laces from your shoes so you are walking not only with shackles around your ankles but your shoes are not flip flopping around. Anyways, the good thing is I have them back until I did a load of laundry and washing machine ate one of the laces. So now

I have to wait until it magically appears or I have to cut the string out of my sweat pants and make a make shift one. Well, I have my clothes back so that is good.

I went to work this afternoon and we got to leave early at 2:45pm. I had o go to the health clinic again today to see a different nurse to be asked about my family medical history. My answers consisted of a lot of 'no's which made me the easiest patient she had had. She asked what I was doing and I told her that I was working and would be starting programming in a couple of weeks and then soon my correspondence courses would be coming in. I had put in a request to speak to the occupational therapist so just waiting for the meeting. The nurse told me if I needed anything like eye exams, dental, therapy ect to just make a request. Some of the girls who have had dental work done here have since had troubles so I am not going to wait on that service as my teeth are good... knock on wood.

I am going o read for a bit and hopefully be able to visit the gym for a 30 minute workout. The gym is small but does the trick. It has two treadmills, two bikes, a stair climber, some free weights and I think that is it. I think I mentioned in a previous letter there is a Stairmaster in the house but I am not a fan, plus it is nice to get out of the house just wait until I have my head set and can sing. The gals will be in for a treat. The gym will clear out.

It is so funny how every one of the girls in the house expects Mea and I are talking about their weight and how they have to lose weight. You know usually girl talk. I just tell them to eat right and work out. I enjoy my walk on the treadmill and hopefully I can keep booking a machine and if not I will walk the yard outside for 30 minutes plus do some push ups and squats and pressed in my room twice a day.

Hardly anyone showed up today for work so tomorrow there should be lots of fun stuff to do. Not much else to report. It was really nice to be able to share this evening, as two weeks is too long. I miss you and would love to be able to see you. Tomorrow will be two weeks since I have seen you and able to hug you. I am grateful we are able to see each other without long commutes.

Funny when I came to the jail, I got a ride in the van and tonight on the news there was a close up of the van. All the different things one experiences in life. Not complaining as I view these things as information I can pass on. We all have a purpose and I am going to make the most of this purpose and sure hope you are going to input this letter onto the computer. 10:00pm but by the time they get to our house it is 10:30ish. Funny they just announced the stand to count.

I was watching TV tonight and the guards came in and we chatted for a bit and had a couple of laughs. They are really nice, some are not very nice but for the most part they are kind people. Everyone has good and bad days but it is all how we deal with them.

November 2, 20xx

Happy Friday! How are you doing keeping busy I hope?

Today I had work. I learned how to sew the outside edges of patches and amazingly I am not too bad at it. I worked with Sally and by the end of the morning I had had enough of her. She made me mad. What happened was the other day I was waiting for a pat down and it was taking a while, but the lady in programs knew that I had to get a pat down the guards were doing the best they could to get some for the pat down and so I just had to wait.

Today, I had to go back to healthcare as the nurse wanted to see me about my results from my mammogram from two years ago, so I had to sign a consent form and to see if I would require another one while I was here. Nothing major so I returned back to work there was a male guard at work but he could not do the pat down but he was here when I returned. He told me I should have gone home and I told him there was still time to do some work and that would not be honest and responsible for me to do that.

I continued to work with Sally when she goes and tells the guard that I had to wait forever for a pat down and missed my appointment. I said that was not true. I did not miss my appointment and the person on the other end knew I was waiting for the pat down. I told her to mind her business about my situation. Then she told the guard that members of our house had grieved the guards. That was between the members of the house and that guard and she had no business saying anything about this either. She is going to get into trouble if she does not mind her own business. Then at work she tells me that I can finish doing the other work after lunch. I am not sure who she things she is, but since she has come into the house she has changed the feeling of the house. I will certainly be spending more time in my room and staying clear of her.

Bob just came to do count at lunch and told me he would call me ups to chat this afternoon. I imagine he got attacked downstairs by Sally as she is very pushy person. I don't even want to go downstairs to see what time it is so I don't have to hear her go on about Bob. If she keeps poking this bear, I am going to tell her in a very direct and firm way, to stay out of my way and my business. I will not put up with her.

There are individuals here that just love to get others into trouble and I want no part of it. I am heading back to work. I loved chatting with you at lunch. The guard came back in to tell us, me and Sally a story about the more secure areas in this jail and some of the crazy behaviours they have to endure. The guard told me he respect my judgment and said he thought I had good judgment. He was very nice and we actually saw eye to eye on all the issues he was discussing which was nice as most of the mates have such a chip on their shoulders and it is not the guard's faults; they are just trying to do their jobs. Jackie, my boss, at work gave me some magazines to read at that the house and then to bring them back when I was done.

Wow, Bob just called me up to the front to chat which was really nice. He told me Wayne was approved on my calling card so I will give him a call once Bob gives me the green light maybe tomorrow. I told bob I had a job a Corcan, that I only had to complete the one mandatory program which started in a couple of weeks but I could work until then and that I would be completing my correspondence course also. He was impressed.

We discussed the concern I had regarding getting forgotten as I am not a pushy persona and I was concerned that because he is others secondary that they seemed to think they had more leverage which as I thought was not the case. Bob told me to have you call and see if you were approved for visits yet. He would also check and get back to me on his rounds tonight. He let me know that you were here to drop off the pen pack and said that all the guards commented on how nice you and grandma are. He said he wished he could have met you but he was in the secured unit. A unit that is not very nice at all. Hopefully visits will happen soon now and you can meet Bob. He told me he was off this weekend and would check in with me next week when he returns but I would see him on rounds tonight.

I find it so funny how insures some people are and how even in here there is always someone who wants to rain on your parade. Earlier the girls were raining on Apples parade and after I had my talk with Bob, Apple asked me how was my visit and I told her about getting my pen pack and phone number for Wayne and how Bob was going to check into my visits and escorted visits. Well, they girls tried to rain on my parade, well at least they tried, and with no luck. Maybe if they changed the attitudes things might go their way, very negative, evil gals. And I am so positive that I think they don't like it and well one does not like it and she is trying to bring others down. Well not me. I will just avoid that gray cloud and she has around her.

I was able to go to the library tonight and signed out some more books so now I would be set of the weekend. It was nice to see you both thru the kitchen window and you could see me from a distance. The person who was waiving with me was Mea. After meeting with Bob tonight our visits should be right around the corner.

I headed to the gym and worked out for 40 minutes and did some stringing exercises in my room. Thank goodness for the gym as some place where no one is yelling. Next week will be the ear plugs for sure.

I am very grateful for Bob and all the members of my team. I have been blessed with these amazing individuals and people who want the best for me and us.

Well I am signing off and I will chat with you tomorrow. I love you both and seeing you from a distance just made it more realistic of how much I miss you. All my love to you both.

November 3, 20xx

How are you both doing and how are things I am so thrilled that tomorrow we can actually see each other in person. Get ready for some kisses. Today was a good day. I woke up and watched some TV went and got my mail, which included some exams I needed to complete and I did some reading. The jail was on a lock down, which meant that there was no movement from our house to the main so that meant no working out, a going to the library or dropping off mail and more importantly no visits.

I cleaned my room and washed and vacuumed the floors and cleaned the bathroom upstairs. If I can't go to the gym then I need to do something physical.

Apple, Sally and I watched some TV. When trying to select a show I saw one that was good, so I said why not watch that. Sally asked if she could watch a show that started at 1:30pm. I said I had no problem with that and maybe we would watch my show until then. Apple said that my show was good and then Sally said no she did not want to watch my show. Apple got upset and told neither Sally that I never get to watch a show nor do I ever ask so that I should get to watch something every once in a while. It was a shock to me that Apple would say anything. I appreciated her two cents and maybe Sally will be more considerate and accommodating to everyone else who don't have their own TVs. She is a bit of a TV hog.

I have no problem reading or writing instead of getting involved in other peoples gong, but Apple really pulled a friend move today and that was nice. You don't know how these people will react and what their triggers are so it is sometimes better to play it safe until you do.

I am not sure why even if you are here treat you that you have to be so mean and selfish. The mentality of some of these inmates is really rude. I can understand why some of these inmates this is not their first time here and it have a lot to do with their attitude. In fact, I would be willing to bet I am the only one here who has never had a criminal record, never been in trouble with the law, and never fled, was fully cooperative and does not have tattoos and piercings all over their bodies. Not that I have anything against that, what I am trying to say is I don't fit the profile.

I am so excited for tomorrow. I am going to read myself to sleep so I can get tired and zonk out. I told Apple about tomorrow and told her I would let her know what to expect for information to tell her family. She should be getting visits soon also, but her family has to travel a fair distance and it is winter weather.

I love you both and again so excited for tomorrow. It cannot come quick enough. Bless you both and you are in my prayers, thoughts and my heart. Today with no movement the valley was that the house was so loud and the peak is seeing you tomorrow, plus I am making my way in here.

November 4, 20xx

Today is our visit day. I am so excited. I called Wayne last night but could not get him on the phone so maybe the number was not added but I will keep trying. Wow, what a crazy day. I was so excited to see you today not only did we have to wait an extra hour but then you received a call this morning telling you that there was a lock down and that visits would be cancelled.

At 1:00pm I moved to the main house and dropped off a letter to you, handed in the package the intake worker had me file out on the history of myself and family and the work safety, food safety and health courses that I completed over the weekend.

I waited and waited eager to see you both. I am sure glad I called to make sure you were coming and that everything was okay. I have to say I was shocked to hear your voice as no one here told me that visits were cancelled. That would be a nice thing for the guards to have done, but if you think about it now we can get our visit at 5:00pm today and that now we know that if you are not here in the 20 minutes after your visit is scheduled I will be on the phone to you to find out what happened. Plus, now we have a new visit scheduled for tonight and one scheduled for tomorrow. I get frustrated sometimes with the common respect but I am looking at this situation as now we have visits tonight, tomorrow and we now know for future visits so it is all good.

This information is useful for Apple who will have family travelling from out of town and what they might have to face. Could you imagine travelling a long distance to find out the jail was on a lock down? The lock downs is usually a result of one of the girls in the maximum security causing havoc and we all get too locked down so they can take the guards over to deal with them. The max is a very scary place and very scary people. You can get thrown in there if you misbehave out here.

I just got back from our first visit and I miss you both already. It is so difficult saying goodbye and seeing you walk away. I pray I will get stronger and so will you and that this will be over so soon. I am grateful to be able to see you tomorrow and will focus on that. I am glad you are enjoying these long winded letters and I hope they will provide you with some comfort on what is going on in here.

My son I trust and know that you can handle and deal with whatever comes our way. You are a strong, intelligent, brave young man and I am nothing but the proudest mom. Mom, I know you have only my son and my best interest at heart and our well being. Thank you for our unconditional love and support. It is because of you both that this journey that we are on will be blessed and we will survive. We will travel it together. We need to count our blessings as there are really so many.

My son I guess we will just have to reinstate movie nights upon my release and catch up on all the new ones we will have missed. Mom we will have Sunday night dinners again soon. I am so glad you enjoyed my home cooking and I am so grateful to have shared them with you both.

I love you both. Big hugs and kisses and the real thing tomorrow when we see each other in person.

November 5, 20xx

Good morning to you both. This morning I had to go back to the health clinic and have an exam completed, which was not very fun but now completed. The machine I was working on decided to break a needle. I have never used a sewing machine like this and my boss tells you to fix it. This is crazy. I have no idea what I am doing, plus this is their machinery. I have noticed the work environment has changed and there is a lot of curing going on that was not acceptable and they are not being punished. But the bosses are now swearing a lot also.

Nice to get to talk to you for a bit at lunch. I sure hope you purchase a lotto ticket as some people here actually won the millions and with our lick we are surely deserving of it. Lots of great things are coming our way. At work this afternoon there were so many girls that myself, Sally and another girl had to do the winter jackets with meant unstitching so that another girl could sew in a zipper. The girls asked me which house I was in so I told her. I was unstitching the seam and ripping just fine and Sally has to pipe up and add her two cents. What is with this lady? She sure is a bossy pants telling me how to do things. Yesterday when you were turned away for visits, Sally was smiling. I was doing my own thing dealing with that situation, but Apple saw and she would have no part in it and actually said something to her. I looked at her and shook my head. The girl beside her did what I was doing and she looked at Sally and told her to mind her business. I looked at the girl and smiled and said she is poking the bear and soon someone will get mad at her and put her in her place.

Well, the house is already tense with her here and now even more so as she woke up with pink eye and went to work and touches everything in the house. Susan said she better not get it or she will snap. What a gong. Deep breathing required again.

I was disappointed not to get our visit last night as you can read in my letter. It sure would be nice to chat with same minded people, but I will go to the gym and we will chat on the phone at 9:00pm and either sees each other tomorrow but for sure on Wednesday. It just gives me something to look forward too. I ran into Bob this morning at the health clinic unit and told him about tour visit yesterday and how you were in tonight. He said he was off at 4:00pm and off tomorrow so maybe the next day you could meet him. Things work out for a reason and maybe tonight's visit got messed p so things will work out later in the week. Who knows? I have been leaning just to go with the flow. I am going to read for a bit and head to the gym for a 30 minute workout and I will call you at 9:00pm.

Just as I was heading for movement, there was another no movement announcement. Gosh those girls in max are really upset. Probably a blessing your visit was messed up for tonight as you would have come all that way to be sent away. I could not go to the gym, so I just walked in the court yard and ended up getting a blister on the bottom of my foot. I took my shoe laces out of my jail shoes and put one in my runners. Mea asked me what size my fee was and said I could borrow her runners until my pen pack came in. That was sure nice.

Gee Mondays are sure hard. I wish this place offered more for use mates. I will have to organize some events. Aerobics, painting, something to fill the time. I told Mea she could be our stand up comedian for a show. We are to be rehabilitated and productive members of society after leaving here yet for some reason, I mean most, and this is just a place to pass the time. I am so grateful I have you both to get me my correspondence, and it would b e wonderful for others to be able to use their abilities and skills. They could have so many skills upon leaving here to ensure that their options would be enhanced upon leaving and hopefully not returning.

These inmates need to be stimulated their minds and working on the body. I am sure if they had a sense of purpose it might change the attitude and outlook on getting and making a difference. Organization, productivity and goals are not high on their lists around here, maybe I could help inspire.

Anyways, even though we could not see each other today, I am grateful we have our phone time and I look forward to maybe tomorrow seeing you. Regardless, we survived and will make it for another day. One more day closer to being together.

Staff count has commenced. I am going to brush my teeth and head to bed. At count Mea tells the guard that Max who was at work had left and told her she was free to go. The guard comes clomping in and announces themselves with a bang of the door. "Staff' they announce, Mea pipes up inmate'. I have to remind myself that even with me being here I am getting information and doing research. I have a good house, and I will have to remind myself that even when the music is blaring and here is nothing but yelling that this house is the best one. I will not let them get under my skin. Speaking of skin I have developed some kind of rash from the second implant the doctor put in my arm to test me for TB.

Grateful for good health, a fabulous, loving, supportive family and friends. You two are my rock and my inspiration each day. I love you so much.

November 6, 20xx

Happy Tuesday! A new day and a new start with a fresh beginning. I am off to work, but first I checked my mailbox as mail had not been done in awhile. There were a decent number of girls at work today. Apple took toady off as she was too stressed, Sally had pink eye and Susan is still off this week. So it was only me this morning, and Mea came in the afternoon. I finished ripping the seams so the zippers could be sewn in. Candice showed how to pin the zippers but I was not interested in pinning used old pins and who know is they have been poked and not cleaned. No way am I going to risk getting any disease. I have a clean bill of health and that is how I will leave this place.

I told Candice this afternoon that I was not comfortable using the pins, plus I knew nothing about sewing. Candice found me another job which I really appreciated. She told me later that the pins had been cleaned which is not true as I have never seen them be cleaned and I did not appreciate being lied too. She also told me that new pins were coming and that everyone would have to pin, well I am not going to risk my health but I will be starting my correspondence soon anyways and not working. The 14th is my last day working. My program is starting in mid November.

It was so nice to talk to you at lunch made the afternoon go quickly knew we have a visit tonight. Plus, it was productive to get the bank stuff dealt with. Funny how you thing that all this rehabilitation information is available here until you get here and they don't offer post secondary, no upgrading, no skills to be taught to help you when you are getting out. Really sad, but I am not going to fall I will get some classes either mailed in or delivered so I can continue my education and be productive both in here and when I get out.

Thank you for getting the property taxes taken care of. Sorry your list keeps growing. I will call Wayne this week. Oh yah, it is only $5.80 a day for working while you are in here so they most I can make are $58.00 a pay period. Plus they take off $7.50 twice a month for your cable in your room. Funny I don't even have a TV, which seems like the government is stealing.

My headache is starting to go away. I am having a tea while I write to you. The guards have just come in. Some are so quiet and others are so loud. I don't mind during the day but the loud ones at night when you are already woken up by the flashlights can cause serious sleep deprivation.

There was a bowl of apples downstairs that were starting to get a bit rip so Mea was going to throw them out but Susan and I said no we could bake a pie or make apple sauce. Then Mea stopped and looked at us and threw them in the garbage. Susan got very upset and threw all the apples in the garbage so now we can't bake anything. Just immature behaviour that goes on in here. What is wrong with some people? You think with all the medication they are on there would be something for common sense. I just took my tea and headed upstairs to write.

I am going to sign off for tonight. Thank you so much for our visit, the water and gum and the chocolate bar, but especially for the company. I love our talks our hugs and kisses and your support. I love you both and pray the angels are around us and god will protect us. I will chat with you tomorrow and call you at 11:30am to confirm our next visit. Each day is one day closer to leaving this place.

November 7, 20xx

Happy hump day. Did you purchase the lotto ticket for tonight's draw?

Funny last night as I was laying in bed I got to thinking about the work pin issue and a part of my personal plan is to not associate with companies and people who would put me in harm's way and yesterday when Candice lied to my back about those pins being bleached that really told me that she has no character about telling the truth and would put my health at risk, so she could have her company pump out product. I just shack my head and I don't trust her anymore. Could be an early day to come home. I love you and will write to you after work.

Work today was fine. I ended up cutting some clothes to help the other girls to complete and order. I helped pack up boxes to get product ready to be shipped.

After lunch we were able to get refills on our hygiene products. I only needed laundry detergent for the house. Tomorrow is canteen day so I will pick up some tide and hopefully my rash will go away. Over the weekend, I will do my bed sheets but the rash is getting better today.

Jimmy came into work today and asked me who the people were visiting me. I said that my mom and my son were visiting. He asked how old you were and I told him 19. He told me I did not look old enough to have a 19 year old son. My reply was well I must look younger with no make-up on and my hair not done. He smiled. The guards see use with our families and it is interesting how some see we as people and others see us as criminals, but maybe these guards have had good or bad experiences either way the brush should be clean and without judgment especially at first glance. Jimmy said next time he would come over and say hi and introduce himself, which was very nice. Maybe Bob will be here tonight also.

We got to leave early from work so that the employees could get home safely, especially with tonight's snow fall it will be crazy driving out there. That is why if you don't feel comfortable driving tonight to make our visit just know your safety comes first. I'll call you at 4:00pm to see what you want to do.

I just took a shower and started a load of laundry. I doesn't usually shower in the morning as I am not going to see anyone but my co-workers. Now I am just watch that I have said that someone important will come to visit.

Just got the dinner call from downstairs. Supper was really good. Apple and I did the dishes and cleaned up as two of the other girls cooked but the other three do nothing. In the morning there are all these dishes in the sink. I used to do them and made the coffee but then I would come back at lunch and after work and there would be more dishes in the sink from the girls who were here all day, so I stopped doing other dishes. If someone cooks for me I will do the dishes but otherwise they can just sit there as I am not their maid.

I just went downstairs to see if Max was off the phone and she is home all day today and no one uses the phone and then they get on it at night when I have been at work all day and take their sweet time. Just like they sleep all day and are up all night. Max and May go to school for two hours and they do nothing all day. Max usually goes to work at the dump, but not today but that might be due to the weather. I am so looking forward to getting my pen pack, my correspondence, and my programs rolling and in place. Living with six other strangers certainly a new growing experience for me and I must not forget that this is for a short time in the big picture. Positive, positive attitude and one day closer to being back with you.

I am so grateful for our visit tonight. I am grateful for all your support, love and encouragement. I am grateful for our health. I am grateful that one day the truth will come out and I am grateful for the support of my team inside here. I will write after our visit tonight.

Well, I just got a chance to call you and confirm our visit tonight. That is too bad they cancelled our visit but I would view it as a small blessing as the roads are terrible and you're safely is more important. We will have our phone chat at 9:00pm. It bothers me if someone schedules a 9:00pm call and books it on the phone time and then someone sits on the phone and don't get off. I mean just total disrespectful and no regards. The thing that so many of these inmates here is no respect and bit chips on their shoulders and the obvious is the foul mouths for ladies they are really showing up the men. I enjoy spending time in my room, writing, reading and keeping out of the drama, gossip and back stabbing that goes on here.

The sidewalks were so slippery around here today that all the people were falling including Mea. She is the girl with the bad shoulder who just can't catch a break. Bad enough she fell when she was out before but today she really hurt her shoulder when she fell.

That is why even thought I would have loved to have seen you tonight with roads being so bad and in terrible driving conditions, I would rather wait and have our visit on Friday. Plus, this gives you some time to get my two letters typed up and tell me which correspondence course I will be taking.

I am going to read for a few moments. The house is actually quiet no one is talking or shouting I say yelling no music is blaring. Serious noise is just beyond words. Oh yes, I do get a pay allowance if I am in programs. All for a good reason things happen and God has a plan no matter what we thing he is doing he is working it out our best. Keep positive and thinking for a higher reason, the path will be in our favour.

Sorry for stressing you out tonight my son. This entire process is very frustrating. I will track down a guard tomorrow and see if I can find the legal aid form for appeals. I will try and get a hold of Wayne. I wish Don would have contacted you eelier instead of leaving your calls unanswered. As I try Wayne's number it still is not working. I need to get some legal matters dealt with. I just feel so helpless that I could be so productive if I had access to the internet to do some of these things myself and not have to burden you with all this stuff. I just can't help but think that if they received the judgment that they would not have given notice to gets their ball rolling.

Hang in there my love, be strong, everything will be okay. We can only do what we can and everything else will just have to wait and God will deal with it.

Remember the important things in life are not the materials things. All my love until tomorrow.

November 8, 20xx

Good morning and I pray you both slept well last night.

I tried Wayne this morning but not luck getting through. I'll put in my request to Bally regarding my appeal form from legal aid and to retrieve my passport this morning. I'll send you some more letters. I will try Wayne again at lunch and then maybe I will have you email him if I can't get in touch with him and let him know I will call him tonight.

I love you both and off to work I go. At least the snow stopped for a bit.

Just got off the phone with you at 11:30am. I tried Wayne again so hopefully I can get a hold of him this afternoon. I'll go and let Candice know that I was unable to contact him and they know and okayed me to get something's sorted out this afternoon.

Today was canteen day, so I purchased some more stamps, envelopes, some lotion, dental picks, some tide, and bounce sheets and some popcorn. The popcorn is a bit healthier then the chips. I really miss dental floss. I also purchased some new pens and writing pads, some gum, q-tips and ear plugs. Funny how some of the simplest things now bring me great joy. Funny how life is. Plus, I needed some ibuprofen for my monthly time. My son the song with the banjo is playing on Mea's TV and makes me think of you. (I will wait for you).

I am waiting to go back to work. You hurry up to wait in jail. This person who need mediations are being called which is about 90% of this jail is on some kind of meds. This morning Max was flapping her gums about how she should get out of here as she was only a drug dealer and that the people who steal or commit fraud should be in here. I just looked at Apple and left the room. First, no point in arguing with stupid or stupid people, second she goes on about how she is going to get out and blah, blah, blah and return to what she was doing before that landed her here. I would rather walk way then subject myself to her nonsense. Remand had more people with character then this place.

I received my items that I had when I first arrived here back today. I was waiting in line to get my canteen purchase and the guard who admitted me poked her head out to tell me she had something for me. I must have left an impression for her to remember me. Probably my body order smell. Gosh, I did not smell my best that day. Or maybe it was my positive personality. Either way she handed me my bible that I received what I had my outing with the Remand girls to the chapel, my contact numbers and my daytime with spiritual Psalms in it for each day. I was so grateful to have the bible back. With it I would draw on my strength.

Great I am going to call Wayne and Susan decides to vacuum. Seriously, they complain about not working and then they complain about working. Bless my room and my peace and quiet.

I wonder if the Remand girl court date went well today. The girls in here are miserable and mean and I miss the gals from the Remand. Talk about mean girls 101 well here I am. I will remain positive in spirit thanks to my wonderful supporters and my lovely family.

I tried Wayne and still no answer. I will keep trying and if you could keep emailing him. My appeal time is running out and there is no help inside here to get this done and my legal team outside they are not returning calls.

Thank you for registering me in the two courses. I'll call you at 5:00 and see if you got in touch with Don. One step at a time and I just wish I could be more help to you both.

I ran the vacuum cleaner over the floors upstairs here. The guards come in with their boots on and track in all the snow and gravel plus all the hair. It will keep me busy to do some good cleaning while I wait to chat with you. I am doing laundry with the tide so hopefully my rash will go away. I normally have a shower in the morning and one at night to rinse off, but I did not a couple of morning and now I have this rash come on so maybe I need to rinse off in the morning all the time. I guess I will just shower twice a day and that will be that. It could be nerves also, after all my body has gone thru a bit of stress in the last few weeks as has yours.

Today was house grocery day that means lots of veggies, milk and fruit. We each get two bananas, two oranges, two apples and a pear. The girls take them and put them in their rooms now. With the house having more people in it we are now getting our own rations to keep in our own rooms. Food can be a real source of anger in here. If someone eats more than their share watch out and these girls are not small and know how to fight.

Max is at the dump tonight so the house is calm. Susan is in a good mood so there is not a lot of tension. We had fish and chips with a salad for dinner. Susan cooked and I did the dishes. Sally never does the dishes. She will only wash her own, and she does not prepare any of the meals.

We just spoke about the appeal and what Don had to say. Unfortunately, even thought I did not commit this crime, I had to commit to the time. One day the truth will come out, but I would agree with Don and don't to appeal to take the change in getting a longer sentence. We can tax Mr. Reck, we can write to the Law Society, we can write to the Chartered Accountants, we can go above the tax officer Martha at Revenue Canada, and most importantly we can publish to book.

We will continue to remain positive and strong. We will continue to write and see each other whenever possible. We will soon have a sleepover in here. We will soon have body guard visits we will soon have unescorted visits and soon we will be back together and with an adventure to tell and a journey to share.

The book I am currently reading is so fitting. It is about a young man wrongful convicted of a murder. The system wears on him, mind you he had some issues prior to his conviction but nevertheless he is trapped in the system. They just want to have someone in jail for the murder. He has the love and support of his family, similar to me, but he gets put on death row waiting to be executed for this murder. It talks about the meals, canteen, dress he is able to leave his cell for one hour a day but the long and short of it is his innocent is vindicated. It took many years but he was vindicated. I thank you for registering me in the courses and speaking to Don. I know what he said comes from a place of concern for me getting more time for this crime that was not committed, so I understand. As long as we are together we can tackle whatever comes our way.

I just took a shower and to into my clean pajamas and my clean bed. I heard the guards come in and did not think much of it but they actually knocked on the door to see if you are okay. Kind of shocking. It is nice to have q tips after a shower. Thank you for my canteen money. I plan on paying you back for everything.

All my love to you both. I just finished watching the movie with Apple and Sally. May was at the main house to play volley ball, Mea is upstairs watching TV in her room and Susan is on the phone. There was an all page for all the mates to return to their houses, and another page for no patio access which means that the guards here are being pulled to the max to deal with those women. It is such a shame that their bad behaviour means we lost our privileges like going to the main house to work out or more importantly for our visits. If these inmates wait to misbehave then they should be locked down in their cells until they get it together not fair that we lose out.

Well let's hope that whoever it is causing the problems gets it out of their system tonight and we have our visit tomorrow. I am starting to realize that if there is a page on returning our unit it is because of the women in the maximum causing problems. No wonder some guards have little patience after what they get to deal with in there.

Thank you for making me smiles. Hearing about the cat being carried around or how Mark is dropping his ice cream and using the 10 second rule makes me smile. Even if there is a hair on it. Yes, I can relate to how messy living with other can be. I will soon have a major lock down in my room. Right now I have to watch TV in the common area but soon that will change. I disinfect the shower before I use it and I keep all my items in my locked room. I have never seen so much toothpaste on the mirror and faucet and for girls their mouths are related to their cleaning habits…just pigs.

I am going to get ready to go to sleep before the guards come upstairs. First night with my earplugs. I will let you know how they work out.

Love you both and miss you so much. Kisses and hugs to you. And know you are in my prayers, my thoughts and always in my heart.

November 9, 20xx

Wow it is a week number three down. Where is the time going? ☺ I found that yester when I was at the house making calls, doing laundry, vacuuming how the time went by so quickly. I can't imagine how time will fly when I commence my studies. Once programs or in my cans program starts, my correspondence, the gym, and my favorite visitors are in place the time will fly by. The day will be productive and the evenings will be enjoyable your visits, homework or the gym. Soon we will have less formal business to attend to and more enjoyable visits to be had. I look forward to our Sunday night dinners again.

Can you look up and I mail me section 312 of the Criminal Code and the Law of Conspiracy please and thank you. Also, if you have not done it yet the Code of ethics and the Code of Conduct for Lawyers or if you can find a piece of paper where I have listed and highlighted them so I can help me prepare for the Taxation appointment. I will ask Wayne if he would be willing and able to attend as there is no harm in asking if I could ever get in touch with him.

Keep buying those lotto tickets. We are surely to be blessed.

There is a nice passage in my calendar I received when I attended the Chapel at the Remand that says" for he that has mercy on them shall lead them, even by the springs of water shall he guide them." Isaiah 49:10. But when I looked at October 19, 20xx it reads for that day "I am a door, by me if any man enters in, he shall be saved and shall go in and out and find pasture." By John 10:9. This journey will be for not and good will from it

Work was work. My brain is turning into porage. As I look outside the jail it seems so peaceful with all the white new snow. They are sewing the zippers into the correctional officer's jackets but they are sewing them in backwards. The bosses are not doing any productivity supervision so now the zippers have to be ripped out and sewn in properly. Mistakes are so easily avoided, yet the individuals who should be supervising seem to be turning a blinds eye. I am so looking forward to getting my correctional path and program and correspondence classes, which I know will be very soon.

I will call you at 11:30am. There is a meeting at the main house for the guards so we have to stay in our houses until further notice.

I asked the guards after work at 3:30pm if lists were visits were still a go and they said "yes". I am just waiting to use the washing machine. People leave their clothing in the machine forever and I have no interest in putting them in the dryer just in case something goes wrong. I am not going to get blamed, so I put my bag for the next in line spot. Work this afternoon was okay. The ladies there this afternoon were ones who were productive with at least most of them. Some are just your typical rude, loud mouths who would rather gossip then work, which is another reason I don't want to work there besides for health reasons. I absolutely have no interest in the gossip. I just want to mind my business as they should mind theirs. At the house I just want to go to my room and read, or write to you. I have no interest in the house gossip. If I am watching TV and someone comes in who wants to speak negatively or gossip, I will just get up and leave. Soon I will have my pen pack or London Drugs order and with more books or a TV so my room will be place of peace.

One of the ladies cut her finger today at work so immediately starting looking for the first aid kit, but apparently it had no band aids. She told Candice and Candice said she had some in her office which was locked and that this lady would have to wait until she was finished pinning a jacket. By the time Candice got finished and went to her office, still not telling the lady to come and get a bandage the ladies finger had stopped bleeding and clotted. As far as these needles being sterilized that is as untrue as they fell on the floor, the entire basket and swept up from the dirty floor. Time to get my path going and my schooling commenced before I end up with a disease.

I enjoyed our visit tonight. It is so nice to just laugh and be surrounded by positive words and environment. Nice that you can now but a name and face together with meeting Jim in person. After you both left he said, I had a very nice family. I told him you were my rock. That throughout this journey, you have seen and been a part of the journey. I expressed how it is unfortunate that so many others have no desire to better themselves even while in here. Interesting how he was the one who commented on the other people having more financial resources. I am beginning to think that more often than not that is how the system plays out. Jim commented on how maybe I was supposed to be here for a greater reason and I told him that whatever my path (our path) maybe that the truth will all come out and that this path will enrich mine (our) lives for the greater good. I also told him that throughout the first part of my journey, I had met many wonderful people, learned more than one can from a text book about the law and found out who I could trust and who my true friends were. This journey has taught me to see people differently and work environments way differently and had I not been blessed with this adventure (our adventure) I would not have been blessed with a strong faith, true family and friends and a story to tell that will one day change people's lives and the justice will be served in this book.

I am looking forward to seeing you again. I will stay in my bubble and focus on the bigger picture which you are.

Mom, I can see not only the moon but dad's star also, so know that he is watching over us. Hugs and kissed and a big smile for today is one day closer. All my love.

November 10, 20xx

Last night I watched the Act of Valard. That was an okay movie. It felt like I was playing a video game. Tonight John Carter is on so I may watch that one even though we watched it together.

This morning I woke up at 8:00am. It was nice not to have to worry about over sleeping and missing work. During the week I am a very light sleeper counting the guards to see if that one was the 6:00am guard, and even getting up and going downstairs to check the time and being thankful when it is only 4:00am, so I know the next guard is the wake up guard. The flash light in the face every two hours is even starting to not bother me is my sleep. Funny how they will keep shining it on you until you move so they can make sure you are still alive.

The sun is shining even if it is a cold winter morning it is still nice to see the sun. The guards did mail so before our visit today I will check to see what jail mail I have received.

The publisher of the John Grisham book is Double Day. A division of Random House Inc. Mom you were asking about this last night at our visit.

The house is quiet right now. The noisy people must still be asleep or have nothing to say as it is too early for them even though it is 10:30am right now, either way a blessing. I'll call you at 11:30am to confirm our visit.

We just finished our wonderful visit. I'll call you at 10:15pm tonight to confirm our visit time for tomorrow. When you were leaving tonight the guard asked me if my son was my brother. I told her not that you were my son. She said she would take what she a complement as I did not look old enough to have a son. I told her she was the second person her to tell me that I did not look old enough to have a 19 year old son. The guard told me to have a nice evening which was very kind.

Thank you for the chocolate and pop. I think I will go to the gun and walk at 6:00pm for 40 minutes hopefully I will get a treadmill otherwise I will book one for when I can.

Well it looks like something else is going on at the max as we were not able go to the main house. So I read and did some squats, push ups and triceps dips in my room. Tonight was fend for yourself dinner night, so is made a spinach salad with mushrooms, broccoli and of course spinach with ranch dressing, bacon bits and a hard bowled egg. Nice and healthy dinner so I will just continue to eat healthy and have a chocolate treat that you purchase for me. Thanks for helping out my sweet tooth.

My son I hope you had a great work shift and mom I hope you had a pleasant time at your granddaughter's birthday. Well would you know it at 7:20pm they called movement to the gym? So off I went to the gym. Apple asked me where I was going and Mea pipes up "to the gym". May baked puff wheat squares and gingerbread cookies so the smell in the house is crazy good, so it is a great time to get out and exercise. Some of the girls have decided to start baking for Christmas and they will complain about getting fat. Nice to have cookies and baked goods but they don't know how to do things in moderation.

Nevertheless, my work out was great. No problems getting a machine. A Russian gal came in and walked on the other treadmill beside me. She walks in and gets on the treadmill looks at me and with a loud voice says "Hi". She goes into her zone and I am in mine. Forty minutes later I hop off and wipe the machine down. There are girls, inmates, hanging out in the supervisor booth watching us work out with the supervisor. Whatever floats their boats? Seriously, these inmates have way too much time on their hands that could be better served. I really like your idea mom about going out into the community to shovel seniors walks or cutting lawns, or picking up garbage, anything for some would be better served then just doing nothing. Plus, it would be paying back to the community but some inmates have a bad attitude. I have had my shower and feel great.

Going to read until 9:00pm and then watch John Carter until our stand to court at 10:00pm and call to confirm our visit tomorrow.

Max is off on a home visit and wow is the house a normal volume and very pleasant.

Well when I called at 10:15pm there was no confirmation on our visit tomorrow so I will call at 11:30am tomorrow and hopefully you will have some news. My son did your friend get his car unstuck down the street? It is nice to see friends helping friends and I am so proud of you and they man you have developed into.

I will call you in the morning. Last night the guards were searching our house lockers. Susan was woken up by it. I heard something going on but it was downstairs and I keep my door locked for safety and security reasons after all this is jail.

All my love and hopefully our visit will happen tomorrow. Stay strong, healthy and safe.

November 11, 20xx

Good morning my son and my mom. How did you both sleep last night?

It looks cold outside today. My room is nice and cool compared to the rest of the house which is like a sauna. I am so looking forward to receiving my pen pack or London Drugs order to get a TV in my room. These girls are not into Gilmore Girls but rather tattoo shows or jail shows. Night and day we are.

I just cleaned the bathroom upstairs and vacuumed my room, Mea's room and the hallway and bathroom. May was not up so she missed out. I have done my share of the housekeeping. Every morning I sweep the kitchen as no on e can eat over their plates, it they even bother to use a plate, just a pig sty, but I keep my area clean and do my par but will make other step up and do theirs otherwise I won't get done and I have no problem saying in my room if they don't want to keep the common area clean.

Thank you for the wonderful visit. Thank you for printing the letters and bringing them in for me to sign. Please mail them off. One more thing can you can cross off the list of thing to do.

I told the girls about the show my son, but they wanted to watch the Amish show and apparently tonight am a two hour show. Soon enough, I will have my own TV so we can watch shows and talk about them.

See you tomorrow at 5:00pm for a visit and we will eat our treats together. Every guard has different rules. Some check shoes, some let you take the chocolate with you. Why are there not one set of rules, one set of protocol, one set of procedures and all I can do is scratch my head. We have been blessed with being able to take chocolate from their machines back before and tonight the guard says no. Oh well, I can wait.

When I got home from our visit Mea had kindly wrapped up some dinner for me. She made fabulous lasagna so I ate, stood for count and had a thirty minute nap. I went to the gym for a forty minute workout as I was leaving I noticed a class being offered for Fork lifting. I will put in my inmate request and see if I can get into this. They usually only except inmates who have parole in six months but who know it never hurts to try and fill out an application and maybe if the course in snot full they might accept my application. There were these two rude girls at the gym tonight. One is a rude girl, who works at Corcan, but I only have two more shifts with her and the other girl was just being rude because of the first girl. I just blocked them out and began my work out. The Russian lady came in and again turned to me said hi and then began her work out. Some people are civil or can be and others have absolutely no manners or social skills, just simply miserable people. Anyways, I finished my book so I am going to have a shower and start my other new one by the same author. I will let you know how this one is.

I love the investment in ear plugs. They will keep me sane and productive.

My saying is this: "the people you associate with can affect your choices and affect your path in life. Good people= good, bad people= bad and that goes for companies and employers also.

Good luck with the home visit tomorrow, I will say a prayer for you tonight.

I popped some popcorn added some pepper and dove into my new book. I am waiting for May to get off her call so I can call you. I am watching the comedy channel for a laugh and to keep my spirits high. Thank you for the words of encouragement tonight. Such a shame when people have to be so rude but I am just going to stay in my bubble and forces on myself and my path. Thank you for your continued support, love and encouragement. I know there are good people out there and I will not let the evil come into our path or yours.

Signing off for tonight, good luck tomorrow. Love you both so much our path is of great victories. Sorry about the envelopes and me addressing them upside down. I am surprised they did not do a moment of silence in here for Remembrance Day and to give thanks for those soldiers who died for my freedom. I gave my moment to them.

November 12, 20xx

How was your home visit today? How was my cat during the visit? Did she make a good first impression? ☺

Sorry our conversation was cut short at 11:30am, but I could not hear you due to the TV being so loud. Good thing we have a visit tonight. The ear plugs are going to be my new friends. I am going to write to Wayne and see what is going on.

You have just left and I have returned back to the house. I had fun tonight with our visit, chatting and playing cards. Tonight it was sad to see you leave, but I just tell myself it is one more visit, day closer to being out and house with you. I try not to feel sorry of myself and try to focus on my many blessings and the fact that we have visits. I know we are unique in our relationship, but I also think of how Apple must be feeling not seeing her kids yet. I would be on the phone every night talking to you and she doesn't do that so I am not sure how close she is to her kids and family, nevertheless it must be difficult for her.

I mailed you another letter and enclosed the one to Wayne. My son could you please get his mailing address and send him the letter. The guards must just love getting my envelopes of letters. I wonder if other inmates write as many letters as I do.

I am very blessed to have a wonderful support and very blessed in being able to talk and visit with you both. I love you both.

Signing off for tonight. I will call you tomorrow at 11:30am to check in and see how you are doing. I will stay strong if you stay strong. All my love.

November 13, 20xx

Today the sun is shining and the temperature is warming up. I just finished my morning at work, so I thought I would write what has gone down since we last spoke.

Last night after you left I was getting ready for bed when things broke loose. Max had a stereo or something that she lent to may and May put it under the sink in the bathroom, but when May went to get it the walkman/ stereo was gone. Not sure what the heck but it sure caused some commotion upstairs. Inmates should not be borrowing other peoples stuff. The guards were searching the house the other night so who knows it must have been confiscated was my theory. This is why

I lock my door at all times. And thank goodness for ear plugs because they were loud last night.

Apple told me today that the girls were asking why I don't sit with them and watch TV. She told them that I don't like all the swearing and the curing, but I enjoy my writing and reading in my room which was the correct answer.

At work today Jim came into the shop. He sat at this long table and ate his cereal. He asked me how my weekend was and I told him great. He asked what I did and I told him I had visits, read, worked out, and wrote letters. He commented on how close my family was and I told him that yes we are a close bunch. He said this, me being in jail must be hard on you both and I answered yes it is. He looked at me and said he would have to get the book. I think my story must have intrigued him.

One of the ladies at work was giving Jim a hard time about his lack of beard growth and how he could only grew four hairs on his face. Then she kept telling him to get to work, he kept telling her that he was working as he finished his cereal. Jackie came by and had a drink of his power drink. Jim commented on how roomer would begin. He looked at me and smiled. I said he would end up getting sick as Jackie was sick last week, he told her he had better not get sick. They act like siblings. Over the weekend Jim saw the movie "Flight" and said it was good. We will have to watch it when I get out. I think it is based on a true story.

Work once again was just ticking along. Candice came in sick and told use she was sick all weekend. Seriously, why do they do this as we can't get sick nor do we want to? I get frustrated when people don't use common sense. Thank goodness tomorrow is my last day and I can forces on my correspondence and my job prospects for when I get out of here.

I am going to read for a bit before returning to the place that makes my brain turn to porage. Thank you both for taking care of the stuff on the outside. I will call you at 9:00pm to see how you are doing.

At 7:00pm I am going to hit the treadmill for a bit and hopefully there is one available. Good thing we heard from Don as my parole officer has not been in contact with me to get the form to appeal and that has to be done by November 19 and today is November 13. I would never have made the cut off due to the lack of speed here. Shake my head

Phew just took a shower after my work out. I power walked over to the main house with Apple, she is going to a Narcotics Anonymous (N/A) meeting. I worked out for forty minutes and it was blissful. One of the mean girls was there tonight but we both kept our distance as I have no time for her to get into my positive bubble. Here comes the Russian lady with her usual, hi to me and off on her treadmill workout. This afternoon at work I was doing some embroidering and Jackie and I got to talking and she said that there are just some really mean girls that she has seen even go thru Corcan and how by the end of their visit some have grown and become nice people. Why do people have to be mean to being with? Why can't people just accept themselves? Love them and quit complaining and comparing themselves with others. Oh well, I can't fix the world but I can be true to myself and maybe some of my positive being will rub off on others, staff, guards, and inmates. I will be the "Ray of sunshine in this dark place".

I am going to read for a bit and I will call you shortly. This new book is really great also. Interesting to find out if we were big winners on the lotto. How did Telus work out? What did Don have to say? You are both doing so much for me and I appreciate everything. You are the best and I am so grateful and fortunate to have you both.

I just got off the phone and my heart goes out to you and your adventure with the truck getting stuck. Getting stuck this winter seems to be a common theme. I am excited to see you tomorrow. Know your visits are what keep me going. I love you both and please stay positive, strong and healthy. We will survive this and be better for it.

November 14, 20xx

Good morning to you both. My last shift at the swear shop, but I can go to work anytime if I have completed my correspondence and want to pick up a shift. Jackie and Candice said they would love to have me back, but my correspondence and my program come first. Yesterday Apple was at her wits end with work and I just reminded her that she would get her path soon and to focus on getting better and her well being. She is funny. She told me that I would be curing within a month of being here and nope not one curse work has come out of my mouth, that is called self control, plus it really sounds terrible and makes me sick, not physically, but my stomach turns. It is very unprofessional and not classy at all like to have Apple's works and hopefully my works of encouragement help her when she is down or discouraged. You offer me words of support and strength and hopefully I can pass them onto others here.

I slept in this morning and by the time I checked the clock it was 6:45am and Max was in the shower, which lasted until 7:10am so I just put my hair up in a ponytail and I will grab a shower after 4:00pm count but before your visit. I don't like being without an alarm clock or at least a clock upstairs. They only clock is downstairs in the TV/ kitchen area. Soon Apple and I will have our pen packs and some comforts of civilization, but until then we will just wing it. The weather is calling for a warm start and then possible a cooling down, but the weather people are so unreliable and don't know what they are talking about as much as lawyers. Heading to work and I will talk to you at 11:30am.

Sorry about being frustrated during our 11:30am call. I will take a look at what you received when you come tonight for the visit. I will learn to just let go and trust in God and the truth will all come out. I will publish this book and as long as we are all safe and healthy we can and will get thru all of this. One day we will look back on this and be better, and stronger, wiser and better because of this journey. I will have to focus on things I can control and outside evils are not one of them. Well this afternoon I will go for these computer testing's to see what I should be when I grew up. Not in the mood but it is what it is, so I will call you at 5:00pm to confirm our visit and see if the truck is ready. Maybe that is why the home assessment lady was asking about me staying with you because they knew the house would be taken. I wonder how they will feel when the truth comes out and his business and all his property is seized by Revenue Canada for all the tax evasion and money laundering and all the other illegal corrupt activities he has conducted for the past 30 plus years. What comes around goes around and his is coming. Karma she is a sure thing.

Well enough of my pity party. I will just remind you as I remind myself I /we are destined for greatness and great things and for making a difference. One positive is now the money spends on property taxes can go to publishing the book. I love you both and don't let their evil interfere in your greatness.

Tell you about my assessment and all the wonderful occupations that God wants me to be. Unfortunately, somehow the class either got scheduled in error, or the program instructor double booked, but the computer choices program ended up being cancelled, which may have been a blessing as I ran into my parole officer who informed me she would be gone for two months. I asked her if she received my require form from over a week ago and she had not. Even if Don was going to appeal there would not be enough time to get the legal aid form and get funding in place for my appeal. Plus, for him to do the actual appeal by November 19 considering today is November 14 would be impossible. But the blessing is running into Bally was to find out she would have a temp dealing with my file until she returned. We were able to discuss a few things that I will chat with you tonight about. I put in another request so her temp can get my passport and my DL as it expires at the end of November. I appreciate her honesty and forthcoming especially in my matter, but after she heard what I had to say she could appreciate my entire situation.

Thank you for taking care of the truck at least I feel better about you driving a safe vehicle. You should go and renew the registration this weekend and you will see if there is anything against the truck. I love you and I am so looking forward to our visit. One day at a time, this too shall pass and we will survive and be better in the long run. God is a good God and he sees all. God will handle and deal with those people.

November 15, 20xx

Hi my son and mom. Thank you for a wonderful visit last night. After you left I had a nice chat with the guard and she explained why I could not take the chocolate bar back. It was nice to have another inmate confirm that one guard says one thing or does one thing but the next does something totally different. She told me she would print off the package which would be lovely. I of course have absolutely no issues with following the rules, just as long as I know what they are. The reason is apparently some girls use the chocolate as bartering items, which would be the same as me purchasing it from the canteen tomorrow. The guard understood what I was saying and I totally understand her position. So I will eat my chocolate at the visit no problem.

When I got to the house, Apple asked me if she could talk to me. She needed someone to talk too. She is missing her family and just needed a set of ears, which I have no problem offering. I completely understand her missing her family and I sure hope that I would be blessed with someone to talk to if I was in her situation. My words to her were not to let the small things into her bubble. She needs to only deal with what and as much as she can and the rest will just have to wait. I don't want her to get too stressed, especially with the stress of not seeing her family that is stressful enough. I hope I can inspire others, and be a blessing while I am here.

You give me the support to deal with things and I consider you both my blessings, so thank you. If I don't tell you in person, I am writing you to tell you that the visitors form is all that is needed to be completed to see me. I originally thought I had to get them to put on my list, but that is my calling card, so anyone can come in they just need to fill out the form and once it clears they can come in and visit on the days you are not visiting which I still hope is often. I love our visits and would not change them for the world. Oh yes, all Bally told me to apply for the visit inside here. She checked and as soon as the home assessment that was done on Monday is completed then that is the green light for your sleep over in here.

I just checked the mail and I successfully passed the WHMIS training a received a certificate...one of many to come and be completed.

I could only purchase deodorant today at canteen as I only had the $4.00 for hygiene items, but that is okay next week I can purchase shampoo and conditioner. Apple spoke to the ladies at the A & D and she told Apple that she was going to try and have our pen packs done by tomorrow. Friday this would be fabulous. Otherwise, we will have to wait until she comes back from her holidays. I keep telling Apple, that this Friday is the day for our pen pack and then when Friday comes and goes. I try and give her hope that next Friday is the one. How wonderful it would be if this was the Friday.

I finished re-writing my day parole form and trying to keep my writing to a readable level. As I was on the phone with you today my son, someone from another house came by and asked if Apple to take something to Mea. Apple left the house or opened the door, not sure what but the guards came and had stern words for Apple. I was on the phone with you helping you with the scanning process and the guards were talking beside the phone, which made it difficult to hear you, but we had our three minute reminder so we ended our call and I quickly went to the washroom and got my tea to call you back. Apple looked upset so I asked her if she was okay and that was when she told me what happened. I let her know that if I get a copy of the updated handbook I would get one for her, especially since we are the new ones here. I suggested that she not talk to anyone who comes to our house asking for someone. If they want to talk with so and so they can find them themselves and that she is not a messenger. Apple was very upset she may be charged, which is as unfortunate as she is just a good person, but this is jail and these people will use you, crush your spirits and some are just pure evil people who are just evil to the core.

I must say that during the day, the house is pretty quiet so my correspondence time should work out fine, fingers crossed otherwise in goes the ear plugs.

Thank you for looking up those addresses for me and emailing Wayne. Thank you for your continued support and encouraging words. When one of us is having a tough day the others are there to lift them up. Again, this journey has taught me so much about not only myself but about others and who I can count on and who truly cares about me and their support. I think that these people will also become even closer to you both and to me in the long run. You just wait our journey will have huge blessings. I love you both. Mom try not to burn the house down and remember to give each other a lot of hugs.

This afternoon Apple and I had to get the groceries from the main house. Usually Mea does this but she was off at an appointment, so Apple and I pushed the cart of groceries to the house and unloaded it and pushed the cart back. For some reason the jail is offering tours. Groups of young individuals have toured Corcan, but anyways there was another group touring the grounds. I told Apple as we were pushing the cart to the main house, we are like monkeys in the zoo. "Look folks there are some inmates. If you are quiet you will not spook them."

Today I also had a BBQ. May had to go to V & C so she asked me to watch the BBQ as Apple does not know how to BBQ. My son they were like Harvey's burgers. I may not have to cook here but I think I have been promoted to the BBQ duty. Good thing they have not discovered my cooking skills.

I will get to the gym at 7:00pm for a work out, shower and watch jersey shore and give you both a call. This new book is really interesting also. It is about a rich company and how the owner is not pleased with the verdict so appeals but pays off the judge. So far it is really interesting and I will keep you posted on what happens.

Tonight with the burgers they wanted bacon, so I was cooking the bacon they told me to add the mushrooms to the bacon grease. So after Mea finished her burger and just as Apple was starting hers she looks at Mea and tells her that the mushrooms were cooked in the bacon fat. Mea was not happy as Apple forgetting she was Jewish and I had not known this. Well, I learned something new today about Mea and I am sure Apple will not forget that again.

The Chaplin, Whitey, asked each house member to fill out the survey from as apparently someone is trying to do away with having a Chaplin in the jail. Wow, that would not be wise or good for the inmates, especially here having Whitey around is such a blessing and a comfort to some inmates to know they can go to him for prayer or a blessing, plus he is a really nice person.

My work out was great. The Russian asked me if I was still working at Corcan and I told her I was taking some university classes. She has a difficult time with English as this is not her first language and that is a shame as I think a lot is lost in translation.

Wow nice to hear we received the books for the courses. I said something would come together eventually. As you were telling me that good news and the Law Society receive my letter, I received your envelope with the Taxation information. Feast or Famine. Tomorrow Apple and I should hopefully receive our pen packs fingers crossed.

It was nice my friend called. I will enclose some visiting forms for her and her daughter if they want to visit me here and a few for others. My most important visitors I already have visiting with so I am happy, but it is nice to know others want to see me.

Tomorrow I will start to work on the taxation information and write to friends. I'll call you at 10:00am to get you up and going. Tomorrow maybe you can take my correspondence to the post office, go to Telus, go to the house, and move the garbage cans. So much to do and I am so grateful you are willing to do this for me. God's blessing to you both.

November 16, 20xx

Good morning mom and my son. One day closer, one day full of adventure, another day blessed.

November 2X says in my daytime is: "let not your heart be troubled, ye believe in God, believe also in me" John 14:1

I like this daytime it has scriptures for each day to inspire you on the work. A nice give from the Remand. Horary today is a visit day. My favorite time of the day.

I just wrote to a friend and sent her a visitation form, so you can just send her a copy of the book, please and thank you.

Well today is my one month anniversary. Time flies not so much. I go to call to V & C to meet with Bally and she informed me that she did receive your message and that I needed to put a request into the acting

Warden to have the boxes of correspondence materials sent in, so that was terrific of Bally was able to get this information to her leaving as today is her last day for a couple of months. She is off on a new journey. Interestingly, was the way Bally looked at my situation? I think she was impressed that I am actually doing something while I am here. I am not like other inmates and I won't be painted with the same brush.

Just after I finished getting off the phone to get the names of the correspondence books to give to the acting Warden. I received a call to go to Trailer four, where I met a staff member who received my request for the correspondence. Funny how things time out. So I told her what Bally had asked me to do and she was also impressed that I was going to do something with my time. She also seemed interested in the fact that I actually have a post secondary background already. It was great seeing her as she is the person I need to do the computer tests to see what it is I should be doing when I grew up...in a career placements so she told me that she had put in the request to re-schedule that appointment and that I should be receiving notice soon.

Gosh this house is so loud. Seriously, they turn their TV on in their room and then go downstairs. Things are going to have to be addressed once my schooling comes. But they don't just laugh they yell a laugh or they just don't talk they yell, but the absolute worst is the swearing and cursing. This just makes my skin crawl at how crude they are, but that all stems from their lack of professionalism and rudeness in behaviour. May was saying she goes before the parole board in January, which would be a 'great', until you find out she has thirty nine charges against her for Fraud and theft and how she is not even twenty one years old and has been doing this since she was sixteen years old. They charges that will hurt her case is the stealing from Corcan and then fact that she has no parole officer on the outside in support of her, but then again I am sure the parole officers get tired of taking a chance only for them to re-offend, which gives the case such as myself a shot in the foot because others are so stupid and spoil it for everyone. Seriously, if these inmates are just going to re-offend them should wait out their sentence with no chance for parole which is the entire house expect for me and Apple. These ladies are just waiting their sentence out as they have breached while out and now have to wait out their sentence. The parole board must get sick of this continued story.

I am just waiting for you to arrive for our visit. So I thought I would write a little. No pen packs today, but maybe tomorrow. I am not sure if she is working tomorrow or not.

Thank you for sending the bills in so I can help prepare for the taxation appointment. Hopefully, Wayne will come down or up to assist you that would be so wonderful if he did.

If you don't hear from him by Sunday evening maybe give him a call. I am not sure what his deal is but this not returning your calls or emails is not very kind of him.

I loved out visit. Thanks for the chat. Mom I will try and write more clearly so you can read my letters better. So when I got back to the house here was a new roommate. As I was walking along the path to the house I noticed a light on in one of the downstairs rooms that no one had previously. As I approached the house you could hear them talking, but that was not new. I walked into the house and Susan was on one couch and Mea and May on another and Apple and a new face on the other and Sally was on the work out machine. No one even looked at me or acknowledged me coming in expect for Sally who gave me a wave. Sally has sure come around and really smartened up. She is actually a really nice person once she removed her chip off her shoulder.

I put my shoes on the shoe rack and put my slippers on and headed to my room on the second floor. I unlocked my room and was heading back down to get my laundry as May was coming up. I asked who the new girl was and she thought her name was Bridget and then she asked me how my visit was. Gosh they are yelling about the mushroom cooked in bacon issue now. All you can hear is Apple yelling she is "sorry" and Mea yelling "whatever."

Anyways, the dynamic has once again changed in the house. This is like a study in human behaviour. My son it is like your psychology class but in real life.

Today Sally was at her wits end with Susan and now they are integrated another person into the mix. I just sit back and watch. I now have become the observer in the house. I have observed Apple's behaviour change as she was trying to become buddy, buddy with each inmate which is feeding off her need to be a part of hence her addiction. She is not one for just sitting being but has to be the centre, but she is now completing with other very strong personalities which could end up getting her into trouble. I know none of these inmates will become friends after I leave here and Apple would be the only person I would consider my closet person but I has always had my guard up not to let anyone in too close and because the dynamics change so quickly so can that situation. I live with people who are criminals and I have to remember that and even though I have a strong faith in people and change I must also be wise to protect myself. My mission is to observe and not to even take part in. Apple will have to learn that on her own.

I am so grateful that you were able to get me the classed to enjoy doing while in here. Thank you mom and thank you my son. I will call you tomorrow and see if you were able to chat with Don. All my love and my prayers are to you.

November 17, 20xx

Good day mom and my son. How has your morning been? How the flu was shot mom? Hopefully you will not have any side effect.

See you at the visit at 1:00pm and I will call you at 11:00am to construct the email for Don. Okay my son it has been four weeks and a day. I'll use the 19th of each month to mark the month passing.

So last night was interesting and I wanted to share it with you. First, I think my letters are so messy because I try to write at the same speed I think and type so I am trying to slow down for you. Okay, here it goes. So I met the new gal. Her name is Bridget. She has been in and out of jail but not at this jail. She is from here and is here on drugs and Fraud charges. She knows many of the people in the jail and some in not such a good way. After I came back to the house from our visit last night I went down to make a tea before returning to my room to read and Apple and Sally were watching TV. They greeted me with a loud "hello" and told me to have a cookie, which I replied politely "no thank you. I had had a chocolate bar at our visit already." All of a sudden Mea and Susan came stomping in chatting about who knows what. I warmed up my tea and started up stairs to read. I asked them if they were still watching the movie at 9:00pm and they said "yes", so I asked if they would call me when it started, they said they would but they did not do it. I luckily went down to check the clock and it was 9:05pm.

Anyways, I was filling my water bottle and I introduced myself to the new girl, who in return introduces herself to me. She seems pleasant, has a history of jail time, and knows a lot of other criminals both in here and out there. Apple decided to go walking with Mea in the court yard along with another inmate from another house. I tried to watch the movie but the other people just kept talking, so I came back to my room and read. I am not sure who to explain it, but there is a definite change in the environment, a shift if you will. I am not the observer but things seem different. I am only concerned about myself, and I just hope Apple is smart enough not to get involved with the drama, but ultimately that is her choice.

Well, maybe the pen pack will come early next week, until then I will still resort to my room for a good read and a letter to you.

Just as I suspected the dynamics are changing. Apple has befriended Bridget and now wants to go to the gym to work out. Sally and Apple want to start to clean out cupboards, move the fridge ect. The apples that were just purchased from the store on Thursday were rotten in the middle, so was Sally's pear. The cucumbers are already mushy. Mea said it was the fridge but the fruit was in a bowl and mine was in my room. May came down while I was making a tune sandwich and asked who took a cookie out of her baggy. She said these cookies were for Mea and if they were bagged not to touch them. I had no idea what she was talking about as I did not have any last night when they were made nor today. The new girl confessed to taking it and after May left Apple confessed to having more than her share last night.

I guess food is the number one tension spot in the houses. I can see that because some people seriously complain about how they need to lose weight they are the first to the fridge.

Thank you for emailing Don again and sorry for being short with you. Max was up last night throwing up and from some reason she has to do it in the sink and so no one in the house could sleep. I tried to put my ear plugs in but I could still hear her, so nasty. I am glad you had a good time at your friend's game. I will see you in a bit for our visit.

Thanks mom for sending the correspondence and photo copying the billings and sending them in. I really appreciate it. My hand writing is still looking messy even when I slow down. Thank goodness for typing, and maybe I should have asked for a typewriter to be sent in.

Tonight when I got back to the house, I was greeted with Apple being silly saying "guess who has family visits" although I was happy for her I was a bit sad to see you go. Gosh those girls must be coming so this is my sensitive week. I have to just be grateful that I get to see you both tomorrow.

I'll meet with Bob tonight so that is great. He is such a nice primary, especially since I am a fish out of water in here. I had so much fun today playing cards and I was so grateful for you to have met Bob. I need to put my emotions aside and focus on the big picture. The guards tonight said it looked like we were having fun during our visit. I told her we were a very close family. She asked who won the card game. I told her my mom but I thing she was cheating and then we laughed. Thank goodness for the kind guards. I told her that you would be back tomorrow and she said she saw that. I told her to have a wonderful evening and she replies same to me.

Well, I am going to get lost in my book until Bob calls me and I will write you later. No sooner then I sign off with you something new happens in the house. So I went down to get a tea and Bridget starts to ask I about movement which I explained to her and we got to talking well she talked and I listened and when I could give her some inspirational advice, I mentioned Joyce Meyer to her that she may enjoy her books. Bridget had read other motivational authors that I had read also. She said she enjoys John Grisham books and she told me, oh heck I forgot but I will remember when it see it. I will take a look tomorrow.

Jim comes in with another guard and in rolls another roommate. She is a native lady and May must know her because when I came upstairs from getting my tea May and her were chatting. I am just the observer. The music is cranked so in goes the ear plugs. Poor Max who is trying to get better from last night's episode of throwing up has to endure the music. Just no respect or manners here. Funny Bridget was telling me she had an encounter with the mean girl at the gym. I told Bridget yes I had encountered her also so now I avoid her because she is a very "mean girl" and if you can't be nice or just civil then you will be a "mean girl" in my book. So now we are almost at full capacity. The number nine for the house which is the number on the wind chime dad gave me and the one with the Dalmation dog in the fire hat. They are just finishing with meds so Bob should be calling me up to the main house soon.

Sorry my son, just when I thought my letter would be getting shorter, well once my schooling starts next week I will get the taxation information and Monday I will start to outline the case, so once I get the bills it will be easier for me to integrate that material. Getting ready to see Bob.

Well I am still waiting for Bob's call, he must have gotten busy anyways that mean I can write to you. Just what you need a longer letter from me well too bad. Xoxo

So I found out by listening that the new girls name is Sammy or Sam and she has moved from another house. Apparently, she requested the move. Both Bridget and Sam seem to be civil enough, but the dynamics of the house are shifting so it will be interesting to see how each character plays out. Now we have five upstairs and four downstairs. They better hurry and finish the house for minimum as this one is at full capacity and with all the new faces that means new mates are coming in whether they are new or returning for another stay either way it makes for some interesting writing. The jail is almost full.

Christmas should be interesting as the girls drew names for someone to purchase someone else a $10.00 item. I am not big on the idea as my family are you and my friends are not here, so I would rather not spend $10.00 to get someone something and spend that money on postage and writing materials. I do not like it when people put your name in on something before clearing it with you, so I will address this matter later this week. I have other fish to fry.

May has just called the girls downstairs "Fart Asses", nice especially when Sally is kindly making banana bread. I went downstairs to pop some popcorn as Bob has still not called and I am getting to a good part in my book. Sally was doing the dishes from the banana bread she made and she told me she would be setting aside some for me. That was very kind of her. She told me that was why last night she kept telling me to eat a cookie because she knew how things work and if you don't take them someone else will.

Overall, each person in the house seems to have a caring sensitive nature. Things turn interesting when they get together. Each mate has the mat mentality and has lost the sensitive human side. They become hard and bitter. Like I told Bridget I am a posit person and I will leave the room when the negativity starts as it feeds on the entire grip and you can see and hear all the cursing coming out. It is so funny how each person I speak to will not use that language and will actually want me to listen to the success they are having, like not only did Apple get visits, but they are next Saturday so that will give her something positive to focus on and how when she was telling me I was sincerely happy for her. I encouraged her to see if the church she use to go has a sponsoring program that may help her to get the classes she need to upgrade. Maybe my positive outlook and inspiration will help these ladies. Some are not going to take any of my suggestions to heart, but that is their choice. I just want to be a positive; blessing and maybe some of it will rub off.

The guards me what I had on my popcorn and I told them pepper, which they seemed to find interesting bit I would be willing to bet they just might try it. One of them just happened to be my secondary. She is a really nice lady.

I got my call to the main house, just before 7:00pm to speak to Bob. I had my list of questions. He told me he would be here tomorrow, Sunday but off until Wednesday. With regards to the passport and DL that if my new parole officer had not had in contact with me by Wednesday to let Bob know and he would get them back for me or find out how to do it, either way he would take action. The visitor's area was full tonight so we just chatted in the hallway, but he was cautious of who was around which I appreciate as this place has so many ears and inmates are all up in other people's business. I told Bob I am a trusting person by nature and this place has taught me not to trust which will be good for when I get out. Maybe, I will be able to spot evil and bad more easily not what I have been here. I informed him on the correspondence and how the warden would sign off on them and then I put in a request to that acting warden telling her the list of books coming in and that as per Bally the warden would sign off on them. I will tell you about that tomorrow along with the visits (escorted and unescorted).

So would you not know it as Bob and I were talking who walks around the corner but Jim? He asks Bob if I was his case load. Bob replies, "Yes" and Jim laughs. Bob and I continued our meeting and Jim comes back and says, "You know I didn't mean anything by my laughing." He chatted for a moment and then moved on but all is good. I told Bob when Jim had told me the day at Corcan. I also told Bob about me taking a leave from Corcan as my correspondence course were coming in and they had told me I was welcome back anytime.

Bob said I should get my correctional plan soon, but each intake worker has so many new inmates to process it could be a bit. Once we have that report and all the other reports, we can move onto the next step.

I also told Bob that I will have my community support come to my parole hearing to show that I maybe here today, but this entire occurrence started in 20xx and I have never fled, moved nothing. I started the civil matter in January 23, 20xx and not until May 21, 20xx, were criminal charges brought against me. Six years later. That my story is not like any other and that each inmate should be looked at individually and not with the same brush. I have no criminal record and even out on bail for four years, I was an active member of my church, volunteering, changing my career path, honest in my mortgage application (like Don said my honesty has been a determent to my case), which I was unable to renew because of my honesty, I went back to school, I worked not one full time job but also two part time jobs at the same time. I have been honest, co-operative, reliable, and respectful and the list goes on. I have not been in any trouble with the law, while on bail and prior. Anyways, you know the story. You have lived it for the last seven years with me.

God bless you for being my rock and my support, my inspiration, my motivation, for without your backing and support I have received from you I do not know where I might be. You keep me strong and focused to endure this battle. Either way I am blessed that you both were a part of it. And should take great pride in knowing the outcome will be victorious.

So I introduced myself to the new girl. She seems nice and quiet. Bob asked me how the house was and I told him loud, but the blessing is that during the day it is manageable and that I had invested in some earplugs, which would be great for my classes. Bob said yes because they were University classes that I would require and benefit from quiet. Sam was busy cleaning her room and getting settled and I was off to see Bob. So when I got back like I said I introduced myself and she seemed nice. It's nice to write to you so I feel like you are a part of this journey with me on the inside. I will try to continue to write from an objective prospective rather than from an opinionated prospective. I may add my two cents in once in a while.

When I came downstairs again to get my tea warmed up Sally was proud of her banana bread and with good reason it smelt wonderful. She looked like she had been crying so I asked her if she was alright. She held back the tears and tuned away. It was only her and I in the kitchen and common area. She told me she had spoken to her dad and that when it comes to saying Goodbye, she said it was hard. I told her I could understand. Gosh, even when I blessed with seeing you both so often it still is painful to see you go and to say good bye. So from now on us will say see you in a bit or talk to you in a bit and no more goodbyes? I asked her if she wanted to go to the library tomorrow at 1:00pm and I would find her a book I told him about she loved that idea. I asked if she had a nice talk with her dad and she said she did. I said to her to just focus on the positives in her talk and that she is one day closer to being out of here.

Funny Bridget was telling me how she has been in and out of jail over her life and she always goes back to those bad people. I suggested she write, "What attracts me to those people" and make it her quest to find the answer. If she can break the pattern she will break the cycle, therefore, become a new person. She said she did not want to put anyone on her phone card as those were her negative people from the outside. I suggested she talk to Whitey and maybe she and he could line up a mentor to help as she said she had no family. Maybe she might meet a good role model thru the church here, someone to give her some guidance, especially with no family in the area or here.

Well, I am exhausted with giving positive affirmations but me sure hope they helped. Funny how they are so open to a positive path, no swearing, and normal speech level nothing to prove until the environment or a person comes in and out comes the potty mouth, loud and negative gong.

Maybe one day that will change, but I will continue to be true to myself and to my family and to my path. I love you both and I will call you at 10:15pm.

God bless Sally she just dropped off some banana bread. I think the house is changing. The environment has shifted a bit and in a positive, giving way. God works in mysterious ways, even in jail.

November 18, 20xx

Good morning to you both. How are you doing today?

This morning I woke up and it was a cloudy start to the morning. After my shower and getting ready for the morning start I headed downstairs to fix myself some breakfast. I was pleasantly treated to Sally informing me has had two hard boiled eggs on the counter for me. She had seen me eating this for my breakfast and it was very kind of her to cook me two. Talk about a blessing in disgust, because as I was pealing the eggs and making the toast May brings down her radio and moves the table. The next thing I see her doing is hair at the table and the music gets cranked up. So now no one can watch TV and no one can eat at the table. I took my breakfast upstairs and ate in my room. This was happening before 9:00am. The three who seem to have no problems making life her more difficult are Max, May and Susan. Max did thank me for helping her yesterday. I offered her some peppermint tea to help with her flu and girls and told her since I was the only other person upstairs to bellow if she needed anything. It was actually quiet when she was sick and May shut her door. That girl needs some 101 in manners.

Well, I am going to read. God has blessed me in finding another author I really enjoy. Thanks be to God.

Thank you for another wonderful visit. I will call you at 10:15pm to say goodnight and check on Olive the cat. Gosh I miss that little rascal. I hope you are showing her my picture so she does not forget me and telling her how much I love and miss her. Mom maybe you could do that.

Oh yah, I remembered something I forgot to tell you during our visit. So prior to our visit while you were getting cleared to come in or pat down. Apple asked me to drop of a request for her which I had no problem doing as I had mail and the request for myself to drop off. So on the bench was a lady who I had had a conversation with and she was from another jail and she told me that that time our first meeting that I was too happy and was too positive that she would come back in a couple of months and see me then. I told her then that I would be even happier because I would be closer to getting out being with you. Well I ran into her today, sitting on the bench and she remembered me not from my looks so much as from my positive up beat manner. I said hi to her and she said she remembered me and I said to her, "See I am still smiling an upbeat." Funny how I met up with her again today.

So back at the house I was greeted with a pleasant hello from Bridget. She was so proud that she had started the Joyce Meyer book I pulled for her at the library and she liked it. I know how much Joyce inspired me and so why not pass on the good help o someone else. The music was cranked in the kitchen so loud I could hear it clearly in my room with the door shut. Reminds me of Mexico and how everyone always had their music cranked. It feels like the scene from the movie, "Along came Polly" at the salsa bar, with Jennifer and Ben dancing.

Dinner was terrific. I think I can cooked this one meal Max just made but I will watch her next time. At dinner May pipes up and tells the girls which consisted of me, Apple, Sally, Mea, Max and Susan if we had any glassed in our rooms as she was drinking from a small glass and she was really mad. Well everyone sees me only drinking from my cup for tea, coffee, and milk. The same cup for all my drinking needs. So after dinner it was May's turn to wash dishes and Sam's to dry. Well, Sam was at church service so I offered to dry for May and said I did not need to but since Sam was out I had no problem helping out. So as I was drying I remember we had smoothie's way before Sally arrived at the house so I looked in the freezer and sure enough there were the glasses in there. I told May some of the glasses were in the freezer from smoothie night. She said someone was hoarding the glasses. Not only are glassing running short but I mentioned to May so are the forks and she agreed. Max was plating food for Sam and for Bridget and she was packing her lunch for tomorrow, she was setting aside food for May for tomorrow also. Then after dinner I made myself a cup of tea and headed to my room to read until 6:00pm and I might pop out to the gym for a bit.

They have the stereo cranked out side my room. So no use staying here too long. I am going to write to Pastor tomorrow and some other supports. I will mail the letters to you as I don't have their addresses. Funny I always thank the chef on for the dinner. No one else does until tonight and Bridget who had dinner later came up and thanked Max. Maybe miss manners are rubbing off on others after all.

I just finished working out, which was great. I washed off today's stink and wrote to Pastor. I am not sure if I asked you to email him, but

I need to write and send him a visitor form. I wonder if pastor has to get the same clearance as others. Well, I guess we will find out.

Hope you had a wonderful evening and I look forward to our good night talk. Bridget was making brownies before I was heading to the gym. Gosh this house is going to make me 300 pounds before I leave. I'll put it away for a special time. I don't have to eat it all today as I have self control.

Tonight I did my laundry as the machine was available and watch the Good wife. Finally I am actually tired. So I am off to bed. I enjoyed our visit today and our talk tonight. You both keep me strong and I am so blessed to have you. All my love.

November 19, 20xx

Well, today I finally received a call to start my program. We have our first session on Wednesday at 8:00am so that is fabulous, especially when Susan keeps telling Apple that we would not get into programs until sometime next year. I reminded Apple not to get sucked into other people's negative attitude and we will get our programs in good time. Sure enough we have our programming.

Last night Apple calls me over as she was on the phone and asked me how you started you visits and did you have to bring a letter. Well, heck if I knew all I know is you telling me you had visits I have no idea if a letter was involved. I am confused because she, Apple, told me they were visiting net weekend, so I don't know but something was lost in translation. I imagine this has run its course on her parents, but they have been down this road before so who knows. I am excited to start programming and I am just focused on my path and that is getting home to you.

Oh yes, I also do my computer testing on Friday to see what career I should be doing, sure hope it's a school teacher, just kidding. Especially since you have spend good money on my legal courses.

A bit about the Women Engagement Program, it is a course for inmates to make healthy choices, to empower relationship choices, identify challenges and obstacles to living without engaging in problematic behavior and developed, reinforce and practice problem solving skills, manage emotions and relationship skills and healthy interactions with other through conflict resolution. I am thrilled to take this course. It sounds like a very interesting, practical and empowering class.

Oh yah the class is twelve session starting on Wednesday for two hours so that will time out perfectly for the correspondence classes to be approved by the warden. I hope this is the only program, but will take and do whatever is asked of me and I get paid while I am in programming just like work, so that is good.

Today I will do some work on the taxation project to get that under way. Well, I have completed what I can and tonight I will go to the computer lab and type and print it out. Once I receive the billings I can complete the task and send it back to you. The computer lab is open every day which will be terrific for my correspondence classes. I hope you don't mind me continuing to write my letters.

Sally mentioned today that her lunch time that the tension is so think you can cut it with a knife. I told her that some people don't adjust to change and because we have come into the house later the four originals have to respect that this is our house also. If they do or not is up to them. Stay out of my path and I will stay out of yours. Funny how May keeps calling the three girls, "fat asses" and how the baked goods are never enough or go missing when her, Mea and Max are feeling the neighbourhood these treats. Interesting how the guards won't allow me to take a chocolate bar for myself but these girls can give out backed goods from our house, which comes out of our grocery budge and not even recognize that there are none left for the house because they give them away. I am living with stupid is becoming apparent here.

The next time she makes a comment about this I may just remind her of the stupidity in her accusing the girls of eating others share when she is actually giving our food away and how that should come out of her share. I am not using baked goods or my chocolate bars so why should they. Just a bunch of hypocrites. I love you both and miss you terribly.

Mom can you look up a couple of items for me on the internet. Thank you and you can mail it in whenever you have time. I think that even if my son is nineteen he is still dealing with a lot and if you could look up on the computer this I would really appreciate it. We just have to press forward and stay strong together and I don't want to over load him too much its hard enough not having me there, I don't want to also be a constant nag. Also, you might enjoy doing some research type work. Thanks a million.

Well I am back writing to you to inform you on tonight's gong. I spend two hours typing the taxation information out when the printer would not work. So I spent tonight and the better part of today neatly writing out what you will need. Once I have the billings I will quickly finalize the package. It will be very straight forward. It might seem like a lot but everything is read into record which will help the Law Society make a case to have him disbarred. One less stinky, spineless lawyer out there. Jill was a huge help and I appreciate her trying to help me tonight. This could be a blessing as now the printer is actually getting fixed. I will print a test copy before doing any of my assignments on that computer. So I look at it as a huge lesson, a frustrating lesson, but at least Brent the computer guy is going to put any documents hat print out in an envelope and that the information will not go anywhere else. The room is also locked so it is secured as secured as jail can be.

Lots of hugs and kisses and all my love.

Ps I thought this computer lab was accessible to the mates but no I had to go into the games room where the mates play cards and do this. I thought the house was loud, not compared to this. I will have to write my assignments out by hand and only go there to finalize them and when I have completed the assignment. Gosh to do anything in here is next to impossible. To try and improve you does not come without major hurtles. To most of the mates here this is a time to relax and live off the tax payer's dollar and with no accountability. I want to make my time her count.

PPS one month today since I have been here…looking at one day closer to being with you.

November 20, 20xx

Good morning to my two wonderful supporters. Gosh I am not in a good mood this morning. Susan and her fouled mouth are going strong. Now she is complaining about the food and how others are eating too much. How if there is baking that everyone should get some, fine, but if they want to give the baked goods out to the yard then it should come out of that person's share, not the house. I'll discuss this with Bob when I meet with him. If they were not complaining they would be dead. Last night while I was waiting for movement to the main house, some girl from another house comes into our house. This is not allowed nor do I like it. I have always locked my door, but I will also mention this to Bob at my next meeting. Maybe the guards should read this letter carefully and know that my chocolate bar you pay for me is actually staying with me.

The house is so loud when Max, Susan and May are here. I don't know why they have to yell. This is our entire house and their Alpha crap is not going to fly. I am glad they are leaving soon because when they re-offend, I will not be here. Gosh this test God has me on is sure building me on so many levels.

I am so looking forward to our visit tonight. Talking to actual normal people who can complete a sentence without a single swear is such a refreshing breath. I am not sure why Max and May and Susan are her but I am blessed they are downstairs doing their swearing talk and I can focus on myself and my list of things to get completed.

I went to get a cup of coffee and Bridget was cooking an egg and Sam was in on the listening to Susan complaining. Mea was on the phone and Max was putting her two cents in, if you want to call it that. Bridget was eating so can you imagine how uncomfortable she felt as Susan was complaining about food, yet she has no problem taking an extra hamburger and Max is saving food for May on the side. I am starting to see the mean girls in this house, but I am grateful for our visiting time that I can write and get my thoughts out on paper and clear my concerns with Bob.

I received a letter from the lady at A&D where my DL is so I will get this to Bob, but she is gone until November 30, so unless Bob can get my DL back I will discuss with you what we may need to do when you register the truck.

I found your news last night about the crooks lawyer moving to another law firm very interesting. Can you look into that law firm? I have never heard of that firm before. I was also glad to hear that the lawyer I met on October 18 was kind to you. Sometimes they can be such jerks and that was my opinion of that day in court but it was also interesting he remembered me and was actually helpful to you. Maybe my story/case is making it thru the law firms. I maybe reading into things but to have the lawyer move or get fired from one lawyer and then who has to go and do the crooks dirty work somewhere else says a lot. Says that this lawyer firm does not like to do dirty works. The universe is catching up with the crook. God is working behind the scene on this matter.

Mom can you mail me some computer paper not a big pack but a few sheets of paper.

Well, that is too bad we could not visit tonight but I hope you were able to get some things done especially since it was not too bad out today and hopefully our visit won't be cancelled tomorrow. It has been a weird day in here today. First they had the movement to work which took forever then they had movement back to the house. So I knew something was up and thought that our visit maybe cancelled because that was just weird. So I am glad I called and we'll talk at 6:00 and at bedtime. They keep testing the fire alarms in the house which is annoying but better to be safe than sorry.

There was some speaker in the gym but I unfortunately missed it. I had my earplugs in and did not hear the announcement. Great to have the ear plugs, a shame I missed the page and a shame I have to exist because of others are so loud or have their doors open and are just rude. Anyways, then there was an emergency count for reach house, which was a first since I have been here. Not sure what that is all about, but usually the 4:00pm count is a stand in front of your room, this count was conducted in the common area/ living room of the house.

I completed the book but not quite the sure I enjoyed the ending. I had hoped that the big company won, but maybe he will like my book. The publisher company he uses was ….

Tomorrow is the start of my program with should be interesting and a nice change. It starts at 8:00am for a couple of hours. Time stands still in here. One hour feels like days. Well no visit means a longer letter. It's unfortunate that the lady from A&D is gone not only because of my DL but also the pen pack won't be delivered for sure until November 30. I am not sure why they don't have departments cover off so things can still flow smoothly.

Just finished dinner which was hot dogs and fries and you can feel the tension in the house. I am staying as far away as possible as I have no interest in any of it. I would prefer to spend my time writing and reading.

I'll write to a couple of supports tomorrow and put it with this letter so you can give it to them next week when you see them. I'll enclose a visitation form for you to give out. Stay strong my little grasshoppers and we will get past this journey. These people are not a part of my social network nor will they after I leave. Apple has even become negative and moved more into the darker side of the house, so I have now kept my distance from her as well. I refuse to get involved with the gossip of jail nor do I want to associate with others who want to be a part of it. I am becoming a person who will become closed off to people, especially in here not that this should not be a good thing, but I just would have thought women with children would be similar, but I guess I was wrong about that. A shame because I would have been a great support for her, oh well her loss. I knew who has my back and is my faith and loyal team and supporter and especially my family and it is not going to be here.

All my love, keeps strong, keep positive and keep praying.

November 21, 20xx

Good morning to you both. Mom before I forget did you ask Pat about renters and tenants as he would know about how to get a good one and may actually know of someone, but more importantly the process.

Well last night we received another new girl, a large native gal who came from Winnipeg so not sure why gals are being shipped so far this way, but she seems to know the drill. So now we are up to ten and there is one room that I did not know what it was for but it is an over flow room so this house can actually hold eleven mates. Not sure what her name is yet but again the dynamics are changing. I love you both and I am looking forward to our visit.

Please type the following for me letter to sign. Thank you. My program starts today and I will tell you about it at our visit tonight. We are having a house meeting today at 4:00pm so that should be interesting. I imagine the four old girls, the original four, will have a lot to day as use six newbie's must be cramping their style. Anyways, no negative thoughts only attracts negative and that is not my style. I love you both and my focus is on my path and getting home to you. Mom I received the mail today and the billings were there so thank you.

Tomorrow is a presentation on Restorative justice so I have volunteered to help assist guest to their seats. The day is spent with guest speakers so that will be motivational and who just wants to attend I would rather help out where ever possible. Get involved in a good way and stay away from the gossip and gong.

I was reading the bible and started to pull out and write down some of my favorite verse to help me on my days to stay positive and up, plus you two keep my spirits high and I am forever blessed for that.

Well the house meeting got adjourned as Bridget and Max were not there. The new girls Sam went off on Sally about how she opened a loaf of bread and now it was almost gone. So we had no soap, dish detergent so today the order was placed and picked up at the end of the day. Apple told May she would get the container but it would be way too heavy for Apple to carry it alone so I told May I would help Apple. May said Apple got called away to a trailer, so I asked May to tell Apple to meet me at the main house and I would help her carry the container.

So long story short Susan brought the container home so none the dishes from the entire day got done and tonight we mine and Bridget's night to do dishes, so I thought I would get a head start so we would have plates ext for dinner. I was washing and blessed Sally was crying. I don't know where Bridget was and so Sally and I went doing dishes minding our business and Sam starts off on Sally over bread, but the funny thing is during dinner I saw Sam consume four slices. She cracks me up because she'll tell me she doesn't eat carbs as she is dishing up the potatoes and leave the chicken. What the heck do you thing bread and potatoes are?

Bless Apple helped me with the dishes tonight after dinner as Bridget was who knows where. So Apple tells me that she asked if she could turn the TV so she could watch it while she worked out. Well it was not there but Sam gets up and turns it back, so within 20 minutes both Sally and Apple have been targets for Sam rage.

May tells me she is moving to another house the "J" house which will help her to get to the lodge she needs if she wants to get her parole in January. I told her she would be missed as she would even if she can bother me sometimes. I hope she gets her act together and I wish her all the best. Plus, the music and TV situation will be a non issue when it comes to my studies. Like I told Bob that if my studies become effected I will cross that bridge with that person so hopefully Max gets out in December and the top floor becomes quiet. God will help me and all good time.

The newest girl is quiet and spends a lot of her time in her room, just like me. I seem to get along with everyone in the house. The person

I avoid is Susan, but I am civil to her, polite and pleasant. I have put myself in charge of the vacuuming and mopping of the upstairs and wiping down the stairs and banister. So that is fine as I can also vacuum my room at the same time.

Oh yes the topic of food keeps coming up in the house, which is making me uncomfortable as I hardly eat anyway, so I will mention to Bob if this is normal. I am going to purchase some soup at canteen and keep it in my room. It makes everyone tense especially when the ones complaining are the ones eating all of it. I just shake my head in disbelief.

I get paid for programs. My instructor is Sara and she said we would probably not have program tomorrow because of speaker, still get paid and now we won't have program until next Wednesday as Sara is off for a few days, but she was kind enough to tell us she would still pay us for those days also. I wish people knew about the story but that will happen all in good time.

The devil must be working today. He must know how he can't break my positive spirits so our visit got cancelled. You are right there are no visits on Thursday. You guys are so smart. Well I remain positive and actually hope that I can be an inspiration to Mea. She was a bit down and I hope I may have been able to have her do something for her to make a difference. Maybe I being here will make each of these ladies motivated to make a difference maybe that is my calling.

Mom I hope you are feeling better and you get past your migraine. Have a nice cup of tea and I will call you soon as the guards do their count. Well one positive is that even though I would have loved to see you tonight and give you a squeeze, we are blessed with being able to talk on the phone and blessed to have one another. I love you both with all my heart.

November 22, 20xx

How are you doing today? How is your headache today mom? My sons please help out Grandma and offer her what you can. I hope you are asked for an interview at the dog kennel and my prayers will be with you. Both way what is meant to be will be and all in God's plan. We may not always like the plan but he knows best all the time.

I have my greeting and seating guests today and I am excited to hear some positive guest speakers. I got to thinking about yester and maybe because I am not your typical inmate and I actually can complete a sentence with no cursing ect, maybe I threw her for a loop but it seems that until you hear my story or once you hear the story everyone is left with the "Wow" facture. Well I am off to the main house so I will chat with you in a bit.

Thursday will be my 41st birthday and silly how it falls on that day. I will not get to visit with you on my birthday and celebrate with you, but then again nothing will be celebrated this year and we will celebrate doubly next year.

I sign up for a volunteer position and today when I went they said I was not on the list. I witnessed her write down my name, so now I can't go and listen to the guest speakers. I will instead have to review my taxation and do the billing portion of that so I can get them back to you. I was really looking forward to going. Well I will complete the taxation project so that is good to be done. I will mail it tonight at movement. I was able to talk to you this morning and get canteen. With the food situation so tense in here, I picked up some popcorn so if things get nasty I can always have popcorn for dinner with pepper on it. I picked up a couple of chocolate bars so if we have to go for more than four days without seeing each other I have some stashed.

I wish I could attend the taxation appointment. If Mr. Reck was smart he would offer to settle because we have a great case of gross negligence and misconduct, unprofessional, breach of ethics and a breach of code of conduct, not to mention the law society is looking into him also. The taxation officer is a very nice person. If Wayne can't or won't go just remember I did this all by myself and the big Q.C. hired a lawyer to represent the firm and him and I also had to go to court and then come back to complete the taxation process. If you need me to clarify anything let me know. You have lots of time until January

23 and I have complete faith in you both. Just stick to the notes focus on the facts, this is law so no feelings or personal ramble just the facts. Remember these terms, gross negligence, breach of ethics, breach of code of conduct, misconduct, failure to communicate, client duress, lawyer buzz words and phrases.

Overall, today was a very productive day. I did the taxation, canteen, moved my room around so maybe I won't freeze, I washed the floors, did my bed sheets, and laundry and wrote to you. The bed is positioned with my head at the window so I can still see the stars at night. Dad is looking down on us. Thank you for all your assistance yesterday when I was a bit down. Sometimes it gets frustrating when you are in here and innocent and you are looked down on even when they don't know the story. You would think that people teaching programs would have more moral training to consider what they are saying and in front of whom they are saying. My information is my private information and she had no right to even say anything about my case or if my lawyer would be appealing. That is between me and my lawyer. And this Institution sure did not hurry up to get me the forms I requested to make the appeal even possible, but that is another issue and I won't go there right now. My writing is getting messy so I am going to take a break.

Groceries just got here and it should be interesting how things go down. Love you both and bless you for starting my canteen fund. Mom keep a total running and one day I will pay you back, maybe with royalties from this book. Grocery day means fruit. We each get two apples, one orange, a pear, and one banana. You eat the banana first because it goes rip the quickest. That was our fruit for this week and I will let you know next week.

I think my room arrangement will be great because now I have the bed against the wall so I can study and spread my books our, which will make for more productive work.

Funny now Bridget and Sally are actually talking to one another maybe they found some common grounds. Back to my book and my writing. May said that the restorative justice was just okay. She said I did not miss anything and the food at lunch was just okay. I thanked her for not telling me it was amazing and rubbing it in my face. I told May I was doing my own Restorative justice in my taxation stuff.

I guess someone from our house has been telling about the food situation at Corcan, well I am not working there so it's not me, not that I would even talk to other inmates at Corcan anyway, so it's either Susan, Mea, Bridget, Sally, Apple, or Sam because they all work there. I have programs and post secondary on my path, but this just goes to show you how crap moves around here and I am just grateful to not be anywhere near it especially when May gets the information and she doesn't work at Corcan. Gossip is like the air around here always on the move and can surround you. See again blessing as I am sure this will be mentioned at dinner. Apple is making a broccoli, cauliflower, potatoes soup which smells amazing. I think I'll go to the gym and try to move these girls out of me. I am excited to hear what the neighbours have to say about their trip. I will write them tonight and put in it a visitation form.

Well, you being the observer the crap seem to come around. Bridget is upstairs in May's room gossiping about I don't know what but May is not quiet and you can hear some swear words coming out so I am sure there will be something at dinner, plus May said we were supposed to have a meeting yesterday which did not happen so maybe tonight. I am not sure if Bridget is stirring up the pot but either way I am just the observer and trying to pass on positive affirmations' to keep the peace, but it may also be good to get some of these issues our especially the food one as that can be huge and is causing a lot of tension. I keep forgetting that these girls are not just the usual gossipy women, but also criminals either way I vote will be interesting.

So we just had our 4:00pm stand for count and Sam comes up saying Bridget such a bitch blah, blah, blah. I was just standing at my door waiting for the guards, doing what was expected of me. Sam walks to her room, which is upstairs and May looks at me with big eyes and what the heck look. I asked May if she was still moving she said "yes". I told her Bridget wants to see if she could have your room. That would be great especially since they don't seem to get along. May started laughing. I asked her if she is sure she wants to move then the guards came.

Susan made the soup and Apple made cheese biscuits which were very good. Sally and I did the dishes. Then I came upstairs to my room with a mug of milk. Meeting will be tomorrow at lunch as Max is at work tonight.

Well I am going to sign off on this letter so I can up it in the mail tonight. Lots of love and blessing to you both. I miss you both more than words can say. All my love.

November 23, 20xx

How are you both? I am doing fine today. Surprise, surprise at 6:00pm last night the page goes out no movement. The guard was very pleasant and apologetic especially since some people have had no movement all day. I want to go check the mail, hand in my visitation form so you could come for a sleep over and pop some more mail in for you.

Guess what I got last night, heat! Not sure if my bed was blocking something or it something got fixed but at 6:00pm my room got warm. Okay that was short lived, as I woke up this morning and it was cold, but I can manage in this temperature during the day. So studying will be easy to not fall asleep.

I was put on the waitlist for the forklift training but better to apply then not at all. This morning I was subjected to a random search of my room. My son you know how I knew was because my closet door was open ever so slightly. I was thankful they did not do a rampage or mess up my room, not like I would have anything in my room that should not be there. I always look my door so nothing strange would ever be in my room.

Let Wayne know I have prepared for the taxation appointment and see if he will attend with you. I am sure he will. Thanks for doing it and I have complete faith in you both even is Wayne can't come, I know you will do your best and that is all anyone can ask for, especially me.

Well my testing on the computer after you finish the math and English part was actually a lot of fun. After you select skills you have to help point you in a Career direction. Allison then asked me to write down three you might be interested in. This was the first time since being here that after I was finished a test that I actually felt inspired to have a career not that completing my legal courses is not top priority but actually gave me hope for the future. So after I publish the books, finish my legal courses, I will have yet another school, work, career goal. I am going to make sure Allison knows how her testing left me feeling which was so positive. The three career choices I selected were Animal Control officer, Radiation Therapist, and Cardiopulmonary Therapist another one that caught my interest was Community health nurse and funeral attendant.

Not sure how many of the other inmates appreciate the test but I sure did and thankful to have had it. Funny one of the jobs was a drycleaner attendant. There were 196 jobs to select from for my skill set, but no judge or lawyer, which is okay because those professions are not human anyway and a funeral attendant would cover the walking dead. Maybe when I get out of here we an open a doggy daycare, kennel, providing you both are up for that.

Sorry for getting all emotional tonight. I thank you for all you are doing and I guess the more I can't get done myself which is pretty much everything the more I ask of you. Plus, like I said tonight is that I don't want you, mom to have my financial burden put on you so I feel helpless. It's bad enough serving a sentence from what I did not do, but it is even worse when you are serving the sentence and not even committed the crime. If I had the money I sure would not be here or worried about money when I get out or paying for bills, so it is extremely frustrating. I thank you for the support and I love you both. Thank you my son, for being a strong young man tonight. Tonight you were the rock; tomorrow I will be the rock. Sunday Grandma you will be the rock. I will call you at 10:00pm. I am excited to hear about your bowling adventure and the new girl.

November 24, 20xx

How are you this morning? Last night after our visit May asked if I wanted to sign Mea's birthday card which I did. As I was signing it

May placed her rose picture on my peg outside my door. She said she would be leaving today. Her bags were packed and she is ready to take the next step to get out. Good for her. I said she would have to leave her forwarding address so we could write, which would be house "J". We smiled. The guards came by, Bob was on tonight. Now when we meet next week he can see how full the house has become and he will be able to assess the usual problems with a full house.

After you left last night I also went to the mail and one of my letters was too heavy so I got bounced back. Of course it was the one with the visitation form and a letter to my friend. I removed the stamp form that envelope and put it on the new one and I am sending it again to you. I will see if I can get the guards to give you the visitors form or I will put it in the mail later tonight.

I received the paper and the letter from the Law Society. I will mention to you at our visit to enclose those correspondence and the taxation stuff. I put in the mail for January 23. I thought the letter from the Law Society was great at least they are doing something, more then I can say for other agencies.

Sorry again about last night, I know this is playing a huge toll on all of us. I was however, very proud of you, my son to bring things back to a place of rational, productive, and manageable position. Now we have a game plan moving forward. I will try to make a list of things that can wait until I get our or escorts and we can deal with that then.

Funny how when I woke up this morning, it was nice and sunny but now it is starting to cloud over. After our visit today I will write to more friends. Once I have Wayne's land number I will call him which takes some of the pressure off you both. To be the middle man can be very stressful and emotionally exhausting so once the news is out and things settle down the normality will sink in. I know your thinking what normality, but who said life was boring was not living it to the fullest. Big missions, reap big rewards.

Yes I am not about to back down over Susan complaining about the food. She makes it uncomfortable for the entire house. I have my fruit and popcorn and I will get my share which is less than half of others. Last night Apple made some carrot cookies, but after our visit I just wanted time to relax so I was exhausted so I just hit the sack. This morning all the cookies were gone.

I can't wait until I have my pen pack or London drugs order. Funny how a few things can make you feel more in your own environment. The other jail they have to share cells so I don't know how those girls are dealing with no privacy or space. I just have to remember to count my blessings. That girl was in the house night visiting again. See you in a bit for our visitation. Interested to hear about the bowling.

That girl at the table behind you my son was the one who was in the house. The one with the foul mouth.

My son my emotions and hormones are all over the place and I am sorry. I miss you terribly and this is very difficult being away from you. Please forgive my sadness and remember it is just me being human.

May is moving out tonight. She has a trail of clear bags with her belongings in them. At count I told her, "it looks like you have your suit cases packed", she looked at me and gave me a big smile and a "yep, my suit cases are all packed."

I just want you to know that I am fine, I will be strong for you and you both and you will be strong for me. God will bless us and keep us.

I will try calling you before you went out tonight, but I don't want to spoil your shift and your date, so just be careful and take care.

Between tomorrow morning and Wednesday I want to finish writing to the outside supports. Sure wish I had a keyboard as I am always aware of how awful my handwriting is. Oh well, I will try and slow down.

Went downstairs but May was on the phone so if I can call I will you know that. I hope I explained the transition thing okay. I have to be myself around you and then mentally prepare to go back. When

I am saying goodbye to you and the guard is getting ready to pat me down, especially when my hormones are off the chart and my mind is transitioning. So we can try the suggestion to say our goodbyes you move to the hallway and I will get my pat down and transition so you can see me walk out the doors and go back to my unit. Good thing we got that cleared up also to find out that the not feeling well had to do with the last night activities.

While I was on the phone with you, Bridget pulled out a bowl to make something or should I say bake something. Well, I got off the phone and headed back to my room to write and to wipe the tooth paste off my nose. Tooth paste is good to help kill zits. Max thought I was or might have been upset so she asked me if I was okay, so I told her what was doing and that was wiping off the toothpaste for my soon to be zit. Mea came upstairs to her room and then it was on. Susan was telling Mea that they were baking downstairs and touching the stuff in the backing cupboard marked "Do not touch". I think this is where the overflow stuff is, but it says "do not touch" so I don't touch. Susan asks Mea what is she going to do about it and Mea replies "what can I do" not sure if anything was dealt with as there is no yelling going on and I will see at movement at 6:00pm when I go to get the mail if any cooking took place, not that is would get any anyways.

Funny how some women or more some people are the complainers about their weight and how they have to go to the gym yet in the house they'll work out on the machine for thirty minutes and then eat all day and night long. For myself, I am feeling bones I have not felt in years as I may still have my chocolate and pop at visits, but I am not over eating or hoarding foods.

I think peppermint tea is the thing for my PMS. At least it has helped right now and that is all that matters. I may turn in early tonight but first I want to get some reading in and wait for movement. Knowing me I will get my second wind in a bit.

I have been notified of my dates for my escorted visits, unescorted visits, day parole, full parole, stat release date and Warrant date. The warrant date is when this is all over and I have served my sentence. I can smell the bounce which means heat is coming up into my room. I put in a bounce sheet in the heat vent and now that the heat is on, I can smell the sheet.

May came back to the house to say goodbye, but Mea did not even go down and say anything to her. I did and wished her good luck. I would see her in the yard and around.

November 25, 20xx

I realized last night after writing to the supporters and family that on my second round of vaccination for the hep A & B is on my birthday. Mea's birthday is today. Hope she has a wonderful one. Its 9:00am and the house is actually at a normal volume level. I wrote down my goals that I want to achieve while I am here and my goals one I am released. This will inspire me to stay on track and be productive and accomplish more, not that I would not utilize every moment I can as of course I would. I am going to write and I am glad to hear that visits are still on for 1:00pm. Mea must be off on a visit as she was called to the duty office. This pen keeps acting like it is running out of juice and then it starts up again.

Remind me of the story about the secret Santa and how upset Susan got. Yah I really want to spend money on someone who has no respect and curses too much. I would rather donate that money. Anyways I will keep in my faith bubble and read.

Woke up last night in a panic thinking that I did not put an address on the Taxation mail, but I am sure the guards would return it to me if I did not. Please tell me when you receive it.

I enjoyed our visit again today and I will call you at 10:30pm to say good night. Kind of funny but my goal sheet for while I am her is also being able to complete these items which is really happening like getting the correspondence, get the pen pack, publish the books, rent the house, complete courses, stay out and way from the gossip, to continue my spiritual/ bible growth, and it is coming to be. My most important goal is to stay connected to family and friends and even that is being completed. I even set a goal to find my love for reading again and I was blessed with that. Funny how some of the simplest enjoyments that you may take for granted are rediscovered in the journey of being in jail.

Time to start a new book, but first I must tell you while we were playing cards at our visit, Mea was waiting to have her pee test done. Max was making dinner and made extra to give to Mea's friend in the yard the lady who keeps coming into our house.

Before I hopped into the shower Sam asked me if I ate cake. I returned the same question back to her. But the reason she was asking was because there was two pieces downstairs and she was asking if she could have my piece which was fine by me. The point is at least she asked, which I thought was very gracious. Some of the other mates would have just taken it, is that not stealing. What a messed up world we live in.

One more day gone and one day closer to being with you. I love you both and miss you terribly. My heart aches for you and I wish us back together. We will survive this and be more grateful for each other.

November 26, 20xx

Good morning mom and my son. How are you both doing today? It is cloudy this morning and it looks like it might snow.

The school here was cancelled so Max is home this morning. The school gets cancelled a lot here, not sure how anyone gets their grade 12 with no school. I never see them studying or doing homework, but maybe they get a lot of class time. Apparently, we are having the house meeting today at 4:00pm, but I am not holding my breath. I am so grateful to have space to escape to with all the negative energy it has no place in my space. I find it hypocritical of people here to complain about the food yet again, and yet they are those ones shovelling it in or dishing it out to the neighbours.

People in here should mind their own business and focus on improving themselves but nope they would rather gossip and create drama, which I want no part in or of. Even the program people like to stir the pot in getting into people's issues. If I want to discuss things I will speak to a professional not an inmate or a person with no skills.

Anyways, I will write to the last of my supporters and at least they will know what I am up to and that I am doing fine. Mom you can give a form to the family members and see if they want to come in and visit. I know my day parole is for June so I will also need to know if they will support me. Anyways that will all come to light and the truth will all come out in that case.

We had our house meeting which not with may have resolved some issues who knows. Someone is sure eating a lot. Apple says she won't eat other people's portions anymore, but the other person who is eating all the goodies at night just sat on the couch and said nothing but when it came to the bread she just told people not to each so much.

Overall, it was a peaceful meeting. I could honestly care less about the food. I will eat my portion. If someone bakes, I will put mine in my room so the last night eater won't eat it. I only care about talking and seeing you guys. The food in here will not keep me going, but your support and love and visits will.

I put in a request for Bob to chat and hopefully he can read my parole form and discuss things this week. Sally says her parole officer is really amazing and that was one of the names Bally has said before she left so maybe Bob can find out, otherwise, we will just have to do it together.

I will chat with you in a bit and please be careful it is starting to snow. I love you both and please stay strong, positive and take care of one another. All my love.

November 27, 20xx

I really enjoyed out visit last night. After you left the guard patted me down and asked if we had a nice visit. She said we looked like we were having fun. She asked me for my shoes and asked if I had the different laces for a reason. When I explained that the washer ate one of them. She laughed and said it's amazing what you will do to survive. I said, yes and you have to make do with certain things. She said exactly. I said you sure appreciate things after you are in here and she said that was also true and the final one was when I told her about the prospect of the adventure. She said no one has ever viewed this as being a journey or adventure before. Well, that is probably because I am not a criminal. The guard just have never encountered someone like me before. I still don't understand why this is not a red flag, but maybe one day they will pick up the book and go "wow, I knew her".

My son I want to tell you how proud of you I am of your new job. Maybe this is a calling to work with animals but either way it is a great new job and adventure for you. Have you ever thought of going into animal control work? Hope your drive to the next town is okay. Gosh you are being blessed with a number of new job selections which is so lovely. We will work our visits around your work schedule.

Mom you be careful going out tonight with Aunt. I received my London drugs order after you left. The lady who I think does the shopping was so very nice. She went over the order and the items she could get and the ones she could not get. I had ordered some face scrub as it helps with my monthly break outs, but since the canteen sells a different scrub I would have to get a doctor's note to get something different. I can get a doctor's note when I get my Hep A&B shot next week. I ordered an alarm clock, a blow dryer, because who knows how long it will be for the pen pack and winter is here and it is not health to go out with wet hair. I have been showering at night and having the night sweets all day long is gross. I am tired of going downstairs to see what time it is all the time so good thing for the alarm clock. If I can return items back to you I will certainly do so. No TV was located at London drugs not the one that can come in here anyways. She said they would try another store so I explained the pen pack situation and she said fir me to let her know. So fingers crossed that the little one you sent it makes the cut in here and we don't have to spend money on purchasing one.

Funny how some people will purchase certain items and others will purchase make up and items that are about their appearances. I guess that makes them feel good and to each their own. I must still be too practical, but then again a TV some would say is not necessary other s would say it is survival material.

I was able to drop a letter in the mail and put in my request to the acting warden and to Bob. If I see him I will let him know to look for the request. Today I will check the mail and writ and maybe meet with Bob and finish my book. Tomorrow it is back to program and a wonderful visit from you.

This morning they fixed the heat so now my room is nice and toasty. I wrote to the family clan and set you a letter. Looking at Psalm 26 really spoke to me: vindicate me, O lord for I have walked in my integrity, I have also trusted in the lord; I shall not slip. I have hated the assembly of evildoers and I will not sit with the wicked. I will wash my hands in innocence so I will go about your altar, O Lord that I may proclaim with the voice of thanksgiving. In whose hands are a sinister scheme, and whose right rand is full of bribes but as of me, I will walk in my integrity; redeem me and be merciful to me. My foot stands in and even place; in the congregations I will bless the Lord. Psalm 23 is also an old favorite.

Interesting as I sit and read the psalms a sense of empowerment comes over me. This journey has brought me even closer to my faith which is so wonderful, wish it was under different circumstances of course.

Just as I am writing that last line flipping the pages of my bible I stumble upon Psalm 64. On day "so He will make them stumble over their own tongues; all who see them shall flee away."

Holy this room is cooking now. I covered the vent and opened the window. Not sure why they can't just turn it up a smig, now they are trying to cook us out.

Bob came by for count and told me he was in the secured unit all day, but would hopefully be able to talk tomorrow. They have some sort of craft thing going on in the gym tonight but I am not into craft and would rather read. Plus, being out canned lead to trouble everyone has nothing better to do then gossip and I have no time for that, nor do I want to start. I will stick to myself and my path. I am not interested in making friends here and by the sounds of things these girls are more interested in gossiping both inside the house and outside. I wish my schooling would get here, I mean cleared by the Warden. This pen is giving me grief. Phew my room is starting to cool down.

There are five rabbits in the yard and I can see them from my window. Oh they are so cute and so tame. Bob just popped into the house and we were able to have a couple of minutes. I was able to tell him about my DL and how we can take care of it on the 30th of the month. I also got to thinking about the passport and maybe on January, after the taxation or before you could go and see if you can get it back. If not I will get a new one when I get out or we will go and get it.

Bob asked about the correspondence and I told him I put in another request and that they should be cleared soon as they were sent to the acting warden, but also attention to him. Bob will look into this matter for me. I told him about the programs persons comment and how it caught me off guard but again once she heard how I had changed and had seven years to grow and how this has been going on for after so many years.

When I told Bob maybe she will read my book and see. Bob smiled a big smile and said "yes, no kidding". I said maybe she was having an off day, but I would view tomorrow as a new day. He told me I have the best attitude. He asked me if I had a visit tonight, I said nope that I was going to the gym. He thought that was great. I told him I have no time for drama or gossip, he totally agreed. He asked about the house and if there was anything pressing. Is said nope we could talk and I would let him know about the two items, but nothing pressing. I told him that the person who apparently was taking over Bally's files was Gail but that was what Mea told me and until it comes from the actual person or Bob, I'll just wait.

I went downstairs to call you but had to wait until 7:00pm so I was watching TV with Susan and Mea. I asked Susan since she worked for the maintance if they could turn down the heat upstairs as now it is a sauna and she was very polite and nice about it. We talked, well they talked about some of their adventures and no cursing was involved. People in here don't swear if they are having a conversation with me, but it is like they have to put on a show by cursing. I will tell you a story about and then someone will not be minding their own business and then the story is spread all over the jail. People need to mind their own business.

Something is going on again as our movement has stopped and all inmates have to return to their units. Poor Bob is over at the max. I pray we can have our visit tomorrow as scheduled.

I will check the mail in the morning and see what surprises are in there. I love you both and I will call you at 10:30pm after the count is completed. Good luck in your interview tomorrow my son and please drive safe.

November 28, 20xx

How are you today? Again good luck in the interview today and please drive safely the roads are terrible today. My program was fine this morning. Max suggested I ask Sara what other programs I should take or if she knew which ones I was to take next as she has read the file on me. Sara suggested that I may want to move the house called the "Humming Bird" but I would probably only need this once. When I told Max, she said no the "Humming Bird" was for people with mental health and serious disorders. Is this lady firing on all cells? Overall, the program today was fine. Hopefully Bob and I can get some time today to chat. I wish the correspondence would hurry up, but all in good time. I will call you at 2:00pm to confirm our visit and our squeeze time.

Mom I received the sin number information and filled it out and will pop it in the mail. Thank you for taking care of that. I will discuss this with you tonight. Funny how people can be so superficial. How they act towards the instructors or guards and how they behave or say why they are not around. Why can't people just be pleasant and themselves all the time. Just things that are said at program which are to their own and I appreciate that but then they are nasty outside. Why can't people just be true to themselves? I guess that is the million dollar question to which no one here can answer. What a gong.

Last night I actually had an okay sleep. At night when movement has ended the inmates talk to one another out their windows. Kind of interesting.

Son I am glad your interview went well and just remembers what happens, happens you felt well about the interview and now just wait and see. Everything will work out.

Today the guards did a random search on some of the girl's rooms. Mine looked untouched but they did mine before so that makes sense. Still have not heard from Bob today. So tomorrow after programs I might pope and see if they need workers at Corcan but who knows what tomorrow has in store. Maybe tomorrow I will receive of my correspondence. That would be a nice birthday present. Please warden and acting warden let me start my correspondence after my mom spent all that money on these classes.

I am looking for to our visit tonight. Thank you for coming tonight in this cold weather. Time with you keeps me going. After our visit I just reflect on how much fun we have and our laughing time. You two crack me up. My son I know you want to move on and start dating and I think that is wonderful I just felt a bit out of the loop. You know I put you first always and hope you know you can tell me anything. Tell me on the phone or in writing, just please keep me in the loop.

I ran into Bob and asked him if he saw the acting warden to please inquire about where the correspondence is in the processing thing. Anyways, Bob and I had a fabulous talk. Bob said he has been stuck in the secured unit and will try to call me up to chat again soon.

I checked my mailbox and funny how it is number 29. Nothing to report. I love you both and miss you even when I just say you. I long for us to be together again and each day is just one day closer to being together. You are the best and I am so grateful for you both.

November 29, 20xx

Thank you both for my birthday card. I read it yesterday just what you wrote and I will re-read it after programs. My calendar says for today is "let not your heart be troubled; ye believe in God, believe also in me." John 14:1. Now what a powerful message this morning, great way to kick start my forty one. I truly think forty one is the year.

You two have been a wonderful support team and I will one day be able to make you very proud of me and will one day be victorious and like Psalm 26 says…Vindication.

I woke up extra early this morning and have no idea why, so I will do some reading from the bible to get my day started on a spiritual note. I was able to read the card and actually felt empowered not sad. And yes I too which I was celebrating my forty one under different circumstances but we will have to celebrate for all events when I get out and spending time with you is more important than anything else. I am so blessed to have you two. I will write to you after program.

One more thing of interest is how in programs we are doing the vision board on my birthday. It is like my own personal gift for our new future and I am able to pick a vision to achieve for us. Just thought of all days it happens to land on today. God must be looking out or dad is here with me in spirit either way it is a nice gift for in here.

All the small things I will make a big positive in here. So I will let you know what I have in store for the vision for the next year. What a nice class for programs today. I really enjoyed making the vision board and it was nice to see that today Sara would speak up with the "F" bomb fight around the room. I like being able to see my vision for forty one come to life. Yes to the healthy life style which was a normal part of our life anyways.

Some with faith, family, cooking, exercise, travel, so the book will be this year and maybe marrying Ryan Reynolds. I put in for sure a golden retriever right my son. Oh happy days, tomorrow we do a session called being smart. Funny the first day of the programs she asked who does not like reading out loud. One I was honest like always and said I don't. Sara said she may ask me to read out loud every once in a while to step me out of my comfort zone. Fair enough.

Well today she asked me to read, after I was done. She said she had jus remembered I did not feel comfortable reading out loud, but how well I did. She was actually surprised. I am not sure what she thought I would sound like, but I do know how to read. So I told her it's like the fear of public speaking. She asked me after I was done my vision board if I was an artist or drawer. I replied no but I do like to take old things and paint them ect to make them beautiful. When Sara was done asking me about my vision board she asked me to explain it to the class. She was yet again impressed that I was done first, had the entire board completed, I did what I was asked to do and followed instructions. She asked about the name of my book. Another lady told her I looked like Diane Lane, which was very kind.

My son I sure hope you are feeling better today. Get some rest. I wish I were there to doctor you. You are amazing about the date thing. Gosh I was the most blessed mom to have you as my son. I love how each day you fill me with strength and inspiration. Thank you for being and saying the right things at the right time.

Mom, sorry to hear about work and the stress you are having. When I get out of here it is my mission to take care of you, and my son and our animal. We will have the book at the publishers and soon after be vindicated. One more day closer to being with you both and I will stay positive and focused on the bigger picture.

Well someone heard my prayer. I just met with the acting warden and she confirmed the warden has approved my correspondence and they were all off to A&D to be logged onto my cell items. This place teaches you patient and then sure enough I was called to go and get my books as I was speaking this to one of the mates. Funny how thing sometimes turn out, but it is a lot of your attitude that will help you endure the journey.

Food delivery day today and I received two apples, two oranges, two bananas and one pear. There is a lot of yogurt in the house these days which is great. The house mom really does order some good food and healthy.

After returning from getting my wonderful news, Sally and Ray were discussing something and were in good spirits for me getting my good news. Nice to have good support from others here and these two girls seem to have kind words for me today.

I calculated the days until my day parole in June and it is 202 days or six months and nineteen days. Well we will take one day and hope for the best and stay strong.

They brought in another lady this evening, she look really scared or really out of it. An older lady is sitting with her in the room upstairs in the room across from me that used to be May's room. Sure hope Bob hears this gong one time but how rude these girls are just no moral compass. Sam asked me if I had a pop she could have until Thursday but I had already opened mine so I offered her a green tea which she humbly accepted. Now we are a full house again. I am not sure where these girls are coming from just hope they want me to enjoy my next path until June.

After programs I came back to the house and showered because in the morning I don't want to go to programs with wet hair so I just wait until after and shower. Today is Thursday not canteen but only hygiene so I showered and then remembered but it was not a huge deal as I missed the call. I got dressed and Sally said I still had time to get canteen so I ran over to the main house after calling to ask for permission. This meant you had to call the wall, and the guard on duty would allow you to move out of the house or maybe not, depending on the guard. As I was leaving after making my purchase a guard commented on my wet hair and how I would get sick running around with it like that. I told her good thing I bought some Kleenex and halls. She laughed at me. If they would do my pen pack or my London drugs order I could blow dry my hair. They should really get more staff to deal with that area of the jail.

Every time Max comes home she sees a new girl. I saw May today when I was leaving V&C and she said hi and I told her we missed her and hoped she was doing well. She looked good. So the new girl is named Cathy but she has a nick name here. She has been here before and has returned on more charges and then she was up for her parole but was denied. I am not sure why these girls think that once they have been given a chance they messed up and come back why the parole board would consider giving them another chance. I think they get a chance to prove themselves so don't mess up and it also shows you are not ready and you just abuse the system. How can your parole officer on the outside trust you a second time and stand behind you to help you in the community. I know whatever I am asked to do to get my parole I will do it. My goal is to be reunited with my family. Sally knows her. I am not sure but I don't think things ended well or on a good note. Oh well, I stay out of their business and they stay out of mine.

Nice chatting with you my son. Hope you are feeling better tomorrow. I will call you at 2:15pm tomorrow afternoon and then I can check the mail from the house. Did anyone get back to you like Wayne? Maybe God will move the A&D along and I can get some of my belongings.

I love you both and not a moment goes by without my heart aching for you. I miss you with every ounce of my being and because of you will get past this. All my love.

November 30, 20xx

How are you today? How are you feeling today my son? Hope you got a lot of rest and are feeling better for your first day at the new job. Congratulations on not one but two new jobs. Mom I need you to please type a letter to the court house if on January 23 they will not release the passport back to you but we will try to retrieve it first hand on January 23.

I had programs today and I will tell you about it more tonight at our visit. Poor instructor every time she talks to me about my so called crime she looks more like those lawyers at legal aid when I was telling them the story. They get that what the heck look and just an unbelievable tail. Today was actually interesting. We learned about risk factors and mine is apparently poor judgment and too trusting.

We learned about protective factors is any strengths, skills, traits, or state which can be linked to a decreased to the probability of re-offending such as determination, positive attitude, ambitious goals, job skills, time management, organization, social supports, spiritual, hobbies, being balanced, having good boundaries, and associates, honest, good work ethics, being a parent, volunteering, helping others, good emotional management, journalizing, common sense, moral compass, commitment, and being creative, which I have most if not all of them.

We heard about triggers and mine would be the crooks commercials, bad news, and certain dates. So overall, it was an interesting session. Sara asked me today so you did not do the crime. I answered her honestly and told her what my lawyer had said the morning of my trial that he did not believe me. Well, he will get his. Funny he will and is actually in hell, just noticed that.

During our break I ran back to the house to go use the washroom and Sally told me I was pages to V&C so I told Sara and she told me I have to plan my appointments better. This was no appointment and I had ten minutes. I think she said that so the others would not take advantage of her as after class she was asking me about my correctional plan interview.

Kind of funny because as I ran to V&C to meet with my replacement parole officer, who was also doing the intake work, I told her that I only had a few moments as I was in program. She seems very nice. The intake interview can take up to three and a half hours and you would have thought that would be done as sooner than now. But a long story straight she told me she was my fill in and how to get my DL sent to you guys. That my interview would be soon and either she or the other lady would be conducting it. I thanked her and went back to programs. Sara was not happy with me having to have met her even on my break. So the next appointment should be scheduled hopefully but not sure what the big deal is or was as I had ten minutes left and it was only a couple of minutes to meet with her anyways. Obviously, many inmates must abuse so much around here so that explains Sara's reaction and follow up comment after program. I think she felt bad but unfortunately, I understood her position and I did not take it personally. Some of the inmates are real head cases in here.

One gal who is really nice was walking with me after class and she told me her house was picking on her, so she wanted to move. My house maybe loud but at least they are not mean and picking on me. I felt terrible for her. She is on new medication which causes her to not feel well and to have mates picking on you also was just terrible. Maybe I can give her some positive motivation to encourage her in the meantime. No love messages today, no mail. I am sending you lots of love and looking forward to seeing you tonight.

I will enclose this ice breaker from Sara this morning about the cat and the dog. It is so cute. Maybe I am here to inspire and motivate others some are far off my radar but some are really in need of just some good positive "hope".

Jim is on today. He asked me how work was and I told him I was in programs and my correspondence classed was just getting cleared so I was taking a leave. I think he may have been bummed out about me not being there anymore, well not for now. I know I just make work fun.

I just ran to the main house and dropped off my request for the correspondence and for the DL to be mailed to you and I ran into the gal who was being picked on. I got to thinking about her and told her that next time I say her I would tell her to keep her chin up. So I did and she smiled and told me thanks.

Sally and I made supper tonight. I told myself I would not cook but no one would help her out so I did. We made hamburger pie and a large salad. It turned out fabulously. No one would help Apple do dishes so I helped her with those also. Next week, Friday, Sally wants to cook with me again which I would gladly do. We work really well in the kitchen together. We will be making cabbage rolls and a large salad. Sam does not like meat so we will make hers with beans and she will be thrilled.

I am excited for our visit. Apple asked A&D about her stuff and she was told she was working on it, but the lady got sent off. Gosh this place takes forever.

I will see you in a bit. I know Max's secret recipe for the meat it is lemon juice, paprika, and two other spices, oregano and parsley but I will have to confirm the ratios before I leave this place.

I will learn all kinds of new recipes and make them for you when I get out. This hamburger pie is a keeper. I am sending this off before our visit, which will be shortly. All my love.

December 1, 20xx

How are you both today? I am sitting at my desk eating my cream of wheat enjoying the silence of upstairs. I was going to read some of the bible this morning and finish my other book before our visit. Bob is on shift today so hopefully we can chat for a moment or two.

Last night after you left I was retrieving my Id and someone stole my chap stick. I am not bringing anything down for the guards to watch so now I have to purchase another one on Thursday. So I calculated the days December 201, January 170, February 139, march 111, April 80, May 19 and June 0.

How are your evenings? How was the drive home? Just think my son if the house is rented no more worries about shovelling.

Sorry my sons to hear you are still not feeling very well. Maybe you can get the doctor to take a look at you.

I told you about Whitey and meeting him in the hallway and how we would meet up next week to talk and to receive my hygiene pack. Nice he remembered me. The DL will be returned next week. It was nice of the guard to write me back her first day back.

Thank you for a terrific visit. I will call y o at 10:30pm. Thank you for vacuuming the house and shoveling it tomorrow. I love you two.

Susan made stuffed potatoes with cheese, veggies and chicken. The chicken had a breading on it that was amazing. She said Ritz crackers works the best with spices. Tonight she used cornflakes and spices and holy it was good. My son gets ready because when I get out you and grandma are in for a treat. I am learning some new ways to cook and you tow will be the tasters. Look out I am going to cook up a store. That is one benefit of living with ten girls, some know how to cook. Either way I am ready to learn and be able to share them with you. Max and I walked back together after our visit. She told me about a church group called Alpha with started in January. So when I speak to Whitey I will get more information about this. It's a spiritual gathering and Max thought it would be great for me. Why not, I would find this right up my alley.

I saw Bob tonight so maybe he will call me up later, here is hoping. I would like to share some good news with him about my DL, passport and meeting with the intake worker. Maybe put a smile on his face for a change.

Can you have my supporters write a letter for my parole hearing? I would need them for February as this is my goal to get things organized and ready. I can ask them also in my letters. I saw Bob as he came by to say good bye and to let me know he is in his favorite unit tonight so we have planned to meet up tomorrow after our visit. Well I will sign off for now and include anything interesting in the next letter. I love you so much and thank you for today. It means the world to me to see and talk to you. I love you more than words can say and I appreciate everything you have done and continue to do. You guys are my rock and I love you.

December 2, 20xx

How are you doing this morning? So looking forward to seeing you both and hoping you are feeling better this morning my son. Looking forward to telling you about when Bob came thru last night and how the showing went this morning on renting out the house. Bob is having a difficult time with why I am here and he is upset with the system. I am sure he hears how people are wrongfully accused and convicted in other parts, but to have one of his own cases be this is testing on him.

We can surely relate as we are living this and have seen first hand how the system can certainly fail. Max was telling me last night about some options moving forward that I would like to let you know, but most of all I just want to see and have a good laugh with you.

Funny last night Max was in Mea's room and had the music blaring her salsa music, but I would now take that over the yelling going on downstairs. My lips were moving as I was reading my new book which was set in Italy and Max and her salsa music kind of allowed me to be absorbed into the book. As we stood for count, Max asked me if I was good at math and if I would help her with her modules. I said sure, but I was expecting my correspondence and I would not be able to help her once those came in. She has until December 19 to complete them. With her working also, she does not have much time. Maybe she should spend less time doing her other activities and get cracking on her school work.

I may be taking these words back later but like I said before they seem normal until they all get together and the foul mouth starts but I might miss Max a bit, just a bit once she is gone. Like you said mom about the devil you know and the devil you don't. I asked Max who sang a song but I thought she was mad because the first thing she said was she would turn it down and I said no, I just wanted to know who sang the song. I told her I was dancing in my room to it. Between the salsa music and this music I will be getting my dance on anyways.

I just finished reading some of the Bible. Interesting how my intentions on going to church today just happened to be the same time as our visit and yet I actually I have been invited to meet with Whitey one on one which is even better. The other girls are going just to get the hygiene pack. Ray pipes up last night and said something to the effect it's not about the service but about them getting something which is so true. How they want something they will use that person to get it. I am blessed for now I can ask and speak to Whitey about the Alpha program and a mentor without everyone around in my business. Just doing some laundry yet again, and doing some more reading.

Here are a couple of good verses from Luke: "for a good tree does not bear bad fruit, no does a bad tree bear good fruit." Luke 6:43

and "But he who heard and did nothing is like a man who built a house on the earth without a foundation, against which the steam beat vehemently; and immediately it fall. And the ruin of that house was great." Luke 6:49

Thank you for our visit. I am so grateful you were able to rent the house out. I hate saying good bye to yea, but I am very grateful we can talk on the phone and see each other so often. This week should have many wonderful things in store for us.

After you left the other girl had something go down and right fully so. She was warned and still she abused her visit time. I see how the guards can get frustrated with some of these inmates. Like I said before I have no interest in getting to know these inmates especially since all they do is abuse the positives like the visitation. So silly but what can you do. I am sure hoping the key will work in the door for the tenants and will save you from having to get a new one. I loved seeing you today. I love seeing you any and every day. We will continue to survive this and be strong, happier, and better for it, plus there will be another book published. Thank you so much and big kisses and I will chat with you at 10:30pm. Stay warm and be safe out in this winter weather.

So Bob popped in tonight. I was waiting and waiting for him to call me up. I was tired of waiting so for him so I had my shower and went downstairs to watch sister wives, which was not on so I go to watch the Good wife and Bob was doing round so we had a quick chat as he was going back to the secure unit after rounds and he wanted to talk so we took a couple of moments. I was able to tell him about the DL and the correspondence being blessed and in A &D. I had a request into that department and she was going to call me up next week so hopefully we can get these classes moving. I asked if he would like to read my parole form and he said we would review it this week. I mentioned to him the program situation and he rolled his eyes at her comment.

He told me the visitor form for the house visit came back to him because the correctional plan had not been completed yet. I told Bob what Bally said about submitting the form as the home visit would have been completed. Bob said the correctional plan had to be completed.

I mentioned that I had met with the parole officer filling in for Bally and how my interview would be done soon. He told me to keep doing what I have been doing and that he loved my attitude and that that would go a long way.

I did not want to utilize too much of his time as he was doing rounds and he had to head back to the secure unit. We would meet up this week to look at the form and to discuss the house questions. Overall, I really appreciate him taking the time for me. His poor partner was not happy about going over to the secure unit again.

I hope all went well tonight with the new tenants, the key to the house, and the post office. Again, I appreciate everything you are doing and I will make it up to you when I get out.

Oh yes, Whitey came in after dinner and told me he put aside a package for me and to come and see him on Tuesday and we could have a chat. Nice of him to do that for me and to also take his valuable time to chat with me.

It sure feels good when your support team actually is there for you. Especially when you are trying to develop trusting relationships and these people are allowing you to trust again. Of course I can trust you and my support team on the outside now I have developed trust for my support team on the inside.

Well, I am going to sign off for tonight and until tomorrow. We will chat on the phone at 10:15pm once the guards have done the rounds. I love you and you both keep me strong.

December 3, 20xx

To my wonderful supporters,

These pens are the worst every, so hopefully either my correspondence comes out today or the pen pack to get some new pens that actually write.

Nice sunny day today. How are you doing this morning? Awesome about the interest in renting the house. I told you about the guards this morning and how I thought it was after their 6:00am walk thru, so I was in the washroom and Max was in the shower and how they made us both get out of what we were doing and sent us back to our rooms until they has done their walk thru. Gosh some are so nice and some are so miserable. I so long for a clock and this won't happen again. I told you about the program and how she got on my last nerve. We discussed goals and how I achieved some of my but one was to write my story. So I had to explain to her about this on going story and how one day we would see vindication.

I was just reading a bit. I had a terrible sleep last night. Funny the guards were shining the bright light in our faces, so one of my goals this week is to get a good night's sleep. I have been using a clean sock over my eyes to cut out the bright light in my face and to get some sleep. I mentioned it at program today. The class like the story so maybe they will do the same thing and then fewer mates will be grouchy from the lack of sleep in here.

It is sad we could not see each other tonight but that will allow you to relax a bit and get some things done. I will call you at 5:30pm to see how the rest of your day went and maybe I will have some news to tell you.

Also, for this morning, Sally's smoke detector went off in her room. She shut it off and then the guards came. I am not sure what she did to turn it off, but they may charge her with interfering with government property. Did you know this is the largest women's jail in Canada? Our program trailer was leaking propane so we had to resume our class in another trailer. I said they should have detectors to keep people safe and the program lady said, "They don't have money to do that". They are not expensive and could save some one's life. It seems like this lady has it out for me or something is up hers, but she is very bitter towards me. During session a girl was asked to mention something positive about her weekend and so she replied that her Primary worker told her to apply for her parole and how happy that made her feel, until the program lady rained on her parade. Why can't the workers here be supportive and encouraging not dismissive. I will pray she is surrounded by positive people and she gets her parole. I don't want to take any other programs here if this is how they operate. This is beyond productive.

Apple received her pen pack today and mine is behind hers, so hopefully it will be processed quickly. Sally was gracious and made me lunch. Interesting how the house mates are actually becoming human and companionate. The house has a good energy right now.

When the guards came by tonight Jim mentioned to his partner how he had been under investigation for eight months here. He seems a little stressed lately. After programs, the instructor gave Apple a book so she would be able to journal in and how she received her pen pack. I wonder if she will give it back tomorrow since she has some in her pen pack that she just received.

One of the girls is serving a four year sentence here for fraud and some weapon offenses. Her and her boyfriend stole $110k. She also has charges from another province. An organization here is trying to get a pen pack together for her, which is so kind of them. She as an interesting tale to tell. Some of these ladies have had hard lives but that does not excuse their crimes. Hopefully since being here this time they will inspire to do more and great things with their lives. As for some they will come back because their attitudes have not changed and they have already spoken of how they will re-offend.

Anyways, I am enjoying a cup of tea as the guards do their stand to count. Tomorrow we visit and I have programs in the morning and see Whitey, but most important is our visit. Wednesday is programs and yes another wonderful visit. Maybe the pen pack will be done and I will have Bob read over my parole application, hopefully correspondence and the correctional plan. Maybe you will receive the taxation information and Wayne will call back. So many things happening plus my son starting two new jobs and mom holding down the fort. We also get to turn in our empty hygiene and get refills. This week is full of blessing and we get to visit this weekend. I am so grateful for you both.

Funny Apple said when she got back after returning the grocery bin that the lady who processed her pen pack had never seen so many items on one cellefex it took the guards a day to log all of Apples items. Apple had packed her pen pack before her sentencing as she knew about the process. I however have no idea what the process is so we are just going through the motions.

Obviously God has us on this journey for a reason and eve as I was heading back to the program trailer after using the washroom there was a small rainbow in the ski. Dad must be with me here or his spirit but it offered me some comfort and hope in this place.

A lady in programs was saying how she is counting for the days, makes lists and sets her goals. She should be in our house. It was said when she said how her family is falling apart on the outside while she is serving her sentence. That must be so difficult to hear. It really puts things back into prospective and then you have these babies crying in the house over the silliest things. This lady is a blessing to know and she tells it like it is. She spoke on how the system sets you up for failure. She could not afford to get help in treatment because it cost too much and you surely would not trust social services with your kids, the system would take them away. She seems to have a tough go of it also. The system can be all encumbrancing of all kinds of people, but it sure does have its fallbacks.

There is one inmate in our program who is in the max secure area and she comes up and we each take turns bring her coffee, but the instructor mentioned that she had a melt down and would not be coming back which is a shame. And the other girl who swears a lot was not there today either so our session was very pleasant. The four that were there were really great and supportive just had a good vibe. Seven more sessions to go.

I asked Sally how this morning went and she told me she was charged with destroying Federal property. I said this is good to know is if the toilet is over flowing don't fix it because you could be charged. After all, she was just trying to turn it off. When the guards came in they broke it when they hit it. My new mode is to just walk away, turn a blinds eye and so on is all the Government is about.

Wow things are coming together nicely. I am so glad you received the taxation information now I don't have to worry it got lost in the mail. Thank you mom for taking care of getting the utilities shut off.

Thank you both for taking care of the photocopying of the taxation package and sending it out. Thank you for taking care of so many things on my behalf.

I was talking to Apple after I got off the phone with you and she was surprised and disgusted with what the instructor said in programs about the one lady, which was absolutely uncalled for. My application is going in and I am determined now more than ever to get back to you. The staff seems to sometimes forget we are human also, and to not be so quick to judge. But one grouchy guard does not mean they all are.

I have made a list of my short term monthly goals and my long term ones. This place will only make me stronger and more determined to get my story out. Justice will prevail and we will be vindicated. One day the story will all come out.

I can't say more than enough of how grateful and how much I miss and love you both. All my love. I carry you in my heart every moment of every day. Not a moment goes by that I don't think of you and wish we were together. I will stay strong if you stay strong, and we will be together soon and better for God's journey.

December 4, 20xx

How are you today? Bob popped in last night to his rounds to say hi and stop and see if I had Wayne's land line yet, so I told him about the land line coming this week. I showed him what Bally put on my application for you guys to come in for a sleep over and he told me that once the correctional plan was done that you would be cleared. So I guess that CA stands for Correctional plan not community assessment. Like I told Bob the right and left don't know what is going on and he smiled and said no kidding. He told me he would get the plan and have to write a report on me also. He asked if he could take the parole application and read it over and return it to me on his night count which of course he could and then he could give me feedback, but at least he is staying involved. So I guess the intake worker will meet with me to review the correctional plan, but my two minute meeting with the other intake lady was months ago. I will just go with the flow and do what I can and leave the rest to God.

Romans 5:3-5 is a good read to remember. Bob came back at count and told me it was really good and we would talk tomorrow.

Thank you both for accomplishing so much last night. I am grateful my son you had a great day playing with you new pals. Mom you bring a smile to my face when you talk of the cat and how she is becoming such a pig and how stinky she is. She will certainly keep you on your toes.

Off to programs this morning. Only six more after today. Another day gone and a blessing to have visits tonight.

Well in programs we were down another person so there was only the three of us. It was hard to get a worked in as those two just wanted to talk about their problems, so today I practiced my listening skills. After programs, I stopped to see Whitey but he was not in this office so I left him a now and came back to the house and showered. Just as I was getting out I receive a page to go to A&D. Guess what I got? My correspondence so happy days. I had a bit to eat and opened up my books. I understood the Women, equality and the law as the manual outlined the flow, but I may have to get you to call on the Civil liberty and Individual rights as I think the study guide and student manual are not included, but we can discuss when you come in tonight. Both ways all is good and now I can start my classes. Thank you so much.

I also saw how much they were and please add it to my bill. The A&D lady will leave my DL for you to pick up tonight at our visit. She also said the pen pack would be ready for Friday and same with the London Drug order. They have to log everything onto your cellefax and with only one person doing this for the entire jail it all takes time.

She told me she was still recovering from doing Apple's pen pack which made me smile.

My son I pray you are having a wonderful day at work and the wind did not ruin your day. Wow I was just blessed with not only speaking to you but I just got paged to Whitey's office. I am so glad you had a terrific day with the puppy kennel and so excited to hear about your day and your stories tonight. It sounds like an awesome group of people you are working with which as you very well know can make the world of difference in the job you have.

Thank you mom for calling to see if those other two guides and manuals were missing. It is sure great if someone would do their jobs correctly and make others lives easier, but it never fails that follow up is just a part of doing anything these days.

On a positive note, I met with Whitey and the other Chaplin and another staff member to receive my care package but more importantly to meet and to talk. I will certainly make every attempt to do church on Sundays if you are not here but my visits with you come first.

Whitey mentioned something interesting about making sure you stay in touch with the outside community because it looks great also for parole. He told me to come on Monday nights or Tuesday to see if I can't hook up with a mentor. Plus, he said I should ask my Pastor to get cleared so he could take me to church on Sundays one I get escorted visits, which would be in April. My pastor could take me out into the community. I have so much to share with you tonight. The care package was lovely it included, shampoo, body wash, lotion, a tooth brush, chap stick, deo, tooth picks, a lovely guide book, fuzzy blue socks and candy canes. Just a nice gesture and very much appreciated.

Thank you for our lovely visit tonight. I really love whatever time we can spend together. I love to hear all the funny things that are happening over there with you two and my fuzzy baby stories. I am sure my little cat is adjusting to all this transitions wonderfully. We are very lucky to have not only what sounds like a fund job with some excellent people.

I will call you at 10:30pm to say good night and to make sure you got home safely. One gal received some good news today as she has been here before but she has a great attitude or at least her comment to me was one I could relate too. I thanked her for dinner tonight and she said you are welcome, but then she said she would be here for a while and I said well good as you are a good cook, stupid me so I went to her right away and said I was sorry for my stupid comment about her being here but that I was glad she was with use if she had to be here. She told me she is been here before so she knows the drill but she told me to use my time wisely as that makes the time go by faster. Which for some reason this week has or is going by at a more normal rate. Soon winter will be gone and moving on to our next season with more change and new beginnings. I have a mission of reach month and a goal to achieve. This will also make the time fly. It really moves slowly and you can almost hear each minute tick by.

All my love and good night to you both.

December 5, 20xx

Good morning to my son and mom. Hope you both slept well and hope you had a wonderful morning. I will try to write with better penmanship for your reading enjoyment. Looking at last night's letter and wow it was really messy. So I will slow down yet again and take my time to write.

Program was good. I am forever learning new techniques with are always useful in life. I have noticed there is a real demand for persons in the legal field. I have enclosed three positions I will apply for once I get out but I already have three jobs lined up so this will be my back up plan. Plus, there is the email address on there and they keep resumes on file for months anyways.

Sally and I had to go and retrieve the new cleaning supplies from the main house. It is really snowing out today. Sally mentioned to me how Apple's attitude has changed since she has been hanging around another house mate. Sometimes we don't realize we are doing things until afterwards and a simply conversation could elevate so much frustration, so I suggested that Sally approach Apple with what was bothering her.

I am grateful for this house as a girl in programs told me that someone in her house has already taken her body wash from her care package. I offered her my friendly support if she needed it. She told me I was her inspiration as I am here and did not even commit the crime. I told her the truth will one day all come out and I would be repaid for all my struggles and my family horrible struggles. I told her that I was telling you guys about who she is related too and how everything happens for a reason. Nice to know that someone else is inspired. She told me she is amazed by my positive attitude and my forward thinking. I told her I have the best support system. I discussed our situation we had a few weeks back and when we were all just so over loaded and how we felt frustrated and things were getting tense. How you my son, said Stop. We all took a deep breath and made a manageable goal list. The teacher said your son said "stop". The programs instructor was impressed that you were so mature in that situation.

I know that each one of use will have a weak day and that is when the others will pull us up and together we will get through this ordeal and soon this will be put a distance memory.

Today was refill day, the first Wednesday of each month. You can exchange your empties for free refills. So today I received deo, toothpaste, shampoo and conditioner plus pads and no name laundry detergent, but nevertheless, it is a welcome treat and free. Thanks tax payers.

I completed unit #1 of the correspondence. I will work on unit #2 tomorrow and hopefully get started on my first assignment for this course. I have to meet with the program director for a one on one at 9:00am tomorrow morning. She asked what would like to go first so I thought why not to get it over and done then I can focus on my correspondence and our visits this weekend. Friday our instructor is not teaching and neither on Monday as the other girls will do their interviews so I have Monday off also. My instructor was kind and will be paying us for those days so that is wonderful. I will have $20.00 on this pay for taking class/ programs even thought my instructor was not there for four of the days. You get paid $2.50 for program days. Again thanks taxpayers. Gosh it would be so much easier if the agency would just audit this company.

Apple made chill tonight for dinner which was really good. I will call at 5:00pm to confirm our visit. I love you two.

Well we just got off the phone and disappointment that our visits got cancelled for tonight. My son thank you for being strong and getting me re-focused. This place is or can be so disappointing, but I am grateful for you positive attitude. I really wish I could shake my pity party, so here I go no more pity party. My son you get a good night's sleep, mom you take a moment for yourself and I will pop some popcorn and finish my book.

I will press forward and maybe one day I can carry the rock. I think that the lack of sleep must be catching up with me also. Every two hours the guards shining their flashlights at you or someone banging around when you are used to quiet really can wear on persons. And another positive is the roads are probably terrible so this will put you out of harm's way and keep you two safe which is most important. I love my supporters. Thank you and be back after I call you tonight. Deep breath! And positive tomorrows!

Well so much for reading, I ended up reading some of the bible and going to the gym. I had not been in a while so maybe that was what I needed to get my emotions in check. So Sally was going to go to the library but Bridget accidently took her shoes so she did not want to wear Bridget's' so Sally stayed at the house and Sam came down and she and I made our way over to the gym. We have to move quickly as our house is the furthest from the main house. I worked out for an hour which felt good and to get out of the house. Sam and I chatted a bit about makeup and then another girl from Corcan came in and asked me why I was not working there anymore. So I told her I have program and correspondence. She said, "Do you mind me asking why you are here?" I said, "No Fraud was the charges." She smiled and said, "You don't belong here." I told here, "that is correct." I told her about my book and how it would explain my journey and your journey also as you are just as much a part of my journey as I am. Heck you two have lived it with me. She smiled and said again "you don't belong here". I told her "thank you". This has been told to me over and over again, staffs tell me this so hopefully the parole board will see this also.

God hears my prayers and we will be vindicated. After I was done at the gym and just leaving, Bridget came in to do some exercising. She is so cute and always just a bubbly person. I mentioned to here she might have accidently grabbed Sally's shoes. She certainly did not mean too. I told her I would let Sally know it was an accident. Funny, but when I got out into the yard everyone is civil to me even the mean girls were very polite. So I got back to the house feeling a bit better talking with Dad and I noticed the girl feeding the bunnies. So I asked her if she can hand feed them and she replied, "Yep". And she as even named them.

I am back at the house and Sally said I was called to the bubble, so back to the main house I went. Praise be to God, I received my alarm clock, which meant a good night's sleep and not having to worry about sleeping in. I received the hair dryer so I could now shower in the mornings and not have fuzzy hair.

Tomorrow is canteen day so I can purchase the necessary batteries for the alarm clock and be set. If I would have had to wait one more day, I would have missed being able to purchase the batteries for two more weeks. Someone is watching over us to ensure we get the end of this journey and something fabulous is waiting. So not only a clock but a radio. I can get music and keep my spirits up and in touch with civilization. I would have much rather seen you two, but all and all tonight was a good night.

Tomorrow I will call you at 1:15pm between my son's two jobs. And again at 10:45pm when you get home from your second job. I will crack the books until canteen time. I was telling my son when I called earlier that I completed reading unit #1 and as I was flipping over the other book I noticed that items I need for my one course I would have to go to the library for are contained in the materials for the other correspondence course, so that is fabulous.

I will call you at 9:00pm to chat and say good night. I love you both and you are always in my heart.

December 6, 20xx

I hope you both had a wonderful sleep as mine was okay. Tonight I will use the ear plugs to block out the guards who seem to either wake me up with the flashlight or the clomping and banging of the doors every two hours.

The house is slim picking for breakfast. No milk, no bread, no eggs, and no cream of wheat. I found some hash browns so I am cooking them up for the house mates who are still in the house. Some people hid bread last night because they knew there would be none come this morning. Either way thank goodness if is grocery day and canteen day. Double bonus! We now have hash browns in our tummy so all is good.

My son my thoughts will be with you today. I pray you have a wonderful morning and day and I pray you stay warm and drive safe. I hope you enjoy the second part of your day at the other new job. I hope you are able to use your I-pad and listen to music while doing your job. I hope you had a good night sleep and I will call and see how your day is going later.

Mom I hope you get some rest and take care of you. With my son working it will now be you and the cat. I am glad we can see each other tomorrow. I am sad my son will not be able to join our visit, but I will give him hugs and kisses on Saturday. Hopefully he won't be too worn out.

I have the program meeting this morning which is whatever. Apple said this morning that my story is like no other and how people are curious. I looked at her and said buy the book and then smiled. Apple laughed and was in a great mood this morning.

Actually an interesting dynamics to see how someone can change or become more like themselves with a few personal items. Apple is so funny she packed over forty books in her pen pack. The A&D said she could have ten and then trade them in for another ten. I said it's like Apple has her own library and there won't be any charge for storage.

Well never a dull moment. I went to do my one on with the program instructor and would you not know it she was inquiring about my story. So half way into a lady came in to tell me I am requested at V&C as two members of the police service were waiting for me. I think God was just telling my instructor that I was telling the truth of my story. So off I went and God even sent me with a nice guard. She walked with me and tells me she was looking for me but she was going to be honest in all her years at this prison she has never seen the police come to the V&C. I asked if they were going to take me somewhere she said NO that would be A&D. I said well, who knows but I just reconfirms to anyone who doubts my story that this is of a high situation. When I went into the area I told the guard this has been the last seven years of my life. She said she would wait for me. I could see three people in the corner table and recognized one as the Detective who had been involved in my case.

I was served with some civil matter documents and then the process server left. So it was me and the detective and his partner, whom I had never met before. They asked me about my stay here. I asked if they had ever been here and they said no. they would not be able to get any further then the V&C are. I am not sure of the words but it was like he knew I did not do this crime and he was there to see if I was alright. Why not just sent the process server? Why do you come into this jail to see me? Do you not have actual criminals to catch? It was God's test to me to see how I would react. Something in the universe is happening.

His partner was curious about my house and the meals. I told them I was taking two criminal justice classes. I think the detective was impressed by my determination. Anyways, I was the bigger person and even shook their hands and the guard walked me to the doors. I went back to the trailer to finish my one on one with the program director.

When I got back my instructor was completely shocked. I was still my positive self. I walk with Jesus and he is my protector. I explained to her that my story would all come out and go public one day. I would be vindicated for this. The odds of this going down while I was with someone who questioned my story were absolutely perfect. It shows each guard, worker, and employee here to what length they would try to stop me. It shows today that my story is very much alive and I will continue to survive with my support team I will mail you the information. One is the Restitution is dismissed by the Crown and the other is a change of legal representation. See if this is the some law firm that they guy from the old firm. I think the law firm fired that lawyer and now he had to move to a new firm.

You see the lawyer can't touch this matter as he knew what I am saying is the truth, and he does not want to be linked to my innocence and his guilty conscience. There is also the application to get the judgement with us knew was coming. Let's get the book going.

My instructor told me as I came back that she had a knot it her stomach over my ordeal. I calmly told her that one day the truth will come out and this is the path to get there. She actually told me I inspired her. She now believes me and was beyond impressed with how I handled myself.

The girls Apple, Bridget and Ray were at the house when I got back. Apple knew a bit of my story and when I told them what happened they were shaking their heads. They think this is such a story and want to be in the next book. They are inspired by our positive and motivation to make a difference. Apple told the girls about when we first met and how she thought I was a bit nut, but she said the more I told her the more she knew I was innocent. Ever today, when I told the instructor the same Accountants, their Accountants did the forensic audit on the books they signed off on; she could not believe no one was not looking at that with suspicion. I was so surprised at the how the mates reacted and how supportive they are for me and us.

Anyways, it was a good morning and I believe my dad was with me. I find it that God's presences are moving and how everything times out perfectly. The girls in the house say I remind them of Erin Brockivich, and funny how when they heard the story that is who I remind them of and very honoured to be in such good company. The instructor said my positive attitude will move millions and all it takes is one.

Good, I did not miss canteen with all the commotion. Funny as I was writing you the song by Fleetwood Mac is on the radio. Kind of symbolic when I was getting my finger prints in my first chapter that was who was on the radio. The part, don't stop thinking about tomorrow, is just words to keep us moving forward into God's plan for us.

I am so happy my son you had yet another great day at your job. I am so thrilled you are enjoying yourself and the staff and the animals. What a difference the day is when you can work with people/ animals that are fun and just good people.

I love how grounded and the right prospective you take on things my son. Yes this is just material stuff and God can replace and replenish all. Thank you for being on the same page as me. This inspires people in here when an innocent person loosed everything and they have the confidence to rebuild. God will bless us as we have the right attitude in his honour. Frustrating yes, but the truth will come out. Mom please don't stress as I am concerned about your health and the stress is not worth it. The restoration will most likely take precedence over the judgment, therefore, they can't do anything for the 3 ½ years, but if the Judge orders the judgment they have to pay out the, but they can't do anything because they have both.

Maybe the next Judge will look into some of this crap and see something stinks, especially with the restraining order was from 20xx and the civil started in 20xx. Either way, again it is material and eventually someone somewhere will look into this, we just have to be the bigger person and do the right things. One day they will meet their maker and have to be accountable for what they have done and let's face it they are living the healthiest life styles and we will continue to be in contact with the correct agencies to heave them do their jobs. One day someone will look into this, someone will do their job and wow the stuff they will discover. One day he will cross the wrong person and they will tell the truth and they will tell what I have been saying all along. It is coming.

My son I hope you can enjoy your next job. We had to leave the house so the drug dog could come in a do a search. I am so grateful to be able to hear your voice and talk. I will tell you more stories when you come and visit. As the house waited at the main house for the drug dog to complete his search Sally and Ray and I were walking and I told Ray to say she needed an interpreter. We all laughed. These girls keep things fun and interesting.

I will call you at 5:30pm to check in on you. Corcan wanted to know when I would come back as one of the girls is leaving, she is getting out. Nice they wanted me back but I have my correspondence courses to focus on. Today was grocery day so we each received our fruit. Our two oranges, three apples, two bananas, and a pear. The banjo song is playing again my son; the "I will wait for you." I just love that song.

My secondary came in tonight and she said she will read my parole application tomorrow. She said Bob is fabulous and I told her that I have the best team of workers. I have been blessed. My secondary told me that she loves that I am always smiling and just have a great positive vibe. She said the parole board looks for the fact that I have a great support system and I have strong ties to the community and that I am not a flight risk. She asked if I was working. I told her I was on a leave and doing program and taking two criminal justice correspondence courses. She said "wow". Plus I was doing many other things.

Bridget and I went to the gym. The mates downstairs at the house were being immature so I am grateful to be upstairs. Someone is going to get hurt with all the running around. Amazing how Mea has a hurt arm yet she is running chasing the other girls.

Tomorrow I am going to complete unit #2 and then on the weekend I will do the assignment. Mom everything will work out I promise you will see my name cleared before you go to the guys upstairs. I am a part of something bigger and one day I will make you proud that I had to go thru this but remember at how far we have gotten and remind yourself that something is brewing. Remember all those years I fought for my son's freedom and how it came. At that time we were so heartbroken and felt like the work was coming to an end. Well, we look back and survived that terrible situation and have been blessed with another mission. That mission enabled children to get out of terrible parenting visitation, this one will be about standing up for the unjust the wrong and making a difference for the greater good. The guards know I should not be here, the mates know I should not be here, and soon things will all come together and this too shall pass with huge rewards.

I just keep smiling at the reaction my program instructed had today. I thought she was going to be able to handle what I have been dealing with the entire time, but her look of shock was a memorable moment for me. She just looked so shocked and for her to be so honest about her reaction made me for just a moment be put in my shoes. I truly think that was a huge blessing. Funny how things work out and they do work out.

I love you both. Tonight at the gym the mean girl was actually nice to me. Maybe I am here to bring kindness to some, well at least today the mean girl was civil and that is a blessing.

All my love and all my heart are full of you.

December 7, 20xx

Good morning to you both this chilly morning. I hope you both had a great sleep and ready to conquer another day. Kill them with kindness is my goal today. For some reason I had trouble sleeping last night but overall it was an okay sleep. I still work up early and did my unit #2 of my correspondence and did laundry. My secondary came by and gave me back my parole application that I gave her to read. She said it looked great. I am just thinking on how to approach my assignment. It has to be 5-7 pages, double spaced. I noticed the printer in the recreational room was working so I will type out one page at a time and maybe this time it will work.

My son I hope you are staying warm enough. I have not been outside yet but it looks very cold. I guess this week was training for our weeks to come with how our communication will change a bit with our phone chats being scheduled times and our visits being on weekends, but still I am grateful for you both.

I love you both and will call you at 1:15pm to catch up on your mornings activities. I learned some new recipes for the coffee, you just add a splash of cinnamon into the coffee grounds and it tastes amazing.

I love to hear your voice my son. You sounded so upbeat which makes me happy and also because tomorrow I can see you. I have no idea how parents let their kids go off to University and not want to move in with them. I have a whole new respect for those parents.

Sally and I made lazy cabbage rolls and spinach salad for dinner. I will make it for you when I get out. My secondary commented on the application and said it was really good but also prepared me for the questions they may ask me, which I answered her honestly. She seemed impressed and so no I will pop it in on December XX.

Did an outline for my assignment this morning. So glad to hear you received the rest of the correspondence materials. We can discuss things tonight when you come in mom, but maybe just put some in the drop mailbox. I have not had an opportunity to go check the mail yet, but will go when there is movement tonight. I guess my pen pack will not be coming out of the A&D this week so something to look forward to for next week.

I just finished washing my bedding. The dryer takes a bit longer than the one at home. Everything is so dry around here. You get electrical shocks when you touch your bedding even when you use the bounce sheets.

Last nights a couple of girls were in the bathroom with the shower on smoking cigarettes that someone smuggled in. I don't know how they do it, but they do it. These girls say how much they want to get out, yet they break all the rules in here.

Today is week seven. One more day down, one more day closer to being with you two and my fuzzy baby the cat. Thanks mom for our visit tonight. I thought it was wonderful. You were so positive in thoughts and how we will survive this. God sees all and knows all, so we will one by vindicated. All my love to you both.

December 8, 20xx

Good morning. One week today we have the Christmas party. Fun stuff! So last night when I was walking back to my room I could see the Christmas lights on the windows of each house. The girls in our house set up the Christmas tree. It was decorated very nicely.

I had a shower and waited until 10:45pm to call you my son and see how the rest of your work day went. Very excited to see you tomorrow and give you a big smooch. Last night during grandmas and my visit the A&D lady came over and let me know my pen pack would be done early next week. This was very nice of her.

I forgot to tell you about this Thursday and when the instructor and I were doing out interview and she tells me a funny story that they look at our ID pictures and she said she has never come across one like mine, where the person is smiling. The instructor said that was the most unique picture she has seen, hence again why I don't fit in here. Funny mom how you mentioned the ICAA last night and I thought they forgot about my letter to them, but everything will all be good. I am going to work on my assignment and when I get the other documentation I will just add the materials needed.

I received the permission slip with the tutor information and stamps today in my mail. Thank you! I will send it back to you in the mail. Well, at least that was quick getting in.

Thank you for a great visit this afternoon. I really miss you two. I will call you at 10:15pm to see you are doing and how your shift went at work. It is going to be rough not seeing you my son. As I was walking back the girl who feeds the rabbits was hand feeding them so as I walked along all of a sudden there was a big rabbit eating leftover salad fixings from last night. He was so cute. I was an arm's length away from him. So close it was amazing.

Yes, I finished my assignment well at least writing it out so I feel a bit home sick. I am going to go make some popcorn and finish reading my book. I will stay strong and positive for you both as you do the same for me. I am wondering how long the Christmas tree will be standing with miss curious.

Mom did you get your Christmas tree up yet? How is the cat with the tree? She must think it is a new toy for her to play on. It was a nice chat we had this evening my son. It is so good to hear your voice and the fun you are having at work. Interesting how things work out. How people can come together? I am looking forward to hearing about your buddy and if he is okay.

I finished another Grisham novel, but I must say I do prefer the legal stories better this one was more CIA and spy based. Still a great book.

I love you both. My son whatever you decide to do either work or go back to school, do what makes you happy and know I support you 100%. I will see you both tomorrow. All my love and stay positive and strong. God's blessings.

December 9, 20xx

How are you this fine foggy winter morning? I had a good sleep and hope you did as well. I had porage for breakfast which really hit the spot. I think I told you about Apple's thumb and how it is infected after being pocked by a pin at Corcan. I got to thinking last night about jail vs. the homelessness and jail is a really good deal. You get food, shelter, clothing and supplies vs. being on the street trying to survive.

Bob is on today, well at least this morning as I saw him leaving the house on his rounds. Gosh I am looking forward to not doing laundry every second day and that way I can time it for when the others do not need the machine. As this is all in good time. Apple told me yesterday she figured out how to get all the channels on her TV so she can show me when I get my pen pack. I am looking forward to you coming to the Christmas party as I am sure you are also happy about. Hoping this week will fly by. Monday I don't have programs so I will go type my assignment. Monday night is the Christmas symphony. Tuesday is programs and mentors night. Wednesday is program and restorative justice is coming in to sing Christmas carols. Thursday and Friday is program and I have to complete as many other chapters as possible in my correspondence. I am looking forward to seeing you today. Who knows what tomorrow has in store, so one day at a time. God is the only one who knows and we need to live in the present.

Apple told me how Ray is reading her "Fifty shades of grey" and how Ray is spending a lot of time in her room. Apple chuckled and said that was a good place for her to be.

We had visits today and thank you for being so much fun. I love playing cards or scrabble and just laughing with you two. We had tacos for dinner which were very good. I am going to go over to the main house and type out my assignment. Keeping myself busy and it is something I can control, plus it will be pro-active and that is always good. The Salvation Army came in and gave the girls a knitted toques, socks and chocolate bars. I was blessed to see you so that is my reward. I guess the best thing is to just survive this journey and to focus on the next moment. This too shall pass and we will be blessed for the adventure. The big lesson is to be grateful for what we have and appreciate each other and love each other.

I went over to the main house to type my assignment but the printer is not working so tomorrow I will get the computer lab and see if I can use their computers. Seriously, I gave the Federal government the company that was doing hundreds of millions of dollars in tax evasion and they can't even get a silly printer but then again they did not want the tax payer's money either. This time I did not waste my time, but spoke to the lady in the bubble. She did some tests on me and was the person that told me about how the police can't say something in a police report without having actually proof, but I asked her about going to the teacher tomorrow and she said yes as she did not think that printer works. I looked over the material from the other course and it looks like there could be materials in it that may overlap and at least some components to help me. These two classes will mesh up so that is a huge bonus.

I am waiting for the guards to come, they are running late and then I will call you to say good night and to see how the rest of your day went. I miss you huge and I am trying to stay strong and positive. Oh the guards are finally here, I must stand for count and then I can call you. All my love....

December 10 20xx

How are you this find, chilly Monday morning? How did you both sleep? This morning I'm going over to the main house and see if I can use the computer lab and type out my assignment. The house mates are up and amazingly for ten women we can function relatively well. I am having toast with strawberry jam and a cup of coffee. I had a good sleep but I am still tired. The call for medication has gone out so that means in twenty minutes the call for movement to school and work will be paged. I will check the mail on my way to see the teacher. And see if there is a Law Society reply from Mr. Reck came and I will call you 11:30am to see how your morning is going.

Thank you mom for coming in on Wednesday and as much as it kills me my son to not have you come on Wednesday for a couple of minutes, I just don't want anything to happen to you and with winter driving conditions and you having to get to your second job I would rather you be safe. Safety first and we will chat on the phone later. Please remember I love you and you are in my heart and you are my #1 forever. Gosh with all the money I allegedly have of theirs, you would think you would not have to work two jobs. Gosh you would think they could have found the actual money. My case is purely a payoff of others to keep me quiet.

We passed the week #7 mark. Well I better get ready for movement. Well I talked to the teacher and seriously they just called no computer lab so I am going over to talk with the teacher about using the lab. Maybe I am here to describe the issues in the jail. Gosh how is anyone able to better themselves when they keep putting up obstacles. Smile, it will all work out as I tell myself over and over again.

I am back and I went over and I spoke to the teacher who said she would look into it and for me to come back on Wednesday. As she sipped her coffee and looked me up and down, all I could think was Wednesday could you move any slower? Oh well, I will hand write this one to you and if you could type it out I would be very grateful. Funny because I explained to her also that the recreation room printer did not work and she really did not care. Gong show, but I will keep smiling and things will just work out. I love you both.

Thanks for our chat at 11:30am. Thanks mom for doing so much for me and for typing out the assignment. Hopefully someone will get on the ball, but I will request a follow up with Bob for this week and see if he has any suggestions or pointers. Max has been putting her two cents into my path, but I will listen and take in what I need. I will discuss any concerns I have with my team, but I know her intensions are all in good spirits and she is being positive about it. I guess I am just a bit frustrated this morning, so I will snap out of it and be grateful.

I wrote to pastor Ken and enclosed a visitation form. I think I did on his first letter but better to be safe than sorry. He is probably busy with Christmas and the church as it is a big time of year for volunteering and Christmas functions.

I just got my hep A&B shot so my arm is a bit tender. Just head the guards go thru and talking about someone's family is being ripped off by a builder. Like the lawyer says there is no justice in our justice system.

Apple mentioned to me that she did her intake interview today with the same person who would be doing mine, so mine should be soon. Then the correctional plan will follow which could be interesting considering I have no addictions and that is all the jail has here, either drug or alcohol addictions. I will just stay positive, focused and honest. So maybe the correctional plan this week, pen pack and Wayne's phone number put on my phone card. He will also be able to give input on the Law Society beef that is if he would ever answer his phone. I am not impressed with his so called friendship.

My son I hope you had a wonderful day at work and remember of all the positives. Tomorrow you get to see you little buddy on four legs. Tomorrow is back to morning program and then tomorrow night I am going to see if I can get a mentor. Funny how jail works, it is so superficial.

Sure gets dark earlier and earlier not ever 5:00pm yet and time to turn on the lights. Tonight they have the symphony coming in which should be nice to see. I completed my readings for unit #3 and #4 now when I get the additional readings I will read those and be all caught up. I need to ask you if you reviewed my stuff I sent you from the dirty Detective and the community assessment report from the jail.

Oh my gosh my arm is so sore from my needle today. I was just going to go to the symphony event but my arm is so achy I am just going to stay here and watch teen mom. I checked the mail but it was not done yet and I don't want to walk around with these people in the yard so I will check it before programs tomorrow morning. Plus, I would just want to read it all night and that would make me want to start my reply to the courts are doing.

Apple said that our fellow program buddy was being picked on in the yard tonight. And when I was coming back from checking my mailbox that one girl was outside waiting for Mea and I said it was chilly out and she replied, "It is f…ing nice out." Nice that she knows how to use her words. Seriously, the swearing in there is so bad. Thank goodness Bob is on rounds tonight. He said he would stop in on his walk at 10:00pm. Nice that he keeps checking on me. I certainly am blessed and that should be my and our focus. I love you both and miss you so much.

Like I said Bob made a point of stopping in and checking in on me tonight. He makes sure I am okay and to tell me he was back on Thursday and Friday and to make sure I had nothing pressing for him to take care of for me.

I was reading the bible tonight and found a huge comfort in Psalm 34, 35 37 and to say from 38 that I will write out and carry with me that goes like this. "Do not for sake me, O'lord; O my God, be not far from me! Make haste to help me, O'Lord, my salvation. Mom if you are in need of some spiritual inspiration look at these Psalms for some uplifting power. The power of our God! All my love.

December 11, 20xx

How are you this morning? Today the temperature is going to be mild. A perfect day to walk your little buddies. The roads sound like they are a mess, so grateful you don't have far to travel but still be careful.

This morning is program. I put in a load of laundry so on my break I can hopefully have it done. I will put it in the dryer before I leave for programs. Tonight is mentor night but I overheard it was a wind up but I will still go and see, after all, Whitey was the one who told me to go. My arm is still a bit sore from my shot yesterday. Thanks mom for taking the cereal over to the neighbours and checking in on the new people living in the house. I am so grateful for you doing all the extras on my behalf. Hopefully you both have a wonderful morning. I will call you at 1:15pm and check to see how you are doing. All my love.

Program was great this morning. I am learning these new skills that can apply to everyday life with are always a great thing to have. It was wonderful to hear your voice at lunch today my son. And that you are both are safe and in positive form. So nice to hear that the cat is meowing like mad. Hard to believe that your friends are already returning from out of town work for Christmas break and that school is done for another semester.

Max is going to take me to the mentor session tonight and introduce me to hers, so maybe there will be a match, which would be wonderful for everyone as Max is going on the 24th and she will need an inmate and I will need a mentor, so I will let you know how things work out.

I was called to V&C during programs so hopefully they will call me again as I suspect it is to pick up the mail with all the correspondence information and the reply from Mr. Reck. Wayne would also help formulate my response but first, I will look at his because I am sure I will be able to pick out a bunch of error, mistakes, and breaches.

I can't believe how the food issue is becoming such a problem here. I am so fortunate to have two oranges and on apple left. It is really uncomfortable.

Gosh Ray is such a hoot. She said her WEP program instructor has them doing lesson five for tomorrow. Bridget said they are graduating tomorrow with a party so that should be interesting. They are doing their course in two weeks, while mine is taking three months. Mea just came to me and asked if I had Christmas cards. There was a bunch left at the house for each inmate and apparently someone took more than their share. What else is new! The nice thing is that for the most part I get along with all the mates here. anyways, I asked Ray what lesson she was on since she had to complete to lesson five by tomorrow, she said she was on lesson one. I told her to take a break and we both laughed. It is so refreshing to find the humour in the stupid.

I did some reading this afternoon and wrote out some Christmas cards. Yes, I did end up getting my share. I completed my program homework that was due tomorrow. For dinner we had hamburgers. Poor Ray and Susan had their meds increased so they become very tired. The jail gives certain inmates medication and these girls just sleep.

I am glad to have visits tomorrow. Just waiting to see if they call movement to the mentors. I received the Law Society information and wrote a reply that I will send to you. I will see what the teacher says tomorrow about my typing out my homework and if I am able to use the computer lab to type this out, but either way no rush as he will hold it open. The Law Society is at least doing something. I am blessed to have a justice also looking into this gong. I put on it a sticky notes to include additional documentation to sent to him in due time.

The additional correspondence information has to be cleared by the school again right and left don't know what they are doing. The mentor thing tonight was invite only so Max was going to her mentor and find out if we could be matched up. I will keep my eyes out on when they meet again and speak to Whitey.

I also wanted to mention to you to send doubles of the letters which is fine and actually I will sent a copy to Mr. Rack's reply to Wayne for his enjoyment. I am not sure why I keep thinking this man will help and that he is a friend, but I hold out hope for him.

I will call you in a bit, oh yes; before I forget she the guard told me to ask you not to use the sticker return address just in case it falls off or something like that…oh yes and thank you for the stamps. The silver lining is that at least the guards are now aware I am taking University courses so maybe they will be more compassionate.

I made mention of how Mr. Reck made the comment that he did not believe me and how he had no intention of defending me. I think this is absurd especially since five days before my trial he did say he believed me and funny once he was paid out to blow my trial that he took his payout money to go and get medical treatment in the USA. Wow I think I know why this member wants me to reply and who goes to the USA for surgery and then a vacation. That seems weird!!!! I wonder if he was on vacation with the crook at his place in Palm Springs that he purchased with the Tax payers funds. I love it when Mr. Reck can feel the pressure and that one day this story will be published. I pray he finds his conscience and one day does the right thing. I am so disgusted with the legal system and the lack of integrity some of the lawyers have. But it is fitting of how Mr. Reck could be bought out to easily, as he is a weak man, some would call spineless. I sure hope he gets good treatment, but God will one day turn this around.

I will call you in a bit to chat either way things will all work out and God will bless us! Hold onto his promises and his word. I love you both with all my heart.

December 12, 20xx

How are you this chilly morning? Probably a bit tired, just like me. Today will be a coffee day for sure. Nice that you only have to work until 7:30pm tonight and you get a free lunch also. Sometimes work does have its perks.

I am still a bit upset with Mr. Reck's letter, but I will do what I can and everything will eventually work its way out. I will go to the teacher and talk with her this morning and hopefully I can use the computers for future assignments, plus I need to get those case studies for my readings.

Good day to not be working your first job. It is nice that you have met some new friends there and so wonderful they employers and employees are good people. Soon I will get my pen pack and we can chat about sports. Heck, I was watching Gilmore Girls waiting to call you and Mea was shaking her head at me. I looked at her and said, "Do I fit in here?"

Funny how things work out with Mea knowing someone and that girls who was defended by Mr. Reck is in here, also Bridget's co-accused is being defended by another lawyer in Mr. Reck's office. Oh well, I will let it go and move forward. No point in being stuck in the past especially when it is thinking about evil people who will have to meet their maker one day and "ha" will be judged.

I am off to programs and I will call you at 11:30am to confirm our visit. I checked the mail on my way to programs and I received a response from the doctor to get the St. Ives brought in and they told me to order it from the London Drugs. The orders from the London Drugs say I have to have a doctor's note. Seriously, this place has no standards or a system that makes any sense and how you do what you are told you still get shut down. No wonder people get so frustrated, yet another day gong in this show. Poor Mea is having no luck with her parole officer. She has put in a request to speak to the Warden, who in turn gave the request back to her parole officer. I wonder if the system monitors face book pages of inmates because that could tell a lot about a person even while they are in here. Employers do that so I would think the Federal Government would be smart to think of that, but then again it is the system.

We got to talking about rates in jail and the program instructor was actually pointed out how I tried to get the system to listen to my story and how I was trying to speak up against the crooks but no one would listen. Heck, if they won't listen to me about a hundreds of millions of dollars in tax evasion case they will surely not care about what I see or hear in jail. Do something about the crooks on the street and don't worry about the inmates. Society has bigger problems with that guy and the higher beings protecting him to protect them.

Apple submitted her application for day parole so that is so wonderful. Bally told me before she left to submit mine, so I will certainly do that, plus both my primary and secondary said a big "yes". I know I am on another path, but it is inspiring to see how moving forward and good it feels.

I have enclosed a cat and dog reading we received today from programs it is rather funny how it nails men and women in this scenario. Nice to hear that this situation has even brought our extended family closer, so that is a real positive.

The A&D lady is here for the pen packs to continue to be processed, so maybe I will get mine today. I thing I may have figured out what is making my face break out, it maybe the new shampoo/ conditioner I received or and it is probably my time of the month, most likely the latter.

I will be going to the main house and speaking to the teacher at movement and if she is gone I will put in a request but I will continue to do my readings and correspondence. Well, I spoke to the teacher who passed on my case file to my parole officer is fine as we then have to speak so that is good and also she will see my correspondence materials. I can also discuss my assignments with her as the teacher told me I could not use the computer lab unless I was supervised but I will speak to Bob and my parole officer about this. It will all work out!

I was able to pop in and say a quick hello to the Chaplin; she was so sweet and asked if I was adjusting okay. She seemed concerned in my doing okay, but she was relieved at my knowing God was watching over me.

My pen pack came in. Thank you so much it is perfect and everything looks great. The TV gets the movie channels. So please thank my sister for allowing me to borrow it. They will be giving you the double items tonight at visitation. I have had to purchase a few things and we can't have double items so I will send them back to you. Thank you for sending items that I have no emotional attachments too. If you think my pen pack will stop me from writing you letters each day well good luck.

Mea received some good news about her arm and so she made us all some cupcakes which was so nice.

Visits seem to be on so I am looking forward to seeing you both tonight. I just finished my program homework not due until Monday but better to get it done now.

Blessed to have done the Law Society stuff last night as you just never know what tomorrow may bring around here. Plus, it is better not to procrastinate. Blessed to have the movie channel as some of the girls can't get the channel

See you in a bit. Gosh to get educated in here is a real challenge, but I will continue to press forward with a positive attitude and take on the challenge. I loved our visit tonight. So grateful we all were able to attend tonight. Saturday will be yet another adventure to tell the grand kids about. I am so glad my son you are having fun at your job. It sounds like an enjoyable place to work.

Tomorrow is canteen day. I will pick up some Clearasil. At age 41 and I am still breaking out. Hopefully the London Drug order will come soon and I can get some proper face cream which wont made me break out or burn my skin. Anyways, today was a wonderful day and a fabulous evening. I love you both so much and I am so lucky to have you both and so grateful to have others that care so much. All my love. Have a terrific evening and I will call you tomorrow.

December 13, 20xx

Good morning to you both. Hope you both slept well last night. This morning was a bit chilly in here. I heard my PW on the intercom this morning. I just wrote a list of things to take to my PO and PW about. Today is a big day in program so I will let you know what happens. Hope you both have a great day at work and I love you both so much and love your continued support.

Programs were empowering. I taught more techniques with just gives me more self power. I will stay positive. Before I went to bed I was waiting for the guards to come and came across this show that spoke to positive thoughts and funny but our instructor and her ex would watch him so she knew who I was speaking of. My instructor again suggests I move into the DBT house for women who have difficulties controlling their emotions. This is called the Dialectical Behaviour therapy. Each woman also receives individual counselling form a therapist. Max was no way that I have the correct outlook and plus I am in the only minimum house and I want to move into a medium house when the correction plan and discuss my options with my PO and PW. I am in control of my emotions and thoughts and I will not entertain being negative or not on my path and keep focused on my goals. This is a money maker to keep workers employed here. They must require a certain quota of mates.

My instructor needs to take a personal day so tomorrow there is not class/ program, so I will focus on my correspondence and readings, just like today. Funny I noticed a reaction when she asked who my PW was and my PO. Gosh they would surely let me use the computer lab if they saw my handwriting. Goodness there is a lot of yelling downstairs, just no respect for the other mates in the house.

Bob came by for count and said he would call me up to catch up on providing everything stays the same and no drama which is out of his control. This meant he would have to go to the max and help out, so we would have to catch up later. Funny Mea's PW was on rounds with Bob and Mea was giving it to her PW and just the facial reactions on Bob's face were so funny. He is such a great person. It is so good to have a sense of humour in here.

A&D called me up to let time know she had not forgotten about my extra bag to give to the front and to put in a request to let her know when your next visit would be after the Christmas party and the goody bag would be there for you guys.

My son I love hearing about your adventures at work. It sounds like a wonderful place and a wonderful fit for you. What a blessing you make me laugh hearing about your stories and the new puppies making a mess in their cages only to go to the school where the kids make a mess and have the Christmas concert and a different kind of mess.

I ran into Jodi who told me to get the teacher to allow me to use the computers for my assignment and she shook her head know I have to find someone to supervise me. Gosh, what a gong show!

Bob just popped in and so we had a quick talk about what was going on. We discussed the computer lab situation and he told me he would check with the teacher, the actual teacher about the computer lab access and supervision situation. Bob's only on until 4:00pm today and it is 2:46pm, but he hopes to be able to get back to me tomorrow to resolve this. He also disclosed that there was an email and Bally was going to be back in January. That was good news as she told me she would be gone for two months. We talked about what the instructor mentioned and he told me they offer good programs but we would wait until the correctional plan was completed. I mentioned what the instructor said about my Pastor and Bob said I had to first go on a couple of escorted visits but with guards which would be great to of course go home and then be able to go to church. One step at a time.

Hey mom I was looking over the new Joyce Meyer book you purchased for me and wow this looks like another wonderful read. So many thanks for putting this in my pen pack. Maybe I will actually hear from God in jail.

Today had been a quiet yet productive day. So nice to be able to watch the news and see that yes there is corruption and even conspiracy still going on. Today is grocery day and so we each were blessed with receiving two apples, one banana, two navel oranges, and five Christmas oranges. Great and health foods.

Apple told me while we were washing the dinner dishes that she was going over to the other house and that she might get full parole on her day parole hearing because she was going back to live with her parents. Something sounds odd, but that is her path so hopefully she is getting the correct information, otherwise, someone is setting her up for failure which is so wrong. I do wish her all the best and a full and productive future.

Tonight was a quiet night. We were unable to collect our mail tonight so I will go in the morning. No programs tomorrow but I will still get up at the usual time. Mea and Sally did some cooking and baking tonight for Christmas.

I will call you at 10:45pm. I hope all is wonderful and you two are staying safe, healthy and strong… all will be wonderful. I love you both more than anything and one day the truth will come out and those who doubted this will be ashamed. Huge hugs and kisses. All my love.

December 14, 20xx

Good morning and how are you both this morning? My son are you excited that your buddy is coming home today as I am sure so is his family and your other buddy.

Well, today is the day they go to court and it is in God's hands as to how this will all play out. I checked the mail this morning and received the ICAA letter and questions to reply too. I also received a Christmas card from that lovely gal friend of mine and which was so lovely. I will write her again. Mom I will let you know that the booklet for the second correspondence course was not allowed in and returned to you, whom I respect and I will tell you why when I see you. When they do search my room if they find anything other than the items on my cellefex I could be charged, so that being said we will have to photocopy the assignment sheets and send it in rather than the booklet it as they consider that contraband and we have to respect that. Plus, the positive is that I don't want any charges, no thank you!

I ran into Bob who spoke to Tara the actual teacher and he told me to go to her room at 11:00am and speak with her about using the computer lab, but Bob did mention to purchase a disc from canteen and save it on it when I do my assignments in the recreation room, even though it is very loud in there, at least it is a computer and Tara said she would print them out for me. I will let you know what the resolution is either way I will get them done and maybe not to my full and best potential but I will pass them and more importantly learn something from these courses. Bless Bob for looking into the lab matter so quickly. He is really on the ball for me.

I was just going over the letter from the lady at ICAA and most, if not all her questions could be answered in the preliminary trial materials, so I think if she could just get a copy of that along with the forensic audit, I have in the burgundy box she could get what she needs from that. Don was the one who told me to file the complaint with them so hopefully they do their job unlike Revenue Canada, so I will take a deep breath now.

I spoke to Tara and she was so wonderful in saying she would print off my assignments and I could put in a request to use the computer lab, so I will do this and it will all work out. Keep the faith!

As I was going up to the main house I offered to check the other mate's mail. Mea said no one loved her so I was able to put a smile on her face with some love mail for her. Also this morning, I allowed Cathy to use the shower ahead of me which made her morning. The small things make a huge difference in their day, which in turn could make the difference in someone else day. A true pay it forward will make a graceful difference in jail or a simple smile and a hello could make a person's morning or day. Kill them with kindness. I will call you in a bit. Hoping your day is going wonderful. Blessed to have you both! Grateful ☺

Had a blah day, so I went to the gym to get out of my funk. Gosh what a terrible event that happened in the States with twenty children and seven adults shot to death. Just unbelievable! I find it so interesting how my tutor was my professor and now is the replacement in my correspondence instructor, this must be a sign from God but regardless it is very interesting how the circle comes around.

I am so looking forward to seeing you both tomorrow for the Christmas party. First time for all of us and last time for us. Bob is off this weekend. He popped in tonight to check on me and told me Tara mentioned I stopped in. She said I was so nice and positive. Bob seemed proud to have me as a mate. I told him I would be putting in my day parole application and hopefully next week the correctional plan would be available. Bob is back on Monday. He told us to have a great time, but he first made sure you were coming to the party. He was surprised I did not have a visit tonight. I told him my son had two jobs and you were here on Wednesday so I got to see you both mid week and Saturday and Sundays of course. I focus on my correspondence to help get me over the difficult time of missing you.

I need to get out of this house so I went to the gym for forty minutes. A girl in the yard told me it was winter and there were no floods because I was wearing my work out outfit which consists of short pants and a sweater. I just shook my head and kept walking. No use in discussing with her or I would be late for my workout. Bad teacher was on the movie channel. Such a good movie and a good laugh, which is always a blessing. I will talk to you in a bit. I love hearing about your day and how you handle life. You clean up poop from the kennel and poop from the kids a school...just a lot of poop. And you handle it with great character. I am so proud of you. You are simply amazing. I love you both and so excited to see you tomorrow.

December 15, 20xx

Good morning to you both. How are you both doing? Sleep well last night, I hope so. I am excited to see you both today as I imagine you are also, plus the new experience of being in jail. Well, what is life without a new journey and experience? I will see you at 1:00ish. I love you both. We will celebrate our Christmas when I get out, just like all the other holidays.

Eight weeks since I came here and each minute is one minute closer to being back with you. The house is buzzing with everyone getting ready. Once again another new experience to observe. No mail today. I went over to check it as I was waiting for you to be cleared and come in for the party. I have heard that every year the jail shuts down as someone spoils it for the group. Someone has something brought in and then visits get canceled. Well that is according to the optimistic Susan. She is always a ray of bright light and just knows how to be a downer. Well she said in years past that is what happens, which does not mean it will happen this year.

It was so wonderful to see you. I waited with great anticipation to see you. I could not wait to my name to be called so I could come up and see you. When it was called, I hurried up to the gym where we would meet but you were not cleared yet. One of the other mates who I work with told me she saw you in the processing area and that you would be here shortly. Funny how the other mates already recognize you from all our visits. You are well known in here. My heart jumped when I saw you. I was so excited to be able to have you experience this journey with me. You were able to see more of the jail then most would be able to. You could see the other mates and their families.

We are just trying to survive this journey and now we see how human we each are. Gosh today was so wonderful and thank you so much for attending the Christmas event here. I am so blessed to have the best support team and to be able to share this journey with you.

Not much to write in this letter as you have just left, but I had a shower and got cleaned up when I arrived back at the house. When I got back here there was a note on the table about having a house meeting and everyone must attend at 3:00pm or we need to find a new place to live. Sally and Ray were on the couch so I asked Sally what went down. She shrugged so I went and spoke to Mea as she wrote the letter. She was laying on her bed and Cathy was in her room. I asked Mea how she enjoyed the party and the three of us had a nice chat. I found out that someone ate the gingerbread house, the candy and Cathy's coffee mug was missing from her room. That was the just of the meeting. Mea said I would have to move out if I could not make the meeting. I told her I would start packing. The three of us laughed. Mea moved the meeting so I could attend. Nice of her. I will call you tomorrow at 11:30am to confirm our visitation. Miss you both and love you with all my heart. God's grace is enough.

December 16, 20xx

How are you today? What did you do last night after the party? Mea is off to visit her nephew. She is so happy which is so wonderful to see. It is nice when people are happy around here. I am just having breakfast, toast with honey and watching 'Gilmore Girls'. I will call you at 11:30am to confirm our visit.

Oh yes, thank you taxpayers for the Christmas party, it was really nice. Sally asked if I would be at the house meeting. I told her that I had words with Mea last night and how Mea told me I had to move out, so I asked Mea if she would help me move out with a big smile on my face. Sally knows what the meeting is regarding. Funny how we were just discussing this would happened at another house. I am not sure who knows about the coffee mug, but I will just wait and see at the meeting. Mea was going to move it until count.

Thanks for a great visit today. Thank you for typing out my assignment #1. Mom, sorry to hear you had such a frustrating morning with missing the granddaughters game after locking your keys in the van while it was running. God bless you for having a sense of humour over the gong. I am so grateful you have each other to help and support each other. Although, I don't get to visit with you this week my son, I will call you and chat and Grams will pass on the smooches from me. Neat how we met the Warden last night and saw her again today. I love that you tow are sharing so much together like Christmas shopping and going to our favorite pasta restaurant. I am envious but very grateful you have each other and of course you had our fuzzy baby, the cat, to keep you busy.

I think we will be having our house meeting after dinner as the guards have not done count and Max is gracing use with her fabulous cooking tonight. Hard to believe Max will be out in just over a week. How exciting for her.

I wonder if Apple is moving. I hope not but I wish her all the best. The guards came by and said, 'Echo is the best house". Well, they had the house meeting and again eating after 8:00pm was on the list, well I don't do that anyways. Apple told me she confronted Sam about this topic which is hypocritical as Apple does this also, the eating after 8:00pm. Apple is not going to move out and she said was going for her full parole in June. I helped with the dishes and came into my room and watched Four Christmases to take a break from the gong and have a laugh.

Dinner was great. I told Max that I wished her well and that I would miss her fabulous cooking. Seriously, Max is an amazing cook. Very loud, but she has come to grow on me. These gals can grow on you, it is like a sisterhood of kinds.

So I got ready to go to the gym, but it sounds like a lock down as they actually came to the house to give mates their meds. So I will just do some simple exercises in my room and make the best of this situation.

Hope you were able to pick up the extra items before you left after our visit. Would you not know it just after I had a shower and got ready to stay in for the night doe they not but call movement to the gym? I wonder if orphans feel this out of place as I do. I love you both and I will call you in a bit.

I was so happy you both had fun shopping today. Like I said material items can be replaced but you two are special cargo and I am so blessed to have you both. Our journey will be blessed as God has wonderful things in store for us.

December 17, 20xx

How are you this fine morning? Well I caught the last couple minutes of the football game and I think that San Fran won over New England, but it was a good try.

Wow, I have so much to tell you. This morning when I went to programs, the instructor informed me that the intake lady wanted to do my interview today at 10:30am. Well would you not know it but last night would have to be a terrible sleep.

I had my intake interview and it was fabulous. Joyce Meyer, church and the intake lady and I had a terrific meeting. The intake lady said my interview was the shortest she had ever done. I am not sure if that is good or bad. She seemed very nice and a gentle soul.

This morning Cathy told me she had to go for surgery. That could be very scary in a place like this. At lunch time Sally waited until I was on board for lunch menu. Today was grill cheese, with banana peppers and tomatoes and tomato soup. So I asked who had not eaten if they would like to enjoy some lunch, well it turned out to be only use three gals, Ray, Sally and myself, but a real blessed feeling to want to take care of your other house mates came over us. Well, just as we were going to sit down to eat; Cathy comes in the room complaining she was dizzy and cold. No one even walked her to the house to ensure she was okay after her surgery. I prepared her some soup and made her a sandwich and made sure she was taking care of before she went upstairs to sleep. It felt good to be gracious and help out someone else. How could they just let her walk all that way and not even ensure she was okay after she had surgery? What kind of people work here?

This morning I was for some reason on a pee run and had to go before my program which never happens but would you not know it I ran into Jackie from the shop. She gave me a big huge and I asked if she would write me a letter as she would be leaving for her trip soon and I would love to have her support for my parole. She said of course she would. She told me everyone keeps asking here when I am coming back as they all miss me. That was so kind.

I will call you at 1:15pm to see how your day is going and pray it is wonderful. Well, my son it is awesome that not only do you enjoy the one job, but you are paid very well there. Thank you for trying Wayne again. I am surprised he had not returned your calls or emails, so something must be going on with him. I am so proud of you for taking on so many responsibilities and working so hard. Thank you mom for looking after my son while I am away.

Today we received an assignment we had to hand in to the instructor and her comment to me was that I nailed it, which was great. One of the gals gave me a Christmas card that was a very kind gesture from her. The intake lady told me I would be able to presume my legal assistant career even with a criminal record. Heck I know Lawyers who have criminal records. The intake lady is very nice and I appreciate her reassuring me about my career path.

Max made a spicy fish soup with I was really good. Hard to believe Max is gone next Monday, then Sally, then Sam, then Susan, then Apple and then my ☺ Gosh you not only count down the days, weeks, and months, but you count down the people and when they get out.

I just helped Mea and Max move some furniture around. Hope your shower woke you up my son, and there are no surprises for you at work today. Big hugs and kisses. I am glad next week we can see each other more with Christmas holidays coming.

I am going to have a shower myself. I can have as many as I would like in here as I don't have to worry about the water bill just the scheduling of them. I received a beautiful letter from a family member. I was called to A&D to get something and I ran into a gal from programs. We had both just gotten out of the shower so we both looked like drowned creatures. The house was so hot, like a sauna in here. I had to open my window to let out some of the heat. Hopefully, the maintance people can fix this as it is such a waste of money.

I put in a request to track down my correspondence notes. Have you received the study guide back yet? The one I had to mail back to you as they considered it counter band and now we would have to photocopy it. I was able to check my mail and I received the letters you sent in with the picture from the family. You know what is so amazing is how much strength one gets from a support system. I am truly blessed. I love you both. I pray for you both to continue to stay safe, healthy and strong.

I still miss you like crazy and that will not change. All I can do is keep thinking we are one day closer for use to be together again. I love you both and my heart is full. I will call you after the guards do the last stand to count.

December 18, 20xx

Good day to you both. How did you sleep last night? Sorry I thought I would write on this sheet to paper before mailing it to save on paper and postage.

Well, today at programs we learned about the medicine wheel, which was very educational. The instructor made an executive decision between relationships and spirituality and how blessed I was for her to choose spirituality and learn about the four sections of the medicine wheel. There is the spiritual, physical, emotional, and mental and when you are in balance life is good, but if one area is out of balance you are out of balance. The 'will' in the middle is your will power and as long as you are in balance your will power is in order. The instructor is bringing in muffins for our last session. This is very kind of her and we don't have to start until 9:00am. We are able to bring back our vision boards that have been hanging in the trailer where we have our program sessions. I asked Ray who read her vision board if she would get my vision board read. I said I would carry my vision board, which was very large around the jail until I found these people. It would be interesting to see what my vision board meant and have some read it like reading cards. Before you know it I would end up in a quiet are of the jail. I did not find the person who read the vision boards but one day it will all come forth.

Bob is on today and he said he would call me over later. Poor guy has had a ten hour shift over at the max, which is apparently just a terrible place. One of the gals in my programs had been there and she described it as being like a pet store, in cages where everyone is on display.

My son I hope you are having a great day at your jobs and mom I hope you are having a stress free day. Well I just went to A&D where I was served with this signed order by the same judge again who is signing all these orders. Does this not constitute as a conflict of interest to not be in front of new eyes? If you pay off one judge you can get a lot of paper signed. This will be the third time he has touched this matter. First was the restraint order, second was the permission for Reck to step down and now this order for Judgement. I also received the consolidated civil enforcement letter and information.

Thank gosh for you two; otherwise, I don't know what I would do. Sure nice of these crooks to do this while I am in prison and can't do anything about anything. Karma, she will come back and get you so be very careful what and how you hurt people. The universe will deal with them. God and my wonderful support team have yet again been here when I needed them the most. Material items can always be replaced but one day these crooks and evil people will meet their maker and spend the rest of eternity downstairs.

Thank you my son for your wonderful phrase today, 'you know who else had a hard road? Jesus, Yes, and my son you are so right and I am so blessed to be included with such wonderful, inspirational role models. Even Ghandi, 50 Cent, Joyce Meyer to just name few had struggles, hardship true tests of character and I always have to remember how I am being watched and viewed from the greatest above. One day mark my words this struggle for justice and for vindication will be for not. One day the truth will come out. I showed Cathy how I can see the crooks back door from the bathroom. Why would God put me here to see this place each day? Cathy thought that was fate.

I think that you my son have the 'luck' in you. I just wish yours/ our life did not always have to be so difficult but in great storms the rainbow will eventually come out. Thank you for taking the $10.00 and purchasing a lotto ticket. Tomorrow is a huge day. First the lotto happens to fall on Wednesday, second it is the 19th which is our lucky number and third tomorrow I am applying for full parole. Tomorrow is my last day of program. Blessed by tomorrow. Isaiah 52:7 is 'How beautiful upon the mountains are the feet of him that bright good tidings.'

Today was also a symbolic as we brought our vision boards back. Maybe this is a sign to make me vision to the universe. Lucky me the guards searched all the rooms upstairs, but not mine. In fact, I got a hand pass wave.

Mom, I will call you at 5:30pm and see how you made out getting in touch with Sharon. Thank you my son I hope you had a terrific day and evening at work. I will call you at 10:45pm to say goodnight and to see how the rest of your day went. I love you both. I did find a way while on the phone to hold back the sadness. I visualized something and it really helped. Well they can try to get blood from a stone, just won't happen and one day God will vindicate me and justice will be served. One day his company will be audited and the truth will come out. I pray for him that he will do the right thing.

How awesome was it for Apple to make me a sleeping mask to put over my eyes so the guards flashlight will not disturb my sleep. So sweet. How blessed are we. God is truly working in fabulous ways. I also go to thinking so much will happen in six months. Maybe it is a blessing I am in jail, so I could not do anything crazy. I will call you at 5:30pm. Max warned me that she may go over her time as she is going to be fighting with someone. I told her she maybe early when she hands up on him. She smiled and got my joke.

Thanks mom for making the phone calls and for being such a wonderful assistant in typing out my assignment and making my phone calls and being my support and most of all for taking care of my special cargo, my son. I am grateful that we have six months so the renters, how are not paying rent, will be able to not be out on the street and how silly they are in having to go back to court over not registering my vehicle properly. As you will see on the personal property I apparently have a 19xx for something and a 20xx other vehicle. Nice to know that this case should go down in history with the most errors and yet no one has been paid off…yah right.

Nevertheless, we will be vindicated later and who knows what can happen in six month. I am grateful that Shana even talked to you. I don't want to stress you out mom and me so appreciate all you have done and continue to do. I went to the gym at 7:00pm. I will not allow them to take my health. So keep smoking, keep drinking, keep having unprotected sex with strangers, and keep eating crap, keep your stress level high and your blood pressure up, one day you will be called out.

Blessed be Sally who asked me to come for a walk to the mailbox. I was watching Fast times at Ridgemont High and I get yelled at that there is someone at the door. Well no one in the yard would come to visit me. I asked to make sure it was for me. Mea said, yes a boy is here. I replied a boy for me. Mea said it was my PW. Bob came by tonight just to catch up with me. How terrific is that. I told him about the interview with the intake worker, and about full parole and that the interview went very well. I told Bob that here was one spot left in the next program and that the instructor asked if I wanted it. I mentioned how I was still looking for the correspondence cases and had put in my request for someone to locate the rest of my materials. I mentioned how I was served again today. He told me that this was absolutely unfair and how they could put me here without finding the money. I think he is frustrated and he sees how wrong this situation is but I reassured him that the truth will come out and that I would publish the book. I explained to Bob that things are material and that things would come back in great fold but I would not allow them to hurt me anymore. I will even come back as a ghost to be vindicated. God has a great plan for us, please hang in there with me I promise you will not regret it.

I love you both and will call you at 10:45pm to see how your day went. Bob told me after the report was complete that we would start to work on private visit in the house. That means a sleep over and escorted visits.

After our chat tonight I must say I am so disappointed in Wayne. He told me about one individual he knew who went to jail and I maybe making more out of this, but he could at least return your calls and emails. But I guess you can't always make sense out of every situation. I hope nothing terrible has happened to him or his family. I will write him again and maybe because I have put out into the universe he will call.

My son I hope you win big on the lotto, because I know I won big in having you. I love you both. God's peace.

December 19, 20xx

Good Wednesday morning to you both. How are you this morning? It looks like another cold day, so my son please dress warmly. Mom you getting lost last night really freaked me out. Please my son mined your grandma. I know mom you asked for directions but it really freaked me out you getting lost, so until I get out please stay close to home that would ease my mind.

This morning my room is so hot it is gross. I think of how people are worried about paying the bills and how we would put on a sweater but not here. I have my window open so I don't sweat.

I went to do laundry this morning as programs does not start until 9:00am and yes our last session, and Susan says that I am too happy in the morning. I told her she could take it to the outside when she goes. I think that maybe some of my manners and happiness is wearing off on some of my mates. I noticed at the gym last night a lot of new faces. Bob said he was at the max on Monday and how depressing it is in there. I appreciate his concern for me being here, but God has a wonderful path for me and for us so I will keep strong and focused as will you and together we will get past this and blessed and blessings will come.

My son I will call you at 1:45pm. I pray you two stay safe and strong and healthy. I love you both and every time I get a bit of a pity party your voice rings in my head…you know who else had a difficult struggle… Jesus…yes you are right. I know god will give us strength and Jesus will walk our path with us.

Our last program session took place and after completing some testing for the government to see how criminals think the course was complete. We each had to come up with one thing we would take away from this session and mine was my tool cards which so many people could benefit from each day in their everyday life and just meeting some terrific women. Maybe that is also why I am here is for the reader to understand that yes there are some terrible situation some of these women have endured but everyone is capable of change, growth and positive resolution and reformation.

At programs we then received a muffin from the instructor. Kindly we sat around and ate our muffin and chatted. Some spoke more than others, but we were just five fabulous women and no one was better than the other. When she got to me to present me with my certificate of completion she said we could get hugs, so after me hugs were handed out. I am certain that this group will go down as one of her favorite groups. The instructor said I could again have the last spot in the next session if I wanted it.

Apple is moving to the other house called the Humming bird and today it is sealed she will be moving. I told her we could meet in the gym and chat while working out.

I submitted for my full parole application this morning. It is now in God's hands, but so is everything we just have to trust in him and keep in faith.

Blessed by that Max, as she folded my laundry for me. I had my items in the dryer and her clothes were in the washer as I was heading to programs so I just asked if she would put mine on the dryer and then she could dry hers. Max said she could fold mine. We got into a no... Yes situation. When I came back after programs there was Max coming out of the laundry room. She tells me we have a problem, and I started with the Houston and she continues to tell me one of my socks went over the back of the washing machine and she could not get it. I thanked her for folding my laundry and told her that I have a real problem with socks in this place. A long story short, Max asked Mea to move the machine which is funny as Mea has a terrible shoulder. I laughed when I heard this talk outside my room door. I came out and we had a good laugh and then I got some tongues and we were able to get the sock. Max was laughing when I showed her the sock. It was covered in dust.

As I was washing the tongues, Bridget told me there was fresh coffee which was perfect timing. She also told me that there was some soup if I wanted it. Mushroom soup with corn and it is actually really good. I was thinking about last night when Bob stopped by. He could not come into the house because he was by himself and how Susan reacted to the cold air and Bob's comment about how grouchy she is. She totally blows things out of proportion. She is a very "me" person. I felt so bad for him and the way she spoke to him. Her lack of respect is beyond words. Anyways, it was cute how things and situations are handled or how they play out especially with different dynamic women.

Just like last night I was apologizing to Sally for "shhhing" her while I was trying to deal with legal matters which by the way was not sitting well with Bob, I mean the legal matters, but I explained to Sally what I was dealing with and she said she was sorry also and was upset I had to deal with this. Bridget came in and gave me a hug and said I was extremely the strongest person she had ever met or crazy, but once I explained how long this had been going on and so on, I had a women looking at me with inspiration. Well, maybe a bit crazy. Blessed be my support system for helping me in this difficult situation.

I was talking to God and reading the Joyce Meyer book and I took a moment to look at the TV directory and Erin Brockovich was on just for me. This was a God's reply to me asking for a sign that I was on the right track. God showed me Erin and her determination.

I just got called to V&C and guess what, the acting warden passed on the correspondence cases. She said she would do a memo for the guards and they will know I have these materials for my correspondence and I will have no grief from them. This is wonderful. Oh another prayer answered. Just know you crook you can take all my assets but just know that the truth will come out. God bless you, my son with all your funny stories and for keeping my spirits high. The crooks year end is September 30 so things can still and will time out perfectly to have them audited by the correct authorities. One day the proper channels will recover all the tax evasion and so on. Justice will prevail and we have a just and righteous God.

Thank you for the great visit mom. Nice to see you and hear what is going on. After you left Sally and I went to check mail but it still was not done, so I will check it tomorrow when canteen is called. My son I will have a smooch for you when you visit on the weekend. Bridget signed me up for a sweat on Saturday, so that could be interesting. Bridget told the elder I would be coming and he said he would read my vision board then, that could be so cool. Gosh it is seriously cold outside tonight.

Stay safe, stay positive, and stay healthy. I miss you both so much today as the first day I was admitted here. One day closer to being back with you. I love you and will call you at 10:45pm once the guards have completed their counts and round at the house. All my love.

December 20, 20xx

Good morning to you both. How are you this cold, cold morning? This morning I was woken up by Sally who was being her usual loud self. As I lay in bed thinking she would stop and keeping my mind in a positive state I just told myself to get up, shower and get my day started, so off I went. I went at movement to get my mail and was blessed with a lovely letter from our neighbours as I read the letter I was filled with joy hearing about their trip. I was watching my church channel while eating my breakfast. I went and watched mine and the rest of the dishes and came back upstairs to my room to read my outline for my correspondence course and thinking I should write to the neighbours and others today as apparently tomorrow there will be a lock down as no movement.

I walked into my room and guess who was on TV... god blessed me with Joyce Meyer 8:00am on channel 120. Oh and her message spoke volumes to me about staying on the path and giving 100% of excellence to the mission. How not to let others steal your joy and to be blessing. A blessing could be as simple as happy in the day. after watching her shoe I went downstairs to thank Sally for waking me up otherwise I would not have found Joyce well would you not know it Ray actually was introduced to Joyce in jail and really enjoys her and I know Bridget also has heard of Joyce and I introduced her to a book of hers in the library. Well, Bridget really enjoyed it and Bridget was no impressed that she was worked up also so when I see Bridget I can let her know that I found Joyce because of Sally waking me up. Before you know it the "E" house could be the spiritual house. Watch the jail will have no movement until 8:30am instead of 8:00am because the inmates want to watch Joyce, and how much happier everyone will be with a little spiritual message to start their day.

Ray was telling Sally and I about a situation she had with her man and it was cute because we played out this situation in WEP so I hope I was able to give her some constructive input on the tools we used and some comfort in not over reacting until you establish all the facts act. I hope she appreciated this.

God is about achieving justice and yes he will. Eventually the evil doers will receive their justice. Justice is coming. A funny story to tell you. I was taking a pee break from reading the Civil liberties and Individual rights unit #1 and Max was coming up the stairs as I was washing my hands. She tells me that there is a new Kim chi noodle soup at canteen. She suggested I should try it, plus it is good to have in case a no food situation comes down. So I of course got to thinking as I see Max walking back to school, how kind some mates are even in jail and how they have my back unlike the evil doers (you know who I am referring too). I guess what I am trying to say is the mates in jail have more character then some of the people who should be in jail. If the real crooks were locked up how different this experience would be. Like I told you about when mates find out my story how they no longer complain about their story. How an innocent person is in jail and maintaining the right attitude how can they complain being guilty. How one can be humbled and full of grace in a system that is so unjust... well that is because I know who my God is and he is a just and he will ensure I receive justice. Thanks be to God.

So I was doing my correspondence when I was called to V&C to be served again. I looked at the documents and it was the same document I received on Tuesday and I told the process server she said that was weird and asked who it was. I told her some black guy. I also told her this was the third time that this Judge had touched this matter and that a Judge should not handle the matter more than once. Now that I have this same copy I will send it to Wayne. The process server was really taken back and confused. Wow they must really want to make sure I am served. Complete harassment! Go the auditing department get in there and audit this company.

Blessed to get a copy to send to Wayne. I sure hope he will contact you after receiving this. Gosh, god must really want me to focus. I get called to V&C again. I helped Mea with the food cart and taking it back to the house and I asked her if I could have them not allowed to come in and serve me. She said this was like harassment. So I went to V&C to see the acting warden and I spoke to her. She told me to have my lawyer deal with this. I told her I was my lawyer. She told me to call the Law firm and tell them to quit serving me duplicate copies on me. She then gave me a long piece of paper confirming my full parole board hearing which will be in May and I would receive a confirmed date. There was a parole officer there when we were chatting and he said I had to wear a lawyer's hat and not an inmate's hat. He must have thought wow... this gal sure is dealing with a lot. But more importantly, God was speaking to me telling me to focus on full parole and he would deal with the rest.

God would deal with the justice and he did not just tell me he showed me in writing. Then my left hand inched and I sneezed twice, which means the intake of money and then a spirit is near me. Wow what a great sign. Thanks be to God. Plus, I was able to write to Wayne and put it in the mail, so maybe it will go out tonight and he will get it soon.

My son you are so funny. I am watching the Seinfeld where George asks out the girl in jail.

Tonight was a quiet night. I did some Joyce Meyer reading as some of the girls were to a Christmas concert at the main house. I took advantage of the quiet. Max told me to talk to the lady who coordinates the work placement; her name is Abby, about working at the garbage dump or the food bank. The food bank is volunteer position with would be so great. So hopefully we have regular movement because being cooped up with these gals will truly test my patience tomorrow.

Guess what is on TV tonight my son? And old favorite 'Speed'.

I completed unit #1 of the second correspondence course. There sure is a lot of reading in this class but the first assignment is only to be five page essays. So I should be able to crack out assignment #1 and assignment #2 for the Women Liberty class and get them on to discs for the New Year, plus spend as much time visiting with you, which is the best.

I love you both and I will call you at 10:45pm to see how work went and how your shot went tonight mom. My son hoping you had a great shift and mom hoping you have no side effects to your needle. I love you and I miss you. I will stay strong and positive for you both. All my love.

December 25, 20xx

Merry, Merry Christmas to you both. This Christmas we will survive and appreciate our many more to come. This will be yet another event we will celebrate with family and friends once I get out. Bless you for being my continued support.

I am just sitting in my comfy chair in my room with the TV on writing to you and wow is there some good shows starting in January. My goal is to get my classes completed by the end for February, along with the program self management and hopefully a couple of other programs like fork lifting, H2S, ect. First aid is an eight hour long course offered on January 16 so I will get signed up for that.

My son an "Under Cover Boss" they featuring Johnny Rockets in Washington the one we went too and gosh the staff is very annoying.

I started a load of laundry while I wait to call you. Ray was asking me about my day parole while I was folding the house dish clothes and towels. I told her that it was my belief to go for it as you can't have any regrets in something you did not try only in things you wish you had done.

Today is a cloudy day, very cold and cloudy. My cycle is still here but getting better each day. I will call you at 11:30am to confirm our visitation.

My son I love hearing about your funny stories and experiences at the kennel. Pets can bring such joy to people's lives, and more often less gong than humans. One support signed her Christmas card to me from herself and her pets. The human's in her life only such the life out of her, but her animals fill her life with unconditional love.

So I got to thinking that everyone in jail is away from their loved ones somehow. We know how the mates are away, but so is the staff who is working to accommodate use also. For some reason, the phone was only taking collect calls or maybe it was only Sally's phone card. I asked what I could do before I go on my visit and offered to do dishes as the other gals would be doing the preparation.

Cathy made a Yule log for dessert; I know dad is with use as a Yule log was what he had on his birthday, which is Christmas. 20xx will be a terrific year and dad is showing me a sign this morning. I loved hearing of how you were playing with our precious cat. I was reminded of her while I watched Shrek and seeking Boots and his big eyes reminded me of her and her eyes going all black before she was going to attach you. Kiss my fuzzy baby okay.

What a nice visit we had. The gals in the house told me to pass on a Merry Christmas from them to you both. When I came back from our visit, I was greeted with Sally informing me that dinner would be 6:00ish as the oven was on a timer and turned off which was fine so I was able to help prepare. I pealed the potatoes and yam; I will make it with the brown sugar. Sally made some Tim Horton's coffee; yes we got a huge container of this coffee. There are a lot of wonderful treats in jail that the average Joe does without. Thanks taxpayers. We made Mochas with hot chocolate and coffee, really good.

At 4:00pm we stood for count and yet again I thought of the guards being away from their families and the gals in the max are away from their families. At the end of the day we are all missing our families and have to sacrifice to be away from our loved ones, but the best think we can do is lean on one another and inspire to dream of how different next year will be. Apple appeared to use the washroom still in her PJ's. Susan asked her if she wanted to come out and visit, she went back to her room. I had asked her before count if anyone had checked on Apple but no one had so if turned out well for her to appear after count. She came into the kitchen while I was making mocha and started crying when Susan started talking about how we are all missing people. I put my arms out to comfort Apple and Susan came and gave her a big huge. I reminded Apple that all these holidays will be celebrated when we get out. Apple went back to her room to get dressed and I came upstairs to write to you but let the gals know to shout if they needed help.

Looks like we will be having dinner together just at different houses. See you at 6:00ish in spirit. I love you both. I will check on Apple in a bit to see if she is okay.

As I was coming downstairs, Ray said thanks and gave me a nickname, so Sally asked where her nickname was. Ray said, "Oh I will give you a nickname." Shrek is on TV, Gosh I forgot how funny that show is. So good to laugh.

Just like when you come and I tell you my story of this morning when Cathy said Merry Christmas but I could not see her and I thought God was talking to me, you two would get a kick out of my stories and I so appreciate that.

A sense of humour is so good for the soul and gosh only knows I have kept mine and will continue to pass it on whenever possible. I love how you have resorted to a big binder for my letters; I am so excited to re-read them. At time it will be difficult as this journey has been very difficult for all involved and I hope one day it will be appreciated and it will return back to all of us. I went to get another mocha coffee and Apple was peeling carrots. She seemed okay. She said she just wanted it to be June. I would agree with that, but I reminded her to enjoy the journey. If anyone knows my relationship with you my son, who is the world to me, I would do anything to be with you, but I will not allow this time to be without merit until we are re-united. I will treasure this time and will treasure our time together even more than words can every say. My point is to be appreciative of the journey otherwise, it is all for not. God has set use on this journey for a reason and we will receive victory and vindication. I just hope Apple can see the many positives right before her and make sure she knew my door was open to her also.

Funny tonight Forrest Gump is on TV. Don't you feel our lives are like a box of chocolates, we really don't know what we are going to get. Dinner was really good. Apple and I did the dishes while some of the other raped up left over's for themselves. I am now going on strike from the dishes. I will do my own and that is it. I asked Sally if she would help do the dishes she said, NO, so I started doing them and had to stop to dry them before I could continue and that was when Apple helped me out.

Meanwhile, some of the girls from another house came in. I am getting really tired of this. I thought I would have a chance to discuss this with Bob, but we never seem to get a chance to talk in private and a lot of the time had to passed so just this morning I was thinking since it had not happened in a while I to let sleeping dogs lie but a new one was in the house tonight. This lady and Cathy were in her room doing God knows what. I looked at Susan and she told me to look the other way. Wow, every time I think Cathy has her kids at heart and she is doing more and more stupid things, but then again it seems like they are not thinking about their kids at all. Why don't they just follow the rules and think about their kids?

I will call you at 10:15pm and see you tomorrow at 5pm. I will call in the morning and late afternoon we can talk about it when I call you tonight.

I was telling Apple about my God story this morning and that gave her a laugh. She knew I was uncomfortable with what was going on in the house. I will have to take this up with Bob and get his input. This is a huge violation and the house should not have to pay for ones actions.

Mea came home from her visit. She told me all about her time with her family and how she was looking forward to coming back. I asked her if she missed us while she was gone and why would she be looking forward to coming back here? I am not sure I understand, but she may have her own reasons.

In April is when she goes up for her release, so hopefully she gets it. I commented how I can't wait for my visits home to you guys and Mea said I would have no problem getting those. She had an unescorted visit today so that is the last step before going out on either day or full parole, but it was nice to hear that she had faith in me getting to see you and our pet. Not that I would ever doubt me not following the rules or what is expected of me as I am all about that. Heck even when I follow the rules and tell the truth I end up in here.

I will call you shortly, and in the meantime I am going to read Joyce Meyer tomorrow until I am blessed with seeing my favorite family. Even though, we were a part for Christmas we still had a lovely visit and spoke on the phone. I wish things were different but next year will be and we will look back on how much more we appreciate everything in our lives. We will be grateful for what we have today and remember all those who were away from their families at Christmas and appreciate what they do more.

Count our blessings and give thanks for everything we do have. I love you both and 20XX will be our year. Merry Christmas my love.

December 26, 20xx

Good Boxing Day morning to you both. Finally hockey is on TV. Happy days! Sally woke me up this morning with her loudness. So I got up and thought I would get some reading in. Hopefully, Joyce Meyer will put me in a good mind set. When I went down to make some tea and porage, I wished Susan a happy birthday. She mentioned how loud Sally was being. I was surprised as she was usually the loud one and now there was competition.

So my son, who are you cheering for in the hockey? I am going for Finland. I will give you a call at 1:00pm and see how your Boxing Day shopping went. I love you both.

I was having words with God and asked him to show me a sign that I was on the right path and that he approved of my/our journey and that he was with me/us and he showed me the TV movie "Horrible Bosses". Of all the movies that one spoke to me especially having one of the world's worst bosses and having so many similar parallels it was a perfect sign. Thanks be to God!

Well this afternoon was a lazy day. I read and had my spirit renewed. I watched some TV and had a thirty minute nap. Around here that is a blessing in itself. Jimmy came around at count and asked if I had a chance to see the family. I said, "Yes" and I have a visit tonight. He said he saw me during one of my visit time running to the main house. He said he was going to stop and get on the PA and tell me no running in the cold, and then he smiled. So kind of the guards to always be waiving at me or stopping by to check on me, it really boosts my spirits. Thanks to the great staff and guards in here.

I am going to see you shortly and I am really looking forward to it. I miss you terribly. Thank you my son for picking up the series 'the Good Wife' for me, you are so thoughtful. We can all enjoy watching it. God they keep slamming the doors downstairs. One day someone is going to get hurt or mad at someone. I am so glad to leave this house and take a break from this immature behaviour. Max should be coming back soon. Like Mea said it will be interesting to see who comes and is her across the hall mate. She is so not looking forward to it. Last night Cathy had a tickle cough so I gave her some of my cherry halls to help her sleep. She was so grateful and we all were able to get some sleep.

The guards tonight were telling me she had booked your visits and she said it was really nice to see you guys visiting me so often. I told her that once school starts my son would only be able to come in on the weekends, so we are getting in all our visit times in now and then I would go back to my correspondence classes. She said what I was taking and she told me she took a couple of courses from that University and we could swap books after I was done. I told her that education was never a waste and how I just completed my first year of the legal assistant. We had a nice chat. She is always so kind to me and I really appreciate that. I am on another level then these mates and I will make the most of my time here.

Thank you for our visit tonight. I love you both and with all my heart and you mean the world to me. xoxox

December 27, 20xx

Hope you both had a wonderful sleep last night. I imagine my son you are still asleep and mom you are up not knowing if you have clients today.

Last night at around 4:00am, so I guess early this morning, I woke up to the temperature in this house. Gosh it was so hot, uncomfortably hot. At 7:00am I got into the shower and on with my day. I am watching a movie called King Ralph with John Goodman in it, it is an older movie and cute. There was just an announcement for no movement to work or programs which means something is going on. Now they say programs will proceed as usual, right and left is not working together. Joyce Meyer is on… oh happy days! And so I will do laundry and catch up with her. Now there is movement to work… seriously. Gong!

Joyce's message today was, we do right because it is right. I will not allow anyone to make me unhappy. Stay in peace and loving and stable. Keep your thinking right. Mom tomorrow will be about Freedom from worry and anxiety that will be a great message.

Great sermon from Joyce, and now I am going to tackle a few chapters of correspondence materials. I will call you at 11:30am to check in and see how your morning has been.

Well I finished reading unit 5 and unit 6 of the Women, Equality and the law and tomorrow I will finish writing out my second assignment and have that ready to go so when I am not enjoying my fabulous visits I can pop over to the recreation room and type it out. This afternoon I am planning on reading unit 2 for the other correspondence course, so I can begin working on that assignment next Monday. I will write them out and then whenever my nights are free I will type them up.

The second course has two assignments which are weighted very heavy. Assignment number one is 20% and the second is 30% but they are only to be five pages and the final exam, is 50%. The other course has two assignments weighted 10% and 15% and a précis worth 5% and a final paper (18-20 pages) worth 70%. Too much fun!

Nice to hear my son that you got together with the boys last night for some quality time and game time. Sorry that call was as loud as these girls act like brainless twits not respectful of people on the phone. Apple has moved out and a new gal has moved in, Max is back for her sleep over so the house is buzzing and of course certain individuals don't know what an inside voice sounds like.

Susan was telling me this morning that she went to make a turkey sandwich and someone left only the bone in the container and left an empty container of egg nog in the fridge. I just shook my head in disbelief. Absolutely, stupidity is going on.

Well off to read for a bit and I call you at 3:00pm. Today is grocery day and that means fruit. Sally called me downstairs to get my fruit and Apple was still here so I was able to give her a huge hug and wish her well and told her we would see each other at the gym.

Mea was bugging Apple earlier about how she was a trader and I could sense that Apple was in a delicate state so I said I would miss her. Mea was not here when Apple had her break down and Apple confessed to me while I tried to help her pack that she was in need of a good cry so I wanted to defuse the situation and Mea could focus on me, which would only take a moment in my world, as then I would be called to V&C and Mea would say "okay, girl what have you done now."

I trucked it up to V&C to be greeted by a nice guard holding a box an addressed to me. Oh my dear loving family who are the most thoughtful, supportive, family ever. I was able to get the letters and picture but unfortunately, the cookies and chocolates would not reach me. I asked if the staff would eat them, but unfortunately not so they had to be disposed of which the poor guard felt terrible doing, but I am so grateful the you my lovely family are thinking of me. It was so kind of this guard to call me up and let me know and show me what my family had sent in rather than just throwing it in the garbage, which some would do. I have a great deal of favour here, and I am so thankful to these amazing guards for being so kind to me.

Wow there is a lot of moving of mates and houses. You can see the guards moving mates to different houses from my room. When I went back to the house, Mea asked what I had done and I told her about the cookies. Max told Mea that if I had any questions that she was just a phone call away. Wow, like I said there is a strong bond you can develop here and one another are actually amazing. I would not have expected to have met so many wonderful women here and hopefully I have been able to touch them in a positive way. Maybe God is using me to help them, but I am also being helped. God is certainly amazing.

My son it sounds like you and grams were having a lazy day watching movies. Nice to have some bonding time. It will call you tonight at 9:00pm so you can get to bed early and be well rested for work tomorrow.

That movie Joyful Noise with Dolly Parton and Queen Latifa is coming on next and it has such a wonderful message. A real family movie which is so refreshing. Safe House is on the is weekend. I am looking forward to seeing this movie. I think you just bought it my son. Well, I managed to get all the reading I needed completed. So tomorrow I can crack out my essay for this course. Hopefully for both but for sure assignment number 2.

The movie Two Weeks Notice is on TV. I am going to go in a few moments to mail this to you and check the mail. I love you both more than words could ever express and I am so grateful and thankful for your support and you believing in me. Your words of encouragement are my armor and without I would be lost. God will bless us!

Oh yes I introduced myself to the new girl who I put where I usually see her which is in the visiting room. She goes by the name of Debby. Anyways, I mind my own business and focus on my path. I love you and will call you at 9:00pm to see how the rest of your day went.

December 28, 20xx

Quote today is, "better to have tried and failed then never to have tried at all" from the movie Lions and Lambs.

Good morning and how are you doing? A bit chilly but the weather channel said it will be warming up. I was watching Joyce and she said this: "Beginning of faith is the end of anxiety". Her message today was so wonderful today. It got up at 7:00am and had a shower. As I was blow drying my hair I could hear a tapping sound so I turned off my blow dryer and answered my door. There was Max standing in the hallway with an armful of goodies. She set on my bed cans of pop, popcorn, some face scrub, shampoo, ect. I thanked her for everything and gave her a hug. Max is getting out today, so I wished her all the best as well. I have learned something new from each of these women, whether it is a new receipt or what to do on the inside, something it is more at test of my patience but that is a self improvement or how grateful I am to have your support when so many have no support so it is a self reflection.

I made myself some toast and coffee before I was going to enjoy Joyce and her daily message while I was making my breakfast Ray and Susan were playing a game. Ray left to go to the main house. Ray told Susan how I was called to the main house last night at 9:50pm to chat with them about the mail I had to add postage to and how they thought I sealed one of the envelopes. The guards seal the envelopes after they have read and approve the mail to go out. The guard asked me why I sealed the envelope which I did not it was already sealed and I was just putting more postage on it. What a gong! I am always in the shower when I get called to V&C and would you think 9:50pm is a safe time to shower as count is at 10:10pm but nope they must see me heading to the shower and then page me over the PA system. So Ray left and Susan got to confessing to me about how she needs to mend fences with her children one of which has just gotten engaged. I hope I was able to give her some inspiration and inspiring words to encourage her. I could not even image after hearing her son's message to her.

The new girl Debbie seems really nice enough but when talking with her she is so focused on the past and can drag your spirits down, so I make my conversations short and will not be bothered with any negativity. I prayed for Apple last night as Debbie said some really scary things about where Apple went but that could just be what she took away from it. It seems like a lot of other mates are so ready to bring others down around here will I don't have time nor the energy to have these negative attitudes be brought into my circle. Stay positive, stay strong and stay in the faith. I love you and I am going to get working on my next assignment.

Well, I finished my assignment number 2 so hopefully I can get a copy of the full case and be able to read it completely, but that seems to be the name of the game around here, you only get half the information to complete the task. I will call you in a few moments to catch up. I am so excited for our visit tonight. I will see you shortly, I miss you guys so much, but I keep telling myself when I get sad that this is one day closer to being with you. All my love, all my kisses and hugs. What is now my test will be my testimonial? Kissed to you both, we will survive this, stay positive, stay strong and in faith. Funny the banjo song just came on, the I will wait song, and this must be a sign from God.

December 29, 20xx

Good morning, how are you both doing? Last night I was watching the Fifth Estate and it was about the lottery. I think the spirits are speaking to me/us. It was so wonderful to see you both and to get a hug and kiss from you. Aunt said in her letter that you are such a fine young man, my son, which I would whole hearty agree. I am so proud of you.

I love that last night we could laugh like we did at home; I love that we will soon be vindicated. I am so grateful to have your love, support and believe in me. I/we are so blessed. After you left last night my son, I tried to get the low down on the card game, but I was told I would be called up when she gets back and she would show me how so I could show you and we could play. I left and quickly checked my mail but nothing and I will check again tomorrow morning when we have a moment. Verna and Debbie were walking in the yard. Verna told me that Apple misses me and I asked Verna to tell me when she saw me. I will try and track Apple down tomorrow. I tried to let Verna know I would be going to the gym back on January 7 but until then I was spending as much time with my mom and my son. I pray Apple is doing great.

I wonder where Bob is these days. Maybe I will see him today. I woke up at 8:00am, had a shower and got ready for the day. Poor Mea has been throwing up all morning so I offered her my gingerale and some peppermint tea, which she gladly took. Hopefully, she can keep this down and get some rest.

No mail for me today, but there is a marathon of Suits on which is fabulous, plus we have visits today so it is a terrific day. One day closer to being out of here. I will call you at 11:30am to confirm our visit.

Wow you both had a couple of late nights. Mom you had time with your grandkids and my son you spending time with the boys. Well the guards tonight were so kind to give me the envelope you could finally get it. This will save on postage and time.

Mea is still not feeling well. I made rice for dinner so Mea had some rice and chicken noodle soup. I asked if anyone had checked on her and Susan did so at least she was being taken care of since our visit. I took her some ice water. She was running a fever so I go her cold cloth and tried to doctor her to the best of my ability. A mother kind of has the natural instinct to assist. Cathy said she wished some was here to take care of her when she was sick, I reminded her that I was here for her and then Susan wished I helped her out, but I did not know she was sick also. I helped Max when she was sick also. Hopefully they will be here for me, but hopefully I don't get sick.

Debbie was asking if I had a nice visit and I told her yes. I asked about hers and she said they were not connecting today, but she had her PFV, Private family visit and she would help me with the paper work if I was to apply. Wow a sleep over would be so much fun and something for us to look forward too.

The girls were talking about the house Apple went to and that house does not sound very nice or mentally healthy. I am sure glad that the program instructor did not make me go there. I have actually not heard anything positive about that place.

Susan made sweet meatballs tonight for dinner. They were really good. Yet another yummy receipt to practice on you. Well I am going to lay down, my head is pounding and with all the sickness going around I can't afford to get sick and miss time with you.

So I found out about the sweat and why women can't do it when they are on the girls, it is called their "moon time". Women are cleansing during their time and a sweat is a cleansing so women are too powerful during this time and over powering to mother earth. Gosh I wish I could over power this headache. I will drink some peppermint tea and relax my mind and see if that will help.

Bridget said my son you will make a wonderful boyfriend and she admires our relationship we have. Well you are pretty amazing. Week ten is over and twenty five more to go on day closer is still one day closer. It seems we are all in need of a good night's rest. My son I am glad you and grandma got the amazing hamburgers. I made Mea some jello as the soup would not stay down so I am going to go get the jello for her and cut my apple up with some cinnamon and sugar for myself.

I will call you at 11:30am. Have a wonderful sleep and stay positive, strong and focused on our journey. I love you more than words can say, all my love. I miss you and can't wait to be together again. Xoxoxo

December 30, 20xx

Good morning to you both. How was your morning so far? I am watching the show Just for Laughs and it is nice to have a chuckle in the morning. Maybe they should put that on at the max for those girls and maybe a laugh would help them cope better.

Last night I had a great sleep. My room was finally cool enough that I could get into a deep sleep. I slept until 9:00am, had a shower and got ready for the day. My highlight is seeing you. I am watching Gilmore girls; I had breakfast which was granola cereal and a banana. I spoke to

Bob who checked in on me to make sure nothing was pressing and to let me know he was off to the secure unit and would be back on Thursday, which would work out perfectly because I should have confirmation of the Self Management program and I should have my women's report and met with my program director so we can start discussing next steps moving forward.

Poor Mea is still under the weather. Bless Bob he asked if she was okay, he is such a kind person. Mea was called to the Duty office for a pee test. She could not supply one as she is dehydrated. I asked if I could get her some more jello which she took me up on. Last night she threw up the jello so I was shocked at the fact she wanted more. I told her she was like a super hero. She laughed at my comment which is a good sign to recover. Mea said she would get to health care and get some gravel. The gals downstairs were so welcoming this morning which makes being here much easier. I have noticed the swearing, cursing, and rude behaviour is starting to decrease around here which is such wonderful thing.

Thank you for our visit. I am not sure if you realize how much your visits help me get through the day. Your visits feed my soul and spirit. Thank you my son for keeping it real about how I am getting garnishee letters sent to the house, even though they have served me in jail and now they are sending garnishee letter to the house. I wonder if someone at the jail said something interesting, but even more interesting is the stupid Detective if they did their jobs correctly would see I don't have any shares in this company, but then again they have the wrong bank accounts for me at the wrong locations. That should be interesting to garnishee something that does not exist. I love what you said my son about them finding the shares. Wow how stupid does the lawyer have to be. They are garnisheeing two vehicles, when I only have one; they are searching for shares I don't own and the keep drawing attention to this incompetent matter. Hard to argue with stupid, and one day this matter will catch the attention of someone who will be able to make sense of this garbage.

The clouds tonight are so beautiful. One thing I have learned in jail is patience and to believe that "He" has something amazing in store for us. Everything will work out and the truth will come out.... very soon. There are many wonderful things in store for us. We will keep our Faith and just you wait and see 20XX will b a year to victories, vindication and true justice. I love you for your continued support, for your words of pure intelligence, your wisdom, your spirit in the entire gong, your keep it real and you point out the letter of stupidity in the entire matter. Why have laws when the crooks get away with all the crap, but they fail to realize there is a God who sees, hears and knows all and he knows the truth and all in good time it will come out. Something is brewing and something is coming out in the universe is shifting. Only a matter to time before they Law Society looks into the lawyer, the ICAA looks into the crooks Accountant, CRA looks into this company and sees all the corruption and tax evasion. It is all in God's hands.

I just got back from church with Whitey. Oh on my walk over Debbie told me she was been speaking to a lady about me. This lady takes Debbie on her visits and is her escort. Her name is Smith and she is excited to meet me. That was really wonderful of Debbie to get this connection rolling for me in hopes I will be matched and get escorted visits. Church was nice and funny how Whitey spoke of how we should be looking at the New Year which is so much about what I have been saying in my letters.

Thank you mom for printing off the case materials for my second assignment. So I wanted to tell you who went to church tonight. It was I, Debbie, Bridget and Susan so soon the whole house maybe going. It was really nice to see Susan there; we actually sat beside one another.

Just waiting for 6:00pm to hit so the football game would come on. So I am going to read until then. Oh yes, before I forget the storey we read in church was all about a group of men who did not have faith in god and how god would be with them and because they would not God waited until they would believe in him by punishing them for 40 years. Number 13 is where the story is. The message is that God will be with you to preserver and trust in your Faith.

Someone new moved in. She came from the Humming bird and I actually saw her at church tonight. Nice to have another faithful person.

The dynamics are changing yet again. My son our Washington team is winning.

Wow me as reading Joyce tonight and was she ever speaking to me. "We make the mistake of holding onto good things that keep us from the better things God has in mind for us." Joyce uses the analogy of a mountain and how God shows us the step one and we trust in him, so we obey and follow but he does not show us the entire mountain because then we might not follow so he shows us step by step and if we obey he will lead us to the top of the mountain, not easy by faith and trust in him and victory will be accomplished. We are moving up the mountain and soon we will be on the top.

"We must sacrifice self-will to have Gods will; we must sacrifice our way to find his way. Don't be afraid of sacrifice; it eventually sets us free to be all we desire to be."

"Character is developed during difficult times. Our call and desires are tested when we are told not time after time and still remain determined."

Joyce refers to Abrahain Lincoln and Thomas Edison in her book and all the sacrifices they dealt with and what the outcome was for them.

"Only determined people succeed." "God usually builds slow and solid, not fast and fragile."

Some really powerful messages tonight which was so perfect as I was so perfect as I was a bit frustrated about all the uncontrollable gong from the crooks, but then I read some of Joyce and what my son said and chuckled over their stupidity looking for something that does not exist and I do not have. Then God sent me confirmation that He was here with us and the nice guard I spoke to today taped on my door window and gave me a wave. I just know that we are so on the right track to something so amazing.

Well, I am going to have a shower and call you shortly. Keep the faith. We had a nice chat tonight mom on the phone. I hope my words of encouragement and the positive visualization left you inspired. My son it was nice that you ventured out with the boys. Hoping you get home at a respectable time. I love you both so much and I have the best support team leaders. You keep me in check, focused and full of love. I love you!

December 31, 20xx

Good morning and how are you both today? I feel a bit home sick this morning but I will just have to shake it off and focus on what I can accomplish today. I just finished eating my eggs and toast that Sally so kindly prepared for me. I have started my laundry and got cleaned up for the day. Are you watching the Russia vs. Canada game? It is very exciting. At 8:00am I will switch it over to Joyce Meyer for thirty minutes of God's word. Wow, my son this game is getting really heated. The score is 2-0 for Canada in the first period.

I figured that after Joyce and while watching the hockey game I could tackle my assignment #1 of the Civil Criminal Justice Course. Next week when we don't get to see each other every day I will print them out and then I will send them off to you to forward on to the University. Last night I had some weird dreams, but I have heard that is common in here.

Joyce's message is to "finish" what you start. Instant gratification and the harvest in the middle and glory in the end. Different between the flesh and the spirit. God will give us the break through. Oh wow, just as Joyce said to me finish what you started a sign came that said Happy New Year on the TV. This spoke to me that God is with us during the 20XX year. Many wonderful break threw will be taking place.

The flesh is a gamble; the spirit will do something over and over and will get huge rewards. If you take God's hand he will walk with you and deliver you. I am going to finish what God has chosen me to do. What a beautiful sunrise. Well I am finished my laundry and Joyce is over so now I will finish my assignment. I have set my alarm for 11:30am to give you a call. Chat with you in a bit.

Yes, finished assignment #1 and now I am going to call you. Happy days!

Wow just watched the hockey game now, but good thing you did not stay out too late last night my son. Exciting to see you tonight and not the same as us being together full time but we will b soon and man will we appreciate our lives so much more. There will be more hugs and kisses. I love you both and every day I am so grateful for your support and love.

This afternoon I helped make dinner. I learned how to make pizza from scratch so when I get out we can make homemade pizza. Maybe God is leading me to a restaurant business or chef position but I am accumulating some new receipts to have my list of things I have learned in jail. I am so excited to see you tonight. Today was such a nice day that I got me thinking that in April I will get visits outside of here to see you so it gave me hope for the next season change. January and February will be busy months March and April will be busy months and then May will be a month of great possibilities and June will be a month full of Glory!

I want to get this letter in the mail before our visit, so I wish us all great health, great wisdom, great new beginnings, great victories and most of all love.

Happy New Year and here is to the 20XX and new beginnings. Xoxooxo all my love.

January 1, 20xx

Good morning my son and mom. Happy 20xx wow the first day of the New Year how exciting. Funny how I am watching Cinderella story. Maybe ours will turn out the be the same ending a very happy ending.

After we spoke last night I read some of the highlighted pages from Joyce Meyer which reconfirmed and further inspired me, but thank you for sending it in with my pen pack. The girls were up past midnight so it was an ear plug last night but I did see the 12:00am so I said a prayer and made a wish.

The sun is out today and the temperature is mild. A nice guard just popped by to give me a smile which is so nice. I keep looking at my vision board and think that this will soon be a distant memory and the vision board will be the new reality.

Thank you for sending in the case materials for my assignment #2, I will complete that one this week. I hope your shift at work is going great and you are having some good laughs. I will call at 1:15pm and see you at 5:00pm. I have to remember to let go of the good in order to receive the great that God had in store for us. I just get tired of evil, bad and wrong getting away with things, but one day the truth will come out and that is in God's hands, but he is not getting any young, the crook I mean, and should be really starting to repent over all the wrong he has done and doing.

The gals are dragging me to bingo at 1:00pm so I will call you before to let you know and after when I get back to talk. Maybe I will be a winner! God sent me a sign this morning a feel good sign "Must love dogs" is on TV. Who is on my vision board who one of the inmates said I looked like plus it is a movie about starting over and find love. Either way it is a cute movie that is a pick me up.

Bingo was a lot of fun. I did not win a bingo but I did win a numbers draw, a bag full of goodies, a folder for my course materials, some facial wipes, buff puffs, crunch and munch, lip balm, pop, a stamp for $1.55, shampoo, juice, yogurt raisins but most of all a lot of fun.

I am excited to hear about your day's events. See you in a bit. Bingo will be an event we will do when I get out. Another day closer to being with you both and I loved our visit tonight. I thank you so much for coming and visiting me and playing cards and spending time with me. I am a bid disappointed in certain people who I thought would be more supportive, but that may have been just because they were busy for the holiday and family commitments, so hopefully the New Year will bring forth some signs of their support. Thank goodness for you both and for other family and friends who have shown their unconditional support? I love you both so much and I pray for you each and every night. All my love.

January 2, 20xx

Good Wednesday morning to my son and mom. How are you doing this fine mild morning? Last night the usual loud girls were up. I have showered, poured myself a cup of java, and collected my assignment and case materials to review. Tomorrow since we can't have a visit being Thursday and that is when the gals from the max get their visitation time, I will go to the recreation room and type as much of my assignment out. Joyce Meyer will be coming on shortly, which is such a wonderful way to start the day, especially in here. I love you both and will call you at 11:30am.

Joyce's message is pay day is coming. Reap what you sew. When you do what is right you will have a reward from God. Sometimes it can take a long time in some situations. Do what is right because it is right, pay day is coming. The truth will come out, these crooks can't hide forever. Look at how far you have come with God. The one who knows the most has to do the right thing first. I am going to do what is right because it is right. Time with god in the morning to get you in the right mind set is hugely important. Today is going to be a great day and it is one day closer to being with you.

Matthew 7:12 "do what's right because it is right". Joyce's message was great ways to start my day I pray you are both having a wonderful morning also.

Wow, I was quiet impressed with my assignment as I read the case point in my essay I had used before when reading the case, maybe law is my path. I completed the Joyce Meyer book and yet another great read from her. One story she share is about how her and her husband Dave, had been wronged and treated unfairly and unjustly in a certain situation so she found comfort in the word in particular Zechariah 9:12 said: "Return to the stronghold (for security and prosperity) you prisoners of hope; even today do I declare that I will restore double your former prosperity to you".

She goes on to say she did not give up hope and held the right attitude and that one day God would give her back double what had been taken from her in that situation. She said that almost a year later to that day, God did an outstanding work and proved Himself true to his promise by restoring double what had been unjustly taken from them and he restored it by the same people who mistreated them in the beginning. God's justice is sweat and to not fail to wait for it. Bless it be God's message. See how others are unjustly treated and vindication comes. Thank you mom for the powerful read. There were many wonderful messages and powerful lessons I will take away from Joyce's book.

What a fun visit. The scrabble queen mom, you rocked it out and so did you my son. We will have to play it again. One of the guards was telling me about another game called Banana you can get it at Chapters. She said it was like Scrabble. That could be a riot to play. I came back to the house and had a nice chat with Bridget. I love you both and miss you already. We will survive this and be grateful and the end of this journey for having gone through the journey and rewarded by the blessed God. You are my heart, you are my soul, and you are my inspiration to be and to be better each day. All my love.

January 3, 20xx

Dear mom and my son and how are you both this mild, sunny Thursday? I woke up at 6:30am and had a shower, got ready for the day, watched some news with was so depressing so I turned to some spiritual TV to get my Holy Spirit in tune for the day. Sally blessed me in poaching me some eggs which was very considerate of her. I am going to miss her, not her loudness but her kindness for sure. I walked to the mailbox to receive some jail mail. I have been placed on the waitlist for a course, I received my statement of funds and last night the guard told me that a letter from a girlfriend was being returned for it did not have a full name on it. Not sure what she was talking about but I will ask you to call her and let her know. It came from her business, but I will call you at 11:30am to check in and see how your day is going to discuss.

The morning has been quiet so I am going to read some of my correspondence materials. Gosh the gals in her have a lot of phlegm. It is really gross. Oh yes, I watched Joyce who filled my spirit to the max. Yesterday we were to have our monthly refills but they pushed it back until next Wednesday and today are canteen day. I don't need much just some little envelopes, ginger ale, gum, and Ibuprofen. I received a box of caramel popcorn which I gave to Susan for her help last week plus her son and her have sleepovers so they can enjoy that treat. Bob is on today so maybe I will see him.

Well I read unit 4 & 5 of the Civil materials and just made me mad at how unjust I was treated over the past seven years but now I have to let it go and trust in God to work and believe and have faith.

I caught the last three minutes of the junior's game and it was really good. I did see Bob and maybe we will be able to sit down and catch up. He said he was on until 11:00pm. That is a long day for him. He always lights up when he says hello to me which brings me so much joy. He is so positive and so kind which is so huge around here. I think this place could use more hope and optimistic vibes. It was nice chatting with your mom and seeking that your day was going well. I am a bit concerned about your migraines and vision and I wish I could do more to help. Please stay positive and try to relax, stay healthy and in the calm. God will bless us with the lotto winnings, or other magnificent blessings.

I will call you at 5:00pm and chat. Today was grocery day so again it is blessed with fruits. I still have some left over from last week so I better get eating it. Mea is great at making sure we eat healthy. She is a great house mom. I went over to the recreation room and typed out my assignment for Civil and the first couple of pages on the Assignment #2 for the course so on Monday I can take it to the teacher and have her print them off for me. At first I was thinking the computer would not co-operate but then it all came together. While in the recreation room, although, extremely loud I also had to content with a couple having a dispute. Even in jail couples fight. I won't disclose what the agreement was about but they asked me not to repeat it which I have not doing as I was more concerned about my assignment. Movement to the recreation room did not start until 7:00pm on Thursday evenings, otherwise, I could have it finished, but the other mates leave me alone except for the usual "hellos". I have the respect of all the mates in the jail and they leave me alone to get my work done. Respect is a valuable asset in here.

The house is changing dynamics again as Debbie is back. I asked how her visit was and she said it stared out fun but ended badly because apparently her boyfriend does not understand her. She can add a negative vibe to the house, so I will keep myself when I came back the house. Mea asked me how my visit was tonight; I told her I was in the recreation room typing up my homework. All the other mates are so pleasant and thoughtful so I will focus on them. I am sure Debbie is just frustrated and disappointed with her visit, especially since she put in a lot of effort to make her family visit time in the house special.

I will call you in a few moments. No Bob tonight. He must have been stuck in the max again. There was a slow movement earlier so that explains a lot. I so love you both and miss you so much. I am home sick for you, but will keep looking at being on day closer to you.

Thank you again for everything. All your support and love is my armour in here. All my love.

January 4, 20xx

Good morning and how are you today? I am going to head over and check the mail. I have showered, made my breakfast that I will eat while watching Joyce Meyer. I was going to go and talk to the ladies at Corcan but they just reported no movement to that area until further notice, so I will go next week then. I asked her if she would write a letter for my file before she leaves for her vacation. One of the staff is taking some time to travel and I would love to have something in writing from her to support my file.

Joyce spoke to me again today about patience and how not to give up. "End result is worth the pain". Diligence, hard work, doing the right think, waiting on God and prayer. To be patient about growth. Do you have a plan for personal growth? Where are you gifted to extend it to others? I would say personal growth could be the same as setting goals.

Me growing me: John Maxwell was on Joyce Meyer's today and his points were these: 1) Law of intentionality the spiritual time with God and making time to do anything, I am going to do this. 2) Law of awareness, knowing yourself and finding your gifts and passion and growth those are your strengths and attitude to make your choices. 3) The Law of reflection allows growth to catch up with use, that growing out of our experiences and elevated experiences, what did you learn? Pulling the good out of you experiences.

Joyce and John spoke to me today. Oh yes in my mailbox was an acceptance to complete a Construction course. Yes another goal I can check off my goal while I am in here. I ran into a mate from programs and she said she had moved into the new house and things were much better for her. Thank goodness. It is nice to walk in the mornings and spread some good mornings and positive smiles to set everyone off on a good note.

Susan has the PFV with her son this weekend. She has not seen him in many months, so she is so excited and I am so happy for her. I could not imagine not seeing you my son for months. Heck, not speaking to you guys when I first arrived here was terrible. I could not even image how they feel. All my love.

My goal today is to read Unit 7 and 8 of the correspondence course. As I completed my readings Bridget is moving to another house. There is never a dull moment in jail and Susan's ex-husband has decided not to bring her son in for a visit and instead of talking about it he just did not show up. I felt terrible for her and for her son. Just a terrible even. Making me even more grateful for you both.

Thank you for a terrific visit tonight and it was so wonderful to see you there my son. Gosh do I ever miss being with you each day. I miss the quiet, I will be so happy to return to the quiet. As I was leaving tonight I walked with another lady from programs and I asked her if she received her report from the program lady yet and she told me "nope" but she ran into the instructor and she told her the report would be done this week. The person who inputs it was away on holidays.

The guard tonight was not new but returning after two years, she seems very nice. I told her she would see you guys a lot. I am glad Apple was out tonight for a visit and even more grateful she is enjoying the new house she is in. The girls at the house said it seems fine at first but then they start to test you and push your buttons. There are two girls from there who have a negative perception of the house, but that could be their experience I am just grateful Apple is happy.

I wish Bob and I could meet up so I could catch him up but I guess all in good time. Well I am going to get my PJs on as I am really tired. I pray Bridget is adjusting to her new house. Sally is out on January 9, January 16 I have first aid, January 21 I have a construction course, you have Taxation January 23 and I have to get two assignments out and start my big one which is worth 70% of my grade and other one for 30% of my other grade. Wow, blink and January will be gone.

I love you both and I am forever grateful for you both. All my love and forever and ever. I will call you at 1:15pm tomorrow. God blessed me today with some visions of places and event that we have attended. I think he is just reminding me that he is with us.

January 5, 20xx

Good morning to you both. I checked the mail but nothing and I walked the yard for a bit to get some fresh air and exercise. This morning was a bit chilly so I will go out later again. I was listening to my walkman and the song "we are the champion", came on which was very inspiring. I am having breakfast now watching "Night at the Roxbury", oh I just changed the channel and "The Help", is on another channel. Wow just some great movies on. Wayne will be calling this week hopefully he commits and follows thru.

I will call you at 1:15pm, my son I pray you have a wonderful shift at the kennel, before you had off to your other job. I am so proud of you more than words can say. I am proud of you both and I am again so grateful.

Bob came by for the 10:00pm count and I mentioned to him about the program. He told me he would look into on Monday and get back to me. At 2:00pm I will head up to the main house and finish typing out the assignment so I can get the teacher the disk to print out this assignment and get it in the mail.

Well I achieved and completed the typing, proof reading and editing of both my assignments. Wow, was it ever loud in the recreation room. Too many loud people in one room really wear on a person's patience. God is teaching me and testing me.

I signed up for another course. This is another Construction course. So hopefully I can add this to my accomplishments. I will see you at 5:00pm mom and my son you at 6:30pm when you get off work. I love you both so much and hold you in my prayers. All my love.

January 6, 20xx

How are you both today? How did you sleep last night? Mine was okay. He usual every two hours flashlight in your face and the stomping up the stairs, but at least I could sleep in a bit well until 9:00am. Then I showered, did my laundry, and wrote to you. Gilmore girls are on and Sally is making breakfast. Gosh I am actually missing her loudness and all. I have found I can take the loudness over the rude, cursing and negativity.

Thank you for waiting an hour last night to see me. Seems that the bullying of certain races is a common factor in certain houses. Other mates have experienced this also, but I appreciate you staying to see me. I also appreciate you my son coming after working two jobs. You must really love me. I am blessed. You two make the justice I am trying to achieve worthwhile.

Celebrate new challenges was on "Gilmore girls". Horrible Bossed is on the movie channel. MMMM eggs, hash browns and sausage for breakfast. Yummy! I will see you at 1:00pm for our visit.

Good to laugh at our visit. Wow you two are such a bunch of fun. You are right my son my focus will be on vindication which is coming. I will drop off my assignment to have them printed out with the teacher and do my outline for my other assignment. That is a huge assignment worth a huge amount of my grade but the outline is very important and worth 5% but it will get me thinking about my assignment. This big one is a 20 page essay and I have a 15 page essay of the other course, so in sum a couple of huge papers to write,

It is nice to have the sun come out. I will go to church tonight to see if Bridget is there and get full of the Holy Spirit. The last sermon was fun so I want to see if this one is better, my own readings do more for me then a group may, but I will try one more time and see.

I spoke to Debbie about Wednesday and she told me about how this lady can take mated home for their visitations as an escort. You have to do so many with a guard and then a qualified escort can take you. This reintegrates you back into society.

One of the guards said she will try to call me up tonight to teach me how to play this game so I could teach you. As I was attending church tonight, Whitey spoke of how he would like to start to study the bible which was one of my goals while in here. I had planned on spending some quality time with God and really devoting my time to getting to know and reading of the bible. Even though we have read and received Christ, it would be nice since I have the time to really spend time with reconnecting with my faith. Whitey is going to spend time each Sunday going over the different sections of the bible, so like a bible study. I did find out that tomorrow night will be the mentor night also, so that is more good news. I don't understand how people can be bored in jail. I am so blessed to be open to all these wonderful new experiences. I dragged Ray to church with me tonight. I think she really enjoyed it, so I will keep motivated her to come with me.

At 6:00pm I am going to walk the yard for some fresh air and exercise. It is really nice out tonight. Well I was just called to V&C and the kind guard showed me how to play this really cool card game. Bridget was also called up so her and I got a chance to talk and every Sunday after church we will walk the yard and share our faith with one another. Cathy came back from an intense work out that will be here all week, so she is going to drag me to one of this session to get a major workout. Sounds like fun!

Anyways, the card game is really fun so get ready. I had a wonderful conversation with the guard also. She is such a nice person. If you respect the guards they will respect you. I don't know if it is because the guards have read my report and know that I am innocent and are showing me favour, but I will think it is because I am respectful to them and therefore they are respectful to me.

Cathy and I just walked up to the main house to purchase some love cards for Valentine's Day, so I can send you some love out.

I did my bedding and washed it all, so my sheets are all clean and fresh. It is only 8:00pm and wow it seems like so much has already happened. So as I was running to the main house to meet the guard another mate stopped me inquire about our house and how the other mates were in the house. I replied that they were all great as I have no troubles with any of them. She told me she had put in a request to be moved to our house. Our house is the only minimum house. When you first arrive you go to a medium house until they assess you and then you move to the minimum house, it is like you last step before you exit. Well I was blessed with going straight into a minimum house, which was unheard of. Well by the time I had returned from playing cards with the guard, this mate had moved in.

So as I was collecting my laundry from the dryer, Susan came out of the bathroom complaining of how the bathroom smelt like "piss". The guards had brought in the new person and I don't think Susan knew but then again I don't think she cares about anyone but herself.

The guards came by with the newbie and one guard stopped by my room to chat. I am having a brain fart but she is so nice to tell me her son is turning 7 and how fast they grow up and how she sees my son and how wonderful he turned out. Wow that was so wonderful. Are you paying them to say that because I have been getting so much fabulous feedback about you two... so fabulous but then again you are so fabulous. The guards are actually commenting on how they hope their children turn out like you my son. You are true gift from God.

The mates in the house are really good about making sure everyone gets the treats. For example I was getting my comforter out of the dryer and one mate Linda told me there was spinach dip and berretta, so I made sure Sam knew. Kindness goes far so why not pay it forward. Funny would it not be ironic if jail was the place of kindness. I am going to watch some TV until the guards to the count at 10:15pm and then I will call you. The count is actually at 10:00pm, but by the time they get here it is 10:15ish.

I love hearing your voice and seeing you. All my love to you both.

January 7, 20xx

Good morning to you both. How was your night last night and how did you sleep? Last night was a noisy night. There were some new guards on training so that meant more feet in the house. A couple of mates had their doors knocked on, which for a light sleeper would wake you up, but anyways it could be worse.

I took my disks over to the main house. The teacher was away so if left my envelope with paper and the two disks in it with her assistant, whose name I think was Janice. I watched Joyce and she discussed revelations and deception and the non-sense in the world today. How to be Godly is an ungodly world. Stand up and suffer for what you believe in. Suffering for the righteousness and for what is right and true. Well, I am going to start to work on my next assignment. And yes, I have to suffer for righteousness and the greater good. God will justify and vindicate. Thank you for suffering with me.

I went to make myself some toast and the new mate who is very old came into the kitchen and started tell me about her life story. But not to sound cold hearted but I have no interest in anyone's story. I just wanted to stay out of the drama and gossip and I have heard she can be trouble maker so regardless of her story she needs to talk to her workers about her situation and mind her own business just like I mind my own business. Study time. I don't ask why people are here I am just trying to make the most of my time.

I just go back from seeing the program instructor and getting my first report while in jail. It was all great. We confirmed the self management which she told me not to be alarmed as they would be on session 6 of the 12 week session but I would just continue along until they started back at one and get all 12 session completed. You have to take it on the outside but why not take it in here also. It was nice to the see the other ladies from program but no Apple as they are only allowed to leave their house on certain times.

Tonight I went up to the main house and engaged in a bible study group called Connecting streams. Three lovely ladies come from an Alliance church and share pray and stories. Once I get my escorted visits they can take me to church, but they were very kind women. It was wonderful to get to meet new people both in the church circle and other mates of faith. I then walked the yard for a while which felt good. I am going to shower and get into my PJs. Sally made cookies so I will put mine away for a rainy day. I am going to miss that loud girl. I was able to see Bridget tonight at church. Speaking of church they ladies close in pray and they asked if I would like to send out a prayer for you two. One of the ladies said I did not look like I had a 19 year old son, and she said she has a son the same age. But you will always be our babies. I will call you at 10:45pm when you get home from work to see how your day went. God's peace!

January 8, 20xx

How are you today and how did you sleep? I slept like a rock. The guards were kind as to not flash the high beam flashlight in my eyes and there was no knocking on doors. Thank you kind guards! We had a house meeting last night over the cookies Sally made. Someone of course took more than their share, yet again. Cathy was the last mate to return to the house so she would be without, so I gave her mine. God bless Mea for she is so tired of one person eating others and I think she was done with this person. Well, during the meeting the person wanted nothing to do with the meeting, but I found out that Debbie had set aside before the meeting dinner for me because she said I did not eat enough meanwhile, one person was throwing out her food. Gong show drama. We have a person eating others sugar treats and that same person is throwing out her healthy food.

Anyways, I am going to check the mail and enjoy Joyce Meyers. No mail. I am not sure if I told you the mate moved in on Sunday has moved back to her house so things are much better. She was the old mate who was really nosey. She got into a fight at her house so they had to put her somewhere, which was this us and now she has gone back to her house.

Joyce's message today was avoiding deception not to blend in. God had the power. Isaiah 10 1:- and 5:1, 5:23 spoke on this topic. Joyce spoke about the first amendments and some court rulings. She spoke of setting precedents and some of the silly Judge. Everyone taking away her right for their own rights. Some of these judges need a little more religion in their lives after all they sit with a sign behind them saying "In God we Trust". Stand up for our rights and God will stand up for you. Making sure you are affecting others they are no infecting you, stay focused and God will walk with you. Stand for what we believe in. I am going to read Isaiah before I start my assignment #2. Do you know what "woe" in the bible means? It is a heated warning.

After the visit I will tell you about Cathy and her visit yesterday. It all ended up positive but the struggle she has had to endure would blow your mind. Jail had opened my eyes to others struggle and how they are dealing with situations out of their controls.

I went downstairs to make some toast for breakfast and Debbie told me she watched Joyce Meyer this morning. Last night at church I mentioned how I just finished Joyce's book and how others were turning into her show. Funny for me is if everyone in the jail turned onto Joyce and how movement would not commence until after she was over.

5:23 Isaiah spoke to me especially about the bible and taking away justice from the righteous man.

My son the song is called "my life" from Eminem and 50 cent. I don't want you to rush here for a few minutes and risk an accident. I would rather you be safe and we chat on the phone after work. This too shall pass and we will survive this injustice, but I won't risk our safety. I will see grams tonight and fill her up to speed and she can catch you up.

Sally is to leave tomorrow, so I will step up and do one meal a week, which is the least I can do as there is one person who will not cook at all. I did not want to cook while I was in here and would pull my weight in doing the dishes more often but we are running out of cooks. Today I finished reading the case materials for my assignment. Funny the case I choice was the only one of the three where the judge overturned and orders a new trial.

Tonight there is a beautiful sunset. Funny also how things in life are looked at differently from this side of the bars. It looks like God put me in this room so I could enjoy the sun for most of the day and the awesome sunsets. Well, I will call you tonight my son at 10:45pm. Hope you are having fun at work and mom I will see you in a half an hour. I love you!

Thank you mom for our visit. I will put in a request to attend the January 23 taxation appointment. The night was quiet; God will bless us, keep the faith and stay strong and positive.

January 9, 20xx

Good morning and how are you today? The weather channel said that we are in for some snow this week and should reach use later today. I am just waiting for them to call movement to go to the main house and pop in a letter, put in a request for the January taxation and to check the mail. Thanks mom for calling the Bailiff and telling him that for the fourth time this "Order" has been delivered. Can you say harassment? This is pure evil, but then again so is everything that this crook and his company are doing and done. The truth is coming out so stay in faith and strong. I am going to watch Joyce and fill my spirits. Joyce's topic was on we learn so we can do. Well we all have a purpose and that is so true, she also talked about deception and compromise.

Blessed Bob just popped in to chat and funny how I just put in the request about the taxation appointment. He will find out about how that process will work and get back to me along with what is to be in the community support letters. I was told to put in for days we would like to have a sleepover in the PFV so we could get that booked. He is so wonderful and he tells me I have a lot of kind words being said which is so inspiring. Debbie and I had a lovely talk about church functions happening tonight. I think I made her day in us chatting about the "Big guy" and I think I filled her with the Holy Spirit. She seems to have a skip in her step as she headed off to chat with Whitey about tonight's event. Nice to see how kindness can spread just as fast as evil and I prefer to spread the love and the light to others.

Even checking the mail in the morning to spread a good morning and a smile to sent one person off to spread that is such a blessing and blessed feeling. I feel blessed and I know we will be blessed and I pray for you each day. You are in my heart and my prayers.

The house is quiet so I will start my assignment and chat with you at 11:30am. Detective came by to see me again and to give me an order to discharge the restraint order in the revocation order. I told him that the order he served me on December 14 has now been served to me four times including my house which he was surprised. Good thing we are paying tax money to have a Detective serve me. Anyways, I was full of the spirit and will mail you this stuff if you could call and tell them to stop harassing me. Funny how he keeps checking in on me and to see how I am doing. Why not just sent the process server? Almost like he has a guilty conscience. He knows I did not do this crime; it is evident in his police report, massive errors and omissions. He told me he was very sick over Christmas and how terrible his Christmas was. Well that is what happens when you have evil all over you and you hang out with the crooks.

Thank you for following up on the phone call to Sharon. I put in a request to Bob to get the number for the ombudsmen so we can have this harassment from these crooks stopped. I also put in to see if we could book the PFV for February 9th weekend so I will keep you posted.

I popped in the mail the gong I receive today and was chatting with a worker here. She is fabulous and we were discussing Christmas and how hers was and how mine was a new experience but I was so grateful to be able to share it with you and she admires my outlook. I told her that you have to stay positive and in faith and have a great outlook with hope. She said she likes how I embrace everything especially when I told her you make of life what you are given. It was nice to see her.

We were blessed with hygiene today. Where were take our empties and receive new refills. I received shampoo, conditioner, laundry soap, deo, and ivory soup, so tomorrow I can save money as I don't need to purchase these items.

My son I did not want to ruin your day and tell you about the Detective showing up again, but I will tell you after work as I will never keep secrets from you and I will always tell you the truth.

Trust and have faith as it is belief that gets us there, god has something so amazing in store and it is coming. Keep your faith.

Well, Sally said she went in front of the board today and she said she was a nervous wreck. This is her stat release date; it can now take the board 14 days to complete her paperwork. She will be shipped off to another jail which is closer to her home. She will then have 8 hours to make contact with her PO on the outside. She laughs at me and my questions; well this is my first rodeo. Bob came by at count. He must have been in the max for the afternoon, but it was great to see him.

I will call you at 5:30pm to check in and chat and then head to church group at 6:00pm. My son I will call you at 8:15pm to chat with you.

Wow what a great church group tonight. Lots of great energy and great people. Debbie told such a blessed story about how she first met me and after words the leader told me I was such a blessing here at the jail. The other leader confirmed I would be attending Alpha on Sunday which is another bible study. This is one that Max had told me I should join as I would enjoy it. I am getting rich in God's word and on God's path. I love you both.

Sally should find out soon about her departure. I gave her a hug and she laughed at me and said I was crazy. All my love and you already knew I was a bit crazy. Xoxoxox

January 10, 20xx

Good morning my son and my mom. How are you this morning? I am going to the main house and see if the teacher will print off my assignment, I dropped off a letter to Whitey and checked mine and Mea's mail.

As I was getting into the shower Susan came up stars to wake up Cathy and then Susan said good morning to me. Getting out of the shower and Mea said good morning. The house is changing slowly but surely. If you stand your ground people will come to you. Did you know Joyce was a bookkeeper? Joyce spoke about being read each day with God. I am working for God and what a great place to do so but in jail. Funny how I have not changed while in here, I changed before I got here, but it was so wonderful to spread my spirit with others and observe the change.

I had such a laugh this morning. As I was waiting for movement along with Susan, Debbie and Ray I entered the room where I was greeted with a nice good morning from Ray and a warm good morning back to her. I told Ray that I tried to wake her up for the church function last night, but she was out sawing logs. Susan said she heard some banging at 3:00am and thought what the heck the guards were doing so she went to the kitchen and found Ray and Sally making porage. Gosh I still can't believe this house and all the funny situations that take place.

Last night at church a mate broke down and expressed in words about how in Cuba, where she comes from, how her people are starving and how grateful we should be even in jail we are provided with so much. I appreciated how she said this as I thought I was the only one.

Thinking of the homeless and how they have nothing to all the items we have in jail. Food, shelter, clothing, hygiene, school, work and these church functions are really enjoyable and a chance to hear others stories and I hope to be the light in all this darkness as God works in me.

Even getting the mail I do purposely in the morning to say hello and good morning to maybe send someone an up spirit to pass on. If we have to be here let's do it in a Godly manner.

Just so you know that I still miss you terribly and long for the day we are together. I will fill my days with productive things and being and bring a new spirit to jail. I will be the best at whatever God has set before me and make Him and you proud.

I checked in to see if my assignment had been printed out but the teacher was not there the other teacher was but she did not know anything about what I was talking about so I politely confirmed she has passed on the envelope and if I don't get anything on Monday I will put in a request to check on it.

I am going to read some of the bible passages from last night and get some breakfast. I love you with all my heart. I think we should write a cook book when I get out and have all the proceeds go to the homeless or create an organization of some sort to help and keep people out of jail.

Ephesians 5:9-12 speaks of walking in righteousness, goodness and truth and expressing the darkness and has no fellowship.

Ya Sally is getting out today at 4:00pm, she will be taking the bus to the station and then off to her home city. I pray she has a wonderful next chapter in life. The other mates told her yesterday she would have to stay until Monday next week, but I had a feeling she would be gone today. There always going to be one who wants to rain on your parade. I am so happy for her as I did with Max. I wish them all the best.

Before I left for programs I gave Sally a hug and told her to write. She would not but I like to leave that door open. Every time someone leaves the house the energy shifts. Mea said we would receive letters that we could not understand or pieces of letters from Sally as a form of humour. We laughed and that helped to break the sadness. We are happy she is getting out, but sad also.

My son I love that you had such a great day with your little buddies at the kennel. When I spoke to grams I could hear our cat talking. My son she has so much to say. Did grams tell you about Pastor Ken? Glad to hear he is better and keeping us in his prayers and with the church.

The program today was really great. It is very similar to the other program. The initial class began with everyone sharing. I spoke to Sam to let her know what happens programs stays in programs, so she will feel comfortable speaking. After class, the instructor and I spoke and she asked me about how things are going so I told her about the wonderful church groups and how to day receiving blessed new about my Pastor's health. I chuckled about what she might have said if I told her about the Detective visiting me again. Overall, it was nice to see friendly faces and get to know some new ladies more in-depth.

Now the house has two empty rooms and blessed them are both downstairs, so no new mates upstairs as I am kind of used to my neighbours. I wrote to Wayne again and another friend today so I will pop them in the mail on my way over to the main for the aerobics class.

Today is Thursday so we received our fruit. This week we received 3 bananas, 2 apples, 2 oranges and a pear. Sally's were left on the table in the common area bowl. When I got back to the house Mea was baking. She told me she making, the cupcakes for Ray as Sally had said she would do them for Ray's birthday which is not until next week. So now Mea is doing it. I am not sure why so far in advance, but should be interesting to see how many are left.

Oh yes, back to the instructor she told me she was starting ballroom dance classes with a guy she started dating five weeks ago. I told her about how my son and I did the ballroom dance class after my boyfriend and I broke up. Something we have in common. Not too many mates who know how to ballroom dance.

Cathy made beans and hotdogs for dinner. Yummy! My son these hotdogs were like the baseball hot dogs. As we sat at the table Cathy asked if I was still going to aerobics class and I said "yes". She let me know she may have a visit but otherwise she would work out with me. We are going to do a work out together during the day which won't interfere with our visitation times. It is more of a muscle building routine, and I think she just wants someone to do it with her and keep her motivated. Well she came to the right person. Right now we have no movement as someone from another house was taken out, so as you know the jail stops until that situation has been dealt with and who knows for how long.

Amazing I come to jail to full fill my wheel which I will have even more of when I get out now that I know about it. God has blessed me with the ability to learn new things and meet new people. He is making me diverse.

Today was hygiene canteen where we get $4.00 from the government, but I was blessed yesterday with hygiene refills so in two weeks I will have $8.00 in that pot so I can purchase a more expensive shampoo and conditioner and treat my hair. I may have to ask Mea to color my grays but I will ask you when I see you if it is necessary.

There was just an announcement that movement has been delayed. Movement to health care just started but then it was put on hold again. So something has started up again. So back to watching Duck Commanders and having a laugh.

Holy what terrific work out! We finally had movement and all ended well. My legs were shacking. The mate who ran the session was amazing. You have seen her in V&C during our visits. She gets visits from her boyfriend. She is also in my program. She could not believe I was 41. After class she asked if I would be coming on Saturday session or did I have visits. I told her we had visits during the day but yes I would love to do this class again. Cathy did not go as she worked out on her own during the day. We are going to do her work out tomorrow together. After I was taking the medicine ball back and chatting with other mates, the instructor asked to spread the news about this class so more would attend.

After Sally left, Sam now spends her time downstairs. We were all waiting for movement and I asked Ray if she wanted to come to aerobics, Mea laughed and asked if I was trying to hurt her. I said no, but I told Sally I would look after Ray. I was washing my dishes after having my apple with cinnamon and Ray was sitting on the couch I asked her if she was missing Sally and sure enough she was. Mea made cupcakes so I took mine and hers to the rooms so no one will eat ours. I am doing laundry, and watching a scary movie.

I love you both and miss you terribly. I long to see and be with you and I am certainly suffering from home sickness. Unless someone has experienced jail, it is indescribable the feeling of emptiness.

January 11, 20xx

Good day to you both. January 11 today and I am just watching Joyce and she is brining light into darkness. Matthew 5:16 speaks to this matter. Joyce also talks of being in peace and enjoying your life and not to let others make you unhappy. Don't change and they will change and to have the power of God. The voice of conscience and the Holy Spirit was discussed and to obey the Holy Spirit. I learned something amazing today about on over anxious conscience and how if you have been abused your shame will bring out the guilt when finding God. God has his eye on me and has something amazing to show me just as he has his eye on you!

I walked over to the main house and dropped off a request for Whitey and a reminder. Debbie told me this morning about an angle in her who teaches piano and vocal lessons. So I put in a request to get my name on the list for piano lessons and to check out the mentor positions. I receive a wonderful letter from a family member. I love you both and I am just about to start my assignment. I will chat with you at 1:15pm and see how your day is going.

I just got back from Whiteys office where he blessed me with news that the lady teaching piano has an opening and another lady has dropped out so I will get the spot. This afternoon I start my lessons. Also, he provided me with a number to pass on to Pastor Ken so that he can come in for visits but also to get him cleared so he can be my escort. It was Whiteys number for them to get connected. He also signed me to receive a mentor I can meet. He asked me how I was doing and how my time was going, so I told him a brief snap shot of the University correspondence, connecting streams and bible studies, programs, construction courses and of course my blessed visits with you. Whitey told me God is watching over me and I told him I have an angel who has my back and wraps his wings around me to give me hugs. I encouraged the new girl in our house to embrace everything this place has to offer and I will try each day to be a blessing. I will call you at 1:15pm to chat.

Piano was so much fun. I learned the keys and the scales so now I have to practice. I need to listen for my name every Friday well at least next Friday as the instructor is not sure at what time my regular lesson will be but she will figure it out. The great thing is I can teach you.

Cathy and I did her work out so now I am good to go on my abs and arms. Debbie and I have made a delicious dinner. Chicken stuffed with salsa, Greek salad and rice. So amazing! I passed on my apple and sugar and cinnamon treat to her. Debbie liked the idea and will try it.

I am glad you had such a great shift at the kennel and it sounds like those cuties keep you on your toes. Thanks mom for finding out the address to complain to regarding the Judge who keeps signing off on all my matters when they can only sign off once. Mea said it is s serious stupid what I have had to endure and I should get these guys, Judges, lawyers, police the whole bunch are being crooks that are the bad ones, and even the crooks are getting away. I told her about the ombudsman and how we only had provincial phone number that does us no good in a Federal pen. Gong! I was able to help Mea out and pass on Don's card as she need as personal injury lawyer. I could really promote Don's firm. Thank you my son and mom.

We all sat down for dinner and that was so nice. I was able to chat with the new girl Natasha, who we all call Nat, after dinner as she is the newbie and hopefully answered any questions. She was very turned off on programming but hopefully she will get inspired. I let her know I would answer any questions she had, but the other girls were so wonderful. I let her know that I would be going to work out tomorrow so she was welcome to come. I let her know that her kids and family could go to Wal-Mart to get their pictures done for their clearance, the library has some great reads, they gym is available and that if she needed anything I was here for her.

I have had my shower and just sitting in my big chair while using my desk chair for a foot stool writing my my loved ones. I love you and just wanted again to sincerely thank you for everything. I could not had done and continue to do this without your inspiration, you are my rock and my determination. I love you!

I will call you at 10:45pm and will write if anything transpires sooner. I am watching the Pink Panther with Steve Martin which is so funny because we were just talking about that movie last weekend. The hamburger part is so hilarious.

Oh am I so sore from working out. Well the "f" house was all sent to sag except for two people. That old lady who was in our house for a bit and a gal from programs. Sam just asked me if I would mind waking her up tomorrow which is not problem. Sam will have to go to work for the Holy Spirit as I was making myself some peppermint tea; she filled me in on her work detail.

What happened tonight was I closed my eyes for thirty minutes and tried to get rid of my headache which did not work so I took some Ibuphen and headed downstairs to make a cup of tea. Nat was in the living room and Mea came down to see what was going on. We all chatted for a while as I waited for the kettle to warm up. Cathy came into the house to tell of the "f" house news. After I had hot water I filled my thermos and that is when it hit me the feeling I get when I first arrived. I grabbed some elastic hair ties, some chap stick still in the rapper, a pack of peppermint tea and a set of ear plugs and headed downstairs to Nat's room. Linda had extended her kindness in giving Nat an envelope and a stamp, which I also offered to Nat, but Linda covered that. Nat and I chatted for a few moments and I let her know I would include her in what I was doing by giving her an olive branch. She commented on the loudness and I reassured her she would get used to it but to get a good night sleep was what I think the essential key to survival here is, hence the ear plugs. I told her if we could not move to the library she could borrow one of mine at least that would occupy Saturday as the library is open on Sunday. So I would take Nat on Sunday. I remember when Apple and I first arrived and how Mea, Susan, Max and May took us under their wings and how grateful I am to them, so to pay it forward to the other newbie's is such an amazing gift.

I will call you in one hour. I am so excited to see you tomorrow. I suggested to Nat to write to her family until she was able to talk to them on the phone, which hopefully will be soon or seeing them in visits. My heart breaks for these moms even if they did commit a crime they are still human. Maybe God wants me to leave this place more compassionate for others.

I love you both and can't wait to see you tomorrow. All my love.

January 12, 20xx

Good day to you both. How are you doing this beautiful sunny morning? I just came back from the mailbox where I received some jail mail saying I have to complete CAAT testing which is a mandatory part of the intake process. The sucky part is that it is next Friday during what would be my piano lesson. Wow are my muscles tender today. It was nice this morning to do something kind for someone else. I checked Ray's mailbox and brought her back some love mail from the outside and brought Debby's mail back to the house so she could continue to walk the yard with another girl. I set my alarm to wake up Sam so she would be up for work she really appreciated that. I am so excited for our visit to give you a big hug and kiss. I miss you and love you.

I was so glad to hear your voice and have a laugh. Before I got on the phone to you, Cathy and I had a quick nice chat about poking the bear. Mea cracked her tooth and Ray was having a sad day so I passed on the Joyce Meyer book and a hug. I will be dragging Nat and Ray to aerobics class tonight. No time for a pity party and I have to be a positive example for the others and that is that.

The Blindside is on, oh such a wonderful sign. I pray they call movement soon to V&C after their second count here, can't they count to 10 in here. I appreciate you both waiting for the visit and to see me. Poor Nat she could not get her call so I asked her again to come up and get some exercise. Mind, body and spirit should be the goal in here. I am so blessed to have you both. I have no idea what I would do without your support. All my love to you and my fuzzy baby…the cat.

At 6:00pm I am going to recruit as many mates to the gym for one aerobic workout. Sam asked me to wake her up tomorrow. I have no problems helping out other mates. We had a great workout and thank you mom for our talk. I know the truth will be coming out and the book will be published. I will continue to follow up and have Mr. Reck disbarred for all it takes in a number of times with other complaints to have this come to light. I seriously would not want to be his age and have all his sins before him as his day will come and to stand before God with what he has done to me and my family is scary. Ps there is a blog where we can write on.

I wrote to the Justice Association and I will go to the press if they continue to harass and intimidate me. I had a real pick me up I will tell you tomorrow. Mea has some kind words for me. Stay positive and strong, God is watching over us and it will all work out on his time. This just goes to show you how useless our legal system is, but it will all come out have faith. All my love and one day closer to being together again.

January 13, 20xx

Good morning and good wondrous Sunday morning. How are you this fine day? I did some praying last night and thought of what you had mentioned last night on the phone. I think you advise was perfect and I am going to wait until the universe catches up with God's intentions. I trust in God's word and everything will work out. I love you!

I will tell you about last night and Cathy's bed and my plant. Those silly girls broke into my room last night and moved the plant, they did not want to make a mess in my room, so kind but they did want to make a point they did know how to break into my room. Wow, they are really talented. The cops should recruit some of the criminals to help them out.

Tonight is Whitey's bible study and after is Alpha with our initial presentation.

I just got back to my room and made a cup of peppermint tea, I had such a full and wonderful day. So ...phew...and thank you for a wonderful visit. I met with Bob and I will meet with him again tomorrow. He asked me to write down my questions for tomorrow but we are now moving on to getting my body guard escorts. I will have more to tell you tomorrow. I have written my questions out to prepare for our meeting as his time is precious and to better utilize it. I hate being under time restraints to chat, especially when you don't know when the next meeting will be. Bob is so terrific about my case; God has blessed me/ us with him.

I came back tonight for count and Cathy and I got to talking and she told me about a book called "The Purpose Driven Life" that Whitey has in his office and that I should borrow and read, so after church Whitey told me about my mentor will be here on Wednesday at 5:30pm and gave me a copy of this book to borrow. Whitey has many resource materials we can borrow during our stay and so I will certainly be back for more. We had such an amazing church service and he explored Genesis Chapter 3 and I would do the book together when I get out.

In the book I borrowed you do a chapter each day and discuss so sure why not we can see how it goes. It is funny that as we sit around the mates look to m and want to know me from a religious, inspirational aspect. I ran back to the house after church and before Alpha to grab my water. The girls were so kind to have wrapped my dinner so I took a few bites and off to Alpha where I met some amazing leaders. They are so kind to bring in treats for the mates. Some of the mates only attend for the treats. I met the leaders and we enjoyed a movie call Soul Surfer and then had a prayer. It was nice to share fellowship with some wonderful people from the outside.

Oh sorry, back to Bob and he was asking about that guy who came in, well when I told him it was Detective; Bob is so confused as to why he is serving me at all. Bob is not impressed with how I am being treated and is having a difficult time processing this story, but the more he sees and hears the more he believes in my innocents. Why are they harassing me and what do I know that is still scaring them?

Back to Alpha, the church has members who will take on mate and pray especially for her. Wow can you feel that energy. I have my church, I have my family, and friends, I have connecting streams, I have Alpha and a special person praying for us and me, that is a lot of prayer energy going out into the universe and I may have forgotten some other avenues, but that is a great feeling to know you have prayer warriors on your side.

I love that even thought I am here that my positive energy is being noticed. My goal is to spread kindness is being met and contagious. I was not going to change my spirit and faith and in fact, it has been strengthened. I pray both had a wonderful evening and had a great steak dinner. Please never forget I am only strong because of and for you. You are my rocks, my inspiration and my being and God will provide us with an amazing outcome. He will bless us. All my love

I mailed the complaint to the Associate Chief Justice so fingers crossed someone will hear my plea.

January 14, 20xx

Happy Monday morning and how did you sleep last night? How is your day going? Thank goodness for the hockey season beginning because I have noticed the news is depressing, the reality TV is silly and the entertainment TV is so selfish, so yes to hockey. Gilmore Girls and the comedy channel and of course Joyce Meyer to get my day started.

Last night at Alpha I told one of the leaders it was my mission to get the jail to all watch Joyce Meyer in the morning to set everyone off on the right foot. Well, Joyce is coming on soon and then it is my day's mission to get my assignment #2 completed and ready for it to be typed. I hoped to get my other two assignments back from the teacher, so I can check it and hopefully mail it out. Bob said he would call me up today to chat. I have connecting streams at 6:00pm and my number one thing that gets my throw the day is my time with you both. I will call you at 11:30am.

I completed my assignment #2 for the Civil liberties and have been blessed with talking to Bob twice. He was on his way to get me an answer about January 23 and found that the PFV was booked for Feb 9 already. I told him to book for any visit weekend and you would work around the booked time, but the sooner the better. God bless him he was going to track down the teacher and see what was going on with my other assignments and disks. I will call you shortly to discuss. All my love.

Well, after our chat at 11:30am, I turned to the bible for some inspiration and Holy Spirit to fill me. As I said in our phone chat that the crooks can take all the assets that I worked two or three jobs to obtain. I did not steal a cent from them, so whatever they take from e now will be paid two fold from them. Funny how our system locks up the innocent and allows the crooks to steal. Vindication is coming! As long as we all stay healthy, strong and trust in God we will win. The truth is going to come out so we just need to be patient and sted fast.

I ran over the PFV form over to the main and God blessed me with running into Bridget. She greeted me with a big hug. After our chat my holy spirit was on the go so I saw Ray who was walking down the path almost to the circle with her head down, so I ran to cut her off and greet her with a "do you need a hug?" she said "yes" so I gave her one. She smiled a big smile and I sent her off to enjoy her day at work. Gosh just going downstairs waiting for the movement call makes me laugh these girls are so funny. Sometimes the small things in live put the biggest smiles on your face.

Yesterday, Bob uses the phrase, "your lawyer threw you under the bus", and so Bob gets it as do so many others. Well if everyone stopped shopping at the crooks store, he would go out of business and that would be justice just starting. I love you both and a smile they cannot take from me. I refuse to allow them to take my spirit...that is for you and God.

At program the phrase of encouragement was from Maya Angelou an activist, "I can be changed by what happens to me but I refuse to be reduced by it."

This is so true. The program instructor put this up and she said to me, using my name this is so true. It was as if she picked the message for me, so kind and today I needed to get a new booklet to continue to write to you and this verse was right there as if to bless me.

A quick note about my day, well the rest of it was like this I met with Bob, had a lovely chat with Cathy and she wanted me to read her information on her case and get my insidght to her rebuttal and we discussed her journey. We had a yummy dinner. Cathy will be using the left over's to make a Sheppard's pie. I spoke to mom and she told me about the bank, I went to connecting streams and received a gift which was a book by Katie Souza based on her jail time. The volunteers are interested in my book. Such a blessing I found this wonderful bible study group. Debbie asked if I would take over her bible study on Wednesdays when she is gone, so we chatted a bit in my room. Oh yes, earlier today Mea called Don's law office and he is sending someone out in a week or so to take up her matter. She is so thrilled to get some help. As back to Debbie as funny we both have the same parole officer who is nice, but there is so few staff that there is a lot of overlap. I just had a shower and sorry for neglecting you my son, I will fill you in tomorrow and she can pass on the information.

When I was talking with Cathy I asked her if she worked out at 4:00pm count, she said all the guards see is me laughing or smiling. Cathy has had difficult road and hopefully I can help her with her appeal and she be granted a new hearing. I love you both so much and you mean the world to me. One day closer to being with you again. xoxoxox

January 15, 20xx

Good Tuesday morning and today is all about Carpe Diem which means to seize the day. Wow is the wind blowing out there today. Please drive safe out here I headed over to the main house and received my assignments and disks back. I spoke to teacher's assistant from the school when I was getting my assignment back and I asked about the CAAT testing. She said if I could prove I graduated me would not have to do the CAAT test. I will tell you where my transcript is and if you could bring it in that would be so helpful.

As I was watching Joyce Meyer she did the scripture from Genesis chapter 3 with the serpent, which Whitey talked of on Sunday church. Bob just stopped by and gave me a piece of paper with the names and addresses of the church groups and filled in the blanks for him. He said he would call me up later to answer my questions. I am so blessed to have an awesome team.

It is Ray's birthday and I am going to have to give her a big hug when I see her.

Thank you mom for the phone call, I am so grateful for all you and my son are doing and continue to do. I will stay strong as long as I know you both are strong. I will stay healthy knowing you are healthy. Don't let the devil steal your day. God has an amazing plan and a wonderful future for us. With faith you will never have fear!

I am going to read over my assignment and bless the teacher for printing this off for me. I am going to do some letters to my outside supporters and my loved ones. At 2:30pm the Lutheran church will be coming in and tonight mom you and I have a visitation date. I will call at 11:30am to check in and chat to see how you are managing. Bob and I are to have a chat and that should be it. I will call again at 10:45pm when my son you are off work to see how your day went.

Debbie asked if she could see me after she gets herself all worked up in preparation for her parole hearing. I told her to trust in God and to stay in peace. She needed to hear that and her energy calmed down.

I love you both and miss you terribly. The guards are having way too much fun with the intercoms. So wonderful for them to be enjoying what they do. God bless them.

My son the guard puppy was out and about today. I could see him or her jumping in the snow as the handler watched. I thought maybe he or she was coming into our house to jump on our beds but thankfully not mine. That puppy sure likes the snow.

I wrote to a few friends and will write to family in the later of this week. The guards have being walking in threes these days. Not sure if they are training or just over staffed. This afternoon I am going to learn new recipes. I am considering doing a cook book on all the amazing food I am learning to prepare in here. This could be another calling.

I realized I had my First aid tomorrow so I made my lasagna for tomorrow night's dinner today in preparation. I did learn Debby's dish it looks delicious. Funny I never was much of a spice girl but I have learned so much from Max, Sally and now Debby on spices. Susan showed me the new life of coatings, especially on chicken. So yummy and I am so excited to cook for you.

I am going over to the main house soon to see and meet the Lutheran student's volunteers. My son I hope you have a terrific day at work and stay in your bubble, stay true to which you are as you are an amazing young man and any mom could be blessed to have you and any person could be blessed to know you. All my love.

Wow the Lutheran students did not come. Maybe the roads were too scary. My room smells like fart so thank goodness the day is so beautiful I can open the window and let some fresh air in. I am not sure what is making that stink but I will be washing my floors incase something got tracked into my room. I am going to now write to another friend as they were on a vacation last time we wrote.

Dinner was terrific. Ray told me that our First aid was cancelled for tomorrow and rescheduled for February 5, but I am going to check with the coordinator to confirm on my way to visits. If it is cancelled then I would be able to call at our usual time. One thing I have learned in here is patience and disappointment. I will call you later my son and mom I will see you in a bit.

January 16, 20xx

Good morning to my son and mom, last night was really scary. Poor Mea was having a heck of a time with all her physical issues that at 9:50am the guards came in, four female and Jimmy to assist her. Because it was a lady Jimmy had to stand back so he and I chatted. I got to know Jim as a strong, willed individual, something we have in common. Mea was blessed she had two baths and after our visit last night she was headed for her third bath to try and relax her muscles and ease her discomfort, so when the guards took her out of the house you would have thought she was headed to the hospital, but nope they walked to the main and ten minutes later Mea was back.

I wanted to make sure it was baking soda as I remembered having this issued after my son was born, but I wanted to confirm and had to wait to help her. I had two ginger ales in my cupboard. I went downstairs and filled a glass with ice and grabbed the pop. Mea was in such pain. I knocked on her door and went in. I told her to drink the ginger ale and I would find out what I used for the bum pain.

Mea drank the pop quickly as she was so dehydrated. Tomorrow I will push the water. I let her know I would find out what it was and she could have a warm bath tomorrow. She had her third bath and thank you for confirming it was the baking soda. I think it helped.

I loved our chat last night my son. I miss you so much and I am so grateful for you. We will survive this and be together very soon.

I buzzed the wall last night and no one confirmed the cancellation. I buzzed the wall this morning and they left me on hold. Debby said she saw a notice on the recreation bubble about our cancelled course so at movement I will confirm. Gong!

The wall asked Mea to buzz them. She just got to sleep, poor gal. Well, I will fill my day with working on my major essay for my correspondence course. I have the privilege to meet my mentor at 5:30pm and church after. The blessing is now I can talk to you before you go to your second job and you are the most important person. I love you my son. I love you mom.

Joyce was bang on and I can truly see my growth with God. I am so at peace as I know the truth will come out and I will stay in Christ. There are two TVs I know of for sure that are watching Joyce Meyer on right now in the house.

Never give up ☺ this situation is not bigger then God. Thanks mom I receive the Law Society letter and this is not over as the writer indicated. I can still continue to voice my case which I will do but I will take a break for a bit, but not for long and I know things will come out and like I said that I will find others who collaborate misconduct of Mr. Reck and the infliction on others. I have a great feeling that this is the right thing to do and that this was not a slam for us but rather a sign that he, the writer of the letter, will entertain my complaint anytime and does not want me to give up. You know me, mom I will have the truth come out, but I am waiting for the proper chain of events to play out. Keep the faith.

I prayed for the house mates last night and especially for Mea to have her pain reduced and to get the help she needed. Well, guess this prayer was answered. I was going to check the mail and offered to check Linda's and Mea's. Mea told me about how she fell asleep in the tub and the guards brought her some preparation H cream. Mea was asking me to call the wall to confirm her UTA to go see her nephew. It is a long story so I will fill you in later but the point is she may be able to get some medication and that her spirits were lifted which can make a huge difference in the healing process.

I was going to start to write my final essay but will instead read the remaining two chapters in the course materials. So that will be my mission for today. Thanks for you both on this cloudy day and missing you huge.

Debby and I went to get the cleaning bucket and she needed to speak to Whitey so I asked for a calendar for 20XX which he so blessed me with when I got back to my room I read the message on forgiveness and flipped throw it to see the pictures and May had three birds sitting in a nest in a purple frame. This reminded me of use three. And June was two bears, a mommy bear and her cub. This saying was "let a man meet a bear robbed of her cubs, rather than a fool in his folly", June spoke to me in so many ways. My son that was your nickname as a young child, your favorite animal is a bear, a mom and cub which is symbolic of our relationship and June is my parole month. Thanks be to God!

I am going to speak to the teacher at movement about the transcript. So glad you are both doing great. After I spoke to the teacher she informed me no test required and that they would get my high school transcript for my. So kind!

So we just finished dinner and everyone was able to enjoy dinner before the guards came by. The lasagna turned out wonderfully. Mea even commented on how she wished she could eat but she is on a liquid diet as per the doctor to help her heal. I told Mea she needs to eat something in her stomach before she had to take her medications. So she agreed to some soup. Sam said she was not feeling well so I suggested the warm salt water and rest. I feel fortunate to be able to help out. I am going over to the main for a mentor at 5:30pm and then to church so I will be back at 9:00pm, have a shower and wait to chat with my loved ones.

The weather is so ugly out tonight. Between the snow and the rain and the warm weather we are going to get cold making the roads and sidewalks a real mess. Please be safe out there.

The mentors came in and I signed up for the next available person. I attended church and we watched another Lui Gigliano video. Bridget was there which was so great. She missed ordering the Valentine day cards and I had three so I gave her one. One was all she needed. If she needed two I would have given her two or all three, but God tested me and I passed. She was so grateful.

As I was waiting for the mentor I sat there in the parole board room and observed. On blessed lady gave me a big huge and told me she loved me. This little blessing reminded me of our next door neighbours. Too bad she could not be my mentor, but I will wait patiently. The other jail mates were just shovelling in the snacks. Seriously, they give other mates at bad impression of where manners come into play. Just rude and I felt so bad for the mentors who provided the snacks from their own money. It seems to be the same race that does this. I told Mea and she says they act like salvages, which is so true. I am really contemplating participating in a sweat, but anyways, church was good. I asked Linda if the volunteer took her out to church visits like Debby. Linda said, 'nope, she only took Debby, which is not very nice". Linda said she got over it and was blessed to have another group of ladies escort her.

I showered and had an apple and orange for my bedtime snack. I will chat with you in a bit. I love you more than anything and one day life will be us being together. My son and mom I could not have been blessed with the better supporters anyone could have ever been blessed with. All my love!

January 17, 20xx

Good morning to my wonderful family. How are you this fine morning? Wow I am watching Joyce and she spoke to me this morning about how I was feeling last night. I will explain further later but the important thing is Joyce spoke to me in her message and how God loves me and you and that is all the matters. God will take care of all our problems and be with us no matter what.

There was a call for all mates to return to their houses so something is going on. I just made some toast with honey and had made a pot of coffee. I will enjoy my toast and coffee. I pray you are both having a blessed morning. I was just thinking it was odd as the guards usually come and check the house, a walk thru, while I was enjoying my God, Joyce and me time and that did not happened this morning. Their schedule is off therefore something is going on. You become accustom to their schedules.

Cathy was heading back to bed and asked I wake her when canteen is called. It seems everyone but me is going to sleep so I will make sure I listen for the house call. Phew that is a lot of pressure. ☺ I love you both and will call you at 1:00pm to check in on you.

I am slacking on my writing so I went to canteen but had to rescan my hand as I had a new number, so now I have to wait until this afternoon to get my canteen, but my call to you would be during this time so I choice to not get canteen. I made the right choice and we had a lovely chat. When you first arrive you are given a temporary number that is your identification number and once all is processed you get a permeate number that is what they had to change over. I am glad your day is going well. We will chat at 10:45pm tonight.

I still have no word on the 23rd. Maybe Bob is here tomorrow. Self management was good. Debby and I had a good chat about last night's session and she said that the volunteer lady is a bully, but I could sense tension so I was right in my gut feelings or my Holy Spirit was telling me something.

There is no intense work out tonight so Cathy and I will do her work out and then I will go up to the main and type out my assignment or at least get as much typed as possible so I can enjoy some hockey on Saturday and not feel too pressured for Saturday, plus who knows around here what can happen, so no sense in waiting. Nat made pork chops for dinner, which were really good. So I will pass on her magic when we talk. I pray you are both having a terrific day. God bless you both!

Cathy and I worked out in our rooms. We open our doors since we are across from one another and we put on the music and we do the workout. It is really hard, but each time it is getting easier and I can see huge results. I can put in my next book about the jail room work out.

Then I went to the main and typed out my assignment. I got it done and some of the second one also, but holy I get having a good time but these inmates have to be so loud. Just like last night the inmates who showed up for mentor's I was embarrassed, seriously where are their manners. So I got a good start on the second assignment and on Saturday I can complete it and hopefully catch some hockey.

I will chat with you in a bit. Much love and missing you big time. God is with us and he has something amazing in store. Peace!

January 18, 20xx

Good morning family and how are you today? Thank goodness it is Friday. I imagine you are both so very tired. I pray that yours and my stress will be all in our favour. I pray we have a terrific day today. I woke up at my usual 6:45am time and showered. I have started my laundry and I am waiting to watch Joyce. Last night I checked the mail but nothing. So your envelope you dropped in the jail mailbox on Tuesday is still having its review.

Joyce moved me to spend more time reading the bible. God bless these guards. There maybe one or two here that are kind of moody, but the majority are just so wonderful and kind. I love when they come by my room and say good morning to me with a wave and a smile. Last night I had someone else approach me to find out about post secondary courses. I pray that while I am here that I will continue to be a blessing to the entire jail. I love you both and so excited that we are one day closer to being together again.

Gosh I was reminded of a story to tell you in full detail when we see each other. I learned how to make Mea's smoothie which are so delicious. I am so happy you are both having a great day. I pray that you be blessed with some wonderful news. I hope I receive a response to my taxation request for January 23 court appearance for being able to attend. I have complete faith in you both and all we can do is try our best and leave the rest in God's capable hands.

I am just waiting for piano lessons to start. The instructor told me last week to wait to be called up so that is what I am doing. I miss you guys and I can't wait to see you tomorrow. One day closer is all I can do but remind myself. Well, I am not sure what happened to piano, so I wrote to Whitey just to confirm the instructor that I am enquiring about my lessons so she does not think I forgot but you would have thought I would have been paged. Next Friday I will go up at movement and talk to her in person, but the upside is I was able to spend a wonderful day with God, the bible and me. We had hamburgers and cucumber, onion salad in a dill sauce and Cathy and I worked out.

I am glad your afternoon was good mom especially when you are going over to my sisters. My son, I pray you are having fun at work tonight and I am so excited to see you both tomorrow. Hockey starts tomorrow also. I will call you at 10:45pm and say good night. All my love!

January 19, 20xx

Good morning my son and mom. Well, today is hockey day, but first my visit with you both. Today is three months and counting down. Every day closer to being with you both. I just turned on my TV and it was for the SPCA and here was a black and white tie cat that looked like ours. Gosh I miss that old gal.

I am waiting patiently to see you. You have no idea how excited I get, my body is like thrilled to know we will be visiting. It is like Christmas or the best time a person can imagine that is what I feel when I get to see you. When my name is called I am out those doors.

Our visit was wonderful as usual. Don't fret about the taxation appointment if I can't go you two will do great. I pray I can attend and it is all in God's hands as we have done all we can do but like I said we will discuss it tomorrow and I have all the confidence in you both.

I received a letter from my cousin today. That was so wonderful for him to write. I am going to do some prayers and bible studies, go to the main at 1:00pm to finish typing my second assignment and work out. I will call you at 6:30pm and watch the hockey. It is so wonderful to have a visit and laugh with you both.

It is 4:00pm and the snow has started again. I just got back from the main. I had to wait thirty minutes as the methadone people get the recreation room after they get their meds. Apparently, they have to wait for this time so they don't throw up their medication and do who knows what with it. It is disgusting to think what they will do around here. Seriously, some people have no boundaries. The recreation room was quieter but I am grateful to have started the other assignment the other day as I don't think I would have finished. I was able to talk to Bridget and we are going to walk on Sunday nights. She has court on Wednesday but hers is for more criminal charges being laid against her, that poor gal. I pray God to protect her.

Wonderful news about being able to go over the billings tomorrow and you being able to bring them in during our visit. I would say that is a great blessing, and what I was trying to impress was that it is important to say, thank you. A lot of these guards don't get enough praise for doing something nice and kind. Thank you guards!

Are you enjoying the hockey tonight, I am. We get to see each other tomorrow. One of us will have the bragging rights on who wins the game.

I enjoyed and evening of reading the bible. Nice guards on tonight. She always comes by my door and waves. That wave makes me feel so special and when I leave here I am going to make a point of thanking each guard personally as they made my stay here that much better.

Looks like you will get bragging rights. Vancouver is not doing all that good but it is only the second period.

I am going to sign off on this letter. Cathy just came in to apologize for forgetting about me tonight and our work out that was nice of her. We had a lovely conversation.

I love you both and I am so grateful to have you support and love and encouragement. You make me stronger and thank you. All my love!

January 20, 20xx

Happy Sunday to you both. How are you doing this morning? Last night I was blessed to be able to be asked by a fellow mate to listen to her appeal for her parole. I hope and pray that I can be a blessing to everyone in this jail. God answered my one prayer last night as Bob is on today as is my secondary. I wrote a request to follow up with Bob and hopefully we can see each other during his rounds. Linda told me about a re-integration program last night that I should become involved in. Linda is such a blessing. She is so kind and will to always help out, without wanting anything in return.

Cathy and I will do our upper body workout this morning she said 11:00am but I am onto sure how late she was up last night and so I don't want to wake her up. I love you both and will speak to you at 11:30am.

Funny how quickly God works. Cathy woke up on her own and blessed that Bob and my secondary both came in so I was able to give him my request.

Thank you for our visit. Wow, we are booked for our sleepovers and I feel so great that we have not bumped anyone out and because of our weekend we get a blessed extra hour. See he is smiling down on us. I am so grateful we were able to go over each of the billing information. I will confirm tomorrow with Bob my attendance.

I got back to the house and the guards were doing over my room items, doing a search but my room was fine as would be expected.

Funny they pulled out my stapler and staples saying they have never seen anyone being allowed this. So I told them it should be on my cell report, which I told them I hang for them and sure enough it was on there.

I attended church and everyone was happy. I thought it was a great service. A program mate asked me if I was coming to the extreme workout tonight, so I will go at 6:00pm for an hour workout. It is nice to support others and the work out is great. A real win-win. I recruited Debby and Nat to come and do the work out also. Cathy is busy with her pal otherwise she would go. I will come back and watch the game and call you. Tomorrow I have another construction course which is all day, a work out, and a bible study group.

I don't understand how Susan says that jail is so boring, when you do nothing you will be bored. I feel pray for people who feel sorry for themselves as they will get left behind and miss out on so much of life.

My son I love you and that you have the confidence you needed today. You two will be amazing I have complete faith in you both. I pray I can attend, but just know you can do it. Spreading confidence is so powerful. Just like the three gals who inquired about post secondary or inspiring Cathy in her appeal. God set us out so be inspired and to do it with good faith in his name. To make a difference and to touch and inspire someone to make a positive, good decision is so empowering. God is working in me with the Holy Spirit to make a difference here.

Off to work out I love you both and I am so blessed. Go Vancouver go!

Wow that was a heck of a work out. I saw Bob in the hallway. Wow he works long hours. Ray completed her quilt and it is really nice. She did a fabulous job. I asked her if she enjoyed her new found career and she laughed. I was serious she is really talented.

I am having an apple and pear and a cup of tea. I am going to sign off this letter and watch the hockey game. I love you both. God is watching over us and has an amazing plan in store for us. I will call you at 10:15pm after the guards have completed their rounds. I miss you and all my love.

January 21, 20xx

Good chilly Monday morning my son and mom. How are you this morning? Last night the guards were coming by every hour or maybe it just seemed that way but I am tired this morning. All I have to do is think of you and how much you both work and I tell myself "mom and my son are tired also, so quit complaining and get on with the day", and that works.

This morning I am going to take over to the main my two assignments and bless the school for printing them out and then wait for my construction course to commence. Maybe I will be blessed with being able to see Joyce's message before this morning. Gosh the devil is sure testing me this morning with rude mates. I will try and call you on my break and hopefully be able to talk to you before you head to your second job. I pray you both have a terrific day and receive blessings and good news.

God is so funny; he puts me in the course with Susan. She is the one mate I am not fond of. Well, I completed the morning of training and our instructor is very nice. He is an older gentleman and has been here before. We will finish our lesion and write our test. You are required to get an 80% to pass, so I pray I get my ticket and pass. I tried to call but no answer so I will try after count if no one is on the phone otherwise, I will call you at 5:30pm and you my son at 10:45pm. I have not see Bob yet so he must be on the late shift which would be reasonable as he worked such a long shift last night. I love you both and miss you.

Oh another thing this morning I met a new mate at this course. Her name is Jane and she seems nice. I spoke to the teacher and she told me to bring my assignments up at next movement so I will take them to her before the course starts again this afternoon.

Well my course was amazing and I receive 100%. The instructor was surprised by someone receiving 100%. Funny how some people were even cheating and I was the only one to receive the 100%. Cheaters never win!

I am so happy I was able to say hi to you my son before you headed off to your next job. I am so full of proud at you both, for all you have done for me, for yourselves and what you continue to do. The other mates are so impressed by you both. I am grateful that the jail provided me with the opportunity to receive some courses while I am here. The teacher said she would have my assignments ready tomorrow to be picked up. So I am on a mission to complete the final essay by the end of February, we will have our sleepover in March and soon very soon visits.

I am just having a cup of tea. Hopefully Bob will receive an answer and information. Blessed to have a great guard here and on my team. I love you both! We had Indian tacos tonight for dinner, yet another meal for me to make for you, connecting streams was just cancelled which is too bad I actually look forward to a night with the gals discussing Katie Souza story. Just something to look forward to for next Monday.

I just got back to my room to write to you and to make my list of things to do each day this week, when I thought I better tell you a funny story. So Sam kept us up last night with her popping of the gum which Mea and I at lunch time had words about, but now Sam is on the phone and I needed to warm up my water for my tea, so in the TV room there is Mea, Nat and Linda and Sam is on the phone popping her gum. Pop, pop, pop and Mea looks at me and mouth to me she is going to lose it. I look at Mea and give her a big smile. Grandma's gum chewing does not even come close to this it is seriously loud. I just imagine her popping that gum all over the phone and wow would she get it then.

Linda is out tomorrow. It was nice to have met her during my journey and I wish her all the luck and the best.

God has blessed me to meet and have a friendship with Ray because I can't paint them all with the same brush, but wow does one race in here think they are superior to everyone else and manners let me tell you right out the door. God had blessed me with more patience because of this journey.

The rest of the night was quiet. I just watched TV and Shameless was on. Mea and Cathy are Shameless fans also. Now I am watching Gilmore Girls, they are not fans of that show.

I will call you shortly, I heard Bob on the wall over the intercom, so maybe I will find out about Wednesday before our goodnight call.

I love you both and missing big time today. Stay strong, stay safe, say in faith. All my love.

January 22, 20xx

Good morning to you both. How are you doing this morning? I am going to walk over to the main and see if the teacher is in, mail you a letter, and check my mail. I will be back to watch Joyce and hopefully meet up with Bob and discuss tomorrow.

Linda left at 5:00am this morning. Last night after we chatted I gave her a big hug and wished her all the best. She told me I would do fine. I was blessed to have met her. Well that is four who have come into this house and left. This house is their last stop. Apparently, that is why our beds are as terrible as this is your way out bed.

No mail, no teacher, but I mailed you a letter. Joyce's message was "we are anointed by the Holy Spirit for hard", which means not to fear anything as God will be with you so you have nothing to fear.

No point is getting upset over something you have to do, face it and do not fear it. You can do it even if you are afraid, just trust in God and God will work for you. Wow, Joyce's message was yet another wonderful fit in what we are dealing with, such a blessing.

I finished doing my morning bible studies. Blessed the teacher for printing out my assignments. Shoot, our visits were cancelled, but at least we can talk on the phone, I have to think positive and not let the devil steal our sunshine. The drug unit is doing a search of our house. While I was speaking to my son, he told me that our handyman came by to get information on how to visit me or mail me a letter. You can tell me when I call at 6:00pm if he did come.

I love hearing about your jobs my son and how much you are enjoying them, well one more so then the other. Whether I can come tomorrow or not, everything will end up in God's hands and God's will. Those who are evil will one day meet their maker, but I pay they will speak the truth and be cleansed before too long. I love you and grateful for our visits tomorrow night. Forces on what we can control and what we are blessed with. All my hugs and kisses.

I am just taking a break and watching Gilmore girls and then go back to studying the bible. I draw close to God's work in my journey. He gives me strength, courage, and fills me with the Holy Spirit. Debbie signed herself up to cook but she is not home yet and it is 3:00pm so Nat cooked up the chicken and I made a salad and rice. Then she gets back to the house and does not ever help. Well at least he house was able to have dinner. Cathy and I worked out and then did the dishes. Apparently, there are seven new mates coming into the jail this week so we will most likely get some new mates. Well I will call you shortly, still no Bob, but shift change is coming at 7:00pm so maybe he is on the late shift. I love you!

I am glad to have a nice talk with you, mom and that you were able to vent out your day. I will one day support you mom so you don't have to work and can enjoy doing something fun. I love you and will talk to you at 10:45pm

Fun how on the news tonight someone from our city won a huge lotto winning. I am reading the book of Matthew chapter 16:22 and it speaks about Peter and his pompous pride and then I turned to the guide channel 5 and it is playing the song I want to learn on the piano. I am glad the Aunt enjoyed the first book and I wonder if Uncle will also since he is a lawyer. Don't worry about tomorrow and the taxation appointment it will all be fine. We have done all we can and we will do our best and then it is in God's hands. Debby is reading a story in today's paper that I will enclose, funny how she told me about this. It is a story of how someone was wrongfully accused and the witnessed lied in court and the truth came out.

Oh wow, you will not believe this I went down to cut the article out and Nat asked me what I was doing, a long story short she retained Mr. Reck also and he bailed on her and dropped her as his client right before her trial. I asked if she would write a letter about her situation and she said she would. I told Nat I was going to find others who were wronged by Mr. Reck and how funny how one is in this house. This is way too weird. Anyways, she got hopped in his treatment of her. She committed the crime, but he did not do his job as they were not going to press charges until Mr. Reck ignored them and this company got tired and pressed charges. He then dropped her as a client the morning of her trial and she did not get a fair trial.

Anyways, the very least this will pay into my next book. Mea and I walked up to the main to sign up for a nail tech class being offered for 4-5 weeks and you get paid for it. So why not! When we got to sing up there was at least 15 other mates that signed up, so we signed up anyways. It is nice that each one of us helps out the other.

My son I pray you are having fun at work. I am so proud of you. I love you both and I am so blessed to have you as my amazing supporters. Nice that my friends from the outside call you to see if you need anything. Nice to know others are thinking about us. I still wish and pray that Wayne will contact you or write.

Well I will chat with you at 10:45pm. If I am going I will go by 9:00am otherwise I will call you so you will know I will not be transported to the Taxation hearing. But either way we will just do our best and pray for God's blessings.

January 23, 20xx

Good morning and how are you both? I am up, showered and ready so if they call I will be ready to go. I guess the rule in jail is to always be ready because no one confirms anything. We have our plan so if I call at 10:00am then I won't be there but if I don't call then they have taken me to sit in a holding cell until 3:00pm the taxation time.

At 7:50am I will go check the mail and watch Joyce and see what the day has in store. I love you both. Glory to God I just checked the mail and blessed that the envelope you brought last Tuesday was there, which I will deal with later. The item that I receive, which was a notice from the sentencing, for me to be there via telephone. This is good news as they went above and beyond to accommodate this for us. So I can be there with you both and we can still then see each other afterwards. All we can do is our best and leave the rest. I trust in God.

Joyce spoke on stepping out even in fear and trusting in God that he will put people around you while you endure your mission that are the right people. She spoke of Timothy 2 and how if someone takes form you that God will ensure it come back to you. I surrendered to God to do what I have been trying to do. I trust in him. God will set everything right. He has blessed us today with me being able to be there, not in body, but over the phone and I appreciate the jail for making this arrangement. I love you and I trust in both of you that God will be with you. Let us count our blessings and stay positive, stay safe, and stay healthy. God has something amazing in store. I will call you at 10:00am and we can talk.

I am so glad we have visits tonight. I am so blessed that my acting parole officer, Sara, was there today as she got to witness Mr. Reck's behaviour. She could not believe his conduct and how he was talking. She was the one asking the questions and talking, yet Mr. Reck thought it was me and he was yelling, yelling at her. Nice to have someone actually witness his evil behaviour and when I tell people he yelled at me until I pled guilty they can now see what I was subjected too. He is an evil man.

Good is certainly doing something and at first I was upset as was Sara at his conduct, but then I receive a feeling of complete reassurance that all was going to work out. Funny how important I am how I have a detective serving me court documents, how the same judge keeps signing off on all the court documents, how this high profile lawyer shows up for taxation of his billings but can't seem to be in contact with me for five months after he threatens me to pled guilty.

Sara said he must be under complete duress and that rightfully so. She was so glad I have faith as she has witness pure evil in motion. She was set back. God is showing people around me what I/ we have had to endure. The song "my life" is coming on the radio. I am so grateful to have my supporters and they seem to be growing. Not too many people have any respect for our legal system or lawyers or judges in here. So funny how much support I have in here and how many people want my story to be told and for vindication. God is working in such an amazing way. I surrender it to Him.

Sara told me to write down everything, which I already do. Sara was a huge comfort especially when he was yelling at her thinking it was me. Mr. Reck is a hurting man and his wrongdoings are catching up with him. I sure hope he appreciates his surgery pay off money to have me in jail and to keep me quiet. This journey just wants me to tell my story even more. You tax evaders, money launders, crooks can only hide for so long and then it will come out. All these people will be found out and the truth will follow. Well, the positive is that I have a date for when I get out and I and Mr. Reck can hash this out then.

Wow what a nice visit I had with you both. I nearly lost my composure tonight my son when you told me you were proud of me. God has something a bigger plan and a change is coming in our favour. At first I thought I wanted the other taxation officer to assess this matter but after our conversation I just may want this to continue with this taxation officer. Like I also said to you guys during our visit if I am grateful to have a great house mates who have my back.

I will introduce myself to the newbie tomorrow; she is probably a bit overwhelmed. My son you were so bang on about them thinking I would hush up. Wrong is wrong and God will be your maker so like I said before these guys are suffering from guilty conscience at what they have done to me and others.

I love you and I am the luckiest person to have you in my corner. All my love.

January 24, 20xx

Good morning to you both and how are you today? I imagine you both are tired from the gong of yesterday and all the excitement. I reflected last night on our visit and again woke up feeling blessed. Mea, Nat and I walked to the main to check the mail. I dropped off my request for the acting warden as per the acting parole officer, Sara's instructions and guidance and a letter to you both. They are offering a construction course, so when I come back I will fill out the request that I will need and drop it off on my way to hygiene canteen.

My mail box was stuffed with all kinds of goodies, a letter from a friend, a pay increase and a letter from the Associate Chief Justice asking for their file numbers so they can investigate further, well at least they are going to look into this matter, which is a blessing.

Today I have self management at 1:30pm and Cathy wasn't to work out, I am going to do some writing to supporters and family and then a bit of bible studying. I was watching a bible program before Joyce started and they were speaking on James 5:1-4 which again spoke volumes to me especially with what just transpired yesterday. Gee I wish Susan would stop being so negative. Anyways, I love you both so much and I am so blessed to have you. All my love!

I was switching over my laundry and Debby was eating her breakfast so I inquired about the bible study she was leading and the meeting last night and how was the video that was shown. She said the video was great and then went on about the lead volunteer so I brought the conversation back to a positive as that is all we can do. Focus on the blessings, the positives and what is good.

I met with a lady who offers the re-integration program that Linda spoke of and she seems very nice. Interesting how Linda's groups of church are reflective of her personality. They are kind, gentle groups and focus on God and good.

Yes it was Bob he came by for noon count and I gave him my request and the re-integration lady information. I gave Ray a stamped envelope and some gum for her birthday. She was so grateful and gave me a huge and more importantly a smile. Self management was great. I am learning about all these resource centres available not that I need them but I will check into them so I can be informed upon my release.

My son I am glad you had a great day at work. Wow the kennel job offers a lot of wonderful perks beside the cute pups and hockey tickets. Mom I know one day I will b able to take care of you so you can enjoy your days volunteering and gardening or just reading a good book. I will call you at 5:30pm to chat. Cathy wants to do a double work out so we can get our legs done and will do our arms and upper soon. I enjoy the upper with the pull ups.

Blessed! Sam asked me to trade her apple for my banana; perfect as I love the apples so can put my cinnamon and sugar on them. Debby made cabbage soup and Nat asked if I would make the pizza dough so for my cook night I told her we could make pizzas tomorrow night. She agreed.

I am so sore, so it is a good night to enjoy a hockey game.... Go LA! I still have a bit of a headache so I will de-stress and get rid of it. The mate who moved in last night is Lisa and then we had another girl move in tonight so we are full and no vacancies. I think the entire jail is full now. Mom I am glad you had a great afternoon or a better afternoon then this morning. I love to know that you and the cat are spending time cuddling. She is so special. I am going to have a shower and use the herbal before the game starts. I love you both and one day closer to being with you. I will call you at 10:45pm to see how your second job went. I am the one who is so proud of you, you both.

Be strong and trust in God and all he is doing. We will survive this journey and inspire others. I just met the other new mate, her name is Lori. She seems nice, quiet and on my level of the house. She has celiac and lactose intolerant so meals will be healthy and interesting. The dynamics are changing again. Mea made coconut, oatmeal, chocolate cookies...mmmm so good! Mom you use to make these for us as kids.

Feels like home watching the game and eating cookies, all I need is you. I miss you!

January 25, 20xx

Good morning to you both. I am just watching Copeland faith program until I am able to check the mail and they are taking about wealth and wealth returning from the wicked to the gospel and how thing come back in 100 folds. Mark 10:2-30, I pray that God will bless us with the 100 fold return, glory be to God.

Joyce spoke on how God will not hold you accountable for what someone else does, he will for what we do and how Jesus believes in confronting issues and how we will put a smile on God's face by doing things that please him. Wow two really great messages this morning. I walked to the mailbox with Mea and we had a couple of good laughs. There is a new energy in the house right now with the two new people, but my room still feels full of calm, trusting energy, so I am staying in there. Today's mission is to write to friends, some more bible study and find out about piano lesson.

Well at movement at 1:00pm I was able to chat with Bob and we had a lovely conversation about the taxation ETA and what our next move is to be. Piano lessons were cancelled so that gave Bob and I more time to chat and for me to help prepare dinner. Debby needed to have a moment of inspiration so I provide it to her and her spirit lifted up. Nat and I made pizza and blessed Mea made the dough for us. I forgot about Mea and how she can't eat ham or pork based on her religion. Good thing she likes me. I have actually gotten along with all the mates who have passed thru this house.

Debby, Cathy and I worked out, well Debby did half of the work out but it was nice she joined us. Gosh, that is terrible that our neighbour is in the hospital. I wrote them a letter just the other day. Blessing that they called you to let you know. I found this journey has brought our group closer together, which is such a fabulous thing inspired of the situation. I have showered, put together our food order for our PFV and will go over it tomorrow during our visit. I am writing you and just having a cup of tea.

I love you both and wish we were together but soon we will be… one day closer. All my love. I will call you my son at 10:45pm to chat. I pray you had a great day. You are both my spirit, my life, my strength, and my amazing support…thank you!

January 26, 20xx

Good morning and how are you today? I am so glad we talked last night so we knew that the visits had been moved to the 9:00am session. I am grateful we were moved and not cancelled. Plus, the positive is that the 1:00pm visit will be full and most likely very noisy. The 9:00am should be quiet and not a lot of swearing at that time. I am not sure why the four letter words are so popular but they are sure used often in here. When the parole board asks me what I have learned while being here is how terrible that word sounds will be one thing that comes to mind. My son and mom you can both have a nap this afternoon and catch up on your sleep before, my son you head off to your third job. Jim came by and was surprised when I was only one up in the house. Visits are my number one priority as is my family.

This afternoon I am going to do to some bible reading and tonight the hockey game is on, plus the movie what to expect when you are expecting is on the movie channel, so I will watch that. My goal this week will be to complete my final essay for my correspondence course. A few more minutes and I will be with you guys.

Well we had our visit and mom I pray you stay positive. I know you are stressed over all the wrongs but we have to stay positive and more importantly in our faith. There is nothing to take from me as I don't have anything because I never took anything. Maybe they should be looking at the other staff member's assets and the one who admitted to the crime and not me with nothing just information on how the crook is doing this and getting away with it. Either way the truth will come out or vindication will come. We have to trust in God as he is the one who will correct all the wrongs that they are doing.

Positive energy, positive thoughts as I can't bear to think of anything happening to you. I already have enough worry with our neighbour in the hospital.

I received a card from your buddy's family today my son. It is almost a month late, so either the jail mail is really slow or the postman is very back logged, either way it was nice to hear from them and I am so grateful for their wonderful support. They are such amazing spirits and offer me/us so lovely words of support and encouragement.

Before returning back to the house after our visit the other mate who was there told me in front of the guard how she is so impressed by my positive being. It always takes me back when people say that, as we left I told her that and she told me it was so refreshing to have someone like me around as it makes her day when she sees me. As we parted another inmate and I checked our mailboxes. She was a bit bummed out so I just let her know she would get some mail on Monday night most likely and we spoke about the movie of choice on tonight. Us gals will be tuning in. Mea is excited as I reminder her. We have been waiting for this movie to come on and it is the small things to find pleasure in. The mate who was having a sad day gave me her number as she was headed to the halfway house.

Mea and I were chatting and I told her how my son's buddies stepmom worked at the crooks and so she knew firsthand what I was talking about and how she had witnessed activities also many years prior to me being there. Point being is he has not changed his way so one day he will get caught. Mea commented on what a small world it is. I am going to make some breakfast/ lunch as it is already 12:00pm and stand for count will be taking place soon. I will go check out the DVD selection for our PFV and do some laundry this afternoon. I love you and will write you later. Hope you both have a great day. I will call at 10:15pm to say goodnight and check in on you.

I checked the DVDs but Mea said here were more so I will talk to the library gal who is an inmate and see what is on the list. Everyone dresses in street clothes so you think they are staff but they are actually mates. Jim was chatting in the hallway with me when he was supposed to be watching the Methadone mates in the recreation room. I love that these guards have such a great sense of humour. He asked how you both were doing and when I told him how proud I was of you both he said he wishes he could trade his kids for you my son.

I noticed there is another construction course being offered, so I will get on that list. Ghostbusters one and two are on this afternoon. Gosh I have not seen these movies since I was a young girl, so I had better watch them.

Tonight I am going to write and watch the hockey game and walk the yard for an hour to get out. Nat and I just walked up to the main and signed the house up for Zumba on Thursday nights. Last week was a no go, so maybe they were waiting for more interest well our house will be there. I ran into a program mate and she and I were going to read the book, "The Purpose Driven Life", by Rick Warren together. So I explained we should start on February 14th but she only has 37 days left so we will start it so she can have it read before she goes. Wow this book looks really empowering. The chapters are short only a few pages each but very powerful material on 'God".

I am going to start to make a list of questions and notes for Parole as to all that I have accomplished so far and add on as to not forget all that I have accomplished in here. I am glad you had a great day the both of you. We need to stay healthy and the stress is not good. I read Romans 5 so if you need some inspiration try to read the bible, and also James 5 or Zechariah 9:12. I am looking forward to seeing you both tomorrow. All my love.

January 27, 20xx

Good morning my son and mom and how are you today? I am going to read the 'Purpose Driven Life as there is a lot of negative energy in the house right now. Debby is complaining about so much and really draining so I am going to read and fill myself up. I am also going to write to the consolidated woman and if you could call her to ensure that it is necessary that I do write that it would be great. Thanks so much as all these tasks need to be completed and it is so frustrating trying to take care of them from inside here. I am so grateful you are doing so much for me, especially making all these calls. They should go after the crooks assets and not the innocent persons… consolidate my butt.

In the Rick Warren book the message is that we are all made by God for God. Nice message isn't? Well I am glad we are back on track for our visits and today was a great one. I love how we laugh and share joy. These moments get me through the week. We had dinner and now I am going to wait for movement to church.

We had a guest speaker tonight at church, which was lovely. She spoke on God's favour, grace and mercy and that was so great. I asked God to show us these three gifts this week. The Holy Spirit gets so stirred up in me these days. God is moving mountains for me and you. The gals in there are getting sick. Nat has a scratchy throat, Cathy a cold, but she will not admit to having a sore throat otherwise I would nag her to do the warm salt water mix, which is like Buckley's awful but it works.

For someone who is of the faith a certain person sure likes to speak terribly of another house mate. I just walk away and I have no desire to hear what she is saying. Anyways, back to church, I sang my heart out and spoke quickly to Whitey as everyone always is hanging off of him, just a figure of speech. Whitey wanted to make sure I knew about the piano last Friday, which was so kind. I asked about Pastor Ken and he has not received any news form him yet but gave me his business card to have him email him, well of course everyone else wanted a card. Bridget was not up to walking tonight and was going to do another mates workout, which I did not feel like attending as I had already done Cathy's workout but we will come later this week and do and we can walk another time.

I think this week will be less giving to others and more observing. More giving to you guys and our path. My goal is to complete the final essay and have it typed out and ready to deliver to the teacher. Of course, I still plan on attending church functions and reading my bible. I love you both and still counting down the days to begin our new journey. God is preparing us for something that is for sure. I will call you at 10:15pm after count. All my love.

January 28, 20xx

Good morning and how are you both? This is a chilly day today. I was asked by Mea to take up the food order which was great because I was able to chat with a lady from Corcan and asked if they would write a letter on my behalf for my parole hearing. She asked if I would come back in two weeks to collect it as the other lady would be leaving on a trip and this way it would get done. All the mates in the morning were so glad to see me.

As I was walking back Bridget was carrying two bags so I helped her carry one to the main house. I offered to bring Cathy lunch for her visit with her daughter whom she appreciated and as it turned out she was able to go to the PFV so that was a blessing. They put mates in the PFV if the jail is full and they use it as an overflow.

I was blessed to see Bob who is going got get all my paperwork in line for my escorted visits. I am blessed that other family want to visit me in here and they have been cleared for that. Hopefully I will receive some more clearances for visitors but that is okay I am grateful to see you two.

Oh yes, I started a parole binder for my hearing. Bob just smiles as I think he is impressed by my determination or either that or he thinks I am a bit crazy. All good! Keep positive and keep in the faith.

This afternoon after I spend the morning writing my essay I started to watch a Steve Martin movie called Sergeant Bilko, and my son we have to watch it. I missed some but it is a funny movie and I have not seen it before. Chris Rock is in it also. Remind me when I get out and we will watch it together.

We are going to work out shortly and then tonight are connecting streams. Mom I will call you at 5:30pm and I pray you both had a great day and received some wonderful news. I read the bible and then headed to church where I was blessed with meeting wonderful women. Her name is Sofi. We were talking and wow she has such an amazing story. Then we go into connecting streams and one of the mates shares her notes from our last session which was very emotional. The ladies asked me to share and when it got to the part about you both, I got a bit emotional. So I am no longer bringing my personal life, matter, situation to this group. I need to say composed and focused and not let my emotions play into this place. I will no longer share my story, but will continue to go to bible studies.

I think it was a blessing that I met Sofi tonight. Debby and Ray were at tonight session, yet not one of them came to say "hey" to me. Sofi had to make a phone call and she put her hand on my shoulder before she left to acknowledge she cared. I don't have to justify how I feel, once everyone read my first book maybe then will understand what if feels like to be here and innocent. Well I shook it off and look at what I am grateful for.

Some really good movies on this month so there is something to pass the time with. I have also learned that there are some people walk with all the scripture from the bible on their tongue but not on ounce of God or the Holy Spirit in their body.

I came back to the house and showered and went to make some tea. I have observed that one individual who speaks the scripture is actually full of evil or has the evil itch in her. I will no longer allow them to drain any of my positive energy, not will I share my store with anyone they will just have to read my first book.

God is mad tonight, the wind is howling and it is really cold out. God bless my family and friends, God bless me/us and may the truth come out soon to vindicate me and may the true justice be coming soon. May justice prevail and may those who have lied be weighted down with their guilt and what they have done. I pray for favour, grace and mercy to come forth and that we are blessed. I am so grateful for the mates who are real and grateful. I love you! I am blessed that God who enables me to see still who are the wolves in sheep's clothing. I will call you in a bit to say goodnight. All my love.

January 29, 20xx

Good morning and how are you? How did you sleep? This morning is very cold out. I am going to go and check the mail and watch Joyce.

Currently I am watching the comedy channel. Funny this is exactly what my soul needed, a good laugh! I miss you both terribly but I will be vindicated as God spoke and his words are the truth, the law not what our cowards on the bench say or the serpents that dress in suits and call themselves professionals do. I am determined that my purpose is to follow God's will for me. Stay strong and positive today.

Joyce's message was on obedience is the root of all character and renew your attitude daily. The other morning God put a smiley face in the sky for me to see. I was standing in the kitchen looking out the window and I looked up and in the sky was what looked like a smiley face ☺ and I even have two witnesses who I pointed it out too. Why should I let others decide how I act? I will not let others rain on my parade.

Cathy just popped in to say hi and to see if I went back to bed, but nope I was watching Joyce. God has an amazing plan in store for us. This morning I continued working on my essay, worked out with Cathy, and read my chapter in the Rick Warren book, where it discussed how to use our talents as this is pleasing to God. As I sat eating my lunch which consists of cottage cheese with pepper, I was trying to watch Troy but it was too gory to watch and eat so I flipped to the Bronx Tale and would you not know it that the scene happened to be right where he is telling his son about not using his talent in such a waste of talent.

My son I know this has to be very difficult on you and I hope you know how proud I am of you. The Rick Warren chapter 3 discussed that "without a purpose, life is trivial, petty and pointless". That knowing your purpose gives meaning to your life. Without God like has no purpose and without purpose like has no meaning and without meaning life has no significance or hope. Hope is essential to your life as air and water. You need hope to cope. If you have felt hopeless, hold on as wonderful changes are going to happen in your life as you begin to live on purpose.

God…is able to do far more than we would ever dare to ask or even dream of, infinitely beyond our highest prayers, desires, thoughts, or hopes. Wow I blinked and it is already 10:30pm. I am going to call you shortly to see how work went. I love you so much! All my love.

January 30, 20xx

Good morning mom and my son. Last night Bob told me he would be calling me up today sometime this afternoon. Gosh the guards here are really committed to some shift work Bless the guards. I pray you both stay warm as it is another cold day. Just know that I get up at 6:45am and on with my day also. We have so much to accomplish while we are on this journey of life. And there is no way I will be sleeping while you two are working hard. I am doing laundry, my essay and church today. I will check in on you at 1:15pm and see you how work went. Joyce spoke on trusting God and not to give up in the hard years and be obedience to God. John 15: 5-6 'He who abides in me, and I in him, bears much fruit; for without Me you can do nothing.'

We just got off the phone at our 1:15pm call and I just love your funny stories of the kennel. It is too bad some people in this world have absolutely no moral or conscience and would leave their sick animals in a kennel so they can go away on vacation. Those people are the ones society has to be afraid of. I wonder if they were like that before they won the lottery. I love to laugh with you and that keeps me so strong.

I pray all things work out with our neighbour and her health. She is in my prayers. I pray the doctors will find out what is going on and that one of them will solve this medical problem. She is a strong, determined woman so pray she gets better soon. She is still there on Saturday you should go and visit her. Guess Who is on right now? Gosh why did Bernie Mac have to go so soon?

I love you both and will talk to you soon. Stay in faith. Jim and a new young male guard just stopped by my room. Well, Jim actually came in and sat in my room and the other guard stood at the door way. We chatted for gosh twenty minutes or so about golf, books, school ect. Jim said he can't wait to read my book and keep asking me when it is coming out. The young guard was impressed at all I am doing while I am here. God will tell me/ us when to release the book and in the meantime we will wait. It is on Gods time.

Gosh I have been blessed to discover channel 37 Avenue. The movies are oldies but goodies. Thank goodness for good movies plus this is a sign as this movie deals with tax evasion situation. In the end the truth comes out and they are vindicated but also learn so much along the way, kind of like our journey.

My son I am watching the last five minutes of a movie called 'Accepted' we will have to watch it upon my release. We will have a lot of movie time when I get out. Thanks mom for taking care of everything and yes send a letter to CRA with their $40.00 maybe that will get their attention. One day someone will do the work and get those crooks.

Nat came in to borrow my hair dryer. Cathy came back to the house and wanted to tell me about her day and then Mea joined in on the visit. My room is becoming a place to share. I am going to get the church group at 7:00pm or when they call it, but first I am going to read my chapter in the Warren's book. I am proud that you both want to join in to do the reading also. We may be apart but we can be connected in the reading of the Rick Warren book.

I will put this letter in the mail when I go to the main house, which will be before we say goodnight my son. I love you with all my heart and miss you beyond words. You are my strength, my back bone, my everything. All my love.

January 31, 20xx

Good morning and how are you doing today? Okay before I forget ask me about the church group last night and I have to read the scripture Ecclesiastes, which is so exciting to read. While I was at church last night I was called to the Humming Bird but I did not hear it in the main house. So when I got back to the house, Mea said that maybe it was Bob so I buzzed the wall and yes it was him so I ran over to the Humming bird and chatted with him there. Bob is such an amazing primary worker and a great person in general, just a great spirit. I have been truly blessed in this journey. I will tell you our good news on Saturday during our visit.

Tonight at church we decided to put on a skit Acts 1 and 2 for the church on a Sunday service so why not. I suggested that Debby inform

Whitey so he could tie in his service or vise versa. Debby made another great point about how Whitey is asked often to be inmates assistants during parole hearings and yet they never attend church, just use him which is so terrible but I guess we all need help and bless Whitey for doing it. So if Pastor Ken can't come in I could ask Whitey and he can see that I do attend his services and attend all the other church functions offered. Wow Joyce was a repeat today which was odd but the message was again perfect "obedience". How whatever is taken away will come back. It feels like ground hog day like the movie.

Be bold and courageous, to take a chance and step out and to trust in God. To hear from God we need to step out and do something. If it is God it will work out, if not then it was not God. Even Joyce was facing fear during her calling. Joyce is a true inspiration. "You have no idea what I have had to do." She said. "Don't give up in the hard years or times, those who think they know everything actual know nothing," were her words of wisdom today.

He is not asking us to do what is easy, but what is to trust in him. Easy to go along with the tired, stay strong and in faith and do what is right? Well, today is canteen day. I don't need much which is good thing because I decreased my biweekly limit to $10.00. Hygiene will be next week and refills will be next week also so that is blessing. I can replenish the shampoos, toothpaste, and soap then. Debby told me that the laundry detergent is actually unscented Tide and we all use too much of it that is why our skin is itchy. So I will make my own liquid tied with some shampoo and scent it as I already have a jug and by next week that jug will be empty otherwise I will just mix it together. I can make my own.

Mea is out each day for the next four days to visit her family and nephew. Cathy, Debby and I finished the double work out so I am tired. I have self management this afternoon and Zumba tonight. This morning I worked on my final essay, which I will continue to do tomorrow morning also. I put in my request to Bob providing him with the information he asked for last night. Gosh, the request box is stuffed. Still no letter from our friends, so I will ask at V & C to see if they are holding his letter

I pray that our neighbour is doing great and she will be released from the hospital soon. Funny story this morning I was coming back from checking the mail and Mea mail and returning her keys and she as she was getting ready to go out today, she left her blinds open. I was bugging her about how she will have to start putting on a show to pay as her nail tech course is now not being paid for therefore she will need to make some money somehow. So this morning I told her she was not going to get any business if she kept giving it away for free. She laughed and said she turns around when she is getting dressed so no one can see. So I smiled and said well then you are keeping them guessing which is good for business.

I hope you are both having a terrific day. I pray we are blessed with great news, great fortune and great health, spirits and full of gods support. I love you both and will check in with you shortly.

Sorry our chat was so short but I am glad we were able to speak and we can get caught up at 8:15pm. They cancelled self management just not sure if it was the main stream or the aboriginal and unfortunately the guard on the wall did not know. So Cathy was heading up to the main and would return to let me know if it is her class or mine. Who has the afternoon off? Cathy in the aboriginal or me in the main stream?

So Ray has had a chance to leave and got to the healing lodge and she has to make up her mind yesterday as they were going to call her up to discuss today. I told her to clear her mind and God would tell you or show you the path to take. Yesterday there was no call to have her go and let them know her decision and today she gets a call to A&D, the arrivals and departures. So we think her pen pack has been processed which would be a sign to stay.

If my program is cancelled I am going to read the next chapter in the Rick Warren book called "seeing life from God's view' and then read Ecclesiastes book in the bible. God is the ultimate judge and to fear God and keep his commandments was the message for today. Otherwise, it will be programs and then the readings.

Today is grocery day also so that means fruit. Self management was cancelled today so I am off to do some reading. A visual I learned is to view life as winning. Life is a test, life is a trust and life is a temporary assignment. Three apples, four oranges, two pears, and two bananas but I traded my bananas for Sam's lovely apples are sure going to miss our trade when she leaves. She is also wonderful for repaying me for items she borrowed. I am so blessed that the gals have respect for me. Bob says I am like an inspiration to some. I am just walking with God.

So I just found out that the PFV house may be turned into to a house unit if we get any fuller and so they have shut done the house for February to review ect, so as it sits we may hopefully have our sleep over in March otherwise the ETAs will be full swing or even better, but my real point is that God has blessed us with not being rude and bumping anyone.

Ray was called and God spoke to her and she is going to go check out the new place, which means she will be leaving us. So sad! When we first met I planted a seed that maybe her mission was to speak to her people and be a role model as to not do what she did, turn a negative into a huge positive. Last night we were talking and I planted that maybe her going was the ability for her to get in touch with her heritage and by going she could do that, but everything in life starts with stepping out. Well, when she told me she was going, I reminded her of the stepping out. She said, "Yes".

I also added that she looked relieved after making her choice and she was very relieved. So tomorrow she leaves, which will be sad but happy for her to step out. Like my first book nothing in the world changes or advances unless we step out and become Gods soldiers to spread his word.

Zumba was a lot of fun and the gals from Connecting streams came and some new members also and that was wonderful to meet some normal faith based individuals. A good work out and a good laugh.

I am glad you both had a great day and both are safe and sound. My son doesn't let the silly people ruin your journey and spoil your spirit. Mom I am glad you are starting to enjoy the small things like watching the cat look for the birds in the window. Don't worry about the sleepover we can book it for another month if we get bumped but everything will work out. All in God's hands. I love you and miss you both. All my love.

February 1, 20xx

Good morning to you both and happy birthday mom! Your birthday will be another celebration we do when I get out. Hope you have a terrific day.

139 days and counting. I am going to check the mail, help Ray carry her belongings up to the main, watch Joyce and finish write out my essay, maybe not in all the order but it shall be accomplished. I love you both so much and pray you will both have a fabulous day.

I think the news should have a section that is all about Good news. When you turn on the TV or read the paper it is so negative if we heard and read more positive or good stories maybe our society would do well.

I received all my intake reports and so now I have to read them to confirm all the information is correct. I am being supported for full parole and day parole from my support team on the inside and the outside. I helped Mea to write a letter regarding her parole. I finished the essay so I will type it out and hopefully take it to the teacher to print it out so I can make all the changes necessary. I was called for piano lessons and have a standing appointment for 6:00pm on Fridays. Oh Sunday I can ask Whitey to sign out the keyboard to practice piano in my room.

I typed half my assignment out and I am just writing to you now. It is 9:30pm as I sit here with a bowl of popcorn and just showered and in my PJs. I will call you at 10:45pm to see how your day went. Just know each day is one day closer to being together. I miss you both terribly and love you with all my heart. Happy Birthday mom xoxo.

February 2, 20xx

How are you both today? I was just reading the reports and overall everything is great. I will ask you if you said something in the report which they have turned around but I understand what you meant, so I will make sure the parole officer does also. They play on your words in here and take your words out of context, so I will get this corrected. Thank my son for your blessed news about being able to visit more this coming week. Never too much time spend with family. This afternoon I am going to type out my assignments and tomorrow finish it for the teacher for Monday to print out. I need to read two chapters in the Warren book.

I got back from typing my assignment out. I still have five more pages to input so that will be tomorrow after church job. I receive a letter from our friends finally the one that was mailed forever ago, so I will write them back on Monday. We finished dinner which was pork chops, broccoli, and potatoes. It is 4:30pm so I will be giving you a big smooch in 30 minutes. I need to discuss with you about getting community letters from supporters, friends and family for my case file.

Wow I love tonight and every time we spend together. I love that we laugh and share and so nice to catch up and so fabulous to laugh. I love you and as I put on my armour to come back here it is just to survive, please know my heart breaks to see you go and for use to be apart. All my love.

February 3, 20xx

Good morning and how are you? How was your night after you left? I am just watching Gilmore Girls and having porage. Cathy let me know that Lori and Susan wanted to join out work out session so now we are up to five who want to get fit. Funny how my smiley faces is the same as what God put in the sky that day. I am going to read my bible and the Rick Warren book and call you at 11:30am. We have visits at 1:00pm so always good to check in before to confirm we still have a date.

Such a nice visit and thank you, your visits will come first to me in here and that goes for all my supporters so just let everyone know I am keeping busy to keep myself positive and productive but my supporters are number one.

Well I guess I have been replaced in the workout and now Debby and Cathy are doing it which kind of makes me think of their character differently but that is okay. I know that work out and I can do it myself. Soon they will see what she is really about and for someone of faith I will act and be right in His name. I am going to go to church and then to the computer lab/recreation room and I will call you at 10:15pm to say good night. Miss you already!

I will fill you in tomorrow but I will write it also, I went to church and Whitey spoke to Pastor Ken who will send his information in this week and be cleared. In the computer lab I was able to finish my assignment and printing it out, so I will proof it tomorrow. I spoke to one gal about church and she came tonight and actually two girls came. Funny about church as we were discussing chapter 12 of Genesis, Bridget says that Abraham reminds Bridget of me. She said I was determined, loyal, and faithful to God. What kind words from Bridget. And how I am in the pursuit of justice also.

Mea made some lovely banana bread so I am going to enjoy it as I watch the super bowl and wish we were together. Soon we will be and I can't even wait. I love you and will call you at 10:15pm. Ps God is listening to me as things again are coming, He is moving mountains for us, and we are so blessed.

February 4, 20xx

Good morning and how are you? Last night sleep was one where you tossed and turned to get comfortable but then it would be too hot to sleep. I am just waiting to see some funny commercials and having a coffee and going to blow dry my hair. I am contemplating if I wi8ll continue to go to the church group on Wednesday evenings as I don't feel like someone who is taking charge of a faith run group is true person of faith or a person of the right spirit. Right now I am out I will spend my evenings walking the yard, reading my own bible, and this Wednesday will be spending that time doing my essay. Anyways, I have no time for others drama or gong which includes negative attitudes. I love you both and thank you for keeping me positive.

Joyce spoke on holiness today. Funny today she was offering her purchase which was the Joyce Meyer Everyday Bible which I am studying. Gosh God is so wonderful and yes I will read today this book. Well I finished my proof reading my essay and wrote to friends and read the Rich Warren book and did a double work out. I love Kelly Clarkson's new song by the way very inspirational and motivational, but I can't remember the name. I will call you in a bit to chat. Oh yes the song is we have to get up and try. And wow Nickel back, we must stand together is another awesome song.

This afternoon was full of bible time. Supper was great and I am so excited to see you. Visits soon! I love our visits. The games we play and just seeing you. I miss you more each day. I will be strong for you always.

I am back from our visit and just had a shower. I dropped off letters to friends and saw a mate from connecting streams asking why I was not there. I told her I had visits and she smiled and reassured her I had not abandoned her. She is a very nice person. Her name is Valarie. Mom, please give a copy of my book to the MLA and see if maybe he can kick things into motion. All my love.

February 5, 20xx

Good morning to you both and hope you slept well. I am glad today I have the First aid course and to get out and so blessed we have a visit tonight. I will go over the mail box at morning movement and check to see if maybe I have been blessed with being able to take some more courses. Tomorrow I will go and speak to the Corcan employers about the letter for parole. I pray for us today to stay safe, healthy and strong. I love you both and will chat at 11:30am or when course breaks.

I just poured my second cup of coffee and Cathy came in with a letter from Family court to notify her on her next appearance. I could not imagine dealing with that also, god bless her. Puts things back into prospective and God will bless us as He is with us.

Well First aid is completed and I am certified. The instructor was great. I saw Cathy come in and get something and mouth Hi to me. Whitey stopped me to let me know that step one was completed and Pastor Ken will now proceed to give him cleared to be my escort. Whitey also let me know tomorrow we would get together to sign out the key board for piano lesions. Look out soon I will be in a rock band.

I am going to work out soon and jumping for joy to see you. Oh yes, Jim told me that there was no receipt book yesterday for the sleepover money to be deposited so hopefully things will be under control tonight when you come in. I will see you soon. I love our time together and value you both. All my love.

February 6, 20xx

How are you both today? Mid week thank goodness. This morning I am going to check the mail, speak to Corcan about the letter of reference, read the next chapter in my book and watch Joyce and read the bible. Well there was just an announcement that there is no work in Corcan this morning so I will speak to those ladies later.

I pray you both have a fabulous day and receive nothing but good news today. I hope and pray that our neighbour is out of the hospital today. As I am doing my laundry this morning, someone is up already banging doors. Seriously, this person has no respect for others. Where is the respect for the girls still sleeping? Just so rude.

Today I should get a call from Whitey, otherwise, it will happen when it happens I am to receive the keyboard to practice on but whenever, it happens will be the right time. I am so grateful to you both. My cheek is a bit sore from the skittles last night but I am reminded of how blessed I am to have you. Vindication is coming and moving of mountains is occurring. Joyce spoke on being consistent to live in Godliness. I even told Mea to turn it on and watch which she did. Joyce was on Colossians 3:1-2 and 3:12. God will bring justice into our life especially if you have a good attitude which in a difficult place, he will bless us. Trust in God and being God's representative.

I finished reading my chapters in the Rick Warren book and wow was it empowering and filling me with the Holy Spirit. I get stirred up with Gods mission in me. I opened the Pursuit of His presence and turned to May 1 which spoke on an Act of Courage and the speak the word was Joshua 1:7, 'I am strong and very courageous'. May 8 was when mouth speaks, minds, listens and the speak the word. Psalm 118.6, 'The Lord is on my side. I do not fear!' I will explain the relevance of this to you later; I just found it hugely empowering to read.

I am getting some information for Connecting streams bible study group. I received mail from my wonderful relatives in the next province over and sending us words of encouragement, strength, and blessings. They had a fabulous time in Hawaii and spoke to other family members and passing on information to all. Uncle is reading my first book and Aunty found it very compelling, so that was nice to hear.

Well I guess all that slamming of doors was that me from Ms. Negativity. So it unfolds like this as was making grill cheese sandwiches for lunch and I saw that Debbie was on the phone crying. Well today is a very stressful day for her so when she got off the phone I asked her if she was okay and to lend her some support. As I was making the sandwiches for Mea, Lori, Nat and myself, Nat tells me all that slamming was her mad at me for doing my laundry. Debby did not know that all her slamming of doors first thing this morning was directed at me. Nat saw me offering her support and told me that Debby was pissed off that someone was doing laundry at 7:30am. I told Nat that for a woman of faith she did not display a Christian attitude in her words or manners. I will continue to spread God's love and behave properly. I also told Nat that she is under a lot of stress and I had offered her words of encouragement, because God would want me to do that. Just because someone else who is to be in faith behaves away does not mean I will be that way. As I am here to make God proud of my behaviour, and to spread his love, and he will show his favour, gratitude, grace and mercy on us/me.

I love that you are enjoying your four legged friends and the job. Animals are so awesome and can spread so much joy. Focus on the positive, on the possibilities, and on His promises. I am glad to hear your afternoon will be a quiet one. I hope you read some of Rick Warren's book. At movement I went and made the corrections to my final essay. Four guards came into the recreation room and watched the Boston/ Montreal hockey game, while I was typing out my essay. Another inmate needs my help with something so I helped her on the computer. They should offer some computer/ typing courses so when gals get out they can do some administrative work. I was happy to help and you know what that mate said thank you after I helped her out.

It was 8:00pm by the time it was done so no Wednesday night bible study group. I did happen to be able to thank the two guards who are kind enough not to shine their flash lights in my face at night and tell them how much I appreciate them keeping me safe and not being rude in the meantime.

I am just watching TV after my shower. Cathy and I did a double work out today so that hot shower felt good on these old bones. Today was also refill day, yes oh happy days. I made my own liquid tide and it smells great. The Dallas hockey game is on. I will call you at 10:45pm my son to chat. All my love.

February 7, 20xx

Good day and how did you sleep? This morning I am tired, my girls must be coming. I am watching the comedy channel this morning, I was watching a good church program, but I needed a laugh this morning so hence the comedy channel. Just got my second cup of coffee and God bless me with a fabulous sunrise so beautiful. I had no mail this morning and now it is time for Joyce. I need to stay close to God especially these days. I want to grow in God and his presents. Do what gives you peace is from Romans 14.

I wrote a letter to the gals at Corcan as it has been tough to see them for the letter of reference for parole. I was just enrolled into another construction course and let the organizers know I was each to complete as many courses as possible. It was nice to see my program instructor back today so self management will be on. I enjoy keeping busy, it keep the spirit on high and feels like you are accomplishing good words and being a blessing.

Today's chapter spoke to the surrendering to God and surrendering to him you problems and casting your care. Mea met with the new warden and she said the warden was very nice. Nice to have a ray of sunshine in here but we may have to land the entire sun. So wonderful. I am back from the long afternoon but accomplished a lot. Self management was great. Had canteen hygiene, so I picked up some cheap shampoo and conditioner as the refill department did not have the shampoo and were doing to deliver it once they came in so just in case good to have a backup. I purchased two popcorns for my movie night Saturday when I sit and enjoy the new feature and have popcorn or apple/ cinnamon.

I wrote to the ladies at Corcan as to what I was requesting and one of the ladies was really upset that they put I had quit on my report when I was on a leave for programming and correspondence and that she would love me to come back anytime. The intake worker made a mistake, well a few mistakes in my reports and it is important to have them corrected. The parole board reads them and they are not correct. So frustrating that you have to continuously babysit and make sure the people in authority are doing their job correctly.

I am thinking Zumba is a no go tonight as they are doing an aboriginal function tomorrow in the gym. Which ties into why that mate needed my assistance in the recreation room on the computer? She is doing the introduction to the lead speaker. So we will see otherwise I will start my parole binder if zumba is cancelled. I will also read or take a walk in the yard, depending on how many people are out tonight.

Sorry back to the lady at Corcan, she gave me a hug and told me she would it, the letter and she was upset at the intake's mistakes. She told me to come back on Tuesday to pick it up, so I have diarized it. It is almost 4:00pm and the count will commence soon. At 4:15pm I will call you and see how your day went. I wonder where Bob is these days.

I miss you two and my fuzzy baby. Cathy is making me work out for a few moments with her. Tonight was a quiet night. I am watching kids jeopardy and wow do you feel the lack of brain area but then I turn to you buck wild and these people are seriously lacking. So a good combo. Some days you feel like mush brain. Tomorrow is 30 days before you come in for a sleep over.

Well I am going to sign off on this letter but I will call at 8:45pm to chat and tomorrow bring on the kisses and hugs, plus a bunch of laughing during our visit.

February 8, 20xx

Good morning to you both. Thank goodness it is Friday. I am excited for our visit tonight; I miss you and being together. I am grateful for our telephone conversations and visits. I am grateful we have a sleepover soon and soon escorted visits and so forth. Thank you!

Today, the presentation starts at 9:00am so I will go check the mail and view Joyce and see what her message is. Joyce said not to be afraid of a little bit of suffering to get the great joy. We only give our own account for our lives. To be a bright light in a world of darkness.

Thanks mom for the deposit for the sleepover. Also, Mea saw Bob in the medication line. She told me he asked how I was doing, which is so kind of him. God is with us during this time and we will and are blessed. Poor Mea is having difficulties getting her passes to go to the hospital to see her nephew. I pray it will all work out. My light was flashing in my room and Cathy told me to call maintance to have them fix it. I replied, No it was my spirits and Mea let out a rude noise. Gosh these gals some days.

The sunrise was marvellous this morning. God sure paints some majestic pictures in the sky. Well, Mea day worked out and unfortunately you had to sign up for the conference but that is fine. In other words I was not able to attend.

I found some enjoyment in reading today. I was reading Joyce Meyers bible version and found comfort in her real inspirational stories. I did my arm work out; it's a bit different then Cathy's. I added a few more exercise. Wow I am still so amazed at the language around here and who is using such words really shows me the "Wolf in sheep's clothing". It is 2:00pm so I am going to take a break and watch Gilmore Girls. Sam and I had words today whereby I tried to fill her with words of encouragement and empowerment for her release. She told me she lucked out and was on the list for today so that was a blessing for you. I pray you are both having a fabulous day and for great news. I am so excited for our visit tonight. Good things always work out. God makes things that are to happen…happen. Soon we will be having our visit. All my love

February 9, 20xx

Good morning and so last night I was leaving a blessed new guard was available to do pat downs as the male guards cannot. She is very nice, but so are most of the guards. She was also funny which a great combo is. Well Sofi and I were leaving together she seemed a bit down so I gave her a "keep your spirits focuses on Him and focused on positives' speech. I almost landed on my butt, as it was so icy out. Pray you get home safely. At the house I flipped on the TV and on sports net they had a feature on the Oil changers and they so reminded me of you my son. All these boys have such great energy and bonding. Guys can have such great senses of humours.

So glad I got a hold of you this morning as I would not want you to worry if I did not call. Today I will try to go to a sweat and check it out hopefully it will be a great experience, but then again if you don't try things you will never experience life.

I checked the mail and on my way over I say Sofi and wished her a good morning and told her to be careful as she was heading to the spot I bit the dust on. She laughed and said, 'yes and I would be there to help her'. She seemed sad and I was glad I put a smile on her face. So I will be heading over to the sweat grounds as soon as they are ready. Cathy said to bring a towel, face cloth and water.

I was just called up to V&C to my surprise. I was able to chat with Bob. He asked me how I was doing and we chatted for a few moments about what has been going on. I am blessed to have him acting for me. I will fill you in later but currently the PFV will be suspended until February 26 but like I told Bob it will all work out. I will fill you in on everything tonight. But we will stay positive and that is all we can do.

Cathy and I did not go to the sweat just because I was not on the list and so she will sign me up for the other ones. If I was to go to one them it will happen. Cathy did not go because I could not go. At 2:00pm there is a band coming in so I will do laundry and then check out the band. I am excited to see you tonight. My son now I will be able to watch the hockey game for a bit. I love you.

I loved our visit. I wrote out why I want to come home to you guys and the bottom line is that you are my heart and my home is where the heart is or hugs, but mostly my heart. I love you both and each day I still miss you and I know one day closer to being with you both. I will be strong and focused, but it still is very difficult as I am sure you feel it also. All my love.

February 10, 20xx

Good morning to you both and happy sunny Sunday. I thing I may have slept too long as I am a bit groggy this morning. Cathy and I were doing out work at 11:00am and then I will call you at 11:30am. I will read my next chapter and then hugs and kisses to you both during our visit.

Thank you for a fabulous visit today. After Bob and I spoke so he told me the request will be going in hopefully this Wednesday but for sure next Wednesday and then would request three guards visits and then the ladies from the connecting streams, Pastor Ken, Whitey, or another volunteer can take me home, but it will all work out and everything has a process so we must be patient and it will all work out.

God is moving mountains. I pray every day for vindication will come but it is coming God hears our prayers, and the truth will be brought forth. So what happens is after the three guard visits, then the escorts can be plain clothed individuals and that is effective May 20ths. They are called ETAs, and then come the UTAs whereby you can come and get me. Bob walked me back to the house as count was about to start and he told me something interesting about the fact we were of similar minds in our faith. I/we trust in God and the truth will be coming out shortly. We will stay in faith and hold tight to God's word, intentions, and plan. Something amazing is in store and coming shortly. I love you both. I am going to go to church shortly and then write to pastor Ken a letter. Hope you both have a fabulous evening. They just announced no movement to chapel, so I will just wait and see if we have service or not.

Well no service tonight. I guess they cancelled it because of the church group that was in this afternoon. Which is fine as I will write to Pastor Ken asking if he would be my assistant at my parole hearing? I am going to ask him how someone is to be remorseful for something they did not do. I know God will show me and tell me, but he is going to reveal it to the people first. Bob is so funny. When he first sat me down he tells me I have to write better as he has trouble reading my stuff. Then he opens the letter and is pleasantly surprised that he can read it. I have been blessed as he told me he knows what I am trying to say. He told me he wants to get me out as many times as possible in the next two months and he knows home would be first.

Hey my son I am watching the Grammy and thinking of you. I really like the song "carry on" by Fun. The lead singer has a fabulous voice, very unique. Hope you had a great evening. I accomplished about half of my parole binder. You get bragging right son the hockey game tonight.

I love you both and I am so grateful for you both. All my love!

February 11, 20xx

How are you today? I am just watching some Gloria Copeland this morning before I head to the main to drop off the house food order. Last night at 10:00pm two guards came by one was Bob to give me back the information he did not need. His present was different, more positive. Bless him for being such a fabulous primary worker.

Today I will complete my parole binder, write to family, read my daily chapter and read Romans in the bible, there is connecting streams and Cathy and I will work out to complete the day. I pray you both have a fabulous day and full of good news. I pray for the neighbour and her health to improve, and home from the hospital. I pray for strength, grace and mercy today. I have signed up for a call for 1:15pm to hear about your day. You have all my love.

Today's message was Joshua 1:8, 'Don't give up…your circumstance will change…. as long as you persevere and continue to be courageous.'

Well it is 12:30pm and I have to reschedule some of my goals for today. I will write family on Wednesday ant that way I will have more things to tell her. I was inspired by Joyce's message and to read James instead, but I have completed my other tasks and everything will get accomplished. Pray you day is going wonderfully. All my love. Nat was also thrown under the bus by Mr. Reck something we have in common. It seems that I have a connection with each one of these women somehow, but a similar act or unjust act, a friend that links us or the system that links us.

It was lovely to chat with you both at lunch. I will call you after work. Debby is getting all her stuff sent to A&D as he is on her way to the halfway house. So congrats to her! So that means that the mates in the PFV will be moved somewhere and movement is all a part of being here. Sam leaves on Thursday so two opening at this house. And still the dynamics yet again change. Sam blew up at Cathy about the workout music, so Cathy turned it up louder. Sam wanted no music until after 1:00pm so that she could sleep. Should be interesting to see who moved in here.

The guards on today have been so kind. Really bubbly and positive and just so nice. I am so grateful to have such kind treatment and so blessed these kind guards are on today. Kindness is contagious. Wow I just got back from connecting streams and the Katie Souza chapter spoke to me along with the Holy spirit before I went saying to me, 'you are a fighter, don't let anyone intimidate you☺ stand up ☺ be strong. I have so many people who know my story and so many supporters and my boss, God is right beside me. It is Nat's birthday and so she asked me to go for a walk with her, so I will check the mail while we walk. I pray you had a fabulous day and I pray for you both to stay strong and healthy. All my love and I will call you at 10:45pm as you will be home from work. Xoxox

February 12, 20xx

Good morning and how are you today? Before I forget last night's Shameless was about Pheona and being her sexually harassed by her boss which was symbolic to why I have to keep strong and press forward for justice. I will stay strong and get my message out to bring forth because God and my fabulous supporters are moving me forward to have this story told and for him to face the truth. So yesterday willing a few hours of Katie Souza spoke to me, a girl in my walk outside asked me what my book's name was and on Shameless the sexual harassment scenario it all came together to press forward.

I am going to check at Corcan about the letter, do the construction course and I will call you on my break to confirm visits and then we will have our blessed visit tonight you and me mom. I send kisses home to you my son. Cathy and I will work out and finish my day with our chat my son.

I learned something about a lady from connecting streams that just goes to show you we all have extreme struggles. I was grateful she shared with us her story and her struggle. We are all here for a reason and no one is better or worse than the other. We are all God's children and it is important not to judge therefore won't be judged. Humbling yes, but so true!

Well this morning was mail and I received a notice that the computer paper stating I have to have special permission to receive computer paper. Good thing I have completed my assignments so my letters will be neatest hand writing as possible. Gosh always one more hoop to jump over. Anyways, I passed my construction course and have another ticket under my belt. Whitey had a keyboard for me to carry back to my room also. Pastor Ken is cleared to come in for visits and Whitey is tracking down the person who will certify him to be my escort also and we can break bread soon.

Tomorrow I have to take Debbie's bible study information up and return it to Whitey and I will have another chance to chat with him then. It is now 5:00pm so I will see you soon mom and I will call you later my son at 10:45pm. I pray your days are full of joy, laughter and good news. I love you both. I will tell you some funny stories that happened today. The girl in the construction course asking me to pray with her and asking for me to bless her as she was cursing at a fellow mate, Mea locking me out of the house while I was carrying the piano and playing a joke on me. She is such a brat. I am grateful no one has taken away our ability to laugh.

Thank you mom for our visit and the words of strength and wisdom. Gosh I am so blessed to have you the big boss in my corner but also to have such a terrific strength in you both. I will speak with Whitey tomorrow and let you know what he says. The book of James is all about watching your mouth and remembers that words are powerful, so fitting. I love you both and you had all my love.

February 13, 20xx

Good morning to you both and how are you this windy Wednesday? Holy one gal in the house needs to be tames by God. Her mood and tongue this morning is seriously in need of being checked. She in her mood tone as I was doing my laundry, "you doing laundry again, you must change a lot you're always doing laundry!' Yes I like to be clean and what is it to her. She is not paying for the soap or the water. I pray for her to get her mind in a kind manner. I am going to check the mail at movement, watch Joyce, read my chapter, and do my questions for connecting streams, workout, speak to Whitey, I am making dinner (spaghetti), I will take a walk tonight in the yard, and read Romans (which discussed Righteousness). Today I pray we all have a fabulous day. I pray for good news. I pray for our strength, our health and our safety and victory. I will call you at 10:30am and again tonight.

Well Joyce spoke to me today, God bless her show with a message for and to me. One section spoke on guilt and you can't live in guilt if you have been reborn and living in the word of God. To have no religion demons, you asked for forgiveness and more on, rather than dragging it on and on and continue to make mistakes in the guilt. Like I said yesterday you have to live in Christ and therefore death in sin, you walk in the relationship with Christ. All your/my sins were washed upon the cross. God is the God of heart and he can't live in you and vise versa if you carry guilt. How to you share his work to others if you have a dark cloud and the devil is dragging you down. God is my life and I/we are nothing without him. Praise be to God, Jesus is law.

There was an Elizabeth Fry sign up form on the table this morning so I inquired information from Cathy who kindly explained how the lady would supply information like my back up plan upon my release, as to help get you started back in the community. I took this information and put it in my parole binder for a backup plan and this would show the parole board I was serious about being returned back into the community and forward in my life. I pray God is moving mountains for us.

I cooked dinner and of course right in the middle I had to run to V & C to add postage to my letter but Emily thought I would require more so she just told me to bring it back to her tonight which I will as there is Chapel at 6:00pm and I need to give Whitey the bible group information from Debby. Alpha that I thought started tomorrow actually commences Sunday after Church. Cathy and I worked out to get back on our fitness track since we were both tired yesterday. So at 6:00pm there is church in the Chapel and then Nat asked to walk which is great to get some fresh air and exercise. I got half way into Romans which is the chapter on Righteousness and will continue later to complete it. I pray you both had a fabulous day and full of wonderful news and joy and laughter. I will call you at 9:00pm and see how your day went. I love you both and miss you terribly. All my love.

February 14, 20xx

Happy love day! Last night service Whitey blessed me and the other ladies who attended service with a blessed cross on our forehead for Ash Wednesday. Bridget and I have committed to doing without starchy carbs (potatoes, pasta, and bread) but we can still eat popcorn as our sacrifice which in no way compares to what Jesus did for us. It is so nice to go out and have such great energy and to share with others to give them hope and love.

Nat and I walked the yard for a bit after and hopefully my words spoke to her by not getting involved with some of the women's drama. She and Lori had a bad relationship so my advice to Nat was to be pleasant and to focus on her own path. I came back and Lori was in Mea's room and Mea called me to do her homework which I won't do but I will help her study. Lori asked me what I had in my hands as I showed her my cards from class and she then pipes up to say they told me I could not take it unless I was getting out in four months, so I said I must be getting out in four months. I don't care what she says; she won't play games with me, and no will I back down to her.

Lori is bad news and bad energy. She is not a good person is not good for this house. Sam leaves today bless her God on her journey and may she never return and have a fabulous rest of her next journey. I love you both so much and really missing you today.

I am truly blessed and you are in my life. Last night at church Whitey spoke of the significance of the number 40, 40 is how old I was when I entered here…40 days and 40 nights…40 years lost in the wilderness and Jesus went without food for 40 days. This number really hit home for me.

Gosh this morning someone was up really early banging around. I can't wait until June to get a good night's sleep with no disturbances. I just came back upstairs while I was down there in the kitchen Susan says to me that I looked like I did not get enough sleep as she yawns. Well, no kidding when you have the rude ones banging around or their inside voices is yelling. I am going to stay in prayer today. I receive a reply from my parole officer regarding my errors in my reports so it was awesome she replied and a blessing that Bob is making the corrections. I received a lovely letter from family. It really is family that keeps you going in here.

Again, happy love day to you both. James 4:1 our value is how we are in Christ. Well, I am going to read and the Cathy and I will work out. I will call you at 1:10pm and hopefully my son you will be there, before you head off to work again and me to programs. I miss you and keep focused on one day closer to be together.

I have got some happy news to tell you tonight about Mr. Reck. The letter indicates that they will keep my file open and that I now will get a letter from my mate to add to this matter. She is going to write a letter before I leave on her experience with this silly lawyer and how he managed to mess her case up. They really need to disbar him now before he fails others.

Program was great. I really like this instructor and this class group is really fun. I got back to the house and Lori starts in on me about how Bob was looking for me, I said he know that I am in programs and well she goes off about how he came looking for me and how she told him I was in programs but he did not know where I was and on and on. So I asked did they have me pages. Lori said no, I asked was it 2:00pm when he came here, she said yes. I said Bob was just probably asking and forgot or was going to tell me something or ask me something that he thought he could say during his rounds and then I walked away. Her body language is very defensive and her attitude is very in your face and rude. All I can say is stay out of my business and gosh I don't need someone jumping all over me once I get back from programs. She is miss busy body and I don't trust her. She is not right in the head

Tonight is Zumba so Nat and I are going. Mea is out visiting her family, Cathy is on a date, and Susan is probably staying in her room. I can't wait to chat with you at 10:45pm. I pray you had a fabulous day and blessed with good news. Today was canteen day and fruit day. Gosh so much happens around her. Bob popped by with another guard and gave me the good news about the PFV and Pastor Ken has been cleared to come and visit me and that Bob would be meeting with the warden next week to discuss my escorted visits. I told Bob to mention that Pizza would be involved to the guard who took me home and try and sweeten the deal. Bob smiled his big smile. I mentioned that I asked Pastor Ken to be my assistant at my hearing. I told Bob I completed another construction course and showed him and the other guard my parole binder they both could not believe my commitment.

Anyway, we discussed the light in the room but I will tell you when I mentioned it was fine and it gave me comfort when the light flickered as if a spirit was in the room the guards got spooked. The story is someone died in that room, but whether it is true or not I did not confirm. I told Bob about Mr. Reck and the movement in that arena and he again smiled his big smile.

I went to Zumba and saw the connecting streams ladies. They gave me a big hug and hoped to be able to take me out this Saturday, but it may have to wait until the following Saturday. They want to take me to their church which would be so lovely.

My son we have to get the CD Konya West second cd Jesus and Lupe Fiasco Loser, I think you would like them.

I pray you both had a fabulous day and so excited to be blessed with what God has blessed me with today. I love you both and I pray you both had a great love day. I am doing laundry again and this time Susan just laughed about it. The mood swings in here are off the chart. All my love.

February 15, 20xx

Good morning and how are you doing? I was so happy after our chat last night, my son I was so grateful that you were looking at how blessed we are. I told Cathy how you know the Konya West song Jesus walks, she smiled and then I spoke of our conversation when I said, my son I feel like we have such disconnect and you said that I was just catching u, well then she laughed. It is nice to see the other mates laugh at our humour and see how united we are.

I pray you both have a fabulous day and full of love, joy and blessings. How fitting is the next chapter of Rich Warren's book, but "What matters most". In the Copeland daily devotional has a message of making the switch and walking in love of God, so a couple of exciting chapters to read. I must practice my piano scales that the instructor taught me a few weeks ago. I was blessed with a visit from my beloved family so I did not attend piano lesson and now I need to practice. Cathy asked to work out at 4:00pm. I will call you both at 1:15pm to see how your morning went. I love you and miss you both terribly. I am so bless to have you both. All my love.

God be with us! No mail today and I pray you both stay safe especially with the freezing rain. Yesterday at self management I leaned it is okay to be happy and a person could not be too happy. Joyce had an interesting message about having safe friends, and in fellowship you can find true people. Trust in god to work something good out of the situation. Romans 11:6-34, 'God's moving the mountains..' what matters the most is love. Time is your most precious gift because you only have a set amount of it. By giving someone your time you are giving them a precious gift. Thank you for extending your time to me. The best use of life is love, and the best expression of love is time, which is now as you don't know how much you have. Life is all about love! Funny how Kenneth and Gloria Copeland daily devotional speaks on the walk in love John 4:16-17 and 15:4-5. So I am practicing piano for tonight's lesson. I have to say one thing before I move on and that is I do not trust this Lori lady in here and after I have a chance to tell you a few things you will see also, but I will mind my business and she had better do the same. Bless you two.

The guards this morning are so cute. The one guard is so friendly she always says hello and good morning and today she must have thought what the heck she is doing now with a piano. I don't have it on but I make my own noise. We should look on kijiji for a uses one or a cheap version as this is really great to stimulate the brain. This one is a Yamaha Piaggero NP-11 digital keyboard and very light and compact version. The guards must keep entertained to see what I am up to next while I am here. Not correspondence, church, working out, zumba, piano then what? Keeps them on their toes.

My son you crack me up and telling grandma about getting a baby grand piano. I love your sense of humour. You keep me smiling. Susan joined Cathy and me for our legs work out. Her mood has changed, Susan's mood as she is getting out soon, so she is actually pleasant to be around well today anyways. Susan has such a contagious laugh which she should use more often. Cathy music is wearing off on me, my son when I get out I will be even more musically rounded then when I got here. At 6:00pm I have piano and then Nat and I will walk the yard. Cathy was in the PFV house today with her daughter so that is a great sign our sleep over is on.

Hey my son and mom, well tonight I had piano and discovered I was playing my left hand scales all wrong, but oh well I will practice and will get them correct. Then at 6:55pm I was back to go for a walk with Nat which we walked a few loops and then she had to go and call her kids. Yes kids come first. So I continued to walk with my radio head set until 8:00pm. I had a shower and popped some popcorn and now I am writing to you and watching Two and half men.

A new girl came in her name is Tara. She is in Sam's old room. I am sure there will be a house meeting soon with all these new mates. Funny how when a new person comes in Mea and Susan is pulling pecking order. Being very immature, silly and weird. They are at least doing this downstairs so the upstairs is quiet where I am, so there is always a silver lining to all life situations. Bless you both.

I pray you both had a great day and full of fabulous news and lots of joy and laugher. I spoke to Bob and he is trying to get things all lined up for Wednesday to go before the warden and the board at the jail. I spoke to a guard also about the paper situation but I will not sweat the small stuff as some of the guards would let it pass but then others won't so I will just place an order with London drugs to get computer paper.

Bless the guards. It is so wonderful when there are ones, who are so able to see things, but I do appreciate to follow the rules and regulations and that is just fine. Overall, all is great. I love you and will chat at 10:45pm. All my love.

February 16, 20xx

Good morning to you both and happy Saturday. Hope you both had a wonderful sleep. Hope your cold has gotten better mom. I am so excited to see you both today and give you both a big hug and kiss. I love you so much and miss you, but I am grateful for my visits with you and focus on the next step of coming to see you and the four legged fuzzy baby. I am going to go check the mail and call you at 11:30am, read the daily devotional and the chapter in the Purpose Driven life. Get him to the Greek is on TV and it is the humour a person needs in here.

I don't want to be a spoiler but I do want you to learn the five purposes: focus on God, face life's problems in fellowship, discipleship helps fortify your faith, minister helps find your talents, evangelism helps fulfill your mission.

Thanks for our visit today, it was lovely. Wow the Lisa situation will have me in my room also. She and I were on dishes tonight together and she sits on the couch while people do their own dishes. I was eating so she could have washed and I would have dried, but instead she allowed Nat to wash so I let Nat know I have got it, same with the new girl.

Well, Lisa sits here so I do the washing and no movement; she gets up so I asked her if the guards were coming she snaps at me. I do the washing and then I do the drying she snaps at me while Mea was in the room, but she does it under her breath but I heard her so I challenged her, she said, why don't you find someone else to do dishes with. Well, I won't accept that attitude. I said I was just drying the dishes I just washed. I think she forgot who she was speaking too. Nat and I will be taking a walk at 6:00pm. The thing is Lisa talks under her breath, but she did it to Mea also. Lori is trouble and so is Lisa. Lisa is bad news and she should not be in this house.

Funny how Fifth Estate is running the Whistleblower episode on February 22, I will make sure to catch it. Anyways, just know that God moves our mountains. I love you both so much and I can't wait for our visit and to be with you again.

I will need character letters for my parole hearing from supporters, and family again. Nat and I had a fabulous walk, I wrote a letter to gal friends and now I am watching the hockey game. I love you both and so blessed to have God and you and fabulous supporters. All my love. Xoxoxox

February 17, 20xx

Good morning to you both. How are you today? I am going to go walking the yard when movement is called at 10:00am and get some fresh air. The new girl, Tara is developing a snotty attitude and I just need to remove myself. Go get into my God space. I am looking forward to our visit. Cathy wants to work out at 11:00am, I will read the chapter, and do my daily devotional, our precious visit and then chapel and Alpha, with two letters to be written. That should be a wrap for the day. I love you with all my soul.

Thanks for you visit. I so enjoy out time together and at the end of each day you are all that matters. I reflected on what an honour it was for the lady here who volunteers to ask me to lead the Wednesday night bible session. And I will mention it to Bob also. I will wait and see if Whitey asks me, but I don't want to over commit, as every night I am involved in something and you are my focus and my priority. Right now I think it is an honour, but my gut is telling me not to over commit. God will be the one to ultimately lead my path. Well I am off to service and then to Alpha. I will call you to say goodnight at 10:15pm. Mom and my son I pray for you to be safe and enjoy cheering on your friend's hockey team.

Church and Alpha were wonderful and so nice to get around others who enjoy true fellowship. I really enjoy Marilyn's energy and I am blessed to be in her group. She asked me also if I would carry Kononia on and I explained to her my concerns. All in God's hands, he will lead me. I love you both so, so much. All my love.

February 18, 20xx

How are you both this fine start to the week? Well happy family day to you both. In here the day is not a holiday, but I am forever grateful to be able to see you tonight, until then I will read my devotional, read my daily chapter, and read the book of Luke in the bible. Which is worse, 'silence of your friends, not the words of your enemies'? I love this line I hear on the housewives last night.

Oh Gloria Copeland it was said you can't be born again, again, which spoke volumes as these people who have returned here can't continue to use God as their crutch if their spirit does not act in line with God's word. Mea returned last night so I would suspect a house meeting is coming which will hopefully alleviate the tension here. It would be nice to be able to be around people with a great attitude. Joyce made a great point this morning which is to look at you so while I am here I am going to stay in fellowship with God and press through for victory with now regrets. To be fully committed to God.

Today was a blah day. I am excited to see you both. You are my inspiration. I love to play games and chat with you both and this is actually the closest we have been. Our bound is nothing but strengthening. I love you both and I am excited to hear about your night and day with the boys. All my love.

February 19, 20xx

Great day to you both. How are you doing? How did you sleep? Thanks for the news yesterday that came from our supporters. I am glad you and the boys will be doing something exciting today. A positive notion was just put into my thoughts that all this will soon come to an end and I will not going to change my positive being because these women have issues. I will continue to be well mannered, kind, and pleasant. I will remove myself from any negativity. I will keep my thoughts purer and focused on God, because He is all that matters. This will also help me/us get past this gong.

I miss you and being with you more than words can say. I love you with all my heart and being. God bless us today. Joyce spoke on resistance. This morning I was blessed again with a letter from the aunts. Joyce made me laugh and truly hit home about how God will test and work for your benefit. I would like to get her CD called guard your heart when I get out. The next two weeks at Kononia, the volunteer is showing a DVD on one of Joyce's messages. When I get out I am going to join Joyce's partnerships to spread the word of God. Well, I am going to go and read and write our supporters back. I love you both.

I attended Connecting streams and met a couple of new women who were so amazing. Funny but fabulous this connecting steams is not doing the Katie Souze story but a bible study so I was so filled. They are very open and it was the first time that you could share openly in fellowship.

I spoke to Bob and so hopefully we can go before the warden tomorrow. I pray we will be blessed tomorrow. My son I am so proud of you and I cherish you each and every moment. I am proud of how you are handling everything and people. I am so proud of your maturity. You are such an amazing person. God puts everything into perspective and after connecting streams and what was shared that really hit home. These women are so broken and the struggles are beyond belief.

I told you when I came here this place would not change me but I would change it. The spreading of kindness and smiles is what this place is lacking and I am filling that void. I pray I am the light in the darkness. We had the house meeting, so I made sure that dinner was ready. Dinner was actually really good. Tara and I had a small chat nothing to long but nice. A nice ice breaker after the house meeting and it worked out. At one point in the meeting there was some tension so hopefully this will be the end of everything and we can enjoy the peace. Peace is wonderful.

I am blessed to have our visit tonight and blessed to chat with you today my son. God is moving our mountains. I love you both and so blessed to have you and all the outside supporters and inside supporters.

See you soon for our visit and we can laugh over cards and other games. Xoxox all my love.

February 20, 20xx

Good morning to you both. How are you this wonderful Wednesday morning? I pray you are blesses with great news today, I pray that we may go before the warden and be blessed with me being able to come and visit you. I love you both and my heart is missing you, but as we move forward one day closer and one day closer to God's amazing plan. We will enjoy each day and be grateful.

I wonder what Joyce has in store for a message today. Her message was to draw close to God and to grow with God. Well, I am going to read and listen for my name to be called up to see if the warden will bless us.

Well God has blessed us yet again. I am so excited for our 1:15 pm call to fill you both in. Bob has blessed us with some fabulous news that the blessed warden offered. I wish I could have extended my appreciation to her personally, but today was not the day for us to have met. Maybe later today or maybe tomorrow but one day I will personally extend my gratitude to her. I pray you will receive fabulous news also. I pray God continues to move our mountains. I just don't know how everyone could not want to be in God's company when he offers and does so much for each of us.

Bob said that he was discussing our application for escorted visitation and telling the warden all I have accomplished and achieved and she was so impressed and asked what I was doing here. The warden asked if she could grant me day parole and that I should not be here. Bob was thrown off by her comments and smiled. He also confirmed my success and how wonderful he thought it was. It really feels wonderful when the people can see you don't belong here.

Bless the maintenance staff for fixing the plugged drain in the kitchen. Tomorrow I will make a point of saying thanks to that department when I go see the gals at Corcan. This morning when I went to check my mail I ran into Apple who I have not seen in a bit and we exchanged hugs and a positive chat. It is so nice to exchange positive inspirational words; it keeps the world a better place.

Kononia is offering a two part DVD on Joyce Meyer so that should be fabulous. I told Bob he and his wife should look into Joyce as he has not heard of her before. It is nice to exchange information that will strengthen people's faith and fellowship. Gosh after Bob told me the blessed news I noticed the sun came out, so I pointed it out to Bob. I have just fixed myself some lunch and turned on the TV and guess what is on Erin Brockovich.

Thanks mom for following up and making the phone calls I can't make in here. I am glad that the neighbours are doing well and in great spirits. I sure hope that the doctors can tell her what is wrong but hopefully it passes and does not amount to anything. Thank you mom for speaking to Pastor Ken. I saw Whitey so I am sure they will connect and I will be blessed with a visit from Pastor Ken soon. Thank you for finding out how my final will proceed in here and we will just wait until Scott returns his phone calls.

Just before we chatted I was called up to V&C and spoke to Bally. It was nice to see her back and that she was ensuring all was good for the PFV and our escorted visits. Nice to have her back. I am sure she had heard or will hear things about the taxation debacle. I often wonder if Sara the acting parole officer filled Bally in on the yelling of Mr. Reck during the taxation hearing. He was completely unprofessional and after hearing him yelling one could see him doing that to me to get me to plead guilty to something I did not do. It became apparent that this man had driven clients into pleading to a crime they did not do. He becomes a different person them most see. He is simply a cruel man.

Well it is all in God's hands. I am so glad we were blessed today and I am so grateful to share the journey with you two. My son I hope you are getting better and your toe is healing. Soak it and if things are still not looking good, you have to get medical attention. Don't leave it. And don't let grandma tell you that expiry dates don't matter, they do. I love you both so much.

I just got back from Kononia where we enjoyed watching a DVD on Joyce. I think the reason Kononia is not working is due to one person. I would wager a bet if I was not there it would probably stop all together. Something was said to me tonight by the volunteer which was very rude but I am not taking it personally as she was saying as though someone else had said it which is gossip and unacceptable so for anything to have been said was not proper. Anyways, like I spoke to the group and said "that everyone is on their own journey with Christ and God and to not compare your journey to anyone else's and vice versa also to forces on your strengths and not compare to others.

Mea just called me to chat with her so I disclosed our good news about ETA's. Mea was loading me up with sports bras and yoga pants, then Susan came in. They were both happy for us. Nice to have good energy and they were genuinely happy which is rare in here.

Tomorrow is Zumba and Mea and Susan said they would be going. Should be a fun time with a lot of good laughs which helps burn more calories. I pray for you both that you had a fabulous day and long for us to be together. I am grateful we will still be able to have a sleep over and body guard visits. Again, my journey is so blessed because I am able to share it with you. All my love and all my heart.

February 21, 20xx

Good morning to you both. I imagine very tired after last night and going and waiting at the hospital for your toe. I hope that the medication will help and kill the infection. I wish I could be there to help with you and take care of you, my son you are still a baby to me. I am so proud of you and of both of you for taking care of each other. Enjoy your morning and I will chat with you at 1:00pm. I pray we receive some blessed news today.

I am watching Gloria Copeland speaking on Revelations and then Joyce Meyer is on. I am going to check the mail and pop in and see the ladies at Corcan. I was going to go at lunchtime but I will go this morning. I will suspect it will not be done, but going to go after programs and give the ladies the morning to get it done. I pray that

Wayne will call you and appear and contact you or me and let us know what is going on with him.

Well, as I was putting in my laundry they announced that Corcan would be closed today, so I will stop and see the ladies tomorrow. God gave me this message loud and clear. Oh my son, sorry to hear your stomach is being affected by the medication for your infected toe. Drinks some ginger ale to help settle your stomach down. I attended Darcy's presentation which she discussed sexually transmitted diseases in the institution. She did a fabulous job and very informative. Cathy, Susan and I finished doing our arms work out and Cathy and I were chatting afterwards about re-integration is next week, next Saturday so I will find out how much notice I will get and we will just go with what happens. This could be an escorted visit out. This Saturday we will have our morning visit from 9-11am and then I will get my sweat in so check that off the list since the other ones have not worked out time wise, but all things will happen the way they should happen.

A mate left today at lunchtime. I pray she has a wonderful journey and wish her all the best with her family, so most likely by tonight or tomorrow there will be someone new and again the dynamics will shift again.

My son I hope you are feeling better and help out grandma. A big group hug is what I am sending you guys. I am going to Zumba at 7:00pm and I will call you at 9:30pm to catch up on the day's events. My son, A Bronx Tale is on. You can have all the talent but if you don't' use it, it is just wasted is what the movie says and that is a sound message. Canteen was today for hygiene and gosh I so appreciate something as simple as a box of Kleenex. My $4.00 purchase was Kleenex, q-tips, and Tums. Next canteen will be purchase popcorn for our sleepover. I need to find out about getting your stuff cleared to come in. Just another adventure we get to share together.

Something is happening as they just stopped movement and told everyone to get home. Back to your units was announced over the loud system. I can't wait to enjoy a meal with you both at home. All my love.

Well tonight we had a lock down with no movement, so no zumba which is very sad. But that is okay as the weekend will be nice outside so lots of fresh air and walking. Nat is watching some TV in my room for a few hours, but she really needs to attempt to get along with the other ladies. As it will make her time here more enjoyable. She is so consumed about others especially and it is only making her look bad. Who cares and focus on your own journey, just like I have told her. She is too busy to worry about nothing. I hope she follows my words and minds her own business and gets her own path. But this one mate is really causing Nat's life difficult.

I love you both and miss you. Cathy told me she would teach me a card game called "tens" the universal jail card game. I will call you at 9:30pm to chat and catch up on our days. All my love. xxoxoxo

February 22, 20xx

Gracious morning mom and my son. How are you this Friday? How is your toe my son? I miss you both and one day closer to being out and together. You keep me strong. Last night I made a rice bag, which acts like a heating pad. Well today I will do some reading, and practice piano for my lesson tonight. I was going to go to Corcan this morning which I will pop in unless it is closed again. I am sure they have not done the letter, but I will check anyways.

Nope no mail and they did not do my letter as one of the girls is really sick and so I will come back on Tuesday and hopefully they will have it completed. No one is in any rush around here to get things done, but then again it maybe a lesson to slow down and enjoy life.

Joyce spoke to me this morning. God will make all correct. Joshua 24:15 "Wait for God. Wait for God...God is moving the mountains. I was walking over to the main and Nat was walking with me, well she started up on the Lori and Lisa and I told her to stop it and don't let them spoil her day. I am going to tell her every time she wants to be negative to stop it. Either she stop it or she will get tired and stop wanting to be around me.

The girl, who wrote a mean letter to Ray way back when, showed me she received a letter from Ray. I was in disbelief but maybe they figured things out. So I asked if it is nice where she is at and a nice letter, she looked at me and says, 'yes' in a silly voice, so I replied well that is nice.

Joyce was about staying focused on God and follows the leadership of the Holy Spirit. Peace be with you! The chapter in the devotional spoke on being mature in your walk. "Be careful how you think; your life is shaped by your thoughts' Proverbs 4:23. I also think 'put on the new self created to be like God is true righteousness and holiness'. Ephesians 4:23. Food for thought.

Interesting how Gloria Copeland spoke on how the devil/ Satan is like a salesman, reminds me of what Nat is doing, but she has two choices one to stop it and get on with life or two I won't be able to associate with her and remove myself. Just like Gloria says, 'so the next time Satan starts his sales pitch, talk back.' I am going to do that when Satan tries to steal my joy or he sends others to do so, not going to work. Get out of her devil in the name of Jesus. Kisses to both of you and hugs all around. God bless us and protect us and show us glory and overflowing grace and the free gift of righteousness.

Well today had such a wonderful ending, me seeing you. I hope you both know who much I appreciate you both and spending time with you. I hate saying goodbye and I hate seeing you leave. I love you more than words can say, you are my everything. All my love. Thank you, thank you for all your time spent visiting me and being my support. Oxoxoxo

February 23, 20xx

Good Saturday morning mom and my son. How are you today? Thank you for coming to see me this morning. My son I hope your toe is doing better today. I am just watching the comedy channel, nice way to start the day with a laugh and a smile. Last night I walked the yard for a bit with my head phones on but it got go crowded so I came in and got ready for count and bed. After count I hit the sack, and silly Cathy wanted to share with me a cologne smell. Nice when mates are just kind. I could not believe that Max is back. Cathy says the return rate is 87%. Why? Has the separation from children and family not been enough to never return? I never want to be separated from you again…ever! I love you both and cherish our relationship and I am so grateful to have you both. I will see you shortly for our visit. My heart is pounding with excitement to see you.

What a lovely visit. Thank you. I have just completed the sweat and it was really nice. The Cookem (Grandmother) was very informative of the entire process which was fabulous to experience the full ritual. How you sit, the offerings of the berries, the peace pipe, the seven grandparents, the meat after, the meaning of each of the four quarters, you say "all my relations' after each prayer. Cathy says each sweat is different, but this one was a very nice one especially for a first timer. I will go into more detail tomorrow at our visit, but just know that the adventure allows for us to experience new journeys. It was also lovely to experience the sweat with a lovely bunch of people.

After our visit this morning the guard said I had another visit tonight. I am not sure if she was mistaken or meant tomorrow or if it was for connecting streams so I have showered and culled my locks just in case otherwise I will be relaxing and calling you at 10:15pm. The sweat really drains you so I hope relaxing is the mode. I know you are not visiting and that is not me for sure. I am doing laundry as jacket smells like fire. Overall, today has been a very blessed day.

Tonight was a nice quiet evening which is just fine as I had a bit of a headache. I am just watching the movie, 'What happens in Vegas', and eating my apple and having a hot chocolate. I hope you both had a great day and evening. I will chat on the phone soon with you. All my love. Xoxoxo

February 24, 20xx

Good morning mom and my son. How are you both today? I am excited to see you both today. I expect the glory of God to rain out over my life like the rain. I am trying to memorize the word and I love this line, so empowering and inspiring. My son I hope you had a great evening with the boys. I hope your infected toe is feeling better. I checked the mail and nothing for me. I am praying that next Saturday or Sunday we can arrange so I could come home for a visit. I am grateful to see you and so looking forward to sharing a meal with you both. Last night I helped Mea organize her peer support cards. As we were doing this and chatting, Lori came back from her visit. She hovers around anyways. She told us she is going to move to another jail closer to her family. Funny how God works. That would be lovely as I know how important family is to me. I am going to do my daily readings and do the daily work out. I will call you at 11:30am to confirm we are still on for visits.

Bless our visit today. I am so blessed to see you both so many times. I am so grateful for your continued support and love. I attended church with Whitey and saw Sandy and her family there. Sandy is a wonderful woman who runs connecting streams on Tuesday during the day and she attends Zumba also. Just a lovely lady.

Gosh, God does paint some beautiful sunsets here. I am off to Alpha shortly and want to get this letter in the mail when I can move. I have put in an ETA request to come see you next Sunday. I love you both and I will call you at 10:15pm to say goodnight. All my love.... xoxoxoxo Remember to stay strong, stays positive, and to say in God's love.

February 25, 20xx

Good morning to you both. How are you today? How did you sleep? Someone here was doing laundry at 5:00am and then Susan was up banging around. Mea asked if I would hand in the food order so I got ready and when they called movement I took up the food order. Lisa was swearing before I left the house about the coffee. She should not be so ungrateful and be thankful someone made coffee. Her negativity is so awful and the swearing is unbelievable. I just have to leave. God I am so aware of the negative speech, of excuse and the swearing and how awful it all sounds. Interesting last night at Alpha how Marilyn mentioned how the world outside is becoming more evil and under attach. God it is time to set me free to go and spread your live and word.

I love you both and pray for a blessed day. I pray you both have
the Holy Spirit fill you and protect you from the evil and cold hearted
persons. Stay strong, and wear a smile to protect you from the mean
people. God blessed me today with some awesome words. Mea said she
only had so many days left and I told her I would be praying for her
and we would spend the day also in prayer and empowering words. She
told me she would like to come and be a support to me. She told me she
would even like to come and wait in V&C if they would not allow her
to come in the room during my parole hearing. Mea said I would get
my parole. She told me I could use her stereo if I wanted to work out.
I told Mea that her words meant so much to me this morning. It was
so wonderful to share kindness and positive feelings. I enjoy going to
connecting streams with a fellow mate from another house. Her name
is Victory and she is a strong desire to know God as do I and to walk a
Godly walk, so we have similar energy. Plus, we like the positive which
helps, empowers and motivates healthy growth. God thank you for the
kind words spoken by Mea. Funny how other mates are supporting my
release. God works in the most amazing ways. So touching. I spoke to
Marilyn and the other Alpha volunteers and God's presents but they
should read my first book and then the second to truly appreciate all
He has accomplished will leave your breath taking and leave you in
amazement.

Well, I spend my day completing my readings, transferring my
Alpha notes, and Mea gave me a manicure. I spoke to my number one
supporters and the two that fill my heart, I cooked dinner which was
beans and wieners, hot dogs, and cob salad, and I worked out. Cathy
and Susan were coming upstairs to work out and Susan announces that
Cathy's moving out. What? Here and I spoke about possible moving but
I thought it would not occur until after I left. We had a good laugh and
its all in God's plan. She needs to do what is best for her and her family.
Time will tell what happens. Tonight I am going to connecting streams,
Wednesday is the Restorative Justice presentation from 7-8:30pm so
that will be good.

I can enjoy Joyce at Kononia and before the volunteer scares
everyone, I will be able to enjoy Restorative justice presentation. But like
I said I can certainly read my bible in my room and enjoy my growth

with God. I certainly do not desire to be in a negative environment. So hopefully the volunteer will mellow out and be more open minded. Anyways, Bob is on rounds tonight so maybe we will hear if the sleep over is a go, fingers crossed.

I pray your day was filled with awesome news, great things, and happy times and most of all love. I love you so much.

Connecting streams was wonderful, they were actually going to take me out last Saturday except there was something that occurred here, but anyways I was just called to V&C and was able to let Bob know, plus clarify that I needed to put in my request for other ETA's so all is good. I am so blessed and grateful to huge a fabulous PW and other wonderful guards here. Thanks god and continue to bless the staff, volunteers, and guards here. I appreciate them looking out for me and with extension you.

I love you both and pray you have a fabulous day also. The guards are looking out for us and that I am so grateful for. I am going to sign off but I will call you in a bit to chat, so just in case I don't tell you everything it is in here this letter. All my love. Xoxoxo

February 26, 20xx

Happy Tuesday to you both. How are you both doing this morning? I pray you both have a terrific day full of joy, peace and good news. I will hand in the request for the ETA's and go and see the ladies at Corcan. I have readings to complete and will chat at 1:00pm. My son I am so proud of you and mom I thank you so much for taking care of my precious son and my cat. God bless that cat for continuing to put a smile on our face. I love you and one day closer to being united with you.

Well I was accepted into fork lifting and confined spaces. Unfortunately the confined spaces lands on the self management date so I will ask the coordinator to please put me on the wait list for next session. I will confirm with the instructor of the program that there is a class as sometimes class is cancelled but I have first committed to my program then to training. I wrote to the coordinator of the training and just let her know it was interested and asked if she would call me to discuss as it is impossible to move and I need to speak with programs which would time out perfectly. You have to secure a spot with a $10.00 holding fee, as some people sign up and don't show up and that has to be in by Wednesday and my time with the program lady is Thursday. So time is ticking and I need to get this sorted out. It will all work out.

I popped in to see the ladies at Corcan and the letter was not done yet but one will be done but I also was asked to come back and that I could pick my days pick my time and drop in when ever. I had time, plus they would be will to pay me incentive pay. So I will discuss it with you both and as it is on the down low we can weigh out the pros and cons. The ladies said it would be awesome if I could come back and how they really need a competent person like me. Bless them. I was thinking maybe Wednesday, but let's discuss it first.

Funny how everyone will sign up for the job jar which is a hit and miss but to commit to work at Corcan, nope they will not. Some of these mates have no work ethics. Thank you for our lovely chat at lunch. I hope Nat make the pizza for tonight's dinner. She and Lori are going to cook together. Hum, now they are friends, thank goodness.

I am looking forward to discussing going back to work with you. Another pro is getting out of here and a change of environment. Jim came by and he was all over our pizza sinner and told me of how he makes his own pizza also. Here I am explaining how I am learning new recipes and he pipes up and says how he has learned a different sort of learning. Shame on him, he is such a silly guy.

Thanks mom for the lovely visit and chat. Well, I will go and chat with the ladies at Corcan next week. This week I am going to focus on finding out about my confined spaces and self management situation, one obstacle at a time. I will chat with you my son shortly. All my love.
xoxoxox

February 27, 20xx

Good morning to you both. Wow already mid week. How are you both doing? I can't wait until we can be together to enjoy a good night sleep. I can wait until March 27 is here and Susan leaves. She is so loud and rude. This morning the swearing and the banging around are really annoying. Last night when I got back to my room, Mea called me in to chat but she just wanted to talk about her disability. Well, apparently that is what Susan has also. I guess I am just tired of the excuses, negativity attitude and rudeness, so that is it. I am doing exactly what I am complaining about. Thank you God for pointing this out. Time to watch the comedy channel and get a laugh in. I love you. I miss you. I am grateful for you both. I will read my devotional, my chapter and the proverbs chapter today. Kononia is at 6:00pm and the Restorative Justice is 7-8:30pm. I pray the duty officer has a pass to come home this Sunday. I pray you both have a fabulous day full of joy, peace, love and good fortune and lots of laughs.

Gosh, Joyce spoke to me this morning about Joy. Use your mouth to be powerful but you need to think about what you are speaking as words are a privilege with huge responsibilities. The tongue is a wild animal and Satan uses people's mouths to hurt people. Enjoy life by keeping your tongue from evil. Judgemental, rude, gossip, telling stories, negative, evil is all the messages Joyce's had on today. God wants us to speak positively.

The more you talk about your problems the more you feel bad about yourself. The more you decrease your joy. The less you talk about your problems the fewer problems you will have. Pray and say. Believe God is working. We receive by faith, and patience. Give god something to work with. See and feel the least when God is working the most. God works in secret. Forces on the good and positive and complaining about it won't change it, praying about it will. God will take care of you. Pray about the problems and be thankful for the positive.

Wow, how truly amazing how god sent me this message. How can you not have faith when you receive messages like this? God is truly amazing.

Gosh, I am really missing you guys today. I will stay strong as you stay strong, and we will get through this together. I will focus on the blessing s and what is the gratitude in all of this. God I pray we can visit each other on an ETA this weekend.

I am going to see if Cathy wants to work out otherwise, I am going to do a quick workout before going to Kononia and the Restorative Justice event. I will call you at 10:45pm and focus on one day at a time. One day closer to being with you. All my love... xooxoxo

February 28, 20xx

Good Thursday morning to you mom and my son. How is your morning going? How did you sleep last night? Did my cat get a good night sleep? Wow what a beautiful sunrise or moon set, just breath taking. Funny how this journey has opened my eyes to all God's beauty. When I get out I would love to have our church help the mates here with a church group, volunteer, or services or items in demand. Did you know Kononia is a Greek word for love? God showed me yesterday that I was to stay in his word, by that one essay I may have to re-due with the correct case study, but he told me that the mates here would be going there. So as I wanted to go for a new environment would actually be with these same people. So essential not getting a new scene but more then with them. I have said I would not do anything until he showed me to go. So all will be revealed. The next training is in March, mid March, so if that is when I am to go, and then I will go. God will reveal. I pray he is moving the mountains. I miss you and long to be back together with you both. I am grateful for all your support.

Last day in this month, and two more until parole. I love you both with everything in me. I pray that we may be blessed with an escort visit on Sunday. Big hugs and kisses.

Good sign they moved the PFV funds. Cathy will check out the game situation. Last night was so much fun at the Restorative Justice. We played Pictionary and met a bunch of wonderful people. Bless these volunteers for their continued support.

At Kononia, the volunteer introduced, 'What on Earth am I here for', by Rick Warren. 'Why am I alive', Jeremiah 20:18 brings that full circle. I did my reading and discover you purpose was illustrated by Rick Warren in stay in Christ, ask your creator, purpose for fellowship. He goes on to provide a better understanding of love each other; Jesus wants you to love each other so others will want to become a part of the family. 1) share fellowship (spend time, share experiences, share support and joy) 2) fellowship of belonging together- love is a commitment 3) serving together- volunteering, contributing 4) suffering together in fellowship-draws you closer together, humanizing and united as Galatians 6:2.

The law of Christ is to love your neighbour as yourself and relationships are more important than anything including more important than money, fame and success. John 3:16 is to love one another. I am looking forward to seeing the entire DVD. I am going to see if Pastor Ken has a DVD or book library otherwise I will check out the library for resources. Wow a week and a day before our sleepover. I am watching TSN to see that highlight we talked about last night, but nothing yet. I think Cathy is moving out today…sad. Susan got a good laugh at my expense this morning saying there were bugs in the cereal and my reaction was grossed out. Funny girl! Zumba tonight, oh happy days. They keep showing the poor guy singing at the ball diamond who forgot the words, poor guy.

I am going to do the daily reading, work out at 11:00am, and call you at 1:00pm, self management at 1:30pm, Zumba at 7:00pm and canteen today. I will get supplies for our sleepover. I pray you are both having a fantastic day and full of joy, love, laughing, great news, blessings and great peace.

The sports central have those two funny guys on and yes they are really funny. I understand my son why you enjoy this show and yes these two make it for the show. So, they almost forgot about the house for canteen. Something that stressed some of the mates out, but not me as the Holy Spirit spoke and said we could get what we need for the sleep over next week. Than we were called up to get our canteen. God is always testing me to see how I handle situations and I pray I will always act with grace and be a warrior for God and be an example to what he wants us to behave like, because he will move and do things for us in our best interest. Cathy has her surgery and Mea received her lab coat. I will call you shortly to check in. I pray your day is fabulous and full of joy.

Self management was great. The ladies are really wonderful. A girl from the programs is leaving Tuesday and is going to leave me her email. The dynamics in the course will be changing in the program. I hope no one from this house is in the program but with more people the course will get interesting.

I was able to speak to the program lady about the confined spaces and I am sure that I will be able to complete that course next time it is offered otherwise, I can take it on the outs. Nice to complete as many courses as possible but all in God's hands. I am grateful for the fork lifting course. Zumba was fabulous. Wow I am certain going to continue that when I get out, so much fun.

I received a reply back for the ETA for re-integration which is on a rotation bases and Tuesday to come home, provided there is staff that could take me. I put in a request for Monday and a second request for Sunday, I gave it to Bob the Sunday one so maybe it is just late in getting to me, but I will locate and follow ups anyways. Mea said she never gets a response. I just did not get a reply to that one. Poor lady replying said to herself, 'I better reply to this one fingers cross and prayers loud to God'.

Lori made some fabulous bran muffins which are so good. I am going to sign off now Mea is trying to write a song about Drugs. She needs help in so many ways. Oh yes you get the bragging rights on the hockey game as Dallas did not show up. All my love. I will chat with you at 10:45pm to catch up on your day. xoxox

March 1, 20xx

Good morning mom and my son. How are you doing today? The start to another month. This month Susan leaves, Cathy is to move out today. She is all packed. I joked with her saying she is like a hoarder with all her stuff. We laughed. Gosh I am going to miss her. As much as we each have our little annoyances, you get used to them. So now two beds will be opened and I sure pray they will be filled with positive, kind people. The house 'f sure has had its gong which seems to center around one individual, that old lady.

I have got to practice piano today and read my devotional, and my chapter in the Purpose Driven book and Corinthians. Gosh I love staying in God's word and surrounding by his energy and I pray he will continue to guide us on our paths. I pray our mountains are being moved. Sandy at Zumba last night suggested I ask Whitey if you could come to our church sessions. Food for thought.

I pray my supporters are writing and Pastor Ken is able to come in. Thank you both for everything. I pray we receive some fabulous news today. In the PDL, Rick speaks on SHAPE which stands for spiritual gifts, heart, abilities, personality, and experience. Stay focused, work hard, set your goals and get results which are a great advice.

My son and mom I love our laughing together. I will cherish our time together so much more and funny how relationships are the most important thing in life next to God. I cherish our relationship and I am so blessed we have each other.

I am excited to see you tomorrow and I pray we will be coming to you guys the Sunday that's if my scheduled body guard escort, providing there is staff. Wow Cathy and I finished our work out. I am going to continue to work out after she moves but by myself. Susan asked us to wait for her so we did and then she goes and works out while Cathy had a nap. Cathy and I eat, Lori made chicken balls, rice and wonton soup. It was really good. She was going on about how she has a bad day and needed to do something. I suggested she may want to walk and get some fresh air. Then she started gossiping about someone from another house. So I looked at her and told her I don't care why people are here and I would not discuss it with her. She shut up. She is real trouble. I am grateful not to have committed to go back to Corcan as she is going there and let me tell you she will be trouble. So when they fire her I will pray and see if that is when I should go back.

I love you both and I am off to piano lessons soon and then I am going to walk for a bit in the yard. I will call you at 10:45pm. I pray you are both having a fabulous day. Mom I hope your cold is going away. One week today you will be here with me. All my love. Proverb 28:6 'Better is a poor man who walks in his integrity that a rich man who is crooked in his way.'

March 2, 20xx

Good Saturday morning mom and my son. How are you doing? I am excited to see you both today. I pray I get to come home to see you tomorrow and my fuzzy baby. I miss her chatting at me and I am sure it would be nice if she chatted at me and gave you a break. Nat asked if I would come with her tomorrow to dye her hair so I explained that I maybe going home but we do have visits booked so I could come up until I was called. I just wanted to make sure she had done it before otherwise I would suggest Mea go as she knows how to do hair dying.

Music lessons last night was fantastic and a real blessing how my note from last week did not arrive until last night into the piano teacher's hands and how wonderful that the time for my lesson had been moved to 1:30pm to accommodate the other person and myself. Funny how God makes things work out when things should work out. This way my evenings are free for visits and my lessons will be a for sure thing. The piano instructor is impressed with my learning and my practicing. Great lesson and hopefully I can continue with her after I am out.

Cathy moved out last night at 8:30pm the guards moved her out. I chatted with her this morning on my way to check the mail and she said she did not sleep well last night. I wonder how loud other housed are, I know this one can be loud but I don't have anything to compare it too. I saw Max last night walking with Mea, as I was waiting for piano to commence. She came and gave me hug and told me about the dog bite. Max doesn't like the house she is in and wants to come back to our house.

When you first get admitted you are put in where ever there is a bed and usually not in a minimum until you have served time in the medium and then once your date is coming up you can transfer to the minimum. It is unheard of to be placed in the minimum right off the bat and because she is returning it will be difficult to move. I walked the yard for an hour last night, it was a beautiful evening. Nat and Carry went in after thirty minutes and me and another mate walked for another thirty minutes. She stopped to talk to some other gals about something and I just kept walking and she caught up.

Like I said I have no interest in speaking or hearing about others situations. I will not get involved with gossip or involved in others situations. If someone asked my opinion about their situation I would give it, but I have no interest in getting involved in the drama. God is going to have to take care of that crooked company getting audited because I am done trying to correct the wrongs in this world, it is not my job. I would rather spread the love and kindness. It is much nicer and more rewarding. I have put my faith in God and he will reward me.

I read my chapters this morning. Oh yes, there was no mail so I will just be patient and see if the duty office received our request. Either way, I am blessed to be able to see you. I love you both and will chat with you at 11:30am to confirm our date.

Fabulous line from The Purpose Driven Life on page 248 is 'Experience is not what happens to you. It is what you do with what happens to you,' what will you do with what you've been through. How empowering and powerful is this message. Time to spread the story and the message on what has happened. Share the journey with others to make the aware.

Mea is out on a home visit. Hopefully, tonight I will be able to attend re-integration otherwise I will walk the yard and read. The move on tonight is "People like us".

Thank you for our wonderful visit. I will call you once I get back from re-integration. I love you both and hopefully I will come home to see you on Monday evening. Bless you both for wanting to get donuts for the home visit. I am a bit nervous but also feel very blessed to be able to go out. All my love to you both.

Wow my first ETA to re-integration was so much fun. The women there were so lovely. Very kind and welcoming. Cathy knew some people who were old mates and I knew May which was lovely to see her and I met a bunch of new women who I will see next time I am able to attend which hopefully will be in two weeks. I would love to continue seeing these ladies and sharing a meal once I am out.

Debby was to go but did not attend. We did a craft which I will teach you. The ladies were impressed with my talent of sewing. One lady shared her story which was very inspiring and lovely. The guard who accompanied us was very nice. It was nice to get to know others outside of the walls. The night was full of laughs, crafts, a great meal and enjoying getting to know a great group of women. Thanks to this journey I have met some lovely new women.

I pray your evening was wonderful and you are safe. The snow is coming down so I pray you are not on the roads. I love you both and everyday this journey shows me how blessed I am. Thanks to the guards and staff who allowed me to take part in this ETA. All my love. xoxoxoxo

March 3, 20xx

Good day mom and my son. How are you doing? Mea and I got a chance to exchange our visit stories this morning. Her family sounds like a real hoot. Just a ball of fun. Wow it is so nice when someone is happy for you and not jealous or envious but just happy because you are happy. Such a wonderful energy. I worked out with Susan and Tara and Lori. Bless Susan she is so funny. As she gets closer to her release day she is becoming more human. Still swears a lot and is very loud but more manageable. So at least I have her as a work out buddy until she vacates in March.

Amazing how God can make the weather so ugly last night and today so beautiful. I read the daily devotional and now just reflecting on the materials. John 15: 'I abide and dwell in Jesus so that I beer abundant fruit'. What a wonderful verse. Such a special message, don't you think? This journey had not only taught me gratitude, how to appreciate blessings, trust in God, strengthened my faith, and exposed me to my true supporters and loved ones, but also how beautiful the world is and how he makes it beautiful each day.

The PDL spoke on using what God gave you and to appreciate your talents, to treasure your gift and not be jealous of others. We are all created special for his purpose and to use and experience new journeys. To master your talents. To figure out your talents. This chapter was a real deep chapter, really makes you explore your purpose and how to serve God's purpose to the fullest.

I love you both and so grateful for you both. I will see you shortly. Thanks be to God. I just came back from church blessed with fabulous news from Whitey. Pastor Ken is coming in to visit with me. Gosh I am so blessed. Then Sandy a fabulous women whom I do her connecting streams with and Zumba with was at church and she put the question into my brain about your attending church next Sunday, so I asked Whitey and he will find out if this is possible. She is getting cleared to be a citizen escort and would love to be mine to take me home. Gosh movement just seems to be filled with blessings. I am so excited for tomorrow to see you and further discuss. I pray it will be a at home in a home visit. I am excited to share with you and with Bob this wonderful news. God is answering my prayers and moving my mountains.

I am off to Alpha soon. Wow my cup runth over. Alpha was wonderful and Marilyn also said she would be my escort. I am so blessed to be able to share this journey with so many. I don't like to see these wonderful people being taken advantage of. I am watching the 'Bible' on the history channel. I chatted with Bob and we discussed the ETAs and what is new. He has my best interest at heart and is so excited to see me out of here. I love you both and will call you in a bit to chat. All my love. xoxoxo

March 4, 20xx

Good Monday morning mom and my son. How was the rest of your evening? How did you both sleep? Wow that was so amazing how you my son taped the 'Bible' series for me. I was thinking how we could enjoy this series together and now we can actually do so. You are amazing. Awesome!

Joyce spoke on fears and doubts and how God admires boldness, holiness, and courageous attitudes. Don't live a boring life; if you do it's your own fault. Step out and do something different. I am so blessed to not have gone back to Corcan yet as there is a real shift in the house energy and I am going to stay away and stay in my room. I know when to step out and when to just listen to God's messages. Joshua and Kaylib spirit.

Live boldly by walking in faith, as fear will come in to form of doubt. Gosh, some of the guards should check their speech and quit using such foul language; they are being to sound like the mates. So blessed that my workers have the proper use of language. God is testing my/our faith and making us waits and stretched. I am keeping the peace and doubt comes in the time of waiting. Faith and patience are the fruit grows under times of trials. Read Colossians 3:12 and Corinthians 16:9.

I am going to do my readings now. Well, I guess we will be doing the home visit tomorrow but at least we got to visit tonight. Forces on all the positives and blessing are God's way of coping and growing closer to him and to us. I love you will all my heart and I pray to be back with you soon. All my love xoxoox

March 5, 20xx

Good morning to you both. How are you doing today? I imagine as tired as myself. I will try to find out about the PFV today. I am going to put in a request to either go to the wonderful church function on Saturday, but if here is no space available then to issue a permit to visit you. It will all work out. This journey teaches you patience. I will chat with you at 11:30am until then I am going to read and at 11:00am do my arm work out. At 1:00pm is connecting streams and then a home visit. Bob is on today so I am sure he will also be looking into the PFV. Oh happy days!

Joyce spoke on how we can't live in fear and doubt. The way I look at this place and life is that kindness is contagious. Joyce spoke a lot on John, which is a chapter I am enjoying currently. Oh yes blessings, I have been placed on the wait list of confined spaces, so I am sure between now and June XX I will be successfully completed otherwise I will do it once I am out. Either way I will either have it as a goal in here or a goal out there.

Connecting streams was fabulous and I saw Whitey and he reminded me that Pastor Ken and that he would be visiting me soon. I saw Cathy in V&C with her daughter which means that the house for the PFV is still out of order. I gave her a hug and told her how much I missed her and she confirmed the PFV being opened I pray my son you will be able to see me on your dinner break tonight. I love you both so much and excited we can share this journey together. I will let you know the good news tonight when I visit with my body guard. All my love xoxoxo.

March 6, 20xx

Hi mom and my son how are you today? A bit chilly out today. I am so grateful for our visit last night. I could not believe how my four legged baby snubbed me on my ETA home, but that just gives me more to look forward to each visit. I love your room my son. So grateful you are in a safe place. Thank you for the donuts last night. I will be so grateful when Pastor Ken can escort me and we can share in prayer.

I am going to do my readings, Pastor Ken is at 11:00am for our visit, work out, it is refill day, Kononia and confirm our DVD selection for this weekend and our sleepover. I pray you both have a fabulous day full of great news and many blessings and lots of love and joy. All my love. 20XX is a year of great grace. Stay in God's love and there is a blessed plan. Keep the grace of God on our mind.

Joyce spoke on prayer on faith, keep the faith. Philippians 4:6-8 "pray and say: pray first and then do the work."

If you believe it, you will receive it. Bless Pastor Ken, we had lovely chat in the chapel and bless Whitey for him arranging our meeting. Pastor Ken will be visiting me once a week, will be shadowing my escort and will be my citizen escort, and has agreed to be my assistant in my parole hearing. I am so blessed and feel so grateful for my amazing supports.

We had a short house meeting and discussed how someone went to work and was saying things to others about our house. Well, it all came back to Mea. So she was not happy that people were talking. Blessed to not be working, mind you I would not be amongst the gossip. I signed up to cook and told Nat I would help her cook. There are two gals who won't cook and one who won't do dishes either. We are also to commit to chores and these women won't do anything. I volunteered to do garbage's. Funny how I am able to help and still do all my commitments. Oh well, I am here to serve. Pastor Ken wants to bring me some new books to read. Susan was having a bad day so I asked her to work out. Clear her mind. She got half done before being called away. Thank you for correspondence with my professors on my assignments. I am grateful for you both. I am grateful for the cat is snubbing you also she has been through so much. We are blessed and God is all we need. He is our love, life and our purpose.

I was asked by another mate to help her do something on the computer, so I told her I would come back after Kononia to help her revise it. After Kononia I went to help her but she was not there. So I will check with her tomorrow to make sure she got it done. Our DVD's are all a go and the gals told me what to expect. Those gals in the organization will bend over backwards to make sure my time here is pleasant. They are so kind to me and they want to also make sure your time here is enjoyable. God's grace is present.

At Kononia, a mate was appointed the team leader which is wonderful. I will certainly help support her in showing up and sharing. She needs a good fellowship in people to help support her journey. I will call you at 10:45pm. I love

March 7, 20xx

Hi mom and my son how are you this Thursday? I am so excited for our sleepover tomorrow. I hope you both have a lot of energy to get through the next couple of days. I will chat with the program director and see if there is a chance to take that course after self management. There is Zumba tonight. I will do my morning reading and work out at 11:00am.

Joyce spoke on fear, which is illustrated in proverbs 15:33. 'The fear of the lord is the instruction of wisdom, and before honor is humility.' Psalm 23, Lord is my shepherd, for you are with me. Romans 8:32 He who did not spare his own son, but delivered Him up for us all, how shall He not with Him also freely give us all things? Romans 8:37 you have victory before it comes. God = Faith and God is with me. Fear= Devil and Satan. Isaiah 30:18 God is looking for someone who's longing for him. God is looking for a believer. God is on my side and I will not fear.

Fear draws things near to you. 10% of people will not accept you. Fear of rejection is a common fear. God gets rejected all the time. Jesus was hated without a reason. Psalm 18:22 God will promote you in due time. Luke 10:10-11 shake it off. When you're confident in God and Jesus you can do anything.

Stop worrying about people who don't like you find the ones who do. Favour is in thinking and mind set. If they reject you they reject Jesus. God gives me Favour. I don't have the energy to be anything else then me. Gosh so much to learn and to grown in with a new walk.

When I get out I am going to write to Rick@purposedriven.com and express my appreciation to all he offers. As we completed the DVD on what on Earth am I here for, at Kon9nia last night I am humbled at that entire God has done and continues to do. There are more free lessons on line so I will check them out when I receive my parole, but you can also look at them if you want.

I spoke to another mate on my way to the mailbox and she let me know she got her letter typed up and that another mate helped her. I let her know that I did go after Kononia to find her, she said she had the mate which was her second option help her, so kind to think I was the first option. But she got it done and that is the most important thing and thanks to that other mate.

As I am writing you I would like to share a story that is unfolding right now. All day has received crunches and she is having a terrible time with them and operating them. Well she is heading to the main and is having difficulties with another mate so I already out is helping her to the main with words of encouragement and being beside her. That is what God is like our support, our advocate, and our words of encouragement. Hopefully this lady will accept Christ into her life and start to be a better person. She causes a lot of trouble in that house and the other ladies are getting upset.

So I found a wonderful radio station that preaches the bible. Oh happy days. I now have a buffer to drown out the constant complaining, swearing, and negativity. How blessed I am, Bob just popped into catch up and check in with me. So, so blessed. I let him know about the PFV and suggested he stop in on Friday. He is so gracious to tell me when his shifts are, thanks be to God and it is not even 10:00am yet.

Wow what an eventful day and only 3:00pm. Sorry I had to cut our chat short at 1:00pm. The reason I was called to V&C was to speak with a lady who does the re-integration. Well, I arrived at V&C and my parole officer came around the corner so I just thought she called me so did the old point at me and she shook her head, no, as I was walking to her. What was even nicer was that my parole officer smiled. She has a wonderful smile when she wears it. I have a great parole officer on the inside. The re-integration lady waved her hands to get my attention. We spoke and a warm hug was exchanged, she would like to come back next Thursday morning to chat again with me. She would be my citizen escort and would love to take me out to re-integration.

We had self management class and that was so lovely. The program lady is ending this session today and starting up again in April. So that being said the Drawing class will be a go. We had an awesome session and celebrated with donuts which were exciting. I will burn it off at Zumba tonight and I have already done my leg workout. It was a great session. The next one will be with other new mates. The positive also is that the lady in my house is in the aboriginal self management and wanted to go into our class but now that it is on hold she will stay in the aboriginal class. Gosh, I need to hold my thoughts before they exit my mouth.

The program lady and I ventured back to the trailer to let the training person know would be in the drawing class, but she was at the main house, so I left her a note. I was able to see the PFV. We are going to have so much fun this weekend.

I love you both and so excited to hug you all weekend long. Well, Zumba was cancelled what else is new. Just hit and miss. So Nat, Carry and I took a walk and a laugh for an hour. Although disappointed no Zumba it was nice to get fresh air and cold air to kill off all the bugs.

Lori says she is getting sick. The last thing I want to get is sick. So such a blessing to get away from her in more ways, but if she is getting sick then time at the PFV will be wonderful. I also find it interesting that she gets all her special flour, bread, ect plus she still gets to eat our food. No cottage cheese, but she gets rice four, which the house already has, plus her own flour. Deep breath! I will apply for more visits our. Family guy is on now and a good laugh. I love you both and miss you so much, all my love. I will call you at 10:45pm. Blessings that I can get close to the Lord, He is my boss, my savior, my security, my strength, and fills me with such love. xoxxoxo

March 8, 20xx

Happy Friday mom and my son, how are you doing? I imagine you are as excited for our sleepover as I am. I pray you both have a terrific day. I will call you at 1:00pm. Susan asked to borrow my curling iron and that will be the last item I will need to pack. I am going to read, check the mail, work out, practice piano, I have piano lessons and the cuddle time. You will officially be inmates. You will walk thru the doors I go through every time I leave you after our visits; you will be inside the jail and will the mates. You will eat jail food and be confined as we are. This will be the closet you will be to being in jail, and we get to have time together without a time limit. We can cuddle and watch TV and play games. I am so happy to have a glimpse of normality and no one better then with you two. We are doubly blessed as the PFV is prioritized for mates to further share this experience.

I have to get on the support letters for my parole hearing so I have made a list of supports to contact to see if they will again write a support letter and employment letters for some who will employee me once I am out. How wonderful today is going? Bob popped by and we chatted. His smile brightens up the room. Bless him, he is a fabulous PW. Actually my team is so wonderful. I have been selected to participate in a spring clean up in May so I was just called and asked to sign up. The warden has to bless it but I am sure it was meant to be and it will all work out. I can invasion the wardens face when Bob takes up my application, "what she wants to do this now?" this warden was willing to let me out earlier or even now, she is so funny. Nice to have a scene of humour in situations, especially ones like this. One lady made the comment she only wants to go if there is food for this volunteer position. I piped up and said this was about giving back, eat at home is what I thought. Most of the ones concerned about food are of a certain race, but not all. That is why God blessed me with knowing some amazing women of this race so that I can no longer group them together. But it gets annoying when you see what and how some people behave. Seriously, these people need to be more gracious about going out and serving.

I received a letter from friends and wrote them back. She is all prepared to write a support letter.

March 9, 20xx - March 10, 20xx

We were blessed with staying in the PFV and snuggling. We had the opportunity to spend some quality time together just the three of us. The PFV is a small house inside of the jail that is used for family visits. There is one bathroom and two bedrooms, a small kitchen and dining room and a living room. It is fully furnished. The outside there is a small patio area and a bbq that you can use. When you book the PFV you purchase food that you bring over and use for the duration of your stay. The house has towels, and blankets, and bedding for you to use.

Once are done you bring up the dirty items and the jail washes them and restocks the house for the next family. We had booked out movies to watch and my son was able to bring in some for us to watch. We played games and just talked. It was so nice and we were blessed to have the time together. it was so difficult to have them leave. Sometimes I can understand why mates don't want to see their families as it makes you very, very sad to see them go. It is like being home sick all over again. But you have to put on your strong amour and get on with it. I try to look at it as a small glimpse of what is to come. I will never not cherish my family or my time again. A humbling lesson that holds great value. Retuning back to my unit was difficult, but I had the love and welcome of my mates who really helped me to get through this difficult time.

I refocused on my time and what I had to accomplish still. My goals would not go unachieved and I had set some great goals. I made sure my schedule was busy and I would be focused on forward movement. I am blessed that my family had the opportunity to see what it is like and for them to get a small glimpse and maybe a more reassuring glimpse that God was protecting me and he was certainly here with us. Not many can say they spend a weekend in jail. The guards were fabulous and did not do their usual stomping and actually did not wake us up and let us enjoy our time together. They were very unobtrusive

March 11, 20xx

Good morning mom and my son, how are you doing? How did you sleep last night? I miss you both and I am so grateful we had this past weekend together. I loved playing games, sharing a meal together, laughing, having and sharing conversations, and just showing love and affection. I love you so much.

Today I am going to do my reading and writing. I will go check the mail and hand in the food order. I will pop in and see the ladies at Corcan on Friday about my letter, but I will see today also. Wow the morning was quiet if Susan does not talk. She has no volume filter. I am also going to do laundry, but that is a simple task. Connecting streams is tonight so that will be wonderful to share fellowship with Deane and Venesa. I will call you at 11:30am. Hopefully the volume here will be manageable so I can hear you during the conversation. I pray you both have a fabulous day full of joy, peace and love, good fortune, and wisdom.

The lady in Corcan was not in yet but I was able to speak to the other worker and let her know I was in the Fork lifting and Drawing course being offered. The lady said their yearend was at the end of the month so they wanted to get out as much stuff as possible. I also mentioned that I did not want to work with certain mates and the Corcan employer mentioned she was in the back and now I will have to take that into consideration before returning.

Joyce spoke on the renewing your thought process. Think on purpose which is a wonderful message and will not allow for those other thoughts in. I finished all my laundry including the bedding, I wrote the letter I will need to type up and mail out to all of my supporters. I swept and did the house laundry. Tonight I will go to the recreation room and type up the letter and attend Connecting streams. I will chat with you at 10:45pm. I am glad you both enjoyed seeing me this weekend. It must have been difficult for you to leave me also. I cherish our time and will cherish it on the outside again very shortly. Keep positive and grateful for all you have and all God has provided.

We are getting a new mate. Sofi is moving in and I am so pleased. She seems so nice. Lori keeps hovering around. She is like a vulture waiting on the prey. I was talking to Mea and Lori needs to come stand there so I left. I told Mea that Lori needs to mind her own business. You see when Mea and I were chatting about when she could do my nails; Lori has to hover so I left. Well, Mea and I were not finished talking but my schedule is not for Lori and not her business but she seems to think she should know where and what I am doing. Wrong! Anyways, I love you both and miss you so much.

I typed up the letter tonight and went to Connecting streams. The volunteers are so wonderful and I really appreciate their presents. Every week someone new comes in, but no one except Victory and I have been loyal followers. These mates always want to share their story but I guess tonight I was just tired of hearing the sadness and the sad stories.

Nevertheless, I just need to shack it off and pray they have a good fresh start. I love you both and will chat with you shortly. I miss you both and move each day. One day closer to being together, but still each day is difficult. God is making use stronger for his purpose and I am grateful for that. All my love. Xooxoxo

March 12, 20xx

Good day my son and mom. How are you? Hopefully you are both having a terrific day and well rested. I pray your day will be so full of wonderful things, great news, and fellowship. I will be heading to the fork lifting course shortly. I will caht with you at 12:00pm or break time. All my love.

The fork lift course this morning was wonderful. I have to head back soon. I pray my son you have a terrific day. I know this has been a difficult journey and I pray God will bring you peace and joy. I love you with all my heart and wish you all the happiness. Gratitude is essenital during this journey. Instead of being frustrated I pray you will be cast it to the Lord to deal with. I pray we can see each other soon. I will try and call you before you go to work otherwise, know the course ran over our window of time and we will chat at 10:45pm. Find love and joy in the smallest places. Makes the search more amazing.

I am glad we were able to talk my son before you went to your second job. I am so proud of you. If you stay grateful and humble, God will do the rest. He was with me when i wrote the fork lift exam. Without him I would never have received 100% on the written protion. I will still require his help for the pratical test, but I have faith he will help me also. All my love and I miss our time together. you are my world and my pride and joy. We are coming to the end of this journey and will be blessed and off to serve God in another adventure/ journey.

Thanks for coming in tonight mom and visiting me. Phew that was amazing how God worked. I am only entitled to go home twice a month that is the standard. Twice a month to go to re-integration, twice a month to go to our church, twice a month home and twice a month to connecting streams church. I count it as a blessing as you would not be home for my visit tonight my son and that would be one visits less to see you at home. I would rather use my last escorted visit to go to church on the weekend rather than waste it on not having there, you there which is so essential to maximum outs from here. I can do eight outings a month. I will ask Pastor Ken if Sunday church at 9:00am is better one to attend with a guard, but I think the ladies form Alpha want me to attend their church this Sunday. I will put an ETA in for next Sunday service after I check with my Pastor. I will call you in thirty minutes to chat. All my love. And God is truly looking out for me and us. One day closer, but my heart still aches for you.

March 13, 20xx

How are you today? What is on your agenda for today? My son you should be at your first job as I am writing you this letter. I pray you have some laughs there. Mom you should be opening your doors to the children and today is a staff meeting day so fun times this afternoon with extra kiddlets on hand. I am off to the driving part of the fork lifting course. I wil put in my request to go to church on Sunday and home March 29. Tonight is Kononia and my turn to cook dinner. Blessed to meet with Pastor Ken this afternoon.

Matthew 6:25 and 28:31 speaks on Great faith and not to worry. I love you both and miss you terribly. We will visit as many times as possible and chat on the phone often. I still have great faith and god showed us again last night of how he is here and there. He is with us and in us. I love you and grateful for your being.

Yes, I passed the fork lifting driving part. The instructor remembered my name even. She said I was a very good driver better than most. The program instructor popped by the loading dock to see how the PFV visit went. So kind of her to follow up on our time together. Funny how life turns out! Too bad you could not have met her, but I am sure our paths will cross again on the outs all in due time.

The negativity in the house is really tense right now. I am staying in my room unless I have to use the phone, washroom, or grab something to eat and that includes cooking. Nice to go to these courses and get away from this energy. I would imagine every house is full of these dynamics but let me tell you it is not good. I love you and will speak to you soon. Keep positive and focused on our path. One positive is even though some negative people want to steal the positive there are some who are motivated by the positive to be positive. Blessed to see Pastor Ken today also. He is such an amazing mentor and a humble man of God.

Gosh, what happened to Pastor Ken? Nice to chat with Bob, but Pastor Ken was a no show. Bob is off for a week and wanted to touch base with me. Blessed to have the escort situation and hopefully the guards will still take me out or an escort. One day at a time. Dinner was great. I made breakfast burritos which is a real hit. I attended Kononia and enjoyed some Christian fellowship. Then I was walking back with the church girls and I was blessed to receive my fork lifting temporary card from the course program lady.

I came back to my unit and before having my shower to get rid of the bone chilling chill Mea told me some wonderful news, well of course, Lori is always around when she sees Mea and I talking. Lori jumps in and waits until we are talking. Lori is a nosy Nelly and I just don't trust her. Bridget shared with me a story about her court today and how she felt blessed to come back to a group of supportive women. After I asked if she remembered when we first met and reminded her of the story of being served and how she told me that I am either completely crazy or I truly love God. She laughed and told me she gets it. She can see how much I love God and now she is in the same place. The shift is occurring and I pray more will shift in this house. I am going to call you soon. Mea did tell me her story and as long as Mea does not put Lori in her place, there will be limited conversations, as I am not in a place to trust Lori or share with her. I love you both with all my heart. Xoxoox

March 14, 20xx

Blessing to you both this morning. How was your night last night? did you got to bed soon after we spoke? I am watching the Copeland ministry on TV. Jeremy Pearson is preaching on how "don't be too proud to receive help when it is offered". Isaiah 64:4 is about letting god go to work for you.

My son please stay warm today. I pray today we will be blessed with great news, joy, blessings, grace and favour and mercy. Last night Mea needed to talk about something and to continue to share what she had started sharing before Lori came and need to be involved but this time Mea shut the door so Miss busy body could not stick her nose in. I pray she would mind her own business. She always has something to come out of her mouth and her two cents are not nice two cents. I pray she minds her own business simple as that. Blessed that Mea knows also that Lori is not right.

I am going to check the mail, write to supporters and family, canteen day is today, practice piano, work out, speak to the re-intregration program lady, and Zumba is tonight. I may have to get groceries but I will let miss busy body do it first. Last night at Kononia, the mate selected to take over had us pick thes lovely cards which have comforting words on them. That was sure sweet of her. Mine was 1 Peter5:7 cast all your anxiety on the Lord because He cares for you. So wonderful but even more wonderful is that is what Jeremy Pearson is preaching on. I sure hope and pray all things are okay for Pastor Ken who did not show up for our time together. I am sure you will hear from him today and hopefully he can come in this week.

Gosh it will be so wonderful when Susan leaves as she is so loud. Too loud, rude and I am so tired of the rude. May she learn to be considerate of others and quiet. I will call you at 1:00pm.

Joyce was amazing today and she spoke on the same verse in Peter, the one I received last night at Kononia. What a sign? Worry, makes you ugly, health problems, and does no good. "I trust God, I don't worry."

2 Corinthians 10:4-5 "God meets all my needs abundantly." Expect abundantly. You need to see things differently; you will look as if you will receive. I will receive vindication and victory. 3John 2:1 talks on take the step in faith change your attitude to receive in abundance. I

want to have all that God wants me to have. God will bless me and us. God has a good plan for me and I am expecting it to happen.

I finished my letters to the family and will purchase a couple of stamps at Canteen. My items today to purchase are, stamps, envelopes, popcorn, gum, and some smelly body wash. I looked over the emails from the University Tutors and have a question for one of them. Not sure if he resent the form request to write the final. I am going to have to look into this.

I think the re-integration will be here this afternoon, and I will work out and practice piano and do my homework for tomorrow's lesson. Zumba is at 7:00pm. I will call you in an hour to chat.

Phew Zumba kicked my butt tonight. They may add another class on Saturdays. The instruction said she would do one Saturday afternoon. Susan and Mea had a fight tonight, not sure what is was over exactly something about food. I find it funny how we all got along before Lori came. I think if we have to fee Lori and her food is more than a certain amount it should come out of the jail funds. We all get a weekly amount which is $35.00 a week for food. Lori east the house food plus she gets special food which cuts into the house budget. You know me I am happy with cottage cheese. I have cereal for breakfast lunch is usually a wrap with veggies and then dinner. I have got fruit and popcorn for my snacks. All I heard was a lot of yelling and swearing and then Susan slamming the door. Been a blessing on the house is quiet. Susan does not manage her emotions very well. Her drama is all about her and the entire house hears about it. She is a drama queen and I think she may need some therapy especially since she is getting out in less than two weeks. Anyways, the house is quiet and there is a blessing.

I am watching the new Community. My son we will have to watch them together when I get out. I love you both. The re-integration program lady did not come today so I am not sure if I am going tout this weekend but it is all in God's hands. My name is on the list. The Bible is on at 8:00pm on Saturday so that is what I will do if I don't go out. I will chat with you in a bit for our nightly talk. The phone schedule seems to be working fine. You mean the world to me and I love you with all my heart. xoxoxo

March 15, 20xx

TGIF mom and my son. How are you both doing? I just want to thank you mom for the letting me know about the response for the ICAA. I am sure that the majority of the people consider this a conflict of interest to have the stinky accountants audit their own unethical illegal work, and according to the code 204.4 it regulates this. This morning it reminds me of the Erin Brockovich movie where the stinky company paid the doctors to report incorrect information well it is true in this situation also. Proverbs 4:23 and Philippians 4:6 are minders from God. I will respond to the letter as it is a conflict of interest and in the hand book it is stated in section 204.4. How a five year span is all one accounting firm can do a company's book. This is how tax evasion never gets uncovered. The same company keeps covering it up. I will read the letter to you before sending it and I will take this matter up the chain of command if need be. I get to or the journalist who wrote an article on the Whistleblower I have sent you the article to read. God will deal with this; I cast this problem unto Him. I love you guys. Jeremiah 17:5-8 speaks of man trusting in man. Perfect message for today. God is never in a rush but he is always on time. Proverbs 11:24-25.

Today I am going to check the mail, practice piano; I have piano lessons, see about my letter from Corcan, and work out. I will chat with you at 2:30pm to see how your morning went. Gosh I am so glad for God's word and these channels to turn too. Susan was on the phone at 6:30 am swearing and cursing at someone. I am so tired of the language. When it gets too bad I will put in my ear plugs.

I am casting my cares onto Jesus. I don't care anymore God will move the mountains and I am don. I will let Jesus deal with this situation. Just like he is doing oath the Law society. I pray God will deal with this Accounting firm and association and I have faith and it will all come together in his plan. I trust in God. The truth will come out. Joyce spoke on being emotionally content. To be happy whether you are getting your way or not. Circumstances cannot control your joy, God is in control. Content and emotionally stable and God will reward us and me later and this happened for a reason. It is all in God's plan even the letter from the ICAA; something amazing is going to come.

John 14:27- "Don't let your heart be troubled. (No fear, no worry, no getting upset). I am content and emotionally stable. Act as if the Pastor was with you. Don't let your emotions control you. Handle anger and pray is the key. Be content and be thankful and grateful.

Being content means trusting in God. Being upset does not help, usually makes it worse. Trusting in god elevates our stress. Be dependent on God for everything. Psalm 5:12 and Ephesians 2:8, 'by grace are ye saved through faith'.

Wow today is already done; I will call you at 10:30pm. I had piano lessons and that was so amazing. I walked the yard with a mate from the house. And went to a group session called Breaking Intimidation which is another faith program. I will tell you about it tomorrow during our visit. I love you and so excited to see you tomorrow. Xoxoxoxo.

March 16, 20xx

Happy days! So looking forward to hugging you my son. I love you and never forget that. I am just waiting for my name to be called so I can come and see you. I am so excited my heart is racing. Oh my name was called so off I go.

I love our visit. I came back to my unit and re wrote my correspondence assignment. At 2:00pm I will go to the main house with Nat and type it out. Hopefully it is not too loud in there. I hope to go to re-integration to get out and enjoy some positive people. The Help is on TV and what a great movie this is. I will watch it for a few moments. Well I was able to do most of my assignment. I was called for re-integration. Myself and Cathy were with a citizen escort. The night was so much fun we watched "The Help" at re-integration also. Three times in one day I was able to watch my favorite movie. Mea was waiting for her search when Cathy and I returned. She was out on a UTA. She laughs at what I think are huge moments.

We each got our stripe search and off we went. It is not a big deal, two guards are present and you strip either starting with your top or bottom. It is the same drill every time you leave. I ask the guards if I should do heads or tails. They laugh. You stick out your tongue and lift it up and down. You pull back your ears, you lift up your boobs, you wiggle your toes and you bend over and spread you bum checks. I am not sure how people smuggle anything in, but they do. I am blessed we got to talk my son before I hit the sack. Be careful driving out there as there is a lot of snow. I love you.

March 17, 20xx

Good winter morning again. Mr. Winter just does not want to let up for Ms Spring. I woke up at 7:00am to get ready to maybe get an ETA to church. An Alpha volunteer said she would be coming to take women to church, so the odds may be in my favour to go. I would love to go and enjoy a full service, but if it is meant to be it will be. I will call you at 11:30am and see you for our visit at 1:00pm.

I am not going to church today, but I do have our wonderful visit and Alpha to look forward to for today. So bless to see you both. Funny how things change on the outsides but remain the same on the inside. So no more pennies in our currency. Things are changing. One thing remains the same my love for you both and our cat. I miss you and thank you for coming in and seeing me today. It means the world to see you.

Church service was lovely. Sandy's husband Rob delivered the message as Whitey was not there. So wonderful that I was on dishes tonight and dinner was late so I did my chore and chapel was cell so Sofi took over so I could attend service. She is so kind.

Off to Alpha and then our chat to close the day. Gosh this headache won't go away, but it is getting better and thank goodness no yelling in the house. Be thankful for small blessings. Sandy commented that she saw I had visits today and that Deanne knows I am on escorted citizen visits. Blessed for these amazing women volunteers to want to take me out of here. All my love! xoxoxoxo

March 18, 20xx

Good morning to you both. Hope you had a great sleep. I pray you both have a fabulous day. It is hard to believe it is already Monday again. The weekend just flew by. God will fill or day with great news today. I am just watching Gloria Copeland about health and her Aunts would use nerve medication. My headache is still there, blessed not as bad as yesterday, but I sure wish it gone. My goal today is to complete my essay, work out, rewrite my Alpha notes, read the daily devotional, cook dinner and attend Connecting Streams.

Joyce show was on God is a good God and a just God, Double for your troubles, and in the mist open our mouth to the devil. Do your act like a soldier, 2 Timothy 2-4 don't worry about world stuff and 2Corintians 10:4-5 God will help you during our wars and the devil will hide in areas of our minds and lie to us. Get behind me Satin is what you tell the devil when you comes about.

God has a mission for us. God wants us to worship him and we are her to serve God. Transform your life to God. We started and we finish it. Don't get entangled in others issues. Don't let them suck you dry. Be strong to live in God's mission. Soldiers live on Guard. Don't do others stuff do your guard your heart. Don't let anger stay in there. Be strong, stay strong. Be a person of purpose. Be offensive to go after the Devil. You cannot be lazy, sleep, passive Christian. Hold our head up. Loving God live on guard.

I finished the assignment. So blessed for your love and support. This afternoon I will cook dinner and work out. My headache is almost gone. Nice to see the sun today.

I went to Connecting streams and continued to read The Key to Your Expected End. The night was lovely until the devil asked too many questions about my life. She kept on prying into my business so I was assertive and told her to mind her own business. I spoke to the ladies at bible study about my ETA's and Friday the 29th. I also explained I wanted to talk with them privately as my ETAs with them is my business and as I told the volunteers that I mind my business and don't look at each person as a criminal but a person, so I don't ask these personal questions. Both told me I was very wise. Funny how I come to jail to learn not to be too trusting, to not be naïve and to test my judgment. Well guess what it worked. I don't trust! Well at least some, but I do have my trust in God and thank goodness for my blessings of you two and my supporters. I will call you soon. One of the volunteers said she would confirm if she could do Friday or Saturday ETA and then we can see each other. All my love.

March 19, 20xx

Good morning my son and mom, how are you today? What is going on in your day today? Today I will do my readings, work out, call you at 11:30am, 1:00pm Connecting Streams, and visit from you mom and then close my day with a lovely conversation with you my son.

Thanks mom I receive your mail from Sunday. I will write a letter back and now I have a hard copy of yet again no one is doing their jobs. How is this going to look when the truth comes out and no governing body would do their jobs? More material for my next book. Surrendered to God is all I can do with this nonsense's.

Blessed my headache is gone, wow what a blessing. Joyce spoke on determined to live in purpose and with no fear. Today was a quiet yet peaceful day. I was blessed to go to connecting streams and enjoy bible study. So wonderful to share with women who can speak a sentence without a curse word. I am surrounded by foul mouth women. Once Susan leaves I pray from a new women who is able to speak with clean words and speak not yell. One more week. I am sitting here listening to a bible session on the radio doing a word find. Soon mom you will be here for our visit. I will call you at 10:15pm my son and chat with you on your day. I miss being there each day with you, but we are blessed to have each other. All my love. I spoke to Sandy and she is to get on the citizen escort band wagon. Bless these wonderful women, bless our visit,

I am so grateful. Today is the five month mark. Seeing the silver lining in all of this and staying positive, staying strong and safe is so important. This will pass and our blessings are coming. All will be blessed.

March 20, 20xx

Good day family, how are you? Last night when I got back to the house, Tara was in the kitchen and she asked me if I could help her with dinner tomorrow, well the long and short is it was nice she thought of me and since she is working I have no problem helping out. I would make the spaghetti and salad and she is so grateful that I just pitched in. Be a blessing each day. Tara gave me a hug and said she wished more people were like me. Well, I think we are all capable of being a blessing but it is whether you do it or not.

My son Hell's Kitchen was on last night. Funny we were just talking about that on Sunday. I miss you guys and our lovely fuzzy baby also. Today Pastor Ken is coming in which is so wonderful. I pray for wonderful news today. Wow can I relate to Paul in the Bible. He is so lovely. All about mercy and kindness, Philippians spoke to me on this topic. Andrew Wommach show today was really great about others critising you as those who come to attack you are the ones who have the weakness. I pray for vindication. I don't care what materials the case made up and that is what they did, fabricated evidence. It is all made up. I will pray and stay strong in God and the word. Bless you both today and every day. All my love.

Joyce spoke on not giving the Devil power and being a soldier in God. Be on guard and on the defensive. Satan will come in quilt, shame, and condemnation and it is time to live in God, righteousness, faith and the word. Jesus has bought us back from the enemy. We are the children of God. I am God's child and how beautiful. You do not have to prove yourself to anyone. You have to live your life free. Wow, thanks Joyce and thanks of this message as it was one I really needed to hear. Christians are not weak and wimpy and have an aggressive attitude. God is working on my behalf and victory is on its way. Be an example. Be stable.

What a lovely meeting I had with Pastor Ken. He always surprises me with his life adventures and his encounters, sometimes people you think you have the least in common with end up having amazing similar adventure. Never look at anyone as though you have nothing in common with as we are all linked somehow. I hate not being there for you to call me or for us to talk right at the moment something happens. I miss you. I asked Pastor Ken about it remorse; he gave me an interesting answer I will share with you. I am so blessed and so grateful. All my love. Good news, the person in the house that is would not work with is no longer working at Corcan. Let's chat and make a game plan.

Nat and I made a nice dinner. I went to the recreation room and typed out my assignment. The printer of course was jammed. To do a simple assignment to better myself is next to impossible. I also typed up the letter to the Judge to look into the other Judge's continuous fingers being in the pot. I don't image anything will come of that as it seems corruption runs deep, but at least I can put it in my next book and know I have done all I can do. Nat and I walked the yard for an hour. Well, we got some fresh air and exercise, but monkey see monkey do, of course the you know who has to pipe up and say she is going to start walking. The house knows it all, the house shadow, the evil one in this house or more commonly known as the one whom I just don't trust. Oh well, she can do whatever, I just ignore her.

Overall, today was a good day. I pray you both had an amazing day. I love you both with all my heart. My son the hockey game is a good one. I miss watching hockey with you, but soon that will be a reality. All my love.

March 21, 20xx

Good Thursday my mom and son. Blessed only a few days until Susan leaves and peace and quiet. I will go and check the mail, I have a manicure with Mea at 9:30am, and I will do my bible reading, and devotional, as well as watch my faith shows. Zumba is tonight so happy days. Gosh, it's showing again oh happy days for you mom. Laura's alarm is going off and she is not shutting it off. Laura is my new mate across from me. She seemed really scared when she first got here and I extended my kindness to her. Funny she is actually one of the mean girls I first met when I arrived. Well I am sure we will be fine.

Well I better go and find her so she can turn it off. I pray you have a fabulous day, with great news, great wealth, vindication, strength, and health. All my love. God is in charge. John 3:18 and Ephesians 6:12 as I put on my armor for God and that you may be able to stand against the evils of the devil. Wow I feel so powerful today. Bless Sofi she is put a reminder letter for the ladies at Corcan, Sofi is a blessing. Joyce spoke on super heroes and I am a super hero. Prayer is power; God is the head of the super hero team.

Mea did a fabulous job on my nails. So excited to show you her great work. Funny how Mea purchased watermelon for the house. Carry, Nat, Sofi and Tara all went to work and I was doing my correspondence homework. I went downstairs to go to Canteen and here was Laura cutting up the watermelon for the other five to enjoy. This afternoon there is a guest speaker that I may attend after I call you to see how your day is going. I love you and pray this snow will quit sooner than later, but the positive is less watering comes this summer. I miss you both. I received a letter from the family and it was so lovely.

Wow the snowflakes are so huge and beautiful like a winter wonderland. This is our old dog's favorite kind of weather. Remember how crazy he would go in the snow.

So, Walter Smith was the guest speaker. He spoke on his journey which had many similar parallels to our journey. He even spoke on how he observed nature and how the goose took off and landed. The snow is crazy almost like another winter is coming. Gosh you know it is terrible when the school staff are told not to come in. oh sorry, back to the another point that Walter Smith made which I have also spend time doing is to set your goals upon being released. He said to spend time reading a bit, spooky is how he also self published his book and he was sentenced on his birthday, March 19, which we have the '19' in similar number circle as this is one of our numbers, but he was wrongfully accused.

The tension in here is crazy. Sofi is talking the Drawing course also, so we are doing it together. Thursday means grocery day which means milk and fruit. Nat gave me her pear and banana. Funny for Lori can get what she wants. Laura does not eat anything but apples so she gets only apples. Nat said she used to leave her fruit she did not use for Lori smoothies. So I am sure this will soon change and maybe she will get fruit she wants also. Zumba was cancelled, rightfully so due to the crazy weather. God bless you both, stay safe and sound. All my love one more day closer to being with you.

Philippians 4:19 'And my God shall supply all your need according to His riches in glory by Jesus Christ.' And you shall receive: John 16:24 'Until now you have asked nothing in my name. Ask, and you will receive, that your joy may be full.' Matthew 6:13 is on forgives us and Matthew 6:14-15 and John 3:16 are must reads.

Phew there is a lot of snow. Nat, Carry and I just came back in from an hour and half walk. The main is shut down so I am doing laundry. Poor Tara is on the phone and Susan is being so loud so I showed Tara how to turn up the phone. Tara said they were being so obnoxious and I said extremely rude. The second time tonight she was on the phone and the rude yelling takes place. Just uncalled for. I will be so happy next Wednesday when Susan is gone. Peace and quiet! Mea goes up for parole in April, so hopefully she will be blessed and then Lori and Lee to transfer and my parole hearing. Please God bless me back to my son and my mom. Big hugs and kissed to you both. I will call you at 9:00pm to catch up on your days. All my love. xoxoxo

March 22, 20xx

Gracious day to you both. How is your day going? The snow has stopped so hopefully that will be it for a while. Today my son I know you have a long day with very little time between your two jobs. I pray you both are blessed today with love, joy, wealth, good news, kindness, fellowship, love and just blessed period. I have been blessed into the Drawing course. I am just watching my faith shows, waiting to be called to the course trailer. Gosh, you know it is bad when the quiet people are sick of the yelling and the women of faith have had enough of the rude behaviour. Blessed to be in this course and getting out of this house for a bit. Thanks be to God. I love you both so much and miss you so very much. I am so grateful to see you tomorrow and all next week. Well as many times as we can see each other. All my love.

Joyce spoke on spiritual war fair. Walk in authority, put on your armour and hold up your weapons. Purposely, but on live with intentionality. Put on the amour of God as you and I belong to God. I am a personal representative of God. God tests me here every moment and I must practice patience and tolerance. Colossians 3:12 God I want to stay calm today. 2 Corinthians 5:17 is to live out of your spiritual not soul. Study the word and be a worshipper. Be happy now, and in self control in the spirit of God and what he gave you. Put on the new man as in Ephesians 4:22.

Our Technical Drawing class is very informative and so blessed to be enrolled in it. Cathy and her girlfriend, a couple of ladies from other houses and Sofi and me are in the class. I know each except one mate. The instructor is so gracious and just a kind man. The tension in here is so crazy. My son I have a new recipe for meatballs. Nat made some the other night and they were so yummy with a kick to them. I can't wait until I can cook for you.

Why can't people just get along without jealousy or bitterness? Wow how much more productive would this world be if we inspired each other buildup rather then cut down. Lori had better soon learn this. I have share a funny story about the guest speaker yesterday. Lori took Carry's seat Nat was holding for her and wow she was so made. I think it is best for me to remove myself from the common area for a while. I just have no interest in the negative energy or the drama. All my love to you both. Bob is on today, bless him and the good guards there are too many to mention by name.

Wow, so I just got off the phone with you, mom and could not believe Mea telling Lisa that is someone gets punched in the face they had better suck it up and not tell the duty office. Mea thinks this is her house, well guess what it's our entire house. She is getting bad inspirations. Bless you two for getting me through this journey. I love you. Oh, yes the lady in Corcan I spoke to also, I will tell you tomorrow. She is so cute.

The bible study on Friday is called Honor Rewards by John Bevere. The volunteers are great but I don't like that the mates for the most part only go for the food not the fellowship. I can't wait until tomorrow to see you. Kiss and hug each other, keep safe, healthy, positive in God's word and blessings. All my love.

March 23, 20xx

Wow good that I was able to type out a letter to my wonderful supporters, family and friends as I had no idea that my letters of support had to be in for the end of the month. Gosh they don't tell you anything and thank heavens for Sofi who informed me on how my letters had to be sent in ASAP. The parole board reads the letters 30 days before my parole hearing which will be in May so I have to get cracking and get my letters. I catch each person up to what I had accomplished and what was still on my list to do before I am blessed with my parole hearing and my exiting this place. Mom and my son if you could collect these letters and touch base with everyone to see if they need anything and express how the time is ticking. Good thing Sofi told me this as I would not have had my letters in time. I love you both and so grateful for your assistance in all of this.

How goes your morning? I am so looking forward to seeing you and so grateful for you both. I finished my cereal for breakfast. Gosh you don't even want to go into the kitchen with Lori around. She is like a shadow, always in your conversations and she is just not nice. Anyways, I am just going to stay in my room, have a wonderful visit with you, type out the letters and hopefully go to connecting streams church and to my reading and walking and work out. See you soon for our visit.

Thank you for the visit and my son for your wonderful time with me. I am so blessed to have my family and friends which have become so much more then friends, but actual family. My friend wrote me a lovely letter and a family member sent me in a lovely card and letter. Jim asked me if I was appealing my gong and when I told him no he looked disappointed. The truth will come out and God has the total control and faith will only get stronger. I pray God will move these mountains and return me to you.

I love seeing you smile and receiving your hugs and kisses. You are my heart and I live for you. I will call you later tonight. I was blessed to go out to connecting stream church. It was a wonderful experience and a lovely worship time, full of singing, a fabulous message, and I am so blessed the volunteers took me out. I am grateful my son you went out tonight with your friends. I will chat with you tomorrow. I love you both with all my heart. All my love. Xoxoxo

March 24, 20xx

How are things? I am so excited to see you today. Will it be scrabble, cards or just talking or maybe all of them? I can't tell the mates how wonderful last night was so I am excited to share it with you during our visit. I don't want to make the mates feel sad about my experience even though I am sure most would be happy for me and not jealous. Yesterday, Mea went home and when she got back Lori was all over her. That woman is just pure evil. I don't even want to leave my room. Yesterday at dinner we ended up again fending for ourselves which is fine. Susan signed up to cook and then does not want to, so Tara cut up some veggies for everyone and Nat asked if I wanted a chicken burger which I don't really like so I had a fish burger. She asked everyone but when it came to eating only Nat, Sofi, Tara and I did. Carry was sick so she stayed in her room. Poor Carry has not been feeling very well. I ate and then went on the ETA. Lori came up to me as I was getting ready for bed and told me she backed muffins and they were on the counter and she was rude about it. Anyways, I took my two and put them in my room. When Mea got back Lori goes and fills her with crap. Lori will make breakfast for Laurie, Susan, Lisa Mea and herself and we don't care at least Nat asked everyone if they wanted a chicken burger. Thanks for the vent.

Today is a new day and God blessed us with a beautiful sunrise. He is such a great Got. Just waiting to see if I am going to church, otherwise I will walk the yard and enjoy God's sunrise. I will call you at 11:30am to confirm our visit time.

Just got back from our visit and no I did not get a chance to go to my church today. I am so full of love from our visit. We have so much fun and laugh. Gosh, it makes me sad when we have to leave one another. I am so missing you. I will hold onto our visits and our precious time. I will cherish our time and ever more when I get more time with you. All my love. oxoxoxox

March 25, 20xx

Today is the drawing course and then visit with my two favorite supporters. So blessed to have Alpha members who truly care about me and support at the house. Nat took fabulous notes for me and made sure to get me a magazine. Sofi and I had a blessed chat about the love of our children. So blessed to enjoy laughing with you both last night. You keep me smiling.

The drawing class was fun. Thank goodness Sofi told me I need to have the support letters faxed to the Parole board thirty days before so now I will have to get you to call and have them sent to you, faxed and send me a copy for our records here. I still take any letters received late to my hearing but I pray we get them all. My son I love your laid back attitude. I asked Whitey to attend and pass on all his wisdom to Pastor Ken. Gosh I pray it all works out. I will be coming home on Friday from 10-2pm thanks be to God. Blessed our visit tonight. I will fill you in on all things again but wrote them in to remind you.

March 26, 20xx

Mercy for us today mom and my son. How did you sleep last night? Again the noise was so loud in here. Someone had their TV on all night and then the banging this morning. One of the guards spoke to me before I left V&C to get my take on what went down last night. I told her that person was so disrespectful to her and I have a hard time with how rude these people are in here. A mate was out of line with this guard and she asked me for my opinion on what I saw. I was grateful to let the guard know she was right in all she did and some of these mates are just stepping out of line.

The sense of entitlement and speech shocked me to no end. I told her that mate should be charged. The guard and the other guard are really kind people and the rude, swearing and especially the sense of entitlement has to stop... jail or not. I am tired of the excuse well it is jail, since when did jail bring out rude, no manners, and all the negativity. I should write a book and call it excuses. Thank you for a fun, lovely visit last night. I love you. I just read my devotional and watching my faith TV then off to course. I will call you at 3:45pm and pray for a fabulous day full of joy, love and kindness. I pray for health, safety, and strength for us.

God heard my prayers, I spoke to my parole officer this morning and we are all set for our parole hearing. She has such faith in me and me in her. I also received a letter for support the one you dropped off from Aunty. Blessed to see you tonight. I was also blessed to be enrolled in the construction safety course for Sunday in April. I am not sure what happened to our drawing instructor but our course has not commenced yet. Hope everything is okay.

Well what a gong about our course but at least we were able to attend this afternoon. Sofi and I did our assignment before our visits. Blessed the fabulous gals who pitched in to help each other the house mates who will extend a helping hand it is so appreciated. Thank you for our fabulous visit. I don't get tired of winning at our games. You make the best visitors and I have been asked if you would come and visit other mates when I am out. I am so blessed. And all my love.

March 27, 20xx

Happy hump day. Wow mid week already. Last night the guards did a search on the house at 1:00am. They were a bit loud but this house is loud anyways. Today Susa goes so maybe it will quiet down and no more yelling or loud banging around. Rudeness is leaving. Lisa should be moving to a different house and Mea goes for parole in April. Hopefully she will be granted parole. I go up in May, and I pray I get mine and blessed to return to you. One day at a time, one day closer to you hope you are having fun with your fuzzy buddies at your job. I love you both.

Oh gosh do I ever have a headache from looking at the blue prints. Susan left and a new girl came into the house. She has been in before and knows a lot of people. Her name is Natalie also. We have two Natalie's' in the house. We have a visit tonight and I am so looking forward to that.

Thank you for this visit. Sorry to hear about the flat tire you got in the parking lot here. You two dealt with it fabulously. All my love. xoxoxox

March 28, 20xx

Good Thursday morning to you both. How did you sleep last night? This house is so quiet now that Susan is gone. No loud yelling, slamming of doors, or just having fits. I actually was so tired that my sleep was disturbed very little. I am thinking of you my son and how your hand is this morning and mom about your garbage filling with water from the melting snow. I pray for you both to be strong, safe, healthy, and in peace. I love you.

Blessed to see my parole officer this morning to get the forms for you both and Pastor Ken to attend my hearing. So now hopefully everyone will get their support letters to me so I can submit them on Tuesday. So blessed to also have Sofi looking out for making sure that I get everything as she knows and has done this before. In God's hands and I trust and pray. I will call you at 1:15pm and thanks again to you both.

Laura and I went to get the groceries today and well you know me it is always an adventure. Bless to run into Bob and he is so amazing. He is always making sure I am okay and making sure I don't have any questions. I told him about the support letters and he was unsure about all that also.

Zumba is on tonight. Nat and I walked for an hour before Zumba and then off we went and we had so much fun. Bob even popped in during and we begged him to participate. He is humble. He said maybe next time and flashed his great smile. So nice to see smiles in jail. Sofi came tonight so now five of us are going from the house. Mea attend another program for herself improvement. It is lovely to see Sandy and her daughter from connecting streams and how she remembered about the drawing course I was taking. She also was informed our ETA to the church she attends and was curious on how it went. I hope I can join them again on another outing.

I hope you both had a wonderful day and evening. I would loved to have seen you again tonight but no visits for the jail except to for the ladies in the max. I miss you guys and so excited to come home tomorrow. All my love. One day closer to being home with my family. Stay strong, positive, and close to God and faith. John 14:12 I do the work of Jesus because it believe in Him.

March 29, 20xx

Home visit. God blessed us and thank you for allowing a wonderful home visit from the volunteer. Thank goodness we found the vehicle the jail supplies. We had to search for it. Thank you my son and mom for supplying a wonderful meal of pizza for us to enjoy. I could have stayed forever and just got lost in our time together. It is so difficult to return back to the jail and leaving you.

Ralph Klein passed away today which is so sad. Tell you a story of how Lisa attached Sofi in the house. My heart is in my throat. Seriously, I am not built to see a women beating up on another women for no reason. Lori is seriously evil to the core. She is trouble and stirs the pot and walks away. Nat and I were able to walk for a bit and get out of the house. Nat and I were watching outside in the common room and we heard a loud bang and thud and so I commented on what the heck was that so we went to go down the hallway and Lisa came out of the area where the bathroom was but we did not notice that Sofi was lying on the ground after her attack. Lisa is three times the size as Sofi and this woman is a time bomb waiting to go off. Sofi was taken upstairs to Tara's room as Lisa and Sofi's rooms are right beside one another. And we called the wall to get a guard but they were dealing with another fight in another house. Lori who is supposed to be Lisa's friend just brushes her off and well she kept filling Lisa's brain with untrue crap about the people she does not like and then Lisa does the dirty work and she did she beat up Sofi really good. Simply both need to leave Lori and Lisa. I will be staying in my room all night until 9:00pm when I call you. Poor Nat had visits cancelled. While Sofi was getting attached Laura was upstairs saying who is slamming doors and Lori says to her their big girls they can handle it.

Anyways, I am okay and this terrible situation actually brought the house closer together with the gals who are normal. Lisa thinks it is a joke and just laughs at it. Sofi went to the main house to get checked out. Once Sofi was out at the main, Lori pops some popcorn and gives it to Lisa like a reward. It was really weird to see. That Lori is pure evil and not even worthy of my breath, so I have no interest in speaking to her ever again. I love you both and tomorrow we will have visits.

March 30, 20xx

Good morning to you both. Thank you for our visit this morning. My son you would have been so proud of me today at bingo. The cards were certainly in my favour. A two time winner plus a door prize winner. You know life is good when you win Gain laundry detergent. I am not sure about re-integration tonight or not but I am sure hoping so. Well yes I did get to go and we made planters at re-integration. It was nice to share with other ladies who have been down this road and to see how they are doing. It was Cathy and I who went out and it is so nice to see Cathy as we spend so much time together and once she moved out we hardly get to talk. The guard are always so nice to me and they love to see me out and about. It was a very nice day, but it started with seeing you and I am always set when my day starts with you. all my love xoxoxo.

I shared my bingo winnings with Sofi and Tara as they did not leave the house. Too scared the other mates will attack them. Gosh, not on my watch. My tiding I gave to a girl in the drawing class really paid off. God does give back in many folds and this is just proof of it.

March 31, 20xx

Happy Easter to you my son and mom. Happy Easter to have visit and be able to see you both. I am up and waiting to see if this morning I will be blessed with going to church. I am getting a bit of a cold so I need to nip this in the butt ASAP. Mea had a wonderful home visit yesterday. Lori was all over her when I got back from re-integration so we could not talk. Nat said the house was nice with Lore at visits and Mea gone home. I need to tell her that I was gone also and she just laughed as she knows I am the quiet one. I wish everyone cold get along but when you have seen evil it is really scary. Anyways, today is about Jesus and how much God and Jesus love us. I am looking forward to next year watching Passion of the Christ with you and other supporters.

I told a mate from the drawing course that she got me sick breathing on me with her cold. She laughed and walked away. These mates don't take me serious or what. At least I was able to get some fresh air this morning in an hour walk. See you shortly for our visit.

Bless you both for your continued loyalty and dedication to me. I can't even begin to express my love, joy and gratitude I have with you being with me. Thank you so much. Whitey had a beautiful service and I just watched The Bible on TV and tired to get rid of my cold. I hope you both have a wonderful evening with turkey and all the fixings. All my love…xoxoxoxxo and I miss you and will see you tomorrow. God will bless us for he is a gracious God.

April 1, 20xx

Wow how are you this morning? Hope the day finds you full of good energy, spirits and great news. I am so excited to see you tonight. Sofi and I had a fabulous chat this morning. She is so wonderful. During our conversation she mention how another mate was appealing her sentence and using Mr. Reck so I will pass on Don's information but the interesting part is how Mr. Reck is not doing his job for this mate either and keeps passing her by. Yet again, not doing his job due to health issues. This is a common theme with this lawyer.

Anyways, I pray I am able to help and pass on Don's information before she gets hooped like so many of us who used Mr. Reck did. I miss you and love you so much. Hopefully you won't get this silly cold I have. I will call you at 1:15pm to chat and confirm our visit tonight.

I went for a walk, had dinner and just waiting for our visit. My silly cold almost gone, but still a bummer to have in here. I am so excited for our visit and so looking forward to seeing you. We have to keep focused on our path and God keeps blessing us. I will pop this letter in the mail before we visit tonight so you can get them. I love you both so much and 31 days until the parole hearing. See you shortly for hugs and kisses. All my love. xoxoxoxo

April 2, 20xx- 30 days until my hearing

Glorious Tuesday my son and my mom, how are you doing? I pray you both will have a fabulous day full of laughter, joy, peace, love and good news and wealth and health. Myself, I still have a bit of a cold. Last night after our lovely visit I made a cold medicine which consisted of honey, lemon juice, and hot water and fell fast asleep until 11:00pm when Mea, Lori and Laura need to be so loud to wake the dead. I was lucky and fell back to sleep rather quickly. Today's events are follows: morning check of the mail, Joyce, meet Bally, laundry, connecting streams, have my joyful telephone conversation with you, write a letter for my passport, write a supports thank you letter, do my room work out, and then visit with you, mom and to sum it all up with a good night chat with my son. Thank you for the wonderful news about my marks. Good has such amazing timing. I will put these in the parole portfolio. I pray we all have an amazing day and god sends blessing and answers to our prayers. Stay in the faith and God's way.

Joyce show was about her new book. Hebrews 3:15 things start today. Joyce spoke on quitting smoking. Blessed be the lord for helping me quit smoking no problem. God wants me to be healthy. Romans 12:21 is worth the read.

Well Bally never called me up, so I will slide the envelope under the parole officer's door. Bob is here today, connecting streams did not happen today and a new gal moved in, the drug dog came by the house and we were each sniffed and then he jumped on each of our beds. Shoot I just washed my bedding.

Blessed to have met with Bally's boss and received the letters of support from the parole board, so that is fabulous to know they received them. Blessed to have a fabulous visit last night and blessed to have had a fabulous chat on the phone with you my love.

I love you and I am so blessed to have you and the supporters. I miss you. Stay strong, stay in faith, stay positive, and soon this will be a distant memory to what God has in store for us. All my love.

April 3, 20xx- 29 days until my hearing

Happy hump day mom and my son, how did you sleep? I was blessed to sleep very well and what a difference that will make to combat this cold. I pray you both have a fabulous day full of great news, blessings and great wealth. Colossian 3:2 set your mind on things above, not on things the earth. Romans 10:9-10, proverbs 18:20 words have consequences, power in the words, 2Timothy 2:16. Habit of being decisive: best thing to do is the right thing, pray, thought, consider, the worst thing to do is nothing. God will show you. Two words God decisions and one work, experience, two bad decisions you learn from them. Don't stay in fear. Making mistakes is a part of life. Take care of yourself be healthy, be full of energy, be happy and be strong.

Proverbs 18:9 Take care of your stuff, and take care of yourself. Joyce told me to take care of myself time to get rid of this cold. Galatians 5:16 stay positive, focus on the good things and taking care of what you have.

I received the support letters that were sent in by you and the information on the exam situation. Yet another huddle I must tackle. I spoke to Bob about this and have a couple of questions for Scott that we can discuss during our telephone chat at 1:15pm. My secondary came by and chatted with Sofi who asked me to speak to my secondary about the gong that took place in the house, so I spoke to her as she is not good energy to me and I want nothing to do with her before and my spider senses are up. Lori and Lisa are bad medicine and my secondary needs to know what actually occurred. Pastor Ken should be here soon so that is a blessing. I love you both.

Pastor Ken did come in. and I received our refills on the hygiene supplies. I am so grateful to have such a marvelous pastor and friend. I am reading the book of Daniel and Sofi said I remind her of him.

Read Hosea about Gods loves us unconditionally and now I am on Philemon about handling relationships. I gave another mate here that is using Mr. Reck for a lawyer; I gave her Don's business card. I walked the yard for an hour and half with another house mate. I was going to go to Kononia but the mate running it is on house confinement and I would rather not be involved in the other women who attend this bible group. I will write you after my second walk of the yard.

Phew I just got out of the shower and wow am I hot. Almost three house of walking and at a good pace. My house mate can really walk and I had a few comments on how quickly we walked from other yard mates. Well my son it looks like you will be the bragger tonight in the hockey game. I am thinking my team did not show up. Funny I have no problem breathing so knock on wood the fresh air healed my cold. I saw a mate while I was walking who is so funny. She says to me as I am walking no wonder your sick, she is such a smarty pants. It was so nice to get some exercise, fresh air and no negativity. Just smiling and laughing. This mate is the one who gave me her cold in the first place. Bob never called me up today so maybe tomorrow. Anyways I will call you in an hour. I pray your day was fabulous and full of joy and blessings and no gong. I love you both with all my heart. Xoxoxo.

April 4, 20xx- 28 days until my hearing

Good morning and how did you both sleep? Be careful later today as they are forecasting some freezing rain and snow. I was watching one of my faith programs but he host and his quest were annoying me. I liked the message from his wife and grandson but he is a different manner. Hope you both have a wonderful day. Last night Nat was done her visit with her mom and so she walked for a bit with my other mate and myself. Nat's mom told her to pray for Lisa and Nat said no way. I told Nat to pray for Lisa that she stay away from me and out of my business. It is the truth. I don't have to like everyone, and I certainly can choose who I associate with and Lisa is not a person I don't want anything to do with. I know what evil is and she is it.

Today I will spend time in the word as that is the best place for me today and every day. The cold is almost gone. Zumba tonight! I will call you at 2:00pm after I get the information on resources in the community. Carry needs it also so I will pick her up the resources materials. Joyce spoke on happiness which was such a great message and enjoy your life and keeping in faith. Trust God and all he has to offer. Be grateful for every journey, live in the faith with no worry, no fear, and no stress. Galatians 5:16 Walk in the spirit and you shall not fulfill the lust of the flesh.

Poor Mea is stressed. She came back and her therapist was not here and she is not sure who will be here assistant for her parole hearing. I hope I was able to provide her with some encouraging words of positive support. As the guards came by. I suggested she put out the message that she was inquiring on peoples where so blessed the guards took action on Mea's behalf. I encouraged her to watch Joyce and to rest and I would keep my ears open for her name to be called up to the main house. Meanwhile, Lisa is being noisy and sneaking around. It is really a sight to see. Anyways, today is about Mea and giving her what she needs before her parole hearing. Time to read.

A house meeting was called for 11:00am but then Mea and Lisa were called away so now it is for 5:00pm. Sofi popped in to ask me if I would go to work this afternoon as the ladies asked me to come in and help with inventory. Perfect timing. So I will check out the back-up plan and gather information for Carry then call you. And then go over to Corcan and put in some hours. I hope I don't infect anyone else with this cold. Mea's parole hearing and my bible reading today were reconfirming my focus. Bless to be thought of by the ladies at Corcan to be asked to help out and again tomorrow, but I have no time or energy to be consumed by the evil. Our house rep came in to air the tension. I said my piece about people minding their own business, so I am done if the others don't want to deal them it's up to them.

I thought Laura was fabulous about getting things out. So at least I have my stuff out and same with one other. But I am done with all this drama. I don't like it nor do I want anything to do with it. Anyways, I will fill you in when we have visits. Zumba is starting soon and I will call you at 10:30pm. I love you both and miss you so much. Stay safe, strong and in faith. All my love. Xoxoxo

April 5, 20xx- 27 days until my hearing

Happy Friday my son and mom, how are you doing? How was your night? Today is the big moment for Mea. I pray she is blessed today with some fabulous news. I just gave Mea some words of encouragement. This morning I am at Corcan, then this afternoon piano lesson and tonight is the bible study. Tomorrow blessed with your visits and walking in the afternoon and possibly church tomorrow evening. Sunday possible church in the morning, a fabulous visit with you and then Alpha and that will be another week gone. Well, I had better get ready to head over to the main house. I pray your day will be blessed, full of joy, peace and love. I pray for our safety and health, all my love.

Work was fine, nice to listen to music and be removed from all the gong of the house. Mea was denied her parole. She was sleeping and wanted to be left alone so I respected her wishes, which were relayed by her rat named Lori. The ladies at Corcan are willing to accommodate whatever work schedule I wish so with the tense dynamics here and with winters arrival again, it may be a blessing to work and wow what an honor for them to want me back.

Yes the ladies are all good with me working a day and half until after my parole hearing. Mea is in good spirits. I am so proud of her for her positive, forward thinking. Nat made a great dinner and Laura made brownies for desert with chocolate chip cookies ice cream cake. I will certainly be walking the yard tonight with my house mates. Carry left Nat and I and went to play cards. I told her she was off to the Casino and we laughed. Sometimes you have to use your imagination to keep things fun in jail.

I am going to church and then I will shower and call you. It is nice to go to worship in the outside world. I miss the fellowship with others. I love you with every ounce in me. All my love. Xoxox

April 6, 20xx

Blessed to you both today. How are you doing? Last night at church one of the volunteers taught me to pray in tongues, which is very unusual from what I am used to but as you read the bible it speaks of this. It is like a secret language to you and God. A bit disappointed in what Nat said to me during our walk last night but she is human and not God. Visitation start soon and that is where my head is focusing. I am so excited to see you.

Thank you for our wonderful visit. I love seeing you both and you are what keeps me going. God will make sure all is in our plan, but you are humans that I can trust. I walked for three hours with Carry. She is such a nice person, no negativity and a drawing giggle comes from her. Nat came out later after her visit. She holds so much negativity about Lori. I suggested she let it go otherwise it will eat away at her. You don't have to be around a person but there are better things to talk about then her. Talk about minding her own business. Grow up already.

Anyways, the gals from connecting streams came to take me to church. What a pair they are. Gosh service was the message I needed to hear. The message was all about relationships, personal advocacy, and total authority. How Jesus stands as our lawyer and not fear, to stay with Jesus and he will lead you. That with Jesus as your lawyer you will always win. I had a lovely time. So excited to share this new church with you both.

I am grateful we were able to speak for a moment before you left to see your friends. Mom I am so grateful for you taking care of my precious little one. I love you more then I can ever express or works could say. Remember for me to tell you about the coffee and Diane. Bless the volunteers who have been brought into my life and yours. God has blessed us during this journey as he will during our next one and the one after that. All my love, stay strong, stay positive, and stay focused stay in faith and stay healthy.

April 7, 20xx

I can hear the church bells ringing. How was your night? How are the boys doing my son? I am just waiting to see if I am going to church service at our church this morning. Nope I guess not. I washed my pillows and did some reading. Thank you for your visit today. I love seeing you I hate seeing you go. I pray we will be together sooner than later. I miss you like the first day, but I am better at handling my emotions. Waiting for count and then off to chapel and Alpha. I will call you at 9:30pm to say good night. All my love.

I am back from church and Alpha and I wrote to Whitey to see f we could meet on Wednesday or Thursday and also to help guide Pastor Ken and I throw the parole hearing procedures. God sent me a wonderful message through one of the volunteers in the form of a card. After our discussion over the video, a pray card was handed out to each of use that I filled out and she then gave me my prayer card back from weeks ago with two powerful scriptures on it. Ephesians 6:10-13 and Romans 12:2. So powerful, especially with our future event. I left early as I don't like talking about parole and another mate was, so I need to remove myself. Nat has negative energy also. She was so mad that Lori approached Whitey after church. I suggested she mind her own business and not concern herself in Lori's. Pray for everyone to have open eyes. Nat is the one who looks bad and petty and the back fire events are happening. A long story short, I am going to remove myself from anyone who is negative energy or can't mind their tongue as I only want to be around positive energy.

I shared with Sofi and she blessed me with reading psalm 91 tonight and I asked for prayer for Sofi tonight. Be a blessing is what life is all about. God blessed you both, God blessed us with vindication, great news, great wealth, great health, great support, please grant me parole and keep us close to you dear Jesus and you close to us. Amen.

April 8, 20xx

Happy Monday morning, the sun is already up and God is painting a fabulous sunrise. Hope you both slept well and pray we all have an amazing day, full of joy, love and great health and fabulous news and vindication.

I am off to work this morning, but first I will check the mail. Mea passed on the food order to take up; I must be re-instated in that role.

Margret Thatcher passed and Rick Warren's son passed on so that was such a shock. I will chat with you at 11:30am, I miss you both.

Work was good in the afternoon, I was even told to slow down as I was making the others look bad. Carry, Nat and I walked the yard. Had some laughs with other mates and I spoke to Bob. Reminded him about parole. He is so funny. He reminds me to tell you what he said about if he came in, gosh he is so funny and the email he received but would not tell me who sent it about my smile. The other guards are commenting on my smile in here. The volunteers spoke about this weekend. Sunday morning will be the visit day, god blessed that visit so I will be able to visit you here Saturday and go to re-integration and then Sunday visit you and do the course Sunday afternoon and Alpha and Whitey service Sunday evening.

We were reading the Katie Souza and in the chapter we are read tonight she said the next three chapters would prepare you for your leave from captivity. These will be very important chapters. I will call you shortly to see how our day and work went. I love you and you are both in my every thought and my every heart beat. All my love xoxxo

April 9, 20xx

I walk in faith and not in sight. (2Corinthians 5:7) what a beautiful saying. I pray you are both having a terrific day. The wind today is very chilly. Mom I received your job posting email and other job opportunities. Work was productive. Another mate had to be put on her place as she asks inappropriate questions so I politely told her it was not her business, that is my business and she understood. Gosh for someone they choice to run the Kononia group she should mind her mouth. Also, she is sticking with Mr. Reck so she will find herself here for a long time.

Just watching the food truck show. Wonton, nutella, and whip cream and my son this is so simple and looks so yummy. This afternoon I am going to call you guys and then Connecting Streams. Mom, you're coming in for a visit and my son I will call you when you get off from work.

Last night the guards kept Mea up with the shining of the flash light, I can so relate. I was so tired I had no issues sleeping. So I found out but want to confirm, but the news is the construction safety is cancelled so our visit maybe longer, as long as the max don't make waves. I pray for Sofi to be healed. She is so much pain and seeing Lisa cannot be easy. She is my strength that is Sofi is my strength.

I pray you both are having a fantastic day, full of blessings, great news, and joy. I will call you shortly. What a blessed visit where mom you could be in the parole boardroom tonight. Never a dull moment in jail. We had to have our visit there as they were processing new mates and could not be during our visit, but at least they accomidated us and visits were not cancelled, but that is where the parole hearing will be held and mom you got to see it first. All my love oxxoxox

April 10, 20xx

Good day to you both. I am reading Jeremiah 29:11, "For I know the thoughts that I think towards you, says the Lord, thoughts of peace and not of evil to vie you a future and a hope." Today I am going to continue in this book and finish Jeremiah off.

The Copeland devotional spoke to me on fact and truth. Fact can be changed, but the truth cannot. Truth supersedes and facts. And watch the truth change the facts. Such a blessing to receive this message today. I will hold this message close always. Blessing to be able to watch Joyce and it was on long suffering is the fruit of the spirit and to be strong in the lord. No quitting and faithful to God. Fruit of faithfulness.

I walked to the mailbox with Tara and Nat and as I was heading back and the gals headed to work, Lisa was heading to the main with her partner Lori. They were spiriting mean comments at Tara. Laura waited for me to pass and we finished walking together. Laura had been up to Medline and said that these two were making threatening remarks about how she should have done more if she knew what she was going to have gotten as a punishment for her attach on Sofi. I think it was a horrible display for when she was released from seg that Mea gave Lisa a hug, but I think it is awful for the institution to allow Lisa to vocalize threats and nothing to be done to protect Sofi or Tara. Lisa needs to be removed from here and soon.

Well the rest of my day consisted of working out, minding Sofi as she is in a lot of pain. She is so silly and said she was going to work this afternoon, well I put a stop to that. I saw my PO she is not feeling very well, and she is still all supportive of me and I signed a go ahead form for my scheduled hearing on May X. Bally will give me a list of questions they may ask me in order to prepare myself. Sofi said she would also help prepare me. Blessed to have so many wonderful advocates that are in human forms.

I made dinner and cut up carrots to send my mates back to work with to keep them healthy. I practiced piano and then taught myself, Mary had a little lamb with two hands. I will practice and show the piano teacher on Friday. I am pretty proud of myself. I made dinner which was chicken, porgies, Caesar salad, and carrots. It was a really big hit. Friday I am cooking again which will be breakfast burritos. At 6:00pm I am going to walk the yard for a couple of hours as it is raining so it maybe slippery and then call you at 8:30pm. I love you both and each day is one day closer to being together.

It is after we spoke at 8:30pm and is so nice to talk to you both and see how your days unfolded. I am so proud of you both and so, so grateful for your support and love. I will call you at 1:30ish tomorrow, but if you don't hear from me just know that self management started up and I will call you at 10:30pm. Funny how you saw a golden retriever walking today down the street as God will show you glimpses of your future and what is in store. All my love xoxoxo

April 11, 20xx

Good day and wow what a beautiful sunrise this morning. How are you both? How did you sleep? The guard's last call this morning was running a bit late, but that gave me some time to say my prayers before having my showers. I pray I will be blessed with parole so I may be with you. I will check the mail, watch Joyce, and continue to read Jeremiah. Self management is to be offered today at 1:30pm and today is Canteen day. I will call you if there is no self management as we discussed last night on the phone. Tonight is Zumba and hopefully it is on I will go and shake my jiggly parts.

Wow how God moves to make sure we can chat. So self management starts at 1:00pm but has been moved to 1:30pm, thanks for Sofi to remind me. So I will be able to get canteen and chat with you. Some pretty powerful information was shared during session today. Nice to see Apple and other mates there and blessed to have Sofi there also. Oh today was grocery day which means fresh fruit. Mea purchased bagels so we each received one, otherwise someone would eat them all. Laura divided it all up. It costs $140k per person here after I watch I would change a few things. Just waiting for Sofi to come back as I imagine she went to work. All my love xxxoooo

April 12, 20xx

Bless you both today and I pray you slept well. As I told you on the phone last night about how much fun we had at Zumba. Gosh we laughed so much. Mea was able to attend the class. Laura was laughing at me and my fancy moves. Nat came and she and Mea stood in the back now helping each other out. Mea kept saying that I would be voted out of the house. The volunteer ladies thought that was so funny. We just laughed and had a blast.

I pray we will receive good news about our home so we can share the good news. Maybe, you could contact the place and we should send a second letter to leave my house alone. God sees all and he knows that these crooks are stealing my house from me. Our system can be such a crooked one. I would love for me people living in my house right now not to have to worry about being evicted from these crooks. Mind you they are not paying anything to live in my house, but still they don't need this stress either. I pray God will take care of those crooks and expose them for all their illegal activities. Why it is the people who stand up are the ones who get punished. Those stories in the bible really hit home.

Joyce spoke to me on having weakness and knowing them. If we don't have weakness God can't help us. To stay humble is to be under the hand of God, under the direction of God. Be a blessing each day and God gives us sacrifices. To not try to defend yourself that we are good people. God's in charge of my reputation. You know your own heart. Be free of impressing others and to be meek is strengthens under control.

Live in the Holy Spirit and be in the fruit of the spirit (2Corinthians 1:8) God uses us when we are humbled and to be submissive and in a good attitude. Come under authority in order to come into authority. Trust God's mission and do things for God not for man. (2 Corinthians 12:79) more valuable in a situation then out of it. My strength is made perfect in weakness. Job 10:16 and 33:16-17 god grows you up. God needs you to have the fruit, rooted and grounded in God.

Pride = problems, humble = solution. God's ability to work in you. I am ready to walk in the fruit outside of these walls and doors. To share God's blessing to the outside community. If I can be a blessing in here, I will do great works out there.

Psalm 57-10 for your mercy reaches into the heavens, and your truth into the clouds. Today I am going to read Revelations. I will call you at 1:00pm to chat. God blessed me by answering my pray and I was introduced to the acting warden and she is my permit queen and how wonderful to have met her. I left her laughing which I have been blessed to do a lot here.

I walked the yard with Nat and Carry and we then went to a church concert. The group was amazingly talented in music. I am so tired of the disrespectful people in here. They attend church functions and are just disrespectful. I know I am a bit sensitive but after all this gong wears on a person who has any IQ, but bless the group who get it. The icing on the cake was Lori was all up in my business, I move right she moves right and I am so tired of this evil person. Sofi and Tara had words of prayer with me and they looked at my parole binder. I miss you both and time for me to come home. Today opened my eyes to others suffering from family stress and what they have been enduring. My prayers will go out to them also. I love you and miss you so much. All my love xoxoxo

April 13, 20xx

Good morning to you both. Again we are in the midst of winter. Nat and I walked the yard for an hour. It was actually refreshing. Apparently, Lori has been going up and down the hallways listening at people's doors. She has been caught by two people. Tara made banana chocolate chip pancakes for breakfast. So nice and very good. I will need to have a nap now. I receive a wonderful letter from the neighbours and they told me about the hockey tournament the young kid was in. When I say young the neighbours are in their 80's, and how he won all three games. He is on fire. When I get out we will have to go and cheer him on. I pray you both are in great spirits and I will chat with you at 11:30pm to confirm our visit.

Thank you for our fabulous visit. You guys are so amazing, your love, loyalty and support fills me up. I hope I do the same for you both. I am to go to re-integration tonight. The weather has started to clear off and so hopefully the roads will be safe. I will call you at 10:15pm when you get off work and I get back. Be safe and have a great day.

Re-integration was a blast. I did improve work which was so fun. Cathy and I went and so did Apple. There were some new faces there and just overall a really great time. Thanks to Sofi for her prayer last night and how Tara's face God put in my sight this morning. How my binder is powerful and now very blessed. Thanks to Sofi. Re-integration is a great confidence booster. I love you and will call you shortly. All my love. xoxoxo

April 14, 20xx- 18 days

Good day! I will be coming home today so let my fuzzy baby now.

Wow what a fantastic day. I was so blessed to see you with the volunteer taking me home to you and then you coming in blessed by the guard on staff, plus to be bless to see Bob and get a beautiful report and the old reports all corrected. I am just amazing at all the mistakes that are made and that it is dealing with someone freedom and life.

Whitey's service was one that spoke volumes about trusting God in the mission he has for us. Interestingly enough, Whitey came up to me after mass to make sure I know we would be in contact with each other this week. So blessed, so blessed to have you.

Sofi is to growing tired of the gong with some people. We had a fabulous house meeting about food and mine is not about food but about being respectful of the people who are cooking to give them the space in the kitchen to prepare the meal. Nothing worse than preparing a meal for twelve and others coming in and out of the area. The kitchen is not very big and really frustrating to be continuously interrupted. Funny Friday's concert would have pushed Sofi's buttons as much those individuals pushed mine. Grateful for prayer. God has been answering mine all in God's time for everything.

Off to Alpha soon and then I will call you to say good night. I love you so much and so blessed to be surrounded by so many fabulous people. Stay strong and in faith and we will be blessed with parole. Be the difference in this world and make it yours. All my love.xoxoxox

April 15, 20xx- 17 days

Good Monday morning to you both. I hope you both slept well last night. As I sit here eating my banana and drinking my milk I over look the court yard where four geese have landed and are stomping around in it. It is funny to watch them interact as well as movement for the individuals going up to the main for medications. They sure are a vocal bird. I am off to work for the day as are you both. I will call you at 5:30 pm mom and again when you get home my son. Seventeen more days and I pray for you both to have a fabulous day full of laughs, joy, peace, wonderful news and kindness. Ps the geese are keeping to themselves in the centre are of the court yard.

The ladies at work wrote a beautiful letter of reference for me. God bless them. Connecting streams was great. It makes you appreciate all you have when you listen to some of these women's stories and what they have endured and suffered with. Gosh these women have taught me so much, but especially how blessed I am to have you both. Laura joined Carry,

Nat and I for a yard walk. Nat and Carry ended the walk so Laura and I continued to get some fresh air and exercise. Laura and I got to know each other a bit more, even though we are across the hall mates. Gosh a person could write a book on each woman's story in here. Just remarkable is all I can say. I love you and bless you for your love and support. I will call you shortly to discuss your day and to say good night. All my love. xoxoxo

April 16, 20xx

Good morning and I am off to work I go. It was a lot of fun full of laughs and smiles. This morning I was blessed with my girls. Gosh being women in jail is hard. Laura got news she was to leave tomorrow but that will now be next Tuesday. She mentioned how Sofi should move upstairs, so I mentioned it to Sofi and she is going to put in a request. You just can't move anywhere you want you have to get permission on everything. Even thought we are in jail you get to know one another so well that some girls end up becoming very fond of and God has blessed me with and for the most part the best mates ever. I pray your day is going well and I will catch up with you on the phone for our chat at 2:15pm.

Carry was checking on her items in the dryer and I walked by and asked her if she had broken it. She smiled and then I told her she would have to help me hang my items on the fence to dry, which she replied she had no problem doing that. Gosh if you are caught by the fence you are in big trouble so it was nice that my mate would get in trouble to make sure I had my laundry done.

Connecting streams was amazing. I am connecting with other mates in here and still I am always amazed at the stories and the struggles these women endure. I pray all will work out. God has an amazing plan in store and my son please try not to get frustrated with people's stupidity, especially when it comes to the crooks and all their illegal group. Don't let them ruin your day, God will vindicate and he is the justice when no other justice will serve. I love you and I miss you so much. You know God is working when the devil is at play. All my love.xoxoxo

April 17, 20xx

Good morning and how are you? I would bet you are a bit tired from all the late night at work. I pray my son you will be blessed soon with a new job opportunity. God is always on time for all new doors to open.

This morning Carry told me we would be walking together tonight. That is great, but then Lori volunteers herself to join us. I will not walk with her. I know the bible tells us to love all even our enemies but I just can't and won't especially so close to my hearing. I am not her walking buddy and that is a big NO.

Tonight I want to go and type up a letter for supporters and to thank each person for their lovely letters. Pastor Ken will be here this morning for our weekly visit. I want to complete Revelations and watch Joyce. I will call you a 1:15pm to chat.

Hopefully Pastor Ken is okay and hopefully he will come in on a different morning this week. He did not show up for our visit. Please call him for me and find out what happened. Sofi is going to read my palms after her visit. I will go and type my letter at 6:00pm movement and then go walking with Carry.

Something happened at the max so no visits and no access to the main so no letter was typed. We did walk however and Sofi did read my palms. She is such a blessing. I am grateful she is so faithful also. I miss you guys and I am so ready to come home. I pray you both had an amazing rest of your day and I will call you shortly to end our day with our usual chat. All my love. xooxox

April 18, 20xx

Gosh my son you have an awesome sense of humour. I am so blessed to have you in my life and mom I love your persistency and you both put smiles on my face. Today I have self management, to finish Revelations, practice piano, and Zumba tonight.

Well I finished revelations and then was called to see Whitey. He was kind enough to share with me the kinds of questions the parole board may ask me and so he also got to know me better as to my story. We will meet again next Wednesday along with Pastor Ken but Whitey will be there in attendance for my parole hearing. Before leaving Whitey's office we had a word of prayer and he asked God to lay his hands on the crooks company and to bring it crumbling down brick by brick. Wow, that was powerful stuff coming from the Chapin.

Sofi and I had further discussion and she and I prayed again together. The self management was cancelled so I was blessed to chat with you. I miss you huge. Carry gave me advice as to just be myself during my hearing. God will bless us, I have faith in him. I walked the yard and read second Corinthians which was way more uplifting then revelations.

Zumba was cancelled so Nat and I went to the recreation room to type a letter. My thank you letter to all my supporters, Nat to a friend and Carry was playing cards with other mates. I told Carry she was at the Casino again. I long for this chapter to be completed and God move us out of here and ready to share God's purpose for me and you in May and to be released. I love you with all my heart.

April 19, 20xx

Happy Friday, I am so excited to see you tomorrow and spend Sunday with you. I pray for vindication to occur, but all in God's hands and his time. I pray for you both to have an amazing day full of all wonderful joys. My son your favorite weather today which is rain.

Today I will finish Galatians, practice piano, and call you at 1:00pm. Tonight will be bible study. Awe my son the puppy sounds so cute you get to interact with. What an amazing number of signs. A golden retriever puppy like the one we invasion in our future. Psalm 82 is a read.

Piano lessons were fun. I did improve together which sounds amazing. The mate I passed on Don's card was asking me questions about Don. It sounds like Mr. Reck messed her up really good so like

me Don could not do anything. Mr. Reck is great at digging your grave.
I sure hope she calls Don's office and gets some good help soon.

The weather cleared up nicely so I passed on bible study and enjoyed
more outdoors walking in the nice weather and fresh air. The bible
study is great, but sometimes it is nice to enjoy what God has right in
front of you to enjoy. I went down to see Sofi tonight when I got back
from my walk and when I opened her door, Sofi was in tears so I ran to
her and gave her a hug. She asked me if I thought she was a good person,
so I hugged her even closer and of course she is a fabulous person. She
explained and I hopefully provided her with words of encouragement,
support and love. By the time I left her, we had learned more about one
another, laughing and strong in prayer. So wonderful to help each other
out and to support and care for one another.

Going to walk again on Sunday. I will say a prayer in the parole
room to make sure God is in there when I am. I pray they have already
decided to bless us with parole and our hearing will not be long.
Nevertheless, I will say a pray with Alpha and next week's bible study
program which is also held in that room.

Chat in a bit to find out about your day's events. All my love. xoxoxo

April 20, 20xx

Good morning. I am just waiting to see you and thinking how
blessed I am. I love you both.

We just finished our visit with you. I am so sorry you are both
suffering with aches and pains. A friend's letter was lovely. This
afternoon I am going to help Carry with her Excel course and so
exciting to go to church tonight. I wonder what message God will tell
me tonight. Thank you for letting me share the Carry toast story. Gosh
that was so funny; Nat was on the phone and Carry making the toast
for me. Laura bless her told me a story about how the others view me.
I guess I am known as the nicest lady here.

Going to connecting streams tonight with the lovely volunteers and then tomorrow home to see you. Bless those wonderful women for doing what they do. Wow it is sure windy out tonight and it is supposed to snow again tonight. I will call you when I get back. I miss you both and love you more than words can ever express. Poor Sofi is going crazy as she can't get a hold of her man. I told her his phone must just be on off mode and not to worry. It is difficult to not get a hold of our loved ones while in here and because it is one way you can't just call us it makes it frustrating to not connect. God's peace to you both. All my love. xoxoxo

April 21, 20xx- 11 days

Blessings to you both this beautiful morning. Church was wonderful last night. These volunteers are so kind to me and gracious to our needs. When I back here after our wonderful home visit, Mea was back and wow very loud in the house again. I am blessed to be able to go home today, as the noise is really unnecessary here. Anyways, so happy to see you and soon to be back with you. The one volunteer is allergic to cats so I pray she can still take me home to you as the other volunteer is off to Mexico. But it will all work out perfectly.

Tonight there is Whitey's church sermon, Alpha and a load of darks in the laundry machine waiting to be done. Tomorrow will be work and hopefully there is a lot to get done. Lots of work makes the day go by faster and that is what you want in here.

Poor Nat is at her wits end. She was to have a visit with her mom this afternoon and V&C said she was not booked in and then to see her daughter but that got messed up also. Just some crazy gong. I pray for her and I encouraged her to go to Alpha and hear the word but she is really upset, which is understandable. I gave her a hug. There were volunteers who did the church service tonight and it was beautiful. Just a beautiful family and I really enjoy this one ladies service to our bible study group. She is the same lady who enjoys Zumba with me on Thursdays.

Well I am off to keep busy and will call you for our nightly chat. I love you so much and miss you like crazy. My stomach is in knots at being here and has the feeling of being home sick is just overwhelming some days. Thank goodness for the wonderful women here and the grace of God, plus I have the most amazing support system and my family are just amazing and they keep me going each day. All my love. xoxxoox

April 22, 20xx

Good Monday morning to you both. I pray you had a terrific sleep and are well rested for the day. I will call you at 11:30am to chat about your day and my son you are only at the one job today so we will get to talk. I am so proud of you both and love you so much. I hope mom you have a blessed morning and son please help out your grandma.

So wonderful my son you got in to the hair dressers and catch up with what is new in her life and then you can tell me. This afternoon work was cancelled. I guess there is no work so I looked over my parole binder. The spring commercials are on TV. I pray I am blessed with parole to enjoy spending time outside with you. I miss you lots.

I spoke to Sofi and she let me know what I will find out by Thursday what time my hearing will be next Thursday. Tonight we had banick burgers and I will walk for an hour before connecting streams with other mates.

Carry and I walked the yard for over and hour and then headed to connecting streams where a volunteer was wearing the perfume I wear on the outside. It is a no perfume zone, but she said she had it placed on her heart to wear that perfume. She sat beside me during bible study and when I asked her if she was wearing so and so perfume she said yes. I told her that is what I wear on the outside and she told me God has told her to spray that on for tonight. How marvellous how He speaks to me. The ladies prayed over me and my parole tonight. I miss you and I am so excited to share my story with you about tonight's events. I came back to the house and helped Mea as she was not feeling very good. I love you both and praise be to God with my release to share our next mission and purpose together. All my love xoxoxo

April 23, 20xx-

Good morning to you both and another fine day. My son I pray you are blessed with a new job especially when you have been getting some bizarre occurrences. I pray you will stay safe and your inner spirit senses will and are telling you to keep aware.

Hebrews 4:12 and Hebrews 11:6. I love you both so much and pray we will be blessed on May 2nd with wonderful news of parole. I will call you at 2:15pm after connecting streams to see how your morning went.

Work was great and blessed that Bob is in today. He is so amazing. I went to connecting streams which is such a blessing to have that group of gals to fellowship with. Thankful and grateful to have been able to chat with you both. One gal is leaving tomorrow and getting out and other mate has left today and another mate is leaving on Thursday. Carry is staying until May 2 and praise be to God mine will be granted.

My son I pray you will get the new job with the City and God will do what needs to be done for all the right reasons. Stay focuses, humble and grateful and remember and focus on what is come not what is now. We have an amazing purpose and it is going to take flight soon. All my love and I will chat with you at 10:30pm and mom I will see you at 5:30ish for our visit.

April 24, 20xx- 8 days

Happy hump day to you both. Last night after our visit four guards came by to clean out Laura's room, but still there are a lot of personal belongings in the room. The guards came back again during the middle of the night and were amazed how much stuff was left, but the room still is not cleaned out and we just got a broken sleep from all their noise. Oh happy days! I will call you at 1:15pm to chat and to share our morning's events together.

Should be interesting to see if Pastor Ken is even allowed in as the jail was just searched we all were taken to the gym where we sat and waited. I was blessed with a lovely letter from relatives to read and I brought my bible to enjoy while I waited. I read chapter on Peter 1 & 2. I was sniffed by the cute golden retriever, yes the drug dog. I spoke to the self management instructor about maybe writing a blurb about me for the people on the board and she graciously said she would.

Lori really pressed on my bottoms this morning, seriously I am encountering some interesting movements and god is amazing to help me bypass the evil. Blessed to have my room not messed up, but then again I have nothing to hide and would never do anything to jeopardize that. Never a dull moment and I am blessed to have gospel music, blessed to have wonderful gals, blessed to have the amazing family, were supporters and to be God's humble servant. 11:00am so I am going to get ready for my blessed visit with Pastor Ken.

1Peter 2:9 'Lord, I thank you for choosing me and making me one of your own special people and for calling me out of darkness into our marvelous light.'

Well, there was a lock down all day so hopefully Pastor Ken can see me another day otherwise I will just have to play it by ear. Blessed to have been able to chat with the SM instructor so the day was productive plus it made me focus on God who I need to trust in. I BBQ dinner, some chicken, corn, beans and rice, and there will be movement tonight so I will walk the yard for a couple of hours and then call you to see how your day concluded. I love you both and I am grateful for you both. Erin Brockovich is on again and this is a fabulous sign to show me inspiration to vindicate. All my love xoxoxo

April 25, 20xx- 7 days

May your day be blessed with peace and joy, laughter and great prosperity. A new mate moved in last night across the hall from me, but I pray I/we will be blessed with parole and entering into our next journey. Praise to be God, and victory and vindication. Sofi will not be able to move in across the hallway from me now, which is too bad. NO one can stop God's plan for us, we belong to God not the world, as this is what Kenneth Copeland preached on today.

I am grateful the teacher her will facilitate my final for my legal class. I had an interesting morning with the ladies at Corcan and a couple of guards letting me know that no one has ever left this institution that proclaimed their innocents. Innocent people don't go to jail, well that is what some may think.

I had canteen and met with Whitey. Sofi did a mock parole hearing and I answered the questions and this afternoon I have SM (self management). Phew and only 12:00pm.

The guards came by to do count and Tara was getting dressed and unfortunately not quick enough and a male guard got a show. So now we call it dinner and a show at Tara's room. That poor guard went red and was quick to get out.

SM was great. My instructor wrote a very nice letter for my hearing. And the teacher sent Bally and email saying she had no issues in supervising my final exam and that she would be honour to do so. God has been so fabulous and putting such terrific supports in here to give me such support feedback. Our new mate is a young girl named Shelly. She said I reminder of a lady of a TV show. So that was very kind. I will have to check out this show. Zumba was cancelled. Nat was no happy.

I walked the yard for an hour and thought I saw Sam and then I heard someone calling my name and sure enough it was her. She was back. I gave her a hug. She has different color hair, so I told her as I gave her a hug that I thought that was her but did not want to go up and give a hug just in case it was the wrong person. We laughed and I told her we would catch up.

Poor Sofi and Tara had words exchanged to them by Lisa. Funny how Lori was just talking to her right before Lisa exchanged words with Sofi and Tara. Nat and I were outside on the patio we saw Lori coming from Lisa. I did not hear the words Lisa said to Sofi and Tara but Sofi was visibly shaken when she returned. The duty officer called Lisa up to the main house. On a positive note we had another new mate, her name is Joy. I met her at V&C when she first came. Both she and Shelly seem very nice and they know each other from the jail they came from. I love you both and looking forward to seeing you on Saturday. I am really missing you big time and I pray so badly for my parole to be blessed. I pray for blessing on us and you are staying safe, healthy, and positive but mostly in the faith.

April 26, 20xx- 6 days

Gracious Friday morning my son and mom. How are you today on this cloudy day? I miss you and I love you both so much and I pray we will be blessed with great news, and my return to you. The desire to do what human's said could not be done. This is my modo.

I am going to rewrite my parole information, practice piano, do my bible reading, call you and have piano this afternoon. Bible study this evening and walk the yard and to close the day chat with you. You fill my heart!

How wonderful the crooks just served me with a court date that is same day as my parole hearing and at the same time my hearing is to take place. How am I supposed to be in two places at the same time and these crooks knew what day and time my hearing was and they did this intentionally? It is my constitutional right to appear for court. They knew all the parole information as they would have been sent this a month ago. This is to fight for our house. How wonderful six days before my hearing? My strength in faith and God is what I turn too.

I pray for my and our vindication and for justice to be served. If that certain agency would do their jobs and look into this crook then they would correct the wrong being done. God will bless us and he is the one in control and I trust him. Gosh my love how God will send blessing on us and show us blessings. My son I hate to hear you cry. Everything that is taken God will replace and replenish. The crooks will one day meet their maker and have to face up to all they have done. Please don't cry, stay strong and the course. I love you and we will survive this and be blessed for all we have endured. I love you! All my love xoxoxo.

April 27, 20xx- 5 days

Blessing on you this beautiful morning and we have visits together. Gosh I love seeing you and so miss you. I spoke to a couple of mates from another house, Cathy and her girlfriend after our visit just walking for a few moments and then Sofi and I had a quick chat and now I am watching TV. Oh yes, I cleaned the bathroom. Blessed Bob approved a raise for me to $6.35 a day. The weather seems to have changed and it looks like rain that will clean up and green up everything. Bless you both. I love you and God will reunite us soon.

Not sure about re-integration as we have been on lockdown all afternoon after a situation in I think I was the `C` house. Nat is looking forward to seeing both her kids tonight and commented on how upset she will be if she does not get to see them, but that is just life and you need to adapt and disappointment is just as much as the joy and flexibility. So hopefully it will all turn out positive because hope is a huge part of any part of life. I am sure we will find out one the guards come in for stand to count as it is 4:00pm. If there is not re-integration I will call you earlier, otherwise, we will chat after I get back.

Nope not going out and poor Nat she has no visits. I will call you shortly. Wow God is mad. The wind is really blowing. God blessed us with our visits. See how amazing He is to us. God is really brought forth some important messages to me and us. How precious time is and how precious family and friends are. I love you both with all my being. xoxoxoo

April 28, 20xx- 4 days

How was your evening and the outing with your boys? I spoke to Mea last night, Nat and I walked for an hour, Lori made cinnamon buns this morning, and I read the bible and devotional this morning. I am so looking forward to our visit this afternoon. I am home sick and really missing you.

Blessing for and to you both! Our friends living in our house can stay there until they crooks evict them and they can take whatever they want from the house. Blessing to the wonderful guards and for Whitey. Lori attended service to speak to Whitey but he was not there so she left. She is using the Chaplin for her evil ways. Whitey is such a gracious man and can see this for himself. Terrible for Sofi but she was not at church tonight as she did another mates hair dye job. We are off to Alpha now.

Alpha was wonderful but sad to come to an end. We had a pizza party and fellowship. Each member received two books to take with them. How gracious of these volunteer to supply these for us. I am going to miss the wonderful fellowship but blessed be to God to grant me my parole on Thursday to continue with growing and sharing with faith. Praise be to God who blessed us all with his blessings.

I am sorry my son we missed each other, Grandma said you were going out with the boys. Thank you both for all your support. I love you with all my heart and our prayers are being answered. Have and hold onto faith. Xoxoxo

April 29, 20xx- 3 days

Crazy weather, rain, snow, dark and ugly day! I miss you and I love you and I pray for us and hold close to God. Off to work soon and I will call you at 11:30am and see how your morning went. 'The lord does great things for me. He has compassion and mercy on me'. Mark 5:19

Work was lovely. This weather has sure made some mates ugly also in their manners. Thank goodness the washing machine is fixed. This afternoon I have to get my needles the cast one they require here, closure. Apparently, there will be ten new mates coming in the next few days, so again the PFV will be closed for all those wishing to book it. I will call you shortly.

The system worked out all the crazy with what is going on at the Law Courts and with all the walk outs, especially with the new provincial jail and remand and the court clerks.

At 7:00pm I will head over to connecting steams, finish my laundry, and call you at 10:30pm to see how your day went. I love you and miss you immensely. Wow the final must read chapter was about how these individuals receive favor and then their expected end was even more amazing…. prison blessed them to be successful with their expected end. This is the Katie Souza book that we are finishing tonight. Very pivotal in my journey and God is showing me and guiding me. I miss you so much today and will call you shortly to have our good night chat. All my love. xoxoxox

April 30, 20xx- 2 days

A bit chilly this morning and so as the snow is still on the ground. I forgot to my thermos in the chapel last night after my amazing bible study so I have left Whitey a note to see if he can find it for me. Bally and I have to meet this afternoon but I will go to work this morning. Blessing to hear about your new job, I knew you would get what doors needed to be open. I am so proud of you. Ephesians 2:7. I will call you at 11:30am to chat.

Well work was fine. Someone jammed our mailbox locks so our keys won't open them. My key won't even go into the hole. Thank goodness one of the guards was coming out so they opened ours up so I got my letters from friends and my marks from the University.

Lisa was doing her usual stare down and made Sofi feel very uncomfortable. I always go first to clear the way and walk with Sofi and Tara for security. Lisa won't try anything if I am there. Sofi was suffering from a lot of anxiety to work so we had a great talk and confirmation that I would always have her back and as it turned out the guards had an encounter today with Lisa.

Bally and I met today. Gosh she makes me laugh. She was shocked about the court appearance for May 2 and will do what she can to get the higher powers to get it adjourned. The crooks could not come to the parole hearing but wow they have a court date for the exact same time as my parole hearing. Pure Evil! Bally even wrote something she will be saying for me on my behalf with she said she does not usually do. I looked for my thermos after Bally and I had our meeting, but no luck.

The ladies and connecting stream gals were so supportive especially when another mate did a speech about if I was prepared if I did not get it, my reply is God goes before me…I trust in my god. Devil can't play in my playground… God has a fabulous plan for each of us… he is my focus…he has a plan and he knows my name.

The more I am here the more the guards, staff, volunteers, and other mates see what I have had to endure and still enduring and the crooks are showing their true colors. God will vindicate us and I and one day the truth of this company all the corruption will come out and I will still be singing my praise to God.

I am going to walk for an hour and get some exercise and fresh air. Glory be to God I found my thermos. A person asked earlier was walking with someone and the person she was with said they had it. It had a dent in it but I am grateful to have it back. While I was walking, I was called to V&C where the lady from E-fry was there. We had a lovely chat and she asked me questions and the long and short of it is she told me to call her when I get to Alpeda and she has a job waiting for me and wished me all the best at my parole hearing on Thursday.

I pray you are both having an amazing day and evening. I love you so much and pray to be reunited. I chatted with a guard about the mailbox situation and phew it was only frozen and hopefully will be working fine from now on. I am grateful my son you got home safe and sound and we were able to speak earlier. Bless you both and all my love. xooxox

May 1, 20xx- 1 days

Happy hump day! Believe in blessings! I pray you both are well rested for the day ahead and you day is full of wonderful news and blessings. Today Pastor Ken is coming in for a visit and I have one from you also mom. I will call you my son at 1:15pm. In Copeland's devotional for today it speaks of act of courage and to stand in God's words. 'I am strong and very courageous' Joshua 1:7. I wonder what Joyce will preach on today. I am going to check my mail and I will let you know.

Luke 15 and Luke 18:9-13 about serving God and love and valuing people. Wow, the devil is working overtime in here; Mea was saying how no one will be getting parole tomorrow, blah, blah, blah. I have my eye on God and he will do what needs to be done. No Pastor Ken yet.

I read to Sofi my address to the board. She is such a blessing. She is my guardian angel in person. There is one part of my speech that I can't get past without crying and so does Sofi. It is all from my heart and anything to do with missing and longing to be with you my son always will make me upset.

Gong today our legal system is a real mess, but press forward and be blessed. Whitey and Bally and my supporters are my inspiration and God will be with me every step. Interesting one year ago today my so called lawyer threatened me until I pled guilty and now tomorrow is my parole hearing. Mom thank you for your words of wisdom and encouragement. Having you be so strong for me, allows me to be me. God bless you both and tomorrow is already set in motion as God has already determined my path and yours.

May 2, 20xx- 0 days- the day of the hearing.

May 2- June 1x= 48 days the number 48 is coming around again and is again a significant number in my path.

Last night was a bit better sleep as the night before the guards were very loud. One of the many things I have learned in jail is how to cope with little sleep, but it will certainly be one thing I cherish once I am out. I was second on the parole panel, with a great spot. I would be more awake and we could get on with the day either way.

I prayed the night before for my primary worker to be able to attend along with everyone else. The people attending are a volunteer from connecting streams, my son, my mom, Whitey, my parole officer,

Pastor Ken and me. Before everyone left for work at the house and one of the mates was leaving the jail we gathered in my room and prayed. The morning was certainly full of peace and then nervous energy and then calm again. My mate was leaving and as the guards came to get her I saw my primary worker. He was not scheduled to work until later that afternoon, but my prayer was answered. I returned to my room to be engrossed in my prayer mediation and on the TV the music channel was the song I love my Fun with was #2 on the charts.

I was wearing the same outfit I was sentenced in which was black jeans, black long sleeve top, black sweater and my runners. I don't wear much make up and even then that is only when I am going out to church. So just a bid of mascara, lip gloss and powder foundation is my fancy face. I felt nervous and when my name was called to V&C a sense of peace came over me like God was with me. The gals here gave me a hug and I grabbed my bag. I had my parole binder, my trade tickets, all legal transcripts and the one I was served with on April 26 at 11:00am. As I was gathering everything Chris Tomlin song whom shall I fear came on and I knew I was in good hands. This is my song!

The crooks served me to appear in court on May 2 at 10:00am as they were going to take my house. Interesting how it was the same date and time as my parole hearing. Pure evil this man/ company is. I wrote, faxed, and mom emailed the Law firm to adjourn it for 30 days. I wrote and faxed the court house last Friday and prayed. My parole officer was in absolute shock at this as they had no interest in attending my hearing but the law firm was okay with adjourning it, but I have a letter saying that the company insisted on proceeding. As my parole officer informed me they, the jail, were not even informed to get me to this hearing, but to do this on my parole hearing date and time was just confirmation as to how evil this man really is. Beautiful how God shows how evil this company/ man truly is. My parole officer would inform the panel of this and this companies conduct.

I took the long walk up to the main, were I was embraced by my supports. The lady who was recording everyone asked my son if he was my brother, which made us all laugh. My mom said she was my sister and then we all laughed again. The lady had a great sense of humour.

We entered the board room where a man and lady sat on one side of the long boardroom table. I sat down and had my pastor on my left and my parole officer on my right. Everyone else sat behind me. The lady read to me all the fundamentals of the process and then the hearing commenced. Bally read a summary of my reports and we were informed that I could only go for my day parole at this time as I was going before my eligible day parole time. My day parole is in June and my full is in December. Traditionally, mates do their parole between the day and full as they will usually be given their day, but I was going before my day they could only grant me my day which was fine. The community is supporting my parole both full and day. I have full support on day and full form my team here and on the outs, which is rare.

The hearing proceeded. I had placed on the table my bible to the left front side of me and my parole binder directly in front of me. A parole hearing consist of three sections: why you are here? Second what have you done while you were here? And third what will you do one released or your release plan? I had a God moment before my hearing where he let me know that my hearing would be all about my alleged crime, as I did not commit this crime and maintain my innocence, yet pled guilty. Most people can't understand why someone would do this. I know this would most likely be my focus and I would only tell the truth so whatever happened…happened. I have all my faith and I work only for God. I will speak the truth. God goes before me, he goes with me and he goes behind me and as he surrounds me the questions began and it is all about my crime.

I took a deep breath and one question at a time. They try to break you and come at you from different phrased questions just like my interrogation, but I stand strong in God's work and I spoke the truth. They had no interest in the seven months here or my release pan and could not understand how I could be okay with paying them for something I did not take. The way I look at it is they need my house so badly then I will give them my house. If they need my vehicle so badly then I will give them that also. If you are thirsty, I will give you drink. If you are hungry, I will feed you. My faith keeps me/ us safe and strong and god will provide. The house and vehicle were both purchased with my wages I received from him and that crooked company, which is all dirty, corrupt money anyways, so if they want their corrupt (tax evaded, money laundered) wage I worked for back then go ahead.

My God will bless us or God will bless the 30 day extension. The really interesting item that was in the documentation they served me on April was a package to list all my assets. Well, they did their big investigation on all my assets so they can go and get all this money, but oh yes they fabricated evidence as I had been saying from the beginning and now they want me to give them my asset information. Just like they said I had two vehicles, which I do not. They want to know about my inheritance I will receive and from whom, so I will let them deal with God on this. This just once again vindicates and justifies what I have been saying all along. I pray blessing s with addressing the courts on this matter.

Anyways, back to my parole hearing, this took over an hour of being questioned and fighting for my freedom and then pastor Ken spoke and then Bally. I read my five page address to the panel and then we adjourned. While reading my letter to the panel I could hear my son crying quietly. Bally spoke to me outside and told me my letter to the board was amazing. She was amazing also with her kind words about me. Pastor Ken has been my anchor for years and his is just fabulous.

We all waited in V&C for 15 minutes before being called back in for the panel's decision. The gentleman read to me their decision. As you can imagine you are just waiting for the yes or no…approved or denied. He spoke for a bit and then my granting of day parole was read. Blessings to that board and tears of joy. I informed the board that I would be their success story, which I have every intention of proving to them.

As we sat after the hearing and enjoyed each other's company, my primary worker came to find out the verdict. He came to see me and let me know that he weighed heavily if he would attend and I can see why he choice not to attend. I respect his decision. He being on shift was so wonderful as it certainly could have gone the other direction. The book was brought in and Pastor Ken made a funny saying I would pay back the company with proceeds from my book and the story.

Blessings to my supporters I have such amazing family as you. I would have had everyone there, just so you know. You may not have been there in person, but your support letters would have been taken to heart and I am so thankful and grateful for you. For you are as much a part of my journey as I am and I am so humbled to have you have supported me. There was a phrase used that my pastor and Whitey picked up on that meant the truth is coming and the panel believed me. I will find the phrase in the transcript, but it was powerful words that were spoken by the parole panel breathing life into my innocence.

As I was reading to the panel my five page address to them, there is a part that I could not get over without crying. No matter how many times I read this to myself, this one part just makes me cry, even thinking about it makes my eyes fill, so as I am reading this part the emotions come and I can hear my son sniffle well that was so powerful to me to motivate me even more to tell this story and I have decided I will type out my second book while I am in the halfway house and get them both published quickly.

As everyone slowly left, mom and my son sat and I enjoyed the peace and gracious news my very wise son spoke these words to me, 'mom remember to enjoy the joy here, but also remember that not everyone may get their parole today.' How humbling and true. Gosh my son is such a thoughtful and godly man. How blessed to even the getting caught up in the human flesh and all the thanks to God that I/ we were blessed. How blessed for my son to speak such amazing, wise words. There was another mate going up right after me and as we were winding down she came into V&C. We wished her all the best and I gave her the Kleenex I had. She was so nervous and asked me for advice. I told her that the best advice is to tell the truth and speak from the heart. What will happen will happen and know that God had a plan for her?

As I walked into the court yard the other mates watched me not knowing if I received it or not. I really wanted to the fist trust from the John Hughes movie but was humbled by my son. I arrived and Nat was in the kitchen and I started to cry. She did not know if I had received it or not, she just gave me a hug. I told her I was granted and she hugged me tighter. Then Sofi came stomping out of her room and gave me an even tighter squeeze and she was crying tears of joy. Sofi and I prayed for that mate who was waiting to go up for her hearing. We all shared embraces of joy at the house.

The volunteer from re-integration was actually outside waiting to take someone on an escorted visit. She is doing a video on how to do parole effectively. She was so happy for us. I let her know that I would be very interested in participating in her video as I can say I have don parole successfully and would love to share any information to fellow mates.

I attended self management and will share my parole binder idea with everyone. I have many guardian angels in here and I am so excited to see you all and for us to all break bread together. The half way house is in town and this hurdle is completed. I will have to stay until mid June. I have to completed one of my correspondence courses final exam and I have signed up for the community clean up which will keep my busy for the next month. My gratitude is over flowing today and I am beyond words to explain my appreciation for my freedom.

May 3, 20xx- 47 days until freedom

Just doing laundry and packing up items I don't use and will see if I can get them cleared and out to you. I am writing in my yesterday journal; need to read about my final exam plus the comments from the instructor on my assignment. This afternoon I have piano lessons, will walk at 6:00pm and 8:00pm and Honors reward bible study is on at 7:00pm. I filled out the forms for the unescorted visits so we can get that process started. I will call you at 11:30am. Joyce's message was so wonderful and relevant. She spoke on how we need not focus on material items but on him and how he will provide all we will ever need.

I was just called to get my release clothing. I saw two other mates there also getting their clothing. The thought of my release is so exciting. I will miss my good friends that I have a church fellowship with, but I am so excited to be back with you and will prepare for my/ our next step and adventures.

My piano teacher did not show up so hopefully all is okay. I completed myself management homework and read with the correspondence instructor wrote. I spoke to Bob about my UTA and told him I put in the requests. I wrote to the teacher here to schedule a time to write my final exam in the University course. Bob laughed at me as I joked to him about the clean up and he said he probably doesn't even have to write a report as I am probably already approved. He is so amazing. I understand why he could not join me during my hearing and how difficult it must have been. He has seen so much here and to have the wrongs win over the just can really play on ones being. He has a terrific smile already, but when I told him I was blessed today with my parole his smile grew even bigger if that is possible.

I was called to V&C to meet with Bally. I thanked her again for everything from yesterday, She is such a blessing. She asked about the court crap and she told me she had not heard anything. I told her we would just keep in touch with one another about that. I told her about the UTA request and she said I would be out before then, so who knows. One day at a time one moment at a time. I will ask the gals about two citizen's escorts for the weekends and like I told Bally I love my new friends, but if I can free them up so that someone else can see their loved ones and I can go home on an UTA then two families could be happy. I know my friends would take me. God is so amazing and so many blessing are being received.

'Faith is being sure of what we hope for and certain of what we do not see', Hebrews 11:1. I also told Bally about what you said to me my son about being full of joy, but how you humbled me. You are very wise.

Oh yes, two new mates moved in. One has been here before and was out for three weeks and now is back. I call her the cuckoo bird. She was involved in a murder and is really messed up. The other lady is an older lady named Janice and this is her first time here. I think Mea got a letter from Laura for me to read. She was asking about my parole hearing and wished me luck. I will get her address and write to her.

I walked for two hours and went to bible study. It spoke on surrendering to God and he will take care of you and your defence.

How to honour your employer and honoring God. I miss you both and I am so excited to see you tomorrow. I love you both with all my heart and can't wait to be with you again full time. All my love. xoxoxo

May 4, 20xx- 46 days until freedom

Just waiting to be called to V&C to see you, so I am reading today's devotional which is so fitting about the transfer of wealth from the hands of the wicked to the hands of the just. Proverbs 13:22 and Ecclesiastes 2:26. See you soon.

I love you both and miss being with you. One day closer. Thank you for our visit. My son I pray you have a wonderful date tonight. I will call you at 4:30pm to chat. This afternoon I will type my last chapter to the second book and a thank you letter to my supporters. I had an ETA to church tonight and that was fabulous. I was inspired with the title of this book or the third book called Justice prevails. I made sure I thanked my volunteer supporters for all they have done and how much their support means to me. One of them confessed that she was holding it together until she looked over at my son and then she lost it also.

Sofi believes my hearing set the tone for everyone that day. The staff and volunteers are still very interested in reading about my story. I will take you and your friends to this church to see how magical it is. We can tell them it is a concert and get them to church and see what they have been missing. I just left speechless after going.

I loved hearing about your date. I am so bless for you. Not many would wait to tell their mom about the date and you waited for us to chat before going out with the boys. You are my life and I am so humbled and grateful. I love you both so, so much. All my love. xoxoxo

May 5, 20xx- 45 days until freedom

This morning as I am writing to you this letter I can look out my window and see gals sunning themselves, playing cards, listening to rap music and it started at 8:30am. Thank goodness only a bit longer.

There is no air conditioning in here so my window is open to get a breeze. I heard last night Carry is on her way back, but I will wait to see her in person. Today I am going to do the laundry, and read the devotionals. Funny it is proverbs 3:9-10 and we covered proverb 3 last night at church.

The volunteer made an interesting remark last night to look at paying back those crooks as a form of tithe giving to God not to them. I love that. She is so wise. Blessed to have visits today at 1:00pm with you and I will call you at 11:30am to confirm.

Time to shut the window as there is too much cursing in the yard. Wow the movie of the week is 'Word' about a writer and how he published a book that was found in a brief case. See you shortly for our game session.

Gosh what a great visit, so lovely to be able to sit outside. Funny how the guards gravitate to us and how they are a part of our circle. Jimmy is such a fabulous person and hopefully we can break bread with him and others soon. Mea told me something interesting after church. Church was wonderful, but no Whitey it was a volunteer and her family that hosted church. The speaker spoke of proverbs 3 again, that is the third time in 24 hours this scripture has been brought to my attention, God must be hinting at me. It is so hot out today and with no air movement it becomes sticky. You are my sword and my armour. I love you with all my heart.xoxoxo

May 6, 20xx

How did you sleep last night, especially in the heat? My room cooled down nicely, but I am convinced that there will always be something to test my patience. The guards on last night had to keep giggling every time they came in. Anyways, one day closer to being with you and that is my blessing. I pray your day is full of greatness. Jeremiah 17:1-8.

My son how was the movie last night? Sorry I missed talking to you. How much sun did you get kissed with yesterday? Today I will work at Corcan and tonight is connecting streams. I will call you at 11:30am as you are working later today. I miss you and can't wait to be with you again. All my kisses.

Connecting streams was wonderful tonight. Some of the gals decided they would write a book about their adventures and tell their story. Wow so similar to my writings. It seems that is all this bible study is turned into now. Poor Mea got home while I was at the main and keeps getting bombarded by other inmates. Some are more annoying than others and this one who is very annoying is in the house next door. So they stand outside the house and yell until that person goes outside to talk to them. Phew it is hot. Today reached a high of 30 degrees. Not sure if it is the heat or what but that devil is sure coming out in some women. God stay close to me and my family, I pray we are blessed and protected with God's army of Angels. I love you and miss you. I asked the volunteer about May 19 and she said she was going to be busy but would ask the other volunteer. Hopefully one will take me home that day for a visit. All my love. xoxoxo.

May 7, 20xx

It was so nice mom to hear how much fun you had last night and how blessed I am as my strong advocate. You told me the gals were going on about the new remand center and how much stupidity was coming out of their mouth and how it filled you with such anger because you were able to now add to your list that you have experienced jail, but more importantly how these were people.

How grateful we are for those fabulous volunteers to take me home to you my son. My son you always amaze me with your strength and wisdom. I am so proud of you and how much you did the right thing and gave your two weeks' notice. I pray we will receive some fabulous news. I pray for vindication, strength, great health, great wealth, and to be blessed. God has a great plan for us. I will chat with you at 11:30am I am off to work and then bible study and them mom you and I will have a visit.

Connecting streams was wonderful this afternoon. I just adore these volunteers who come in to share fellowship. I made a homemade card for a couple of the gals to say goodbye for when I leave. Funny at work I have everyone saying ya-no. No Carry yet. I thought today she would show up back here. Sofi and I shared a prayer and she discussed some issues weighing on her heart. Tomorrow I will go into work to help her out and hopefully elevate some stress not cause her more. I am just waiting for our visit mom and having a coffee.

Miss you, I miss being with you sharing your lives, but soon enough. God is never late to do anything. All my love. xoxxooo.

May 8, 20xx

How are you this morning? Bless the guards last night they did not even wake me once which is amazing especially here. God is sure amazing as getting a good night sleep was one of my many prayers. I am off to work today. Sofi is very busy and I have offered my hands to help her out. As I tell her I maybe more of a liability and she is so kind to dispute that remark.

My son for you gracious services and thank you for telling me the story of the two people walking the golden retriever. Soon that will be us as you said. We will be blessed with that chapter so soon and thank you for including me. The key to success, proverb 4:20-23 keep in the word.

Work was fine. Sofi got her pen pack today, Lori has left for the humming bird and Apple moved in. I am cooking dinner tonight which will be breakfast burritos. The dynamics are changing again. I miss you.

Only six weeks left. Apparently, this place is getting packed so anytime they want me to leave, I am ready. Blessings to Whitey he popped in to Corcan and I expressed how I would love a moment of his fine time to express my deep thanks for everything he has done and he told Sofi he would love to write a chapter in one of my books. Wow thanks that would be huge. During Nat and my first break we came into get a drink before going on our second hour of walking and Apple decided to stick up an attitude at me. I just left and walked again. When we came in there was a new girl who is lacking some basic skills, so this should be fun. All my love.

May 9, 20xx

Today seems to be a sunny start. I will focus on writing a couple of letters, studying, canteen, self management, and stay in the word. I will walk tonight for a bit. Yes, Boston is leading their series. I was able to complete everything I had to complete today. Bless the wonderful mates who work at canteen. I missed last week's hygiene and needed some ibuprofen so they allowed me to make that purchase even though it was a regular canteen day. I purchased stamps so my letters of thanks were mailed out.

Poor Nat received a decline to attend her nieces wedding. I presented to her what I thought she should do which Sofi thought as very reasonable, but right now she is busy dwelling in self pity. I told her she needs to be proactive. Unfortunately, she refuses to do the community clean up which does not look good and has refused to do other things, so the warden really has nothing to go on in granting her this pass.

Self management was okay. I feel for the instructor some days and today group was seriously wasting her time and mine. I only have two more and then Thursday will be doing community clean up and then it will be June. I will see if Nat wants to walk and get some fresh air and exercise. 7:15pm a great movie is coming on. Just watching the Wedding singer and missing you. I love you and one day closer to being back with you my son. Faith is Gods amazing plan. I saw Whitey again and he asked about how to get a copy of my first book and we will have to make sure he gets one. All my love. xooxox

May 10, 20xx

Today is going to be a cooler day, but still a nice day. What is on the list today? I will check the mail; hopefully A&D will have an answer so I can send you the items I won't need such as my winter gear. Then I will watch Joyce, read my devotional, and study. I will write something to you, practice piano, and do my work out. I have forty days so I will start the work out again. Today is also piano lessons and bible study tonight. God is amazing. I am so blessed to have such amazing supporters. Agape= I will love you regardless (unconditional) I walk in love and I never fail because love never fails.' 1 Corinthians 13:8. Colossians3:15… let the peace of God rule in your heart…'.

I am so lucky today Sofi asked for prayer with me. I am blessed to have her in my live. I love fellowshipping with her and privileged to be able to help but to be asked. Piano was wonderful. The instructor and I enjoyed catching up with each other, not actual piano but a fabulous chat. She is really a kind and gentle person. So wonderful to share life with fabulous people. Mea and I made ice cream sandwiches. Chocolate chip cookies and ice cream. Yummy, for Sunday dinner or mom day. We will celebrate once I get out. Like you said mom we have some celebrating to do. So excited to break bread with everyone. I love you.

Tonight has been very quiet. No bible study so I read another chapter in my study notes and painted my nails. I put together an envelope of bible verses for Sofi to give her inspiration after I leave. I walked to the main and ventured to the library to show Tara where the John Grisham books were located.

The jail is packed again; even the PFV is being occupied again. I met to let Bob know if the warden wanted my room I would vacate with notice. I will mention it to him next time I see him or just in passing. I am sure he is over loaded with newbie's or more common returns. I just shake my head unless it is going return with is also possible.

I was just watching hockey and Boston is still in their series. I really like the Leafs goalie he is gracious. I will call you at 10:30pm. I pray blessings over you and may we be receiving some fabulous news and vindication being served. I love you and I am so excited to visit tomorrow. All mylove. Xoxoxox

May 11, 20xx

Just going to walk the yard for an hour before your visit mom. I am so excited to get two visits today and so blessed you are coming here. My son I am looking forward to our visit later tonight. It is supposed to be hot today so maybe we can work on our farmer tan from last week.

Thank you for taking the time to visit. I pray you understand mom the importance of not speaking our business while you are here. Also, I will discuss mother's day with my son. I booked him in for tomorrow. I truly appreciate all you do for me and for my son. You are a huge part of each journey so don't lose sight of that. We are the three amigos. Sofi is such a blessing. My feelings of being tired of being here are normal. I am going to be sad to say "see you in a bit" as she is like a sister to me.

Blessing son our lovely visit tonight my son. Thank you for expressing to grandma how we are a tripod and how vital we are to one another. I am so grateful you wanted to visit me tomorrow on mom day instead of going for dinner. I am so blessed to have your love as I would go to the ends for you. You are my heart. As we pass on into the next phase of our journey, I am so grateful to be doing it with you. God has placed amazing new friends in our lives. I love you and miss you. I am watching your favorite movie, Troy, and one day soon we will watch it together. Tamo xoxoxoxo.

May 12, 20xx

I pray mom you have a wonderful day full of joy and peace. The day has started out cloudy and bright but hopefully the sun will come out this afternoon. Happy mom's day!

This morning I will read some materials for the final exam, do laundry, and call you at 11:30am to confirm our visit. I had a blast at our visit I love playing scrabble with you, my son and I laugh while grandma makes up the words. Wow the wind sure picked up but at least the sun came out. I am so blessed that you will be coming back in a few hours my son. The lovely guard said she would keep the game out for us to play. They are truly wonderful to me. There are so many blessings here, you are my biggest blessing. God has been so amazing during this journey. I am going to the chapel and then I will see you.

I am sitting here in my room watching hockey and can't wait to be able to do that with you in our house. I just love how our visit are always with a guard joining us during our visits. The lime green jacket only he would have one of those. Gosh Jimmy is so funny. Yes my son

I love how you thought of Night at the Roxbury. I love seeing you both today. I am so grateful for so many things but God has truly blessed me with your love and support. Thank you both. All my love. xoxoxo

May 13, 20xx

Thank you for coming in yesterday and making my mom's day special. Today I will go to Corcan and work and then connecting streams. I will call you to chat. I am so looking forward to our chat time. I miss you terrible today. I just got back from the morning at Corcan, which was fine. I am looking forward to chatting with you both. I miss you lots today.

Sofi asked me to be in her wedding party as a bride's maid which is so honorable. So we will have to save our pennies for that even in 20XX. Lisa called Sofi a Bitch as we were heading into Corcan. I did not actually hear it as I was handing in the food order, but I walk in the doors first and knew where she was. I left Sofi know the line, I put the food order in and turned to Sofi and Tara had passed me so I was last in the walk line and the look Lisa gave them especially, Sofi was evil. Sofi told me what she has said. I expressed why there is no guard there is the morning especially since Lisa obviously can't hold her tongue and the jail knows Sofi is being harassed by Lisa. A guard there is essential just to defuse what could be another messy situation and we need to air on the side of caution would be my mind set. I will be calling you soon. I love you and miss you big time today, so your voice will cheer me up.

Oh one piece of news, she did get a new lawyer. God is amazing. Wow the wind is blowing and the afternoon God showed his presences to me again. I was called to the duty office while at work, so I went and was served with the order. Just as I was asking if Bally was here, she came around the corner. I asked if I could speak with her for a moment and she said for me anything, everyone else can wait Bob had let me into the building so he asked what was up and I told him no idea just got called to come up. He was finding out what was going on and met with Bally and I which also served a great purpose to discuss with Bally my UTAs. I was reading the order and they discussed. Bally read and told me to get a request form, quickly filled it out and she signed it and then the call was put thru. Bob came by at count and told me we would chat.

I let Corcan know I was going back to make a call. Mea and I read it and Sofi and I read it and then I called home a second time. After I read the order over again the order was not as bad, still bad but God has a fabulous plan and he will still bless my son and I with a house. All in God's plan and not sure that they realize they just inherited a money pit. Father give me strength to forgive them as they don't know what are doing is a song I heard.

Connecting streams was interesting. The volunteers said May xx works for her which will be when we celebrate my son's birthday. There is a person who wants to publish their book, the same girls want to write the book in here and the volunteers have found a person to publish their book for them. How wonderful.

I really enjoy fellowshipping with Sofi and after Connecting Streams I really need to pray with her after all that occurred today. I feel the disconnect from the volunteers and apparently, that also happened to Sofi. Wounderful how God puts people here to shares the same experiences. I will call you soon and I love you forever. xoxoxo

May 14, 20xx

How did you sleep? Mine was okay as my mind was racing. I find it amazing how the occupants of my house actually have a story about the crooks and how this man has removed something from the mother of my occupants. Funny this crook has stolen from others I know. So to have them have an experience and know this man's character is so incredible. That is such a blessing as we actually have yet another person know how crooked he is first hand. God will handle these and he will enable the occupants to save some money and he will provide them with a place to live all in good time. We will go over the order tonight. I love you and thank you for speaking to the occupants.

Yes the process server is not to threaten or harass, not a part of their job so shame on her for doing that to the occupants. The court expects people to be respect the process well then these process servers better do the same. Just like when they harassed me and then they wonder why they get the attitude, will it very well maybe deserved.

My son I am grateful for you continued wisdom. You are my role model and you humble me. Are you sure you are not an angel sent from above sent from God. I know you are created by him but wow how blessed am I to be in your wisdom. I love you.

Off to work and then to connecting streams this afternoon for bible studies. Sofi offered her vehicle should you need it as she can't us it. What a blessing! I come to jail and find my sister. How great is that? Connecting streams was good, so grateful for the volunteers so amazing how Sofi has experienced so many of these experiences and the feelings I am going thru. We are blessed and so grateful for each other. God is so amazing and I love seeing how he works in others lives. Wow you know it's a God moment when Mea even says "yes".

We studied Joseph and the entire gong he had to endure from his family to being sold to going to prison, to God showing and building his character in Joseph for God's purpose. God has a fabulous purpose for me and you and we are being shown favour for our loyalty to him. God's grace is enough but he then keeps loading more and more on. We are blessed so we need to be a blessing.

Our T-shirt business is one project we will start and spread God's love. Bless you mom for coming in. It was wonderful to sit down and read the order. Gosh those kids are so misbehaving. Those parents are so disrespectful to everyone who is trying to have a visit. They should not be allowed to visit if the parents are not going to parent and the screaming is just mind piercing. So unnecessary. I spoke to Sofi and then Nat came in. I thanked Sofi for all her support and then we all had some good laughs at some of my silliness. It is good just to let things out. I will call you shortly to say good night. All my love. xoxoo

May 16, 20x

Happy Thursday to you both! How is your morning going? Some crazy speeding or stunting out the back of the jail was taking place this morning at 6:15am that was what woke up the house. Hebrews 11:3 and Romans 12:14 are reading to keep in mind. The stunting reminded me of the Indy. This morning my son you are working with the puppies.

It is so nice to see how a little puppy can put such a big smile on your face. I will call you at 11:30am. I love you and have a terrific day. Mom I pray you day is full of joy and peace.

Today is hygiene canteen, I will study, read the bible and I have self management which I need to chat with the instructor about my last class next week. It is also grocery day which means fruit and then I may go to the gym as the other girls are doing their hair tonight. They can purchase hair dye at canteen and then schedule the salon to apply the dye. I am excited to work out with my music and in my bubble. I pray you will be blessed and at peace with your new job today. God is amazing and has opened these doors for you.

I checked the mail and bless by the duty officer spoke to the volunteer about the 20th which she could not take me home but the acting warden will ask her about the 28th. The other volunteer said she would take me home on the 26th so hopefully she will keep her word. Well, of course no one word really matters anymore. The volunteer has said she is now busy and cannot take me home on the 26th, which is so frustrating.

God has foreseen this of course hence the job where we may be able to see each other during the weekdays and evenings now. They weeks will fly by and I will stay in a positive good attitude. Yes, I am a bit frustrated about not seeing you as much on my ETAs home but I am blessed to see you and we are on the last stretch of this journey. God has pulled me to him and we will stay in faith and follow in the right attitude. John 5:15. Time for me to get some studying in.

Next week is my last class in the self management class. One more door closing, actually two as I write the final for my correspondence course. I will have to ask Bob if I have been selected for the work clean up and about my UTA. Hopefully I will see him soon. The gals are sad about my last self management class, but I need my doors closed.

Nat and I walked for an hour and then the four of us were going to go up to the main but the movement was all weird due to a concert going on in the gym. So I am doing a load of darks and watching the hockey game. I saw Carry in the yard during our walk. Nat gave her the raspberries and I would not do that so I said hi and once she is settled we can chat. I wait for people to tell me what they want I don't get in to their business.

Nice to be able to chat at an earlier time. I will call you at 8:30 pm and I am so excited to see you tomorrow. Remind me to explain the "E or" or what I call the pity party gong. I sure hope I am out of the halfway house when she gets there. Seriously a woman this age should have some better coping skills so I pray she will advance in here.

I love that you and grandma went and got the bedding plants together. Last shift with the puppies tomorrow and then your orientation at your new job. This job will open so many doors and is a blessing. I love you both and miss you so much. All my love. xoxoxo

May 17, 20xx

The sun is shining this morning. Last shift at the puppy kennel and off to your orientation. Grateful for our visit tonight. Bless you both and blessings on you both today. 1 Corinthians 13:1-8 'love is everything; love never fails and walk in the love of God. Today I will study, do the whites, piano and chat with you at 11:30am and see you at 6:00pm. James 1:2-4 we count it all joy while I am in the midst of my trials. I let patience have her perfect work in me that I may be prefect and entire.

The morning was spent reading and studying. I got over an hour lesson for piano where we actually learned piano. Sofi made chicken empanadas and they were so yummy. The gals keep giving me their fruit. Nat her bananas, and pears, Sofa her apple and pear. Gosh I love the fruit. We eat very healthy in here. Great the washing machine is leaking. There are a couple of gals in the house that are a few bricks short of a load in here. One won't do dishes only rinses them and the other is not all there just simply lazy. So just when I said I had not seen jimmy around guess that comes by for count. God is so wonderful. He puts a smile on my face. God is always listening and he is moving our mountains. I am blessed to see you shortly for our fabulous visit. All my love. xoxox

May 18, 20xx

Going to walk the yard for an hour and them blessed with morning visits with you both. See you very soon. I just love our visits. Thank you for offering to help Sofi move. This afternoon Nat, Sofi and I got some sun and I did some studying. It is almost 3:00pm so I will be calling you soon. Still a bit burned about the so called friends on the outside but she has to make her own bed, but goodness you would think you would get tired of all the gong and games. I sure wonder about people sometimes.

Weird evening at church I could feel the vibe on the volunteers as soon as I saw them. One volunteer could not wait before she let me know she was not taking me out on the 26 of the month and the other volunteer just said no she was too tired, and then they started complaining about my Pastor and how he must be gay. They knew how important this visit was to me as it was your birthday and then they pull this. I did not appreciate them putting me in a place where a mate was just released. I was going to church but this was not appreciated and could really put me in a bad position. What were they trying to do? I actually like the person, but if the jail knew that these volunteers were doing this it would not end well. And the final straw was when the volunteers put on a show for the guards. What the heck is going on?

I came back and spoke to Sofi to find out how her night went which was a gong also. The devil is working overtime and that devil can get away from me and the people I love. Bless you my son as your words of selective hearing are actually what I needed to hear. Funny as I sit here and write this entry, I reflect on the message tonight and how he spoke on how our society is spinning out of control with divorce, depression, massive debt ect. Well society would be less depressed if people would speak of love. As Christians these escorts should watch their words. The next outing I am going to opt out of as I did not sign up to go to be their punching bag, but I am not anyone's. I love you and miss you. All my love. xoxoo

May 19, 20xx

I pray you both had a fabulous sleep and my son you had a wonderful evening. I am focusing on our visit today. I am going to walk, so I am going down stairs to wake up Sofi. I would slip her a morning letter but I better make sure she is awake. After Sofi and I walked we sat with Carry and Nat where I found out that I had given the wrong address for the half way house. I did however get some useful information about the halfway house and the rules and policies I must follow while there. I loved your reaction my son to my mistake on the address I was given but it puts a smile on our face.

I was getting a cup of coffee and Mea was cutting up her fruit when a new mate asked to speak with me about her parole hearing in June. I looked at Mea as parole hearings are at the beginning of each month. Then she went on to ask me or tell me she wanted to know what I told the parole board. I told her she need to discuss this with her team as I had no interest in knowing anything about her crime or situation as that is her private information. Then she looked at the other new girl and shook her head. I spoke to Sofi and apparently this mate did the same thing to Sofi already. Things are getting more nutty. See you soon for our visit.

I love our visit and our time. I am getting excited to go on to the next chapter of our adventure. I love you both and a new receipt to consider is potatoes wedges, mushrooms, cheese, tomatoes. It is like potatoes skins slash nachos. It is Mea's creation. Blessed to have the snow stop and our table in the yard open up for us to enjoy. Nat is not happy as we walked back for count that her team member did not say hi to her mom while she was there on visitation time. Gosh the simple things are really bothering her. I am doing my darks now and waiting to head to church at the main. I will call you later to say good night. I miss you and being with you. All my love. xoxoxo

May 20, 20xx

Blessed this morning and Joyce on the TV. Her message was so relevant especially after our telephone conversation last night mom. I am full of hope and joy and peace. God has an amazing plan for each one of us if we will allow him to work. If I have a chance to visit my son or and you that comes first. I go to church for the fellowship, message and worship but I will not put myself in harm's way. Mom I miss my son and my time with him is precious so please respect that. I still participate in all my usual activities but I will not jeopardize because someone does not know the rules or have my best interest. No matter how many times I explain this to you, you are not listening so you have to trust my following the rules.

Zechariah 9:12 one day the truth will come out and vindication is coming, today is going to be my day... I keep hoping. I believe God's word and God's promises. Remember your words are like a sword so please mind your mouth and fill them with kind, loving ones. I love you and I know you are coming from a place of love, and I love you for that. Thank you my son for breathing life into this situation as I am so upset with the way people are talking to me and I need to be more at peace.

Thank you for the chat at 11:30am, you put things always in perspective for me, my son is wise beyond his years. This afternoon was spent studying and I did my bedding as the washer was free. The jail supplied sidewalk chalk to do a house drawing but no one was into doing it. I thought we should do a zoo, but my idea was voted down. Oh well, now I am just waiting to see you as it is almost 5:00pm. Today's devotional was perfect, 'I forgive others, as God for Christ's sake has forgiven me.' Ephesians 4:32 and yesterdays was 'The lord delivers me out of all my per seditions' 2 Timothy3:11. See you soon. Xoxoxo

May 21, 20xx in memory of Dad

Good, Good morning. I believe in Jesus. I am sent by him. I fulfill my destiny John 17:18. I pray your day is full of love, hope, many blessings and safety and great health. Today maybe a day a full of wonderful memories or a day of sadness, but we can get threw anything and everything together. I love you both. My son I pray your day is wonderful at your new job. Full of fun and joy. Mom I pray your day is full of love and amazing news. I am off to work this morning and bible study this afternoon and maybe a visit tonight. Surplus of prosperity Deuteronomy 28:11

I got Scotty's work number should we need in the future. He remembers me and will help us out should we need it. What a blessing. Work was quiet. Poor Sofi's tailbone is causing her a lot of discomfort so she stayed home. The teacher here called me to ask if I could write my exam tomorrow or next week as she would not be here on Thursday. I am so grateful for her supervising so I will write it tomorrow afternoon.

I saw dad's memorial in the newspaper. It brought a tear to my eye. I cut it out and put it in my bible cover. This is the bible; I carry it with me everywhere, which means he is also with me and us along with God. I will spend the afternoon studying and call you at 3:00pm. Mea is going to ask the lady at A&D about the items to send to you. I absolutely loved our visit. I loved the sharing and who exciting, nervous and proud you were about starting your new job. I love how you mom were more receptive and open and how you even approved of the garage sale when I get out. I spoke to Jimmy as I left to return back to my unit. He mentioned he would be my escort. I am glad you were able to find out your new worksite for work. This will eliminate a lot of nervous energy knowing where to go. All my love. xooxxo

May 22, 20xx

How are you this morning? I pray my son you have a fabulous first day on the job. I have asked the angels to stand watch over you and you also mom. I pray we have a fabulous day full of blessings. Gosh the guards were noisy again last night and I even put in my ear plugs. Apply started off the morning banging on her TV which is extremely annoying so I can see why the other mates is not impressed. No respect for others.

Today Pastor Ken is coming in at 11:00am and I am studying until 1:00pm at which time I will write my final exam for one of the correspondence courses. I love you both and will call you at 5:30pm.

Well, today I spend the morning studying and unfortunately no Pastor Ken, so I will ask you to call him to ensure all is well. Chaplin Whitey came and visited me at the house what an honor usually we are called to him, but he took the time to see me. God is amazing.

I wrote my final which I think went well. The teacher is such a kind person to allow tm to write and to accommodate me. She is truly amazing. I spoke to the lady at A&D just before my exam and she let me know that I could bring to her my items for tomorrow morning and they would be ready for pick up on the weekend. Wow. I am just so grateful to the wonderful staff here. I am so blessed and humbled.

I have not found out if I am approved for the cleaning up but I am hoping to be able to volunteer my services back to the community. I was able to help a mate with some legal advice. Everyone should get a limited power of attorney in place prior to coming to jail. Bless Don for informing me on that.

I am excited to see how your day went and I am pleased to hear it was a hit. This is a wonderful fit for you. I love you and miss you so much. All my love. xoxox

May 23, 20xx

How are you? My son I imagine you are tired today as your body adjusts to your new job. Philippians 4:19 and Ephesians 3 are chapters to read. I look forward to being able to help out. Today I will take up some of my items to return them to you. Hopefully the lady at A&D calls me up early to get this done. Then it is canteen day not that I need much just stamps. I will vacuum the stairs here and this unit. The last self management class is today, which is a bitter sweet as I enjoy and cherish the instructor. I will call you at our usual time and then my son I will call you at 6:00pm as you will be home by then. Thank you for calling Pastor Ken and making sure he was okay, nice to know he just got busy.

I should find out if I was approved for the cleanup. I pray for huge blessings on us today. Glory be to God! I spoke to a mate and asked if she went to bible study on Monday which she did but she left early. I asked if they read the next chapter of the Katie Souza book. She told me nope that they just sat around talking so next Monday I won't be behind. I was going to read on to stay on track so now I can read another book instead.

The last SM class and so grateful to be done with that. A few individuals really make that class difficult. I just find them to be rude and not at all there. I feel for our young couple living in our house, and hopefully they will stay as it would allow them to save some money. I wish I knew my son was home safe and sound. The weather channel is forecasting rain all weekend long. Yuck I pray my son you get home soon and safe and sound. I will call you again at 9:30pm and chat with you then. Peace is with us and blessings are coming, keep the faith! God is so amazing and his plans are amazing also. All my love. xooxoxo

May 24, 20xx

'Grace and peace have been given to me from God my fathers, and the lord Jesus Christ' Ephesians 1:2. Peace be with you both today. So grateful for you and I spoke to Mea about our situation and she told me they can't do this as there is nothing in the order first and she will get me a number to her good friend who is civil counsel. This would elevate a bit until I can deal with this matter upon my release. I love how they do this in the most evil way, but God will set all things right. Keep in faith and let god move these mountains. The truth will come out and god will bring forth all righteousness and honor. The evil will be revealed and god is showing their evil.

Well, we got the phone number for the lawyer so we can get a lawyer involved should we need one. I will write the justice at the court house also and see what can be done. This is so wrong and against my Constitutional Rights. Work said I could work full time plus still do the bible study and piano lessons with excused absences.

Tonight I will go to the bible study and then at 8:00pm type the letter but wait until tomorrow to include the garnishee gong.

Mom you make my heart skip when you asked if I wanted to speak to my son and told me he was fired. You are so funny. Piano was great. I will call you shortly and will read the letter to you I will send to the justice who is overseeing my complaint against the system.

Sofi and I spoke about how we miss our families and are grateful to be put together to help get past this journey. I went to the bible class and enjoyed a video. I left at 8:00pm to go and type up the letter to the courts. Gosh that room is so loud. Absolutely, brain piercing! These women are so rude their mouths are jaw dropping and loud, but I got it typed up and finishes. Blessed to chat with you and my son and sending you all my love. xoxoxo

May 25, 20xx

'I expect the glory of God to be poured out on my life like rain', Zechariah 10:1

I forgot to tell you that the lady at A&D called me up to have my items sent out. She got them packaged up and they are at the front ready for you on your next visit to take out. God is so good and funny how I was waiting all day and just given up thinking about it when it happened and then I get the call to bring the items up. Blessing to Sofi as she helped me take the stuff up. The lady at A&D is becoming a parole officer in here for a month and then hopefully the community. She is such a kind person that maybe god will put her in my path for my journey out there.

I left my thermos in the recreation room after being distracted by all the noise. So I am going to walk up this morning and find out when the room is open to go and retrieve it. Everyone knows it is mine so hopefully no one will take it. I placed it behind the monitor as there is no desk space and forgot all about it. Time for me to leave it in my room, but I was full of the Holy Spirit as I was on a mission from God to get those letters done to the court house.

Not sure if you are at work my son, it is not raining here but that could be different story where you are. Blessed to have your visit tonight. Phew my thermos was there. I will leave it in my room as obviously I am full of the Holy Spirit after church and not focus on material stuff. I am excited to see you both tonight. I pray that the acting warden gave the volunteer the heads up I would not be going tonight to re-integration.

Nat was very upset as she was denied her wedding request and Mea go to go to her function. What Nat does not realize is Mea is also established her UTAs extra and Nat has done one ETA plus refused to do the community clean up. I am blessed to have visits and your support it is time for me to get out of here.

I am so grateful the guards will allow us to visit and so wonderful how quiet V&C was tonight. The guards would usually cancel the visits but they stay for us, how wonderful. I love our time together and our quality time playing scrabble. Thanks for taking the boxes out with you tonight. This will be less to move when I am released. I pray that God will lay his hands on the crooks company and crumble it to the ground. Expose the company for all they have done and are doing. God hear my prayer

As I returned back my unit, I saw a guard and she asked me about you and how you were doing. They see you both so much that you have become well known in here. All my love. xoxoxoxo

May 26, 20xx

I pray for us today. I wrote to the acting warden asking she not put in a permit for connecting streams on Saturday as your visits come first. Hopefully we will be blessed and Wednesday I will receive my UTAs so that I can come home and go to our home church but on Saturday evenings will be able to enjoy re-integration and Connecting streams my frustration is with the volunteers and they don't want to take me home to my church or home and only to their church which is nice, but my heart is at my home church so as I said I pray for the UTAs se we can have our visits and I can go to my church. I am up, showered and ready to go so now I have to wait. If nothing goes forth by 10:00am I will call you at 11:30am and see you for our visit at 1:00pm here.

Thank you mom and my son for your words of encouragement. I am so ready to leave here and back to my life. Poor Sofi is being exposed and her face is breaking out bad in a rash. I am so annoyed with the noise and lack of respect by others. Sofi is deadly allergic to peanut butter and just touching it can cause a reaction, but these women still don't get it and insist on having it in the house. One day closer to being with you and I pray Bob is able to have the UTAs put forth and the wander blessed them.

Going to the chapel soon. Thanks mom for calling Pastor Ken about Wednesday as I will be on the community clean up so not to worry about this week and looking forward to seeing him next week or at church on my UTA. I will call you at 9:30pm. Hope you enjoy your BBQ tonight. All my love. xoxoxo

May 27, 20xx

All blessings to you both! I am off to the community clean up. The ground is looking wet so hopefully the bugs won't be bad. I will call you at 6:00pm. Luke 21:28, 'I look up and lift up my head for my redemption is drawing near!'

I am calling to be excellent. The clean up was great. The nuts and bolts were the guards were awesome. Would you not know but we started out at the crooks business cleaning up this curb side filth. Tara fell twice and Sofi left as her nut allergies were flaring up, we had coffee break in the morning and afternoon and a fabulous lunch at a little café. The weather was perfect. I got a bit burned but it was really great to help clean up god's world.

My son all I could do while enjoying my walk today was thinking of this day 20 years ago and how blessed and grateful to have you and wonderful the world is today for you being in it. God has an amazing plan for you and me. So get ready we are going to be blessed over and over again. I love you so much and will chat with you at 6:00pm. So glad you both had great days. Shoot Bob is not here until 8:00pm walk so I cannot talk to him until then but I will next time I see him and find out about the UTAs. All my love. xoxoxo

May 28, 20xx

Happy birthday today is your 20th; the world would be changed forever at the birth of you. I love you! Grateful for the day you were born. I am so glad I was able to wish you a happy birthday this morning before you headed off to work. I am writing you this letter at 7:04 am to you, you are such a gift to this world and this world is such an amazing place because you are in it. You bring such wisdom, joy, laughter, love, patience, kindness, hope, and adventure to each person's life you touch. Never forget you are blessed and will continue to be blessed along with a blessing to others. You are unique, special and created by God for an especially for his purpose. You are so loved and cherished. I love you more than words will ever be effective to express, but I would not change one thing about you as god created you perfectly. I love you and will later see you, but my thought and prayers will be on you and with you all day.

As you head to work to fix God's earth and I head to clean up God's earth, keep focused on his plan and hold close to the promise that we will be blessed and that he has special purpose for us. We will be rewarded in so many blessings and to focus on that. I love you!

Thank you for coming in to see me on your birthday. I appreciate both of you so much and I promise you your loyalty and support will not go unforgotten. You both mean the world to me and my son I am so blessed to be able to call you my son. I love and cherish you both. I am so proud of you and thank you for everything. Mom thank you for thinking of me and purchasing a gift from me to him. I sent him a birthday card but it is very kind of you to make sure he had a gift to open. Justice will prevail in this story and vindication is coming. Thanks be to God. All my love.

May 29, 20xx

One day closer to being with you and no words can express my heart longing to be with you. Proverbs 10:22, 'the blessing of the lord makes me rich and the adds so sorrow with it.'

Don't chase success let it chase you. Today's devotional is yet again a blessed one. We are destined for great success, all the riches and to be blessed huge by God. I am off to the community clean up and my son and mom I pray your day is full of love. I was warned about how the clean up in the past years has gone very wrong and that some of the mates have ruined it for others. I will not tolerate any nonsense and no mate will jeopardize my freedom for their selfishness. Jail can be a very 'me' place, but I have no use for those kinds and if you want to go you will follow the rules and be a team player. I am aware of the reputation of the mates and will not be around or near the bad ones.

After each day each mate is strip searches and hand swipes are taking. This traces any drugs on your hands, which is scary as you can pick up traces of drugs on so many places and especially on the garbage. I don't touch door handles or chairs and try not to touch any place other might have touched. I am used to these procedures are I have to be searched after all my outings and follow the rules at all costs.

Clean up was great. The weather was great until late afternoon and we got everything done. I ran into Bally this morning and bless her she said we would chat but she had not forgotten about me and has no concerns about me. I finally got to see what who and who the warden was. We got back to the jail and then Tara and I wiped down the hallway walls and stairways. The jail was having a clean day so if you were not out in the community picking up garbage you were to be cleaning up the house. All mates were to do this and then the massive amount of garbage was hauled away. I think visits got cancelled again; poor Sofi always gets her visits cancelled.

Oh the guards each day were fabulous on our community clean up. We had so much fun. Laughing and doing god's work. The only mates that could be out were the minimum mates so there were eight or so of us who got the pass to go. No we did not have to wear the orange jump suits, but our regular clothes which are just like other people, jeans, sweats, t-shirts, runners, ect

I am grateful you both had a great day. Awesome that the taxation department called to schedule when I can come in and get your money back from the sneaky lawyer. God will open one door and close another.

With all the fresh air and hard work I expect us all to sleep well tonight. I will call you shortly to catch up. Never judge a person and you will not be judged. Vindication is coming. All my love. xoxoxo

May 30, 20xx – fingers and toes count down 20 more days.

I am off to work today to be a blessing and help out as much as possible before I leave. Sofi is swamped and stressed so I am offering my hands to help. Today's devotional is about stepping out and doing, which is so true and what I am trying to do. Work was productive and a bit tiring.

Cathy showed up with her girlfriend and told me they were purchasing a ring and planned on getting married. She also told me she won her appeal that I helped her with, so what awesome news. I did not make a huge deal of it as she was telling me by Sofi and they don't get along. Jail teaches you to be more aware of your surroundings and I am more mindful of others feelings. Cathy may have won her appeal but her girlfriend does not want her to go so she is a bit upset. And as happy as you are for others, there is a lot of jealousy and evilness here. I have taught my son to be kind in all cases.

I spoke to Sofi after when we got back to the house to make sure she was okay. She was happy to see me but expressed how much she will miss me when I am gone. I understood, but she was my sister and we will be carrying on like sisters if she was in here or we were out there.

I was a bit taken back that the volunteer called you mom and I think that is crossing a line. I am not happy with this game and don't want her to be doing that. Not cool. I am not comfortable and my trust is being tested and I am not impressed. Please don't talk to her again as she could be up to something and I am now more cautious of this and not wanting to let her play games. Nice that she call but too tired to take me out when I wanted to be with my son on his birthday. I am done with her, and so should you be.

I am just waiting until the 10:00pm count and then I will call you to say good night and see how your day was. You are probably tired so I will make it quick. All my love. xoxoxo

May 31, 20xx

I was up to make sure Mea got off to work. Poor gal chipped her tooth and her filling fell out and of course it is right in the front tooth. Copeland is a repeat so I am going to watch the sports highlights. It is hot and muggy in my room which is really ugly. Maybe I will get word on my UTAs today. I am off to work soon and to fill some orders for Sofi so she can be stress reduces. Piano lessons this afternoon and laundry. You are in my thoughts and my heart is aching to be with you my son. 'My continuous praise and thanksgiving to God give him the opportunity to intervene in my circumstances and bless me.' Psalm 145.

Work was interesting. Two groups of ten parole panel individuals came by Corcan to see what we do and to begin a tour of the jail. I was chatting with the acting warden and found out no one went before the warden, so hopefully next week the UTAs will be blessed, but as we were chatting some of the tour groups gravitated over to me where I was chatting to get to know me. It was lovely to speak to them but also to speak to the acting warden was a voice to tell them I was getting out very soon. She is so kind. Funny how when I first got here one of my mates was always watching the cooking show Chopped and now I find myself enjoying that show.

Thank you for dealing with the entire house gong. That realtor is such a snake. I expected the crooks to use him as they are two of a kind and best buddies, but it is conflict of interest and not in my best interest for him to sell my house. Do the courts not understand this and the conflict of interest? 'Let a man meet a bear robbed of her cubs, rather than a fool in his folly,' proverbs 17:12. Justice vindicates my name and righteousness prevails. All my love xooxxo

June 1, 20xx

I received the mail this morning and inside was one request of my requests to the duty office letting me know that the volunteer would not be taking me out as I had received my parole and you could visit me here so she will only be taking out the women who are less fortunate. Nice volunteers! Funny how they called you on Thursday the next day I asked not to go to connecting streams. My request was dated to the 29th and the volunteer called you on the 30th, oh well moving on. These women I shake my head at, but God is amazing and had a plan in store. Apple got called up to the duty office and she was to go home but then she came back. This place teaches you how to cope with disappointment but I think I have learned to trust in God even more. My request maybe blessed for tomorrow home visit, but one day at a time. I love you. 'Fight for that expectancy in the name of Jesus. Take your hope, fill it with faith and storm, the gates of hell.' They will not prevail against you is the meaning. Hebrews 6:16-20, 2 Kings 4-5, Ephesians 6, and 2 Corinthians 10:5.

I am watching the movie 'Big' which I have not seen in years. Nice to have this old movie on and the time to enjoy them. I hope you had fun with the boys tonight. And I pray tomorrow I will be visiting you. I love you both. I will call you shortly and catch up on your day. All my love xoxoxo

June 2, 20xx

I am up and ready to go waiting to see if a guard will bless me with my ETA visit home. Hurry up and wait is what jail is all about. Blessing and thanks be to God who waits with us. I would go walking but I am not getting wet especially if I maybe going home so I will pass until further notice. I am sure a walk will get in sometime today.

Pray and believe, for god will deliver and he will bless us in abundance. Romans 8:17-18 comes to mind. We have stared in the suffering and now we share in the abundances of his glory. Glory be to God. I love our visit today. You two made it so much fun. It would have been nice to go home but I will take whatever time I can with you. I love how that old man was telling that mate to say with the lawyer she had and yet there are two people in jail because of that lawyer that I know about. Mea agreed that the lawyer is just going to sell her out and she will be deported, which is exactly what will go down.

Off to service soon just waiting for count to clear. I will call you at 7:30pm and then bring on the hockey game. Apple is following Mea around it is so funny how Mea will want to tell me something and before it was Lori who would be there now it is Apple. DBT really paid off these women are still needy.

So church was packed and there was only two seats so Whitey graciously gave me his so that Nat and Tara and I could sit together, right in the front row and funny how we Lori goes and sits right beside Nat. God has such a sense of humour. The gab squeezed down and Whitey was able to sit beside me. Alpha was having a meeting but nothing was said until church and I had a telephone call time booked. Why don't they say something before to let the mates know? The volunteer for the connecting streams during the day told me this week would be the last session.

Apple was telling Mea what cake she wanted for her parole cake. Mea bakes everyone a cake upon receiving their parole. I did not get one but that is okay. The sense of entitlement is wearing on people, so done with this gong show. I am just spending time writing and away from her. I understand she is nervous about her hearing, and if she gets it will actually be out before me. The people that she was involved in who passed away, well their family members will be at her hearing along with the media.

I will call you soon and chat, I miss you so much and I love you with all my hearts. One day closer. All my love. Xoxoxo

June 3, 20xx

I pray you both had a terrific sleep last night. The guards were so loud last night, so sleep was interrupted and very lacking. It looks like the rain is coming today my son just not sure when it will get here. I am off to work today and I will call at lunch time 11:00am. Tonight I will go to connecting streams and say hello to the volunteers but I have scheduled our phone cell to see for the house appraisal appointment went. I pray that God will be there and that he will handle this situation. I pray for angels to shelter and around you both and the people who are occupying our house. I pray if God intends us to keep that house he will. God controls all, sees all, knows all, hears all, he is for us and has already gone before us in this situation and has blessed us. I love you both and so grateful for you both.

'The shield of faith, where with ye shall be able to quench all the fiery dirt of the wicked.' Ephesians 6:16. God satisfies my mouth with good things. He renews you like the eagle's' Psalm 103:5 Work was fine. Thank you mom for taking care of the taxation. Well of course, the crooked lawyer is out of the country until August. So maybe he won't come back but nevertheless, we will take the August appointment and I will get a copy of the January appointment transcript to send to the Law Society.

I love Bally she was the one who called me up to V&C to get my release papers in order. She is so amazing and making sure I am ready to go. The health care cards and the paper work in order and filled out the mate at work will be writing a letter about the crooked lawyer also. So we will see and I will forward it on to the Justice looking into the complaint.

The front door flew open again this morning. It is like a sign from God that he is opening my doors. Like I have said the guards just shut the door and it bounces back hence it opens up. Thank you mom and thank you for taking care of the appraiser and the crooked realtor. I love you both and I am so grateful for you and your love and support. All my love. xoxoxo

June 4, 20xx

Sleep was blessed to me last night as the guards on shift were respectful and gracious in keeping quiet. I just love the verse from proverbs 17:12' let a man meet a bear robbed of her cubs, rather than a fool in his folly. 'So personal to what we are going through. This morning is the final test for the self management and this afternoon is the last connecting streams bible study.

Get out of my garden is the title of today's devotional and speaks on satin and how he will mislead you and your words. Focus on God's glory. The devil is a thief and a liar.

'I am sober and vigilant. I resist the devil steadfast in faith.' 1 Peter 5:8-9 and Romans 8:17-18 and 2 Corinthians 9:8. I pray you both have an amazing day full of blessings. The instructor and I just had our self management appointment. I completed the forms and testing. She told me this would be it and I commented back until I was out. I was talking about how I had to take self management on the outs, she laughed and said no this is it for my fraud and I said but I didn't commit it in the beginning. She knew I did not do this alleged crime. We chatted after and she asked me if I had ever been bullied while here and I explained how blessed I have been by everyone here. Other mates respect me and they are very gracious to me, including the staff and to my family also.

She told me that my walk has brought her back to God, wow that is so wonderful and just the blessing words I needed to here. Thanks be to God! Work was great. The mate wrote the letter about the crooked lawyer for me to submit to the law society. I will send it out in this letter.

Connecting streams was so relevant about forgiveness and then the volunteers ended up being there at the end of our session, the ladies who would not take me out anymore. So prevalent to today message. Genesis 45-50 is the words to be read. I love God! I saw Bob for a brief wave as he was heading one way and me the other. Blessings are coming in huge amounts. Thank you my son for visiting for a bit especially after a long day at work in the hot sun. Thank you mom for staying and visiting. I pray for you both and it is so difficult to see you go and one day soon it will be a memory. All my love. xoxoox

June 5, 20xx

My son will already be at work as it is 7:15am and mom you will be attending to your work. I am watching my show and it was said that God offers you favour when you are on the right mission. I love that. I pray you we are on the right mission and will receive all kinds of favour, mercy and blessings as there is nothing better than receiving them from god. I love you both and I pray we will be blessed with the UTAs today. Peace and grace cover us today. I am off to work. Pastor Ken should be coming in today for a visit. It is empties day, so if I don't call you at 11:00am, I will shortly after that.

'You must not fear them, for the lord, your god himself fights for you.' Deuteronomy 3:22. Work was okay. Glad we got to chat and great idea about the letter to renew my licence. Pastor Ken must have gotten lost, as he did not show up again. Apple received her parole. I will need to find out about my UTAs. Nat is crying on the phone so after count I will check in on her. What people need to realize is that everyone had their own path and to be happy for people on their path? Bless others as you would want them to bless you. Nat received some gong news today, seriously we are people and the lack of professionalism is head shaking. Sofi has her visit finally which has been a gong to get to see her boyfriend.

I saw Bob and only three emergency situations were brought forth to the warden so we will have to wait until next week, but I did put my request in for a male guard to take me home. He offered to and that is such a kind gesture. Gosh I don't care if they are male or female I just want to go home. This guard is the one who was there while we were chatting the other day during visits. I chatted with Nat and she got some good news so that offset the bad news.

I hope you are home my son as it is raining here. I will call you at 6:00pm to chat and then I will type up the letter for the Drivers licence and will send you a copy to see if you can renew it otherwise we will have to wait until I get out. All my love. Xoxoxo

June 6, 20xx

Well what a difference a moment makes in here. after we hung up the phone last night, I walked the yard with Nat and ran into Bob who told me someone took up my application for UTAs to the warden and he will pulled the report to see what came of it and see me during the 8:00pm rounds. The male guard who would take me home was with Bob doing rounds so I asked him if he would take me home and he said of course. At 8:00pm I received the news and was blessed, we received clarification about what to do and the male guard was still prepared to take me home and looked forward to the pizza and movie idea. How absolutely gracious the guards are here and how wonderful the person who took up my UTAs. I pray that the duty officer will issue a permit for Sunday to go home and see you.

I pray for all the blessing for us, to be surrounded by angels and that god will continue to show us favour, mercy, grace and huge and many blessings. I will call you at 6:30pm with more fabulous news. Off to work, canteen, fruit day, and blessings. I had a dream about the crooks and how they were caught.

'I lay aside every weight and sin which so easily besets me. I run with patience's the race that is set before me', Hebrews 12:1, James 1:4, and James 1:1-8.

The peanut butter gong is on again. Everyone got pay sheets but Tara. Jimmy came to Corcan now we can rest easy; he wanted the guard to pat him down upon him leaving. He has such a sense of humour. Bally came to tell me that my outside parole officer will meet with me tomorrow. Blessed to chat with you both twice tonight. I was able to fix the printer in the recreation room and help out fellow mates here. It feels so wonderful to help someone else and not leave until they are helped. I love you so much and so looking forward to coming home. All my love. xooxox

June 7, 20xx, I worked half a day and had piano lessons. June 8, 20xx I attended re-integration on an outing pass with another mate. June 9, 20xx, I had a blessed home visit on UTA 9-9. My son and mom came and picked me up so I could spend the day with them.

Words cannot even begin to describe the emotions you feel leaving the institution and when you have to come back. It is like a home sick feeling. An inmate learns to become two different people, one to survive this place and the other to deal with society. I miss my family so much and long to be back in the real world. I pray that God will vindicate my name and bring justice to this company. Every day is one day closer to leaving here. I am blessed to have been granted my parole and that the panel believed in my innocents and they believe that one day the truth will be told. I enjoy ever moment I can spend with my son and miss him. I am so grateful he is such a strong and wise young man that this journey will only better equipped him for life.

June 10, 20xx, I had work and then attend connecting streams in the evening. On June 11, 20xx I work and went home on UTA. It is funny how things move so slowly when you first arrive and now so quickly. I am so grateful that I was granted my parole, as if you are denied you have to wait until you receive the privilege of your ETAs and UTAs again. Being denied is not only upsetting but it puts you back and that can be heartbreaking also. You have to have the warden approve your access out of the institution again and that in its self is a process. I admire the strength these women have and until you have been in this situation you can see how one copes in certain times. I understand frustration and anger at the system, as I have been subjected to this miscarriage, but it is with my faith and my strength in God and what He can do I put my trust.

June 12, 20xx, I worked all day. Pastor Ken was a no show, but I am so blessed he stands beside me and believed in my innocents. He is such a wonderful person and God has placed him in my life. I am sure Pastor Ken is dealing with other matters and his blessings are being shared to someone else in need.

June 13, 20xx – 6 days left

I received my self management report from my instructor to review and to read. And I had my last canteen day. This afternoon I will go to work and keep productive. The guards asked me about my UTA and how that went. It was kind of them to ask. I have another UTA tonight.

My instructors words of my innocents were so wonderful and a gift from God. God speaks of my vindication through other people and I hear his messages loud and clear.

We had a great visit tonight on my UTA and things are feeling still weird but as time passes this feeling will also. I am so grateful we have somewhere to go and blessed to have so many wonderful supporters, loved ones and met so many amazing people along the way that will not be forgotten.

June 14, 20xx

Last day at Corcan and I am grateful to have had this job and the opportunities to learn a new skill. I pray blessings on us today and the angels to stand guard around us. God has an amazing plan for everyone. He has gone before in everyday, every year in all. This is the last Friday here. Proverbs 17:12 'I will be vindicated in Jesus name.' Work was good, Whitey stopped in and we chatted. He will visit my at the half way house. Work asked me to come in Monday which I will for the morning only. Tara made chocolate chip cookies and apple cake which are so good. I must remember my yoga pants are what I have to wear out of here.

Gosh Nat is becoming so rude. She is continuously slamming the laundry door. One hand left to count down. I am off to work. Tara was doing laundry and dropped her underwear on the stairs, first a peep show and now she is leaving her under on the stairs. Good thing I notices them before the guards saw them and of course I gave her the funny face when I gave them back to her. She laughed.

The day is done and I am going to take a shower and get ready for bed. I will chat with you shortly and see how your days finished off. I love you so much and miss you so, so much. All my love. Xooxxo

June 15, 20xx- 4 days left

The morning involved a walk in the yard with the gals. I will call you at 11:30am. I am so ready to commence a new chapter. I packed and did laundry this afternoon. I was blessed to see Bob and know he will be on this Wednesday so we can say our 'see you' on my way out. He seems so excited to kick me out and likes to voice it. God bless him, he is my guardian angel. Thanks for your lovely visit. I love Bob's spin on the half way house and how excited Jimmy was until I mentioned the going away party he must be throwing for me. I don't think he wants me to go, so sweet but I would not want me to go either. I was going to bring some of me to this place and I succeeded. I pray I provided this place with some joy while I was here. I love you and will see you in twelve hours for a visit. All my love.

June 16, 20xx- 3 days left

Home for an UTA! Happy dad's day, we love you and forever missed in our world. It was a beautiful day with TV time, dinner, preparing the taxes, and watching the Hobbit, but the best thing was spending time with you both. Hugs and kisses and just chilling.

Coming back here is the usual strip search and being processed. The guards are always so gracious to me. I spoke to Sofi and Mea as they are having a difficult time with me departing. I know they are happy but sad to see me go. It will be difficult to say 'see you later' to them but I will certainly keep in touch and we will be breaking bread on the outside. I will call you shortly to say good night and sending you my love. All my love. xoxoxo

June 17, 20xx- 2 days left

I am off to work and I will say see you later to some people. I chatted with the guards at A&D to see when I should bring up my stuff and she told me they would call me. I did some laundry and chatted with you on the phone to confirm our visit and then before you blinked it was our time for a visit. You have to be back in the jail for a length of time in between the UTAs so it is wonderful for you to come and see me on those off times. I talked to Nat as she is a bit negative but it must be as her parole hearing is coming up shortly and her nerves are acting up. Tonight is our last visit here so enjoy as we are closing that door. All my love xoxxo

June 18, 20xx- 1 day left

Today I am saying my goodbyes. I was to have an UTA but that got messed up so maybe you can come in for a visit. It is supposed to rain tomorrow so maybe no work and you can be there with grandma to pick me up upon my release. I know you want to be there, but if you have to work well then you will come to the halfway house and we will have dinner there. My release papers are wrong, they have the wrong date. Thank goodness for Bally to get that all corrected so now they are correct.

I had to take all my boxes up and thank goodness for Sofi's help. The guard, Sofi and I whipped the process so that all my items were ready for tomorrow's release. Gosh this is very stressful as everything is last minute. I have nothing left but the items that were given to me. I will borrow my mate's blow dryer in the morning as everything is packed and has been processed out. It was so kind of you both to come in and for the final, final visit. I love how we have been blessed in this place with such amazing grace. Tomorrow is the day.

June 19, 20xx -0 days release day.

John 13:34 'focus on love and everything else will be taken care of.' This place was dark when I arrived and I hope I left it a bit of light. God's peace and grace to everyone who touched my life while I was here.

Today is my release day and my heart is bounding out of my chest. A lot of tears were shed these last couple of days. I love these mates and they love me. We have formulated a strong bond and this is life changing and forever. The guards called my name to the duty office where they led me back down the hallway I had come in. I pulled my cart of boxes out the doors and the guards unlocked the gates for me. I knew the guards and so they wished me well and gave me a huge.

Mom and I loaded up the boxes and off to see my outside parole officer and then to the halfway house to start another chapter in our journey. My son had to work, but would see me for dinner tonight. Justice will prevail and after seeing God's hands at work, you can only hold onto his love and have faith in this journey and his plan for your purpose. All my love. xoxoxo

We all endure struggles in life, which we tackle with courage. One day during afternoon church service, a mate came in with her girlfriend broken. She told the circle how her son had been murdered in a gang related altercation. This was her only son and she wished to attend the funeral. The then acting warden denied her request. The blessed guards offer to take her and gave every possible scenario to have her request accepted, but with no luck. Could you possibly imagine being in her shoes. The heartbreak was beyond anything I could have imagined. Humanity was not extended to this grieving mother. I hugged her and she wept for her loss. No on should ever judge another person as you yourself could one day be in a situation that could change our life forever. I heard once that everyone has made or done something that could have landed them in jail; the only difference is they never got caught. What would have happened if you did? Someone drinks too much or someone is in the wrong place at the wrong time or someone has an angry outburst. These cold be your situation, so a humbling piece of advice is to stay humble. What is your test today will be your testimonial tomorrow. God sees all and He will be the judge.

Release day:

After packing all my belongs up and taking them to be proceed, you are left with next to nothing as upon your exit you leave with new release clothes and that is it. Your pack is been proceeded for departure and you leave whatever you had the night before behind. So if you had a tooth brush to use for that morning, you have to garbage it. I was blessed to have mates that would lend my shampoo, tooth paste, and some items I was just about out of anyways so no wastage. I relied on my mates to make sure I was up, but that night I did not sleep very well anyways with all the excitement of my departure.

I waited until movement and my name was called. A bitter sweet as I was so excited to be leaving, but I had met so many wonderful women who I could call my sisters and now I was leaving them behind. There were tears of joy and sorrow. I knew that my journey would continue with some of these gals.

Today I would be processed out. I made my way up to the main house at movement otherwise the doors would be locked and I would have to wait to move. My mom would be waiting to pick me up. My son had to work but I would meet up with him later that evening. I hugged some mates who did not live with me and said my goodbyes to the great guards who I had the pleasure of meeting.

My PW and SW were not there to say goodbye to me. Some of the guards who I would have like to have seen were not there, but I also think it may have been difficult for them also to see me go. They surely wanted me to go, as I should never have been there, but after getting to know me it may have been difficult to see me leave.

After waiting in the hallway to be processed out, a guard finally came by to take me to departure. All my boxes were there waiting to be loaded up. It was nice to see that as I have heard nightmare stories over the disorganization that can occur as the arrival and departure area is not very big. Gate after gate you had to exit through. My mom was there waiting. I exited from the side doors and we loaded up my boxes and off to the parole board office to check in with my parole officer. I can't even begin to explain the emotions one feels. Knowing that your freedom can be taken from you in a moment is a real scary feeling, almost makes you sick. I was blessed and my trust in God was strong to know he was with me and has and would continue to protect me. God is my vindicator. He is a righteous and trusting God. Our journey is already determined and knowing he had already gone before me, makes me feel safe.

I had met my outside PO once on the inside for a brief chat and she seemed very nice. The Parole office building was an old building with lots of character. I probably drove past this building a number of times and never knew it was what it was. Of course, we were running late from the hold up on departure so we quickly made it to the office. Mikki processed me into the system and gave me a piece of paper to carry with me at all times. We would meet and she would check in at both the halfway house and with my supporters to make sure I was doing okay. Mikki gave me her cell number and her office number on a business card and she would be in contact with me to schedule our next meeting. We left and headed to the halfway house to check in. This is where the next chapter of the journey starts and where vindication is found.

CPSIA information can be obtained at www.ICGtesting.com
Printed in the USA
LVOW08s0511260315

431978LV00001B/12/P

9 781503 544734